"[Lutz] steps smartly out of her comfort zone to write a dead-serious thriller (with a funny bone)"

MARILYN STASIO, THE *NEW YORK TIMES* BOOK REVIEW

"Binge-worthy fare, especially for those drawn to strong female protagonists"

BOOKLIST, STARRED REVIEW

"This tenacious and resourceful heroine will keep you chasing, rooting, lip-biting, and above all reading until you reach the ending you never saw coming. My advice: buckle up"

TIM JOHNSTON, *NEW YORK TIMES* BESTSELLING AUTHOR OF *DESCENT*

"A sharp, clever, and utterly compelling thriller about a woman running from the mistakes and misfortunes of her past. Terrific"

CHRIS PAVONE, *NEW YORK TIMES* BESTSELLING AUTHOR OF *THE EXPATS* AND *THE ACCIDENT*

"With whip-smart writing and a breakneck pace, The Passenger*'s clever plot twists and sharp characters are sure to keep you guessing long into the night"*

KIM McCREIGHT, *NEW YORK TIMES* BESTSELLING AUTHOR OF *RECONSTRUCTING AMELIA*

"Suspenseful and funny and utterly riveting! I devoured The Swallows *in one delighted gulp. You'll laugh out loud, even as you anxiously flip the pages"*

TESS GERRITSEN, *NEW YORK TIMES* BESTSELLING AUTHOR

"In her witty and charming style, Lutz offers a genre-busting work of fiction…this novel keeps readers on the edge of their seats"

BOOKLIST, STARRED REVIEW

"An offbeat, darkly witty pre-#MeToo revenge tale"

KIRKUS

"Wes Anderson meets Muriel Spark in this delicious and vicious Battle of the Sexes set within a private school. Wickedly fun and wildly subversive but packing an emotional punch, The Swallows *is as powerful as it is timely"*

MEGAN ABBOTT, BESTSELLING AUTHOR OF *DARE ME* AND *GIVE ME YOUR HAND*

"[Lutz] takes no prisoners"

PUBLISHERS WEEKLY

PRAISE FOR THE AUTHOR

"Told with enormous verve and at a breakneck pace, the story twists and turns like a corkscrew"

DAILY MAIL

THE SWALLOWS

ALSO BY LISA LUTZ
AND AVAILABLE FROM TITAN BOOKS

The Passenger

THE SWALLOWS

LISA LUTZ

TITAN BOOKS

The Swallows
Print edition ISBN: 9781785656279
E-book edition ISBN: 9781785656286

Published by Titan Books
A division of Titan Publishing Group Ltd
144 Southwark Street, London SE1 0UP
www.titanbooks.com

First Titan edition: September 2019
10 9 8 7 6 5 4 3 2 1

Names, places and incidents are either products of the author's imagination or used fictitiously. Any resemblance to actual persons, living or dead (except for satirical purposes), is entirely coincidental.

A CIP catalogue record for this title is available from the British Library.

Printed and bound in Great Britain by CPI Group UK Ltd.

FOR ANASTASIA FULLER

PART I
IN THE DARK

Now this is not the end. It is not even the beginning of the end. But it is, perhaps, the end of the beginning.

WINSTON CHURCHILL

MS. WITT

Some teachers have a calling. I'm not one of them.

I don't hate teaching. I don't love it either. That's also my general stance on adolescents. I understand that one day they'll rule the world and we'll all have to live with the consequences. But there's only so much I'm willing to do to mitigate that outcome. You'll never catch me leaping atop my desk, quoting Browning, Shakespeare, or Jay-Z. I don't offer my students sage advice or hard-won wisdom. I don't dive into the weeds of their personal lives, parsing the muck of their hormone-addled brains. And I sure as hell never learned as much from them as they did from me.

It's just a job, like any other. It has a litany of downsides, starting with money and ending with money, and a host of other drawbacks in between. There are a few perks. I like having summers off; I like winter and spring breaks; I like not having a boss breathing over my shoulder; I like books and talking about books and occasionally meeting a student who makes me see the world sideways. But I don't get attached. I don't get involved. That was the plan, at least.

I came to Stonebridge Academy because it was the only place where I was sure of a no-questions-asked job offer. The dean of students, Gregory Stinson, is an old family friend. I don't know if he offered me the job knowing everything or nothing. Back then, Greg never spoke of unpleasant things.

Why I wanted to give it another go is beyond me. It's not like I thought of teaching as my life's work. I doubt I'll ever have that. Maybe I just wanted to wrap up my career in education with a memory that didn't make my skin crawl.

It was July 2009 when I first laid eyes on the campus. During my preliminary visit, Greg and I hammered out my contract in his musty old office, which overlooked fifty acres of dense woods. Under the thick brush of summer, I couldn't see the veins and arteries of the interconnected hiking and cross-country-skiing trails that Stonebridge boasted of so proudly in its brochure. It seemed like too much space for four hundred or so high school students. Despite the classic prep school architecture—cathedral buildings, everything stone—I had heard rumors about the lax academic environment. Warren Prep kids had called Stonebridge students "Stoners." I considered that detail its most attractive quality.

Greg was sure I was perfect for the libertarian style of his school, and his certainty compensated for my hesitation. We discussed my course schedule for the new year. I would teach three English literature classes and one American lit.

After that, Greg took me on a brief tour of the campus. His office and several classrooms were housed in an imposing stone structure that had no formal name. Later, I learned that the students called it Headquarters. It was the only building on campus without a literary appellation. You know the game where you take your first pet's name and add the street you grew up on and, *voilà,* there's your porn name? I think Stonebridge used a similar formula for naming their buildings and recreational grounds. Take the last name of a British (or occasionally Irish) poet or author and add *House, Manor, Hall, Field, Commons,* or *Square* to it. The center of campus was Fleming Square; students ate in Dahl Dining Hall; Tolkien Library and Samuel Beckett Gymnasium flanked Fielding Field.

Across from Headquarters, adjacent to Beckett Gym, was the headliner of the tour: the Oscar Wilde Bathhouse. We passed through double doors with a sign that read NO STUDENTS ALLOWED, NO EXCEPTIONS. The marble compound, which housed a whirlpool tub, sauna, and steam showers, was apparently an extravagant gift from a former student.

"If this doesn't seal the deal, I don't know what will," Greg said.

I had a feeling that Greg was using the bathhouse as camouflage. I suggested he show me faculty housing.

In silence, Greg led me across the square to a four-story brick building. There was a heavy drizzle outside, which made everything look like it was on the other side of a cheap, transparent shower curtain. We strolled past Dickens House, the boys' dormitory. And, yes, they called it Dick House. Next to Dickens was a similar four-story brick structure. The sign above the door read WOOLF HALL.

"Yes. After you," Greg said, opening the thick paneled door.

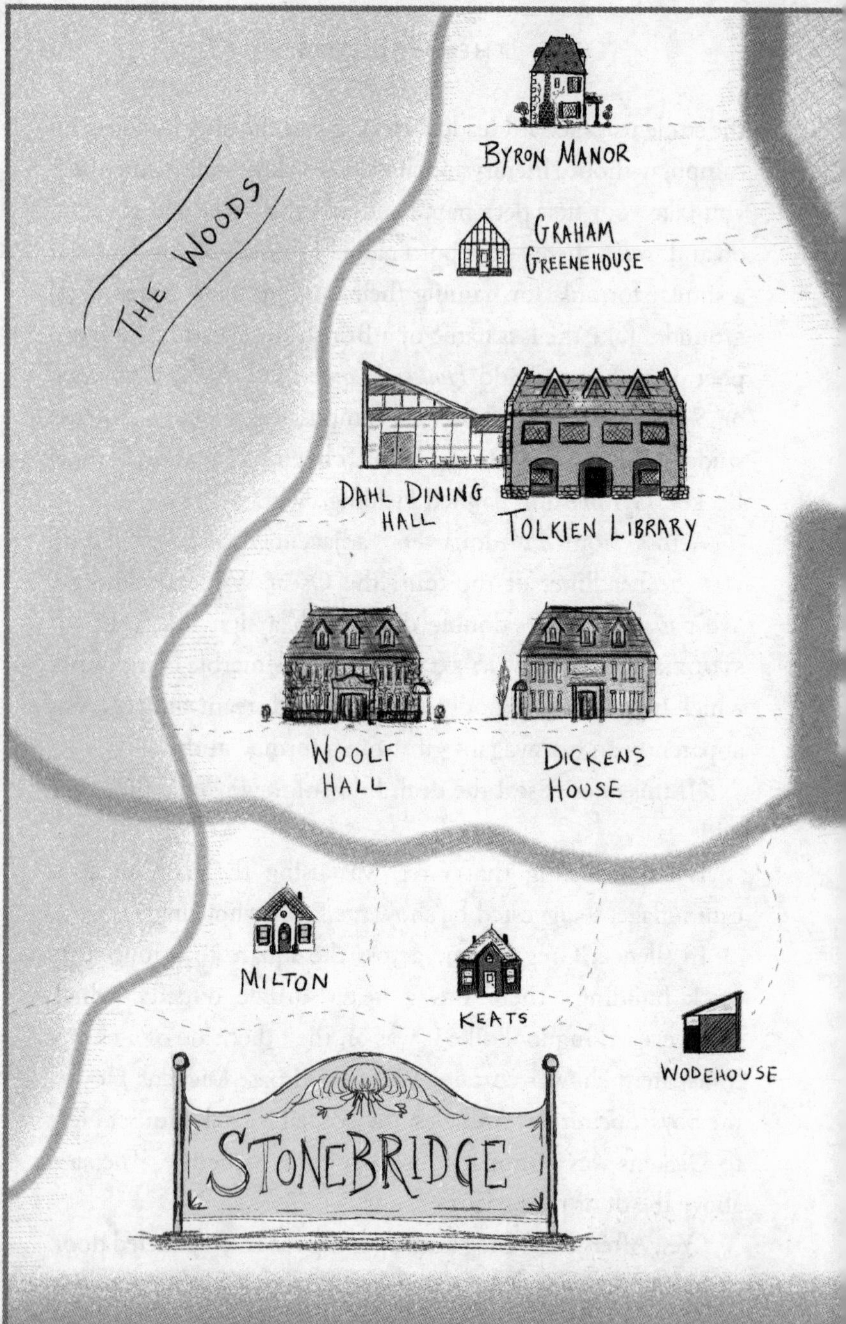

Byron Manor
Graham Greenehouse
The Woods
Dahl Dining Hall
Tolkien Library
Woolf Hall
Dickens House
Milton
Keats
Wodehouse
Stonebridge

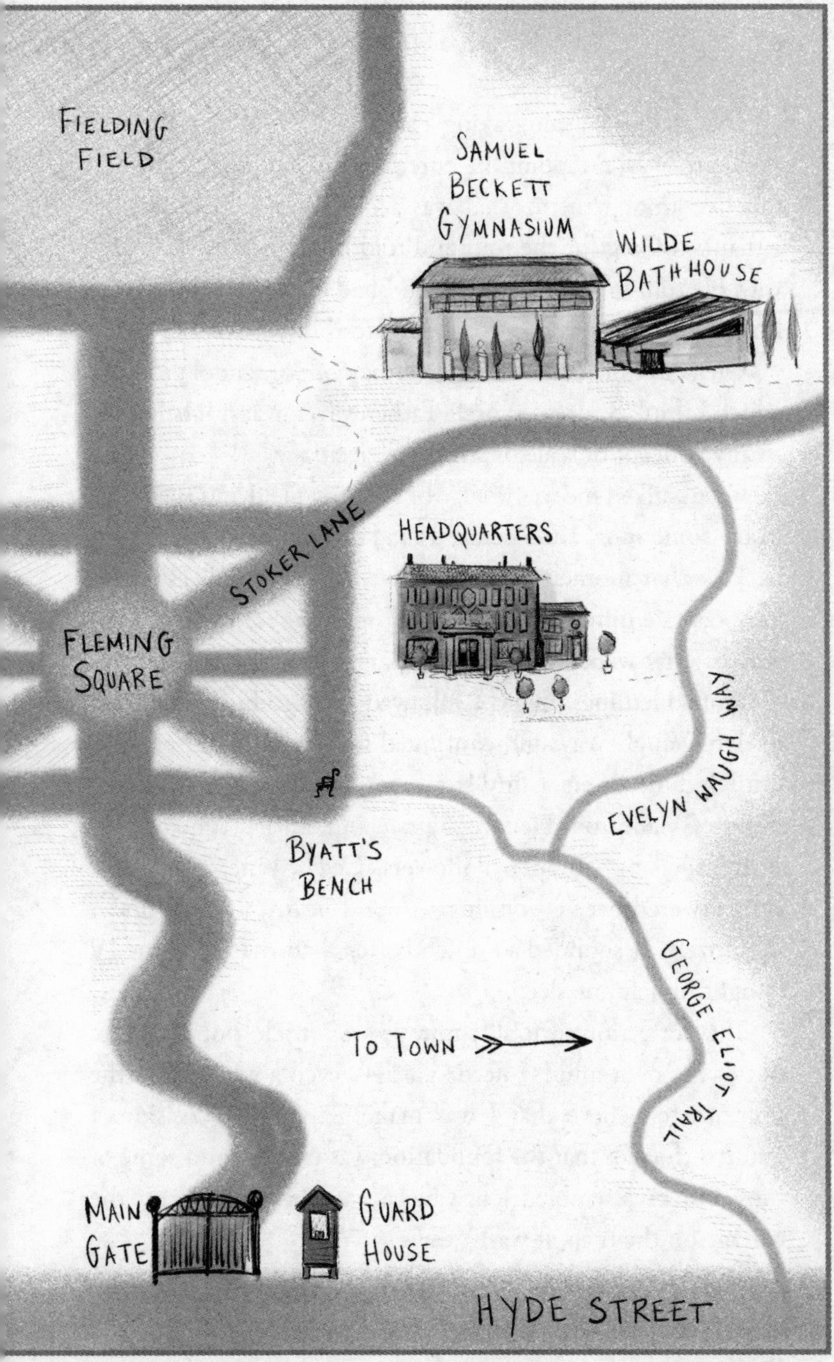
FIELDING FIELD
SAMUEL BECKETT GYMNASIUM
WILDE BATHHOUSE
STOKER LANE
HEADQUARTERS
FLEMING SQUARE
EVELYN WAUGH WAY
BYATT'S BENCH
GEORGE ELIOT TRAIL
TO TOWN
MAIN GATE
GUARD HOUSE
HYDE STREET

"No thanks," I said, taking a step back.

There was no point in entering the building. I would not live among them. That was a deal breaker, I explained. I thanked Greg for the tour and told him I had to be on my way. He told me I was being rash. I had driven two hours; the least I could do was take some time to think it over.

Greg gave me a hand-rendered map of the school grounds, which I think he drew himself. Either way, it was not beholden to any concept of scale or structural accuracy.

Greg walked me to the edge of Fielding Field and suggested I take some more time before I made a final decision. I come back to that moment again and again. So many lives would have taken a different course had I not gone for a walk in the woods. That walk changed everything.

From Fleming Square I followed George Eliot Trail past Evelyn Waugh Way, and continued for about a quarter mile, until I came upon a tiny stone cottage. It was at least ten minutes' walk from Fleming Square and, at that time of year, surrounded by vibrant wildflowers. Cedar, pine, and maple trees towered over everything. A pond nearby rippled under the drizzle. It sounded so much better than that machine I'd bought to help me sleep.

The perfection of it all I now see as a trick, not of nature but of my own mind. I needed a sign, even a wink, from the universe to believe that I was making the right decision. I ignored the fact that the foundation was cracked and some of those stones resembled Jenga pieces. When I looked for the cottage on the map, it wasn't there.

For someone looking for a place to hide, that was as good a sign as any.

I returned to Greg's office and told him I would take the job if I could live in the cabin with no name. He said the place wasn't habitable. He mentioned the absence of a shower. I reminded him of the bathhouse. He continued to resist. I told him those were my terms, take it or leave it. Greg reluctantly agreed.

I returned to campus on Labor Day, after dark. Classes were to begin the next morning. I picked up the key to the cottage from the guard at the security gate and followed the blue ink on my annotated map. A muddy fire lane took me just shy of twenty yards from my new front door.

Inside the cabin, I stood on the cold stone floor and wondered what the hell I was thinking. I was struck by a fresh memory of the perils of dorm life and forced myself to feel at home. I wiped down the cabinets above the kitchen sink, which contained a sparse collection of dishware and an unopened bottle of bourbon. I pulled the bottle from the shelf and noticed a small square of folded paper attached to the neck. I unfolded the paper and read the note written in small block letters.

WELCOME TO STONEBRIDGE. BE CAREFUL.

I sat outside on a rickety chair and considered the message. Was it a warning or just a piece of advice? I drank half the bottle as I tried to decide. Then I crawled into bed and fell asleep.

The next morning, regretting the booze, I washed up in the kitchen sink, mourned the absence of coffee, and dressed in the first shirt and pair of jeans I could find.

I stumbled through the woods to Headquarters and entered Agatha Christie Admin (aka AA). Ms. Pinsky, the school secretary, handed me an envelope that contained my class schedule for the semester.

WITT, ALEX (FALL 2009)
Instructor Schedule

PERIOD	COURSE	ROOM
1. 8:00–9:10 a.m.	CRWA400–Advanced Creative Writing	203
2. 9:20–10:30 a.m.	CRW100–Creative Writing, Elective	203
3. 10:40–11:50 a.m.	PHYSED501–Fencing, Intro	GYM
(no number)		
12:00–1:00 p.m.	Lunch	
4. 1:00–2:10 p.m.	Office Hours	
5. 2:20–3:30 p.m.	CRWAW410–Advanced Creative Writing Workshop	203

After I reviewed my schedule and noticed the bait and switch, I asked Ms. Pinsky if Dean Stinson was in his office.

"End of hall. On the left," she said.

I stormed in hot. I shouted some things, including *fraud* and *liar.* Greg had a student with him, whom he quickly dispatched. I waved my class schedule in the air and then smacked it down on his desk.

"I teach English. Not creative writing. We had a deal," I said.

I braced myself for a fight. Instead, Greg sat down in his chair and deflated. I swear, he lost four inches with a single sigh.

"Oh my," he said, cradling his head in his hands. "My apologies, Alex. Len said that you wouldn't mind the schedule change. I tried to reach you repeatedly. Len said you were at the monastery."

"You spoke to Dad?"

"I did. Len insisted that if I simply presented you with a new schedule, you wouldn't notice the difference."

That trick worked once, maybe twice, when I was fifteen and smoked a lot of weed. I was stunned my father had the balls to provide tactical advice against his own daughter, and lousy advice at that. I sat down in one of the well-worn chairs across from Greg's desk.

"You can't change my schedule because my father told you it was okay," I said.

Greg scrunched up his forehead like a shar-pei. Then he leaned back in his chair and crossed his long legs. I could tell he was settling in for a lengthy negotiation.

"I should not have listened to your dad, but I am in a terrible bind."

"What happened to your previous writing teacher? Did he die?"

"No, no. Of course not. He is still on the faculty and I'm sure he'd honor our old agreement, if need be. However, he is currently working on a novel and feels that teaching writing at this time is stifling to his art."

I liked the dead version of him better.

I wasn't going to do any favors for an unpublished hack who thought of himself as Van Gogh with a laptop.

"I know this is all last minute. And I deeply apologize. But I need you to be flexible here, Alex. In fact, if you do this for me, we can forget about fencing."

"I already told you I don't fence. You can't expect me to teach something that I don't know how to do."

"Okay," Greg said. "Fencing is off the table."

"It was never on the table," I said. "Back to writing. I've never taught creative writing before. And I already prepared my literature curricula."

"According to Len, you don't really need a lesson plan."

"If you mention my dad one more time—"

"Okay. Okay," Greg said, with just the right dose of panic in his voice. "If you agree to the switch, you are released from any supervisory responsibilities."

One of the worst things about private school employment was the boundless chaperoning responsibility tacked on to a full teaching schedule. I was unlikely to get a better deal.

I entered my class, Headquarters room 203, without a word about my tardiness. I wasn't going to start the year in their debt. This time, I would not let down my guard. This time would be different.

As I gazed at my students, I had the same thought I always had on the first day. They looked so young and innocent. Then I found a dead rat in the bottom of my desk drawer and remembered the tenet I had learned over the last eight years. The young may have a better excuse for cruelty, but they are no less capable of it.

For someone looking for omens, it's odd how many exit signs I chose to ignore.

If a century of tradition were the only thing my time at Stonebridge brought to an end, I'd be okay with that. It's the two deaths that keep me up at night.

GEMMA RUSSO

I remember everything about that first day.

Ms. Witt showed up for class *fifteen* minutes late. She had on a pair of old Levi's, a wrinkled light-blue button-down oxford shirt under a threadbare gray cardigan. She wore mud-splattered red Jack Purcell high-tops. Her straight brown hair hung loose and tangled, like she'd just rolled out of bed. She looked like she didn't care about anything. She was definitely pretty, but she wouldn't cause any traffic accidents. Her features were all kind of standard. From a distance, she was just another white woman with long brown hair. But, up close, you could see her wide brown eyes tracking everything. And when she flashed a smile, I saw her twisted tooth. It made her look dangerous or something. I liked her right away.

But when she found the dead rat, that's when I knew she was special.

I'd heard that morning about Gabe's planned prank. He was so stinking proud of himself, everyone knew. When Witt opened her desk drawer, she gave up nothing, like a gangster. She squinted, at first, like she wasn't sure what she was looking at. Then there was the recognition, an eyebrow raise. Not even a millisecond of fear. The rodent was contained in a Ziploc bag, which Witt removed from the drawer and held from the corner edge.

"Is Ratatouille, may he rest in peace, property of the biology department or nature?" Ms. Witt asked.

Her eyes scanned the classroom, waiting for a response.

"We dissect mice, not rats, here," said Bethany Wiseman.

"Thank you," Witt said.

Gabriel Smythe was being a total spaz. His attempts to tamp down his laughter made it look like he was having a seizure. Witt lasered in on him.

"You, with the tie around your head, what's your name?"

"Uh, uh, Cornelius . . . Web-ber . . . Mc . . . Allister," Gabe said.

Gabe's fake names are always unfunny because he takes so damn long to come up with them.

Witt dropped the dead rat on Gabe's desk and said, "Please take this creature to his final resting place."

"You want *me* to bury him?" Gabe said.

Gabe was totally freaking out by then. His face was bright red, his zits even redder. The class was dead silent.

"Well, he's not going to bury himself," Witt said.

Jonah let out a guffaw. I saw a slight smirk on Witt's face.

"Chop chop," said Witt.

Gabe quickly stood up and took the bagged rat out of the classroom. Then Ms. Witt returned to her desk and completely ignored us, as if nothing had happened.

My phone buzzed with a group text from the Ten.

Mick: Holy fuck. What was that?

Adam: That was kinda hot, right?

Tegan: Damn she cold

Rachel: What is she wearing?

Hannah: Weirdo

Mick: Def hot

Tegan: moths r obv drawn 2 her

Emelia: pretty, needs blush

Hannah: needs more than blush

Jonah: I think I'm in love

Mick: u r freak Jonah. Wish I could see her ass in those jeans

Jack: gd mouth

Rachel: sm mouth. Think it could hold your entire dick?

Hannah: OMG. Can u see that snaggletooth? Bitch could cut you

Emelia: 2 early in the day 2 think about Jack getting blown

Jack: never 2 early

Jonah: I like her teeth

Adam: Jonah = lunatic

The Ten refers to the top ten percent, give or take, of each class, which generally works out to around ten students. No one's a Nazi about the precise number except Mick Devlin, who really likes it to be exactly ten. The tier has nothing to do with academic credentials; it's a pure social hierarchy. Members come and go depending on a voting system that is so nebulous, I wouldn't be surprised if there were some preppy wizard from years past pulling the strings somewhere.

This is the current roster of the senior Ten, in no particular order, along with their primary role in the organization:

Emelia Laird—hot girl you can bring home to Mom
Tegan Brooks—girl goon, gatekeeper
Hannah Rexall—dancer, humblebrag virtuoso
Rachel Rose—hot girl you don't bring home to Mom
Jack Vandenberg—he who provides alcohol, enforcer
Adam Westlake—spokesperson, man about town
Mick Devlin—dandy, editor in chief
Jonah Wagman—jock, nice guy
Gabriel Smythe—court jester, suck-up, moron
Me—she who does not belong in this picture

None of the Ten mentioned Witt's father. It was unlike them not to run a background check on fresh meat. As soon as Dean Stinson dropped her name, I did my research. I decided to keep that information to myself. But I had to chime in to the chatter to reinforce my shaky position in this ridiculous club.

Gemma: I want to be her when I grow up.

* * *

Ms. Witt didn't say anything until Gabe returned to class. His shoes were muddy and there was a stripe of dirt on his shirt.

"It's done," Gabe said. "He's interred behind the greenhouse. I gave him a eulogy and all. Would you like to hear it?"

Gabe glanced over his shoulder at the class, waiting for a few laughs or any nonverbal sign of encouragement.

"No," Witt said. "We weren't close."

"Well, he's in a better place now," Gabe said, still trying to dig out of the ditch of submission in which he'd found himself.

"Take a seat, Cornelius," Witt said. "I think we'll start class."

Witt wrote her name on the board.

"This is apparently advanced creative writing. I am Alex Witt. Address me however it is done here. Alex or Ms. Witt. Whatever. I just found out this morning that I'm teaching this seminar, so don't expect a thoughtful syllabus at this point."

Carl Bloom's hand shot up, angled forward, like a Hitler salute. I've always meant to caution him about it. Never got around to it last year. Maybe this year. Carl has the unfortunate distinction of walking and talking like a nerd and yet struggling in every one of his classes.

"Ms. Witt," he shouted. "Why isn't Mr. Ford teaching creative writing anymore?"

Witt glanced up at Carl and then jotted something down in her notebook.

"That's a *great* question. You should ask him. Over and over again," she said.

As Witt scribbled some more, paying no attention to us, half-assed whispers circulated the latest information on Ford.

Mel Eastman, who always knows the most while seeming to gossip the least, informed us all that Ford had taken over Ms. Whitehall's core curriculum.

"What happened to Ms. Whitehall?" Ephraim Wiener asked Mel. "Did she die?"

"Not unless you killed her," Mel muttered below his earshot.

I think Ephraim Wiener would have preferred that. Then he could finally stop pining for Whitehall. Boys are like that. They'd rather you die than reject them.

Mick Devlin stood up from his seat in the back row and ambled up the aisle with that lame half-gangster lean/limp he'd adopted late last year. When Devlin reached Witt's desk, he extended his hand like one of those stock Wall Street–movie douchebags and formally introduced himself.

"Mick Devlin, Madame Witt. At your service."

"Mick Devlin?" she said. "I'm going to remember that."

Most people call him Devlin. Some girls call him "the devil," and some mean it in that captivating bad-boy way. I don't. Devlin's eyes landed on Witt with generic lust, but his half smile, so boyish and goofy, balanced him out. Tegan once pointed out that the top and bottom of Mick Devlin's face should have belonged to two different individuals. She demonstrated with his school photo and a pair of scissors, cutting his face in half just above the nostrils.

"See," she said. "They don't belong together."

It was true. If you looked at him divided, neither part was particularly appealing. But I don't see what the other girls see when they look at Mick. Emelia thinks it's his eyes that give him power. From what I've heard, it's his giant penis.

What also gives Mick power is his role as editor in chief. Every male member of the Ten is called an editor. It's so stupid, I'm not even sure how to explain it. They don't edit the school newspaper or a magazine. They manage an exclusive website that only select Stonebridge boys can see. It's called the Darkroom. Suffice it to say, there's not a whole lot of "editing" going on.

Witt tilted her head at Mick's hand, looking confused or suspicious. Eventually she took it, but I could see he held on too long, like he does. Witt gave him a withering glance and he quickly let go.

"How *old* are you?" Jack Vandenberg said in that frog-deep voice of his.

Witt's eyes narrowed as she determined the identity of the questioner. Jack, the biggest man on campus, is often mistaken for a teacher by the freshmen. Of course, he likes the tiniest girls. He won't even look at a junior or a senior . . . with one exception. He likes the little bric-a-brac girls—small-boned, flat-chested. I have a theory that Jack is an undetected pedophile. In ten years, he'll still want the same kind of girl. If you're eighteen and date a fifteen-year-old (who looks thirteen), you can slide under the perv radar. But later he won't have the age or discipline to hide his sickness.

"Name, please?" Witt said, annoyed.

"Jack. Vandenberg."

Witt consulted the attendance sheet, nodded, and then cast her eyes on the rest of the class.

"I'm not going to take roll. There are nineteen students on the attendance sheet and nineteen in the class. I need a seating chart to learn your names."

"I can do that for you," offered Sandra Polonsky.

That's Sandra's thing, acting like everyone's valet. One time, I sat next to her at lunch and told her to quit being so goddamn submissive. She thanked me for my advice and then bused my tray.

"No thank you," said Witt. "And you are?"

"Polonsky. Sandra Polonsky."

That was also her thing, saying her name like she's James Bond.

Witt drew on the whiteboard a four-by-five grid so uneven that it suggested a neurological disorder. Witt regarded the grid, tilting her head like she hoped that would square it. She picked up the dry eraser and began vigorously deleting her crooked lines.

"Just be grateful I don't teach geometry," she said.

Some of the nerds started shouting their names. Witt winced and said, *"Shhhh."*

"What was that on the board?" Adam Westlake said in his sweet, harmless voice.

"The aforementioned seating chart," Witt said, taking a step back and regarding her work.

Adam approached the front of the classroom as the new teach finished wiping the board clean, and he picked up another dry-erase pen.

"Do you mind?" Adam said, uncapping the pen. "I have a steady hand."

Then he flashed his dimples, which works every time.

"By all means," Witt said, stepping aside. "For the first week or until I learn who ninety or so percent of you are, I need you to sit in the same seat. I learn better visually. So sit wherever you like, and then write your full name down on the corresponding chair."

She turned around as Adam completed an almost perfect grid, as if he'd sketched it with a ruler the size of a human.

"Well done, um . . ." she said with a question mark at the end.

"Westlake. Adam Westlake."

Maybe everyone introduces themselves like James Bond.

Witt pointed to the top and then the bottom of the board and said, "This is the front row, and this is the back row. Write down where you plan to sit for the next few weeks until I know who you are. Sort this out while I get a cup of coffee."

Witt picked up her bag and headed for the door. A few of the front-row obsessives charged the board to claim their real estate. Witt lingered at the door.

"I want to be clear on something," she said. "I'm going to learn the name that corresponds to the board. And I'm going to grade that name. If you get up to any nom-de-plume shenanigans—and I'm talking to you, Cornelius—I'm cool with that, but you better be prepared to live and breathe under your assumed name. You can *never* go back."

When Ms. Witt walked out of the room, I felt as if she had taken all of the oxygen with her. I knew then that things were going to change.

Ms. Witt was my friend, my ally, my confidante. She charmed, teased, amused, incited, and befriended us.

Alexandra Witt was the pied piper of Stonebridge Academy.

MR. FORD

The first time I saw Alex Witt, I thought she was a student out of uniform. I would have paid good money to see her in uniform.

She walked into the teachers' lounge looking lost. I asked her if she needed any help. She said yes, she was searching for coffee. I pointed her in the right direction. She got up close to the coffeepot and was watching the drip, like a kid staring at her pet goldfish. I thought maybe she didn't know that it was the kind of carafe that you could pull out and pour as it brewed. That's how all of them are now; how could she not know that? Finally, she removed the decanter and poured herself a mug. She took a sip and scowled. She held on to the sink for balance and looked down at the drain.

Then I realized who she was. There was only one new hire that year. It was odd that she didn't introduce herself. Women always do that.

"Hi. I'm Finn Ford," I said.

She put down her mug and glared.

"You. You. You're the one."

She started pointing at me, angry. I said I was sorry. I wasn't clear what I was sorry for. But I have a policy to always apologize to women. She was going on about all of the lesson plans she had pored over for the lit classes she thought she would teach.

"Dean Stinson said you were cool with the change," I said.

"Did he, now?" she said.

She was so pissed off I wouldn't have been surprised if she pulled out a switchblade and held it against my jugular.

"I'm really sorry," I said.

"I reread *Moby-Dick,*" she said. "I can't get that time back."

I loved *Moby-Dick* and asked her what she would change. She said she would have had Ishmael shove Ahab overboard around page 200.

"And then what?" I asked.

"Who gives a shit?" she said. "Finn Ford. Why does your name sound so familiar?"

"Because I'm the asshole who inadvertently made you read *Moby-Dick* for nothing."

"Moby-Dick for Nothing," she said, smiling. "Now, *that* book I wouldn't mind reading."

I liked her then. I thought she was crazy. But I liked her. She was stuck on my name. Fuck. I tried to get her off topic. She seemed easily distracted. I like that in a woman.

"I heard you staked your claim to the Thoreau Cabin," I said.

"What? No. It has no name. Besides, that's the wrong name, if it has a name. Everything on campus is named after writers from the British Isles. It's bullshit if you throw in one or two American names, just out of convenience. Besides, it's not on the map."

"That's what we call it," I said. "There's a pond nearby. We have a name for that too. And if you want to talk about boring books—"

"Why is this coffee so bad?" she said, as she took another sip.

"Because it's bad coffee," I said.

"Your name. I know that name. It's going to drive me crazy," Alex said.

"Are you really planning on living in the Thoreau Cabin the entire year?"

"Stop calling it that! I've been there one night. I wouldn't put the address on my tax return."

"I think it's safe to say that place doesn't have an address."

"Finn Ford, Finn Ford. You wrote a book, right?"

"I did."

"I think I read one of your books," she said.

I told her it was physically impossible to read more than one. She asked me to remind her what the title was.

Tethered.

She made a different face, reminiscent of my editor's. I have a visceral memory of our fight to the death over the title. It feels like a migraine in my solar plexus.

I was pleased she'd read it, even if it did slip her mind.

"*Tethered.* Yes. I think I liked it. Oh yes. I remember now. The ornithologist was weird. But I hate birds.

"Can I have that banana?" Witt asked.

There was a banana sitting in the middle of the table.

It wasn't my banana. It was probably Martha Primm's, and she would have been pissed, but I told Alex she could have it. She devoured the banana in four impressive bites. She didn't do that thing women do where they cover their mouth while chewing.

She tossed the banana peel in the trash and said, "Give me the lowdown."

I asked on what. She wanted to know the social hierarchy at Stonebridge, the predators and prey. This woman really got to the point. I was curious how that characteristic translated in the bedroom.

I considered her question. Some days it seemed like they were all predators. The image of the serpent eating its own tail came to mind. I told her she'd have to figure that out on her own. I felt proprietary all of a sudden. The inner workings of this academy had taken me years to dissect. I wasn't going to give it up for nothing.

Witt took another sip of coffee and winced. I admired her commitment to caffeine. She asked me what I was working on now. I told her I was working on a novel about a guy trying to assassinate a whale who ate his leg. She laughed. Then she asked if I was a Phineas or a Finn. I told her I was just Finn. She asked if I had a middle name. "No," I said.

Finn Ford makes me sound like enough of an asshole. Witt looked like the kind of woman who wouldn't give a Phineas Finn Ford the time of day.

"Okay," she said, smiling. There was something about her mouth that turned me on. I wanted to lick her snaggletooth.

She asked me when I decided that teaching writing was

derailing my writing. I wanted to kiss her, partly so she'd stop asking questions. I told her I'd decided at the end of last year. I suggested that maybe the dean forgot.

She topped off her coffee and headed for the door.

"If you don't want to answer a question, I'm cool with that. But don't lie to me. You're really bad at it," she said.

ANNOUNCEMENTS

Good morning, students of Stone. This is your old friend Wainwright back for another year of enlightenment, education, and entertainment. The three E's, if you will. It's a sunny seventy-two degrees on this eighth day of September, 2009.

Today's lunch menu is a choice between a tuna and kale casserole and falafel for the vegetarians. If that menu doesn't turn you vegetarian, I don't know what will. What was that?

[inaudible]

Since it's the first day, I'll keep my announcements brief. But before I go, let's welcome the new creative-writing and fencing instructor, Ms. Alexandra Witt.

[inaudible]

Ah, really? Scratch that. Only independent-study fencing. How does that work? I sure hope there's more than one person enrolled.

This is Wainwright signing off until we meet again. Which will be tomorrow.

MS. WITT

I was hunting through the desk drawers for a dry-erase pen when I found the dead rat. I didn't jump, because I didn't know what it was. I'd drunk way too much of that warning bourbon the night before and I needed coffee. After I registered that a dead rodent was in my desk drawer, it took all of my energy to remain calm. The prank was a power play. If I gave it up on the first day of school, I'd never get it back.

I may have looked ice-cold on the outside, but it felt like my entire body was in revolt. When I tried to draw a grid on the board, my hands shook uncontrollably. A boy offered to help. That's when I left. I needed a moment to regroup, alone. Away from them.

When I returned to the classroom, a gravelly male voice was droning on the PA system. I thought he said my name, but there was no reaction among the students. They just kept staring at their laps, tapping away.

I opened my notebook and copied down the seating

chart, making a few annotations on the ones who'd already made an impression.

Three girls huddled together in the corner, trying to pretend that class wasn't in session. They were like the three bears, in cascading order of size. The tall one wore combat boots and had brown hair streaked with blond and blue stripes. She was attractive, but her heavy eye makeup and rainbow hair only distracted from it, which I assumed was the point. The second-tallest girl was her opposite, classically beautiful without any adornment. Her shiny brown hair hung just above her waist. She wore only a dab of lip gloss. Her eyes were dark as coal and her cheekbones jutted out like a paper airplane. The small one appeared almost malnourished next to the other two. In my notebook, I jotted down my first impression of the trio: *rebel, beauty, wallflower.* Their names I parsed later: Gemma, the rebel; Emelia, the beauty; Tegan, the wallflower. Their fist-tight conspiratorial whispers suggested they ruled as a triumvirate; I assumed one of them was queen. I couldn't decide whether it was the rebel or the beauty.

The caffeine kicked in. I remember looking out onto a sea of wool. It looked scratchy. Unlike Warren Prep, which had a pajamas-to-class non–dress code, Stonebridge students sported the old-school button-down uniform. The girls wore a tailored light-blue oxford shirt with a slim crimson tie, which most knotted in a lazy half-Windsor. Of course, the schoolgirl look wouldn't be complete without that short tartan skirt. Some of the girls were bare-legged, some wore black tights, and a few sported those iconic kneesocks. I often marveled at how private school uniforms hadn't changed despite the masturbatory energy they evoked. I wondered how many of the mothers had borrowed their daughters' uniforms to liven things up in the bedroom.

The boys wore yawn-inducing navy-blue slacks in cheap polyester, with a fat blue tie slashed by diagonal stripes. Although one boy, I noticed, sported a red bow tie instead. I have a theory about bow-tied men. They're either good or evil, never in the middle ground. I also have a few strong and well-documented theories associating personality disorders with specific tie knots. If time were infinite, I would write a dissertation on the subject. Suffice it to say, keep your distance from any man wearing an Eldredge knot.

I erased the whiteboard and wrote down five questions.

1. What do you love?
2. What do you hate?
3. If you could live inside a book, what book?
4. What do you want?
5. Who are you?

"*Who are you?* is a weird question," said the girl in row 2, aisle 3.

"You're right," I said, consulting my chart. "Melanie Eastman, is it?"

"Let's go with Mel," she said. "What do you mean, *who are you?*"

Mel wore her thick black hair in a sloppy ponytail. She

had on dark-rimmed specs and her wrists were adorned with bands of beaded bracelets.

"It's best, I find, if you interpret the question yourself. But the first thing you need to know is that the assignment should be completed anonymously. Do Not Write Your Name on Your Paper."

I instructed my students to type their papers in a font of their choosing, to include the class name on the top right corner, to print it, and to deliver it to my box in the Agatha Christie Admin office. As always, the students had more questions about the assignment than the assignment itself had.

How long do the answers have to be?

However long the answer is.

What if it's one word?

Then it's one word.

Can you answer a question with a question?

I don't know. Can you?

So the assignment is really anonymous—you'll never know who wrote what?

Yes.

I started the Q&A's in my second or third year of teaching. It's a tradition now. I give it to all of my classes. I've adjusted the questions over the years. But it wasn't until I made the assignment anonymous that I learned anything useful. I can usually identify the authors within a few weeks. So, no, it's not really anonymous. I used to feel guilty about filleting my students like this. But it's better to know up front who they are and what they're capable of.

Some students still used quill and ink in class, others brought their laptops, but the universality of the mobile phone could not be denied. I don't, as a rule, prohibit the use of phones in my class. As the students' primary form of communication, the devices are much more useful as a bargaining agent.

I wrote my number on the board.

"If you need to reach me at any time, here's my mobile. The first time you text, please provide your name. If anyone texts me any anonymous weird shit, I'll track down your number and give you a D+ on everything you write for the rest of the semester. Also, please use normal spelling. I'm not fluent in text-speak. Got it?"

I could have sworn they were all looking up at me, but my phone began to vibrate like an old washing machine on the spin cycle as one text flew in after the next.

Sandra Polonsky: I'm done with the assignment. What is next?
Adam Westlake: at your service.
Jonah Wagman: I already like you better than that Ford fellow.
Tegan Brooks: Will we turn in ALL of our assignments anonymously?
Enid Cho: Will there ever be a syllabus? Will it be on Blackboard?

Blackboard is Stonebridge's proprietary communication portal. Students and faculty use it not only to convey personal messages but to disseminate campus information and to deliver class materials that, in my day, would have been hand-collated and stapled by the instructor.

I replied to Enid's text, informing her that I was undecided about the syllabus. Then I read through the influx of new numbers and questions. Most texts consisted only of the student's name. A few added smiley faces or winks and some used punctuation in a code I didn't understand. A few students said they'd finished their Q&A's and asked what they should do next. It's not like I had a creative-writing lesson plan up my sleeve.

"I don't know," I said. "Write something until the end of class. Or pretend to write something."

I got some blank stares, and a few of the front-row kids pulled out notebooks and pretended to write. But mostly it was heads down, hands in their laps, tap-tap-tap. I was witnessing the brink of a complete restructuring of communication. Just a few years ago I would have had to tell my class to be quiet over and over again. Now I missed the ocean-like sound of whispers.

The tapping stopped. The room fell as silent as a snowstorm.

A howl pierced the quiet. It didn't sound human, at first. I looked for the source. It was Gabriel Smythe, laughing like a goddamn hyena, aggressive and fake. No real person ever laughs like that. Others slowly joined in like an ugly orchestra. The din of adolescent cruelty. I looked around the room at the smirks, smiles, and other unmistakable expressions of *schadenfreude*. No one tried to hide it. That pitiless, joyous sound was so familiar, it triggered a fury and nausea deep inside me.

"What the hell is so funny?" I said.

They quieted.

Row 2, window seat, raised her hand. I consulted my chart. Her name was Kate Bush, like the singer. I still can see the humiliated flush on her face, the unmistakable color of shame, her body betraying her, as her classmates' laughter blared like a stereo system. It was like watching *Carrie,* minus the buckets of blood. Her arm wrapped around her belly, like she might be sick.

"Go," I said.

All eyes followed her out of the room. When the door shut, the laughter returned at a lower volume.

The girl in the last row, second aisle, was sitting slumped in her chair, scrutinizing everyone in the class. Her expression was like fury in a cage. I checked the seating chart and took note. Gemma Russo was not laughing at all.

"CREATIVE" WRITING Periods 1&5 seniors only	EPHRAIM WEINER twitchy
KATE BUSH Shamed	ENID CHO Remarkable posture
NORMAN CROWLEY Kind face	RACHEL ROSE Pink Scarf
TEGAN BROOKS Snide	JACK VANDENBERG Giant
EMELIA LAIRD bearly	GEMMA RUSSO Rebel Didn't laugh

CARL BLOOM Allergies	SANDRA POLONSKY Eager
MEL EASTMAN Smart, questions big hair bracelets	BETHANY WISEMAN No impression
ADAM WESTLAKE Red bowtie good or evil?	AMY LOGAN boys uniform
JONAH WAGMAN Thoughtful	HANNAH REXALL lithe, blonde
MICK DEVLIN limp or gangster- walk?	GABRIEL SMYTHE Rat boy Bad clown

NORMAN CROWLEY

I heard the howl first. Then I saw Kate, her face brick red, as she walked past my desk and out the door. She wiped tears with her sleeve. My phone was buzzing the whole time. There were already like twenty texts on the subject. I clicked on the first message.

A picture with a caption:

Kate's Bush.

She was toast. In just a few seconds, I could see her entire senior year playing out.

By end of period, everyone would have seen her: Kate Bush—her own name biting her in the ass—lying on a twin standard-issue Stonebridge bed. Naked, legs spread. Her head thrown back, as if she were following someone's instructions.

The comments flew into my text thread, like a gunman pulling the trigger until the chamber was empty. It was like my classmates thought they'd cease to exist if they didn't add to the noise. I don't even know why I'm in the group text for the Ten. I think it was Jonah who added me. I'm like the bcc of the group, if you could bcc in texts. That kind of sums up who I am at the school. I'm the guy you don't see who sees everything. I'm not invisible in that cool superpower kind of way. I'm just not important to anyone, unless they need something from me.

Rachel: Has she ever met a rzr?

Hannah: OMG!! It really does look like a sm animal

Mick: the horror, the horror

Jack: I want to bleach my eyeballs

Jonah: Looks like my dad's old Playboys

Gabriel: Can't deal with unshaved girl

Adam: A man w/out options can't afford 2 have standards

Ms. Witt told the class to *shut the fuck up*. She'd already earned major respect for the way she handled Gabe's epic rat-prank fail. Everyone was super quiet when Kate slipped back into the room.

Tegan dropped a scrap of paper in front of Kate and quietly said, "Ask for Olga. You'll be like a dolphin when she's done with you."

Tegan is a master of the sneering whisper. There's no way Ms. Witt could have heard what she said, but the new teach stared her down. I imagined seeing flames in Witt's eyes. For a very short, satisfying moment, Tegan looked scared. I wanted to say something. To tell the Ten what a bunch of dickwads they were. I wanted to tell Kate I was sorry. I didn't say anything, as usual.

I completed Ms. Witt's strange, anonymous assignment:

What do you love?
Bright Eyes, Reservoir Dogs, PB&J sandwiches, CS
What do you hate?
The Darkroom
If you could live inside a book, what book?
Tinker Tailor Soldier Spy
What do you want?
For my real life to begin
Who are you?
I'm a coward

GEMMA RUSSO

Stonebridge has a little brother/little sister program. As a junior you get a freshman all to yourself, and that person stays your charge until you graduate. Some of the upperclassmen abuse this tradition, using their little sisters or brothers as personal assistants or valets. Others just pretend they don't exist. And, I suppose, there are a handful of students who take the job seriously.

I entered Stonebridge in sophomore year, but I was still assigned a big sister. She was a junior at the time. I think Dean Stinson was trying to engineer a friendship. Or, at least, give me a leg up with my acquaintances. Christine was one of the junior Ten and, as far as I could tell, on her way to becoming the queen of Stonebridge. I don't know if Dean Stinson was fully cognizant of her status or simply understood that she was a girl who fit in. At first, Christine ignored me. Later, when she spotted me making inroads with the Ten, she began to acknowledge my existence. In the end, when her status at school had taken an unfortunate detour, she tried to warn me.

Christine was the first person who told me about the

Dulcinea Award. It's named after some beautiful woman in *Don Quixote.* It's weird that I've never seen that book on any Stonebridge reading list. Christine said the boys score the girls on their blowjobs and pronounce a winner at the end of the school year. Only the girls don't know they're competing and the winner of the Dulcinea Award never learns of her victory. At least, that was how it had always been done, until the boys started getting sloppy.

The sloppiest of all had to be Kingsley Shaw, Christine's steady boyfriend. One night, after they'd messed around, he went for a shower and left his laptop open, with Christine's score sheet on full view. She couldn't figure out what she was looking at, at first. She saw a lot of numbers—sixes mostly. It wasn't until she read the comments section that the full impact hit her.

Christine was so angry, she had trouble focusing on the big picture. She got twisted up by the whole scoring system.

I remember Christine saying, "When you put your mouth on someone's dick, that's an automatic eight out of ten, with the only possible deduction coming from permanent damage."

Christine confronted Kingsley, who owned up to not just his record keeping but to the larger conspiracy and made some kind of joke about there always being room for improvement. Christine told Kingsley that she was going to destroy him and every one of his cohorts. But she didn't know what she was up against. She confronted the editors, without allies or backup. The editors responded with a full-blown attack on Christine's character. They painted her as a queen bitch who spread nasty rumors about all of her friends. She was shunned and shamed until she transferred to a local high school to finish up her senior year. I've learned from Christine's mistakes.

My little sister is Linny Matthews. Linny, a fifteen-year-old waif who wears her hair in a short bob with bangs, looks like prime bait for the editors. She's also crazy smart, willful, and has an unusual talent for persuading people to do things they don't actually want to do. I've told Linny everything she needs to know to stay out of the Darkroom, including not talking about the Darkroom. Linny's contribution to my cause, however, is limited to a few administrative assignments. She has three years left at this school; I won't put a target on her back.

Linny has independent-study Latin after lunch. I tracked her down at Milton Studio, where she was lying on top of a long desk, wearing an eye mask. Stonebridge doesn't offer any formal Latin classes, so Linny can do what she likes, wherever she likes, during that period.

"Wake up," I said.

"I'm awake," she said, as she bolted upright and whisked off her eye mask. *"Quid novi?"*

Linny occasionally throws around conversational Latin to maintain her cover.

"I need a meet with Kate Bush," I said.

When I saw the photo of Kate, I knew it was more than a nasty prank. I had to enlist her as an ally.

"Tragic," Linny said, shaking her head with a look of pity and relief.

There's always some grain of pleasure in another person's

shame. It's impossible not to think, *Thank God it wasn't me.*

"Text me if you see her," I said. "We need to have a private, unobserved conversation."

I knew that if I asked Linny to keep an eye out for Kate, she'd stalk Kate until she found her alone. I find it better to give Linny assignments than to leave her to her own devices.

Linny checked her watch and slung her backpack over her shoulder.

"That's it?" Linny said.

"That's it," I said.

Sometimes I worry about the transactional nature of our relationship. Then again, that's how so many of mine are.

I left Milton Studio and returned to Headquarters to deliver my assignment to Witt's box. As soon as I relinquished my Q&A, I had my doubts. Anonymous or not, maybe I shouldn't have told her who I was. Besides, I am many things, not just one.

I'm an orphan. I'm a retired pot dealer. I'm an independent contractor. I'm a double agent. I'm a dissenter. I'm a ticking time bomb. I'm the enemy who hides in plain sight, looking for others like me. I'm an agent of revenge who will bring the Darkroom to its knees.

MS. WITT

At lunch, I grabbed some kind of vegetable stew from Dahl Dining Hall and strolled the short distance to Tolkien Library. The librarian sat behind her desk, hovering over a thick book with her head low and her arms guarding the edges, the posture of a convict during chowtime. I saw no reason to interrupt her, so I dropped my stew on a long wooden study desk and roamed the aisles.

First I heard the patter of the librarian's pumps on the linoleum floor. Then I saw her, gazing at me from the other side of the bookshelf.

"There's no food permitted in the library," she said.

"I'm sorry," I said, framing my head between a gap in the reference section.

The librarian leaned in with a scrutinizing gaze.

"You're not a student."

"No," I said.

"You're Len Wilde's daughter."

"I usually go by Alex."

She marched around the stacks to the section I was

investigating and handed me my stew.

"Hi. I'm Claudine Shepherd. Librarian," she said, shaking my hand with perfectly manicured nails. "You can call me Claude."

"Hi, Claude," I said.

My general opinion of librarians tends to be a step above that of the rest of the population. The reasons are obvious: They're book lovers with, often, an evangelical desire to push reading on anyone within range. I was inclined to like Claude Shepherd, head librarian (only librarian), even before I met her. And when I first laid eyes on her, I liked her even more. She was a librarian out of central casting. She wore a tweed pencil skirt, a light-blue blouse with ruffles, and three-inch pumps that echoed through the library as she stalked the aisles of her domain. Claude looked like she could rule the world without breaking a sweat. And yet there was warmth behind her sharp edges.

"I bend the food rule for faculty, but absolutely no tuna fish. Ever," Claude said.

"That seems reasonable."

"What are you looking for, Alex?"

"A book," I said.

She smiled. "You're in the right place. What kind of book?"

"Some kind of creative-writing exercise book."

"Aren't you the creative-writing teacher?"

"Debatable. That's why I need the book."

Claude immediately pulled two paperbacks. One was called *Just Write Something Already* and the other *In Progress*.

"This is all we've got."

"Thank you. Do I need a library card or something?"

"Nah. I know where to find you," said Claude.

"See you around," I said, as I hooked the books under the arm that wasn't holding stew.

"Do you drink?" Claude said.

"I do."

"Excellent. The town of Lowland, Vermont, has exactly one thing going for it. A bar. You will come to love it. As it is the only place you can go to escape the students. It's called Hemingway's. Don't ask. A few of us are meeting up for happy hour on Friday afternoon."

"I'll try to make it," I said.

"You'll *try*? It's Friday in Lowland and you live in a shack. I'll see you there," Claude said.

My last period of the day was something called advanced creative-writing workshop. When I reviewed my class roster, I noticed that the students were the same ones from my first-period class. I tracked down Greg to get him to explain it to me. He said the group of nineteen would be working on longer-format projects—screenplay, novel, one-woman show . . . anything they wanted to do.

I couldn't decide if having the same students twice in one day was a recipe for disaster or immaterial. But I played up my disappointment when Greg gave me the scoop.

"You might start looking for my replacement," I said.

That afternoon, as the students filed into the classroom,

they flouted the morning's established assigned seats. I shook my head, said no, and waited until they rearranged themselves. I did notice that at no time did anyone sit in the front row's window seat.

"Looks like we're going to be spending a lot of time together," I said.

"I, for one, am looking forward to it," Mick Devlin, the one who wore his tie like an ascot, said.

I had no lecture prepared and they'd already completed their Q&A's, so I just grabbed one of those writing books, leafed through it for a few minutes, and delivered their next assignment.

"Write your origin story in five hundred words or less. This time your name should definitely appear on your paper."

"Origin story?" Hannah Rexall (lithe, blond) said.

"Like we're superheroes?" said Adam Westlake (bow tie and dimpled smile).

"Precisely," I said.

Carl Bloom (red nose, allergies?) insisted that he needed more than five hundred words. I insisted that he did not. Gabriel Smythe's hand shot up. I nodded for him to speak.

"Five hundred words or less could mean only five words or ten words, right?"

"Yes. Although that would probably be a crap origin story. How about we say between four hundred and five hundred words. Due Monday. One more thing," I said, remembering my primitive living arrangement. "You have to deliver hard copies of all of your assignments to my box in admin. I can't access Blackboard, or the Internet for that matter, from where I live."

I sat back down at my desk while they groaned their disapproval. My phone buzzed again.

Jonah Wagman: Are you the daughter of Len Wilde?

If I were to write my own origin story, I suspect it would be more about my parents than myself, which, come to think of it, is vaguely pathetic.

My father's nom de plume is Len Wilde. Forty years ago, my dad published his first and only novel under his real name, Leonard Witt. *Darkness, Behave* was well reviewed, but the sales were modest. While Dad wrestled with his sophomore effort, he supplemented his income by teaching and taking on the occasional magazine assignment.

Dad's popularity rose sharply, about five years after the first printing of *Darkness, Behave,* when a well-known filmmaker adapted his book for the screen. In the novel, people fall in love and out of love and think an awful lot about murder but never, in fact, commit murder. The filmed adaptation took Dad's characters and gave them a plot. The resulting movie was a taut thriller and a huge box-office success, which made the paperback of *Darkness, Behave* a massive bestseller. While Dad relished his newfound wealth and celebrity, he was chastened by the knowledge that his success did not directly correlate with his work. Such a motif would become his lifelong curse.

My father met my mother, Nastya Lazarov, a few weeks

after she defected to Canada, while his first book clung to the bestseller list. Nastya was an alternate on the Bulgarian fencing team. She jumped ship, so to speak, the day after the opening ceremonies of the 1976 Montreal Olympics.

My mother's true passion was escaping Eastern Europe, not swordplay. She'd simply chosen the sport that gave her the best shot at making the Olympic team, which was phase one of her plan. My father interviewed her for a magazine piece. These were the first two lines:

> Leonard Witt: *Do you like fencing?*
> Nastya Lazarov: *Not particularly.*

They married a year later. A few years after that, in another Olympic year, I was born. My mother never competed again. Although she occasionally gave pricey private lessons when we were low on cash. I don't have memories of my parents during their honeymoon phase. I'm not even sure they ever had one. My mother always said that my father's most attractive quality was being American. If pressed, she'd mention his smile and blue eyes. But marriage was simply security for her. Whenever I'd ask my dad about the early days, he'd first comment on my mother's beauty, then he'd undercut the compliment by mentioning one of her quirkier flaws. She fenced left-handed and, according to my father, had a bizarrely lopsided musculature, which, he claimed, made her left breast at least a full cup size smaller, and significantly higher, than the right one.

My most vivid memory of the pre–Len Wilde years was

my father reading his work in progress to me at night, as a bedtime story. He'd edit as he read aloud and would often ask the seven-year-old me for her opinion. I never got a full grasp of the story, since Dad read it to me piecemeal. My best guess was that it centered on a janitor who haunts an office building and habitually relocates the personal items of the senior executives.

Later, I learned that Dad had been at that novel for more than ten years. It had surpassed six hundred pages with no end in sight. One night, when Dad had drunk himself into oblivion after finding a gaping hole in the plot (no easy feat with a plotless novel), Mom snuck into his office and removed every digital and hard copy of Dad's work in progress, tentatively titled *The Marauders of Main Street.* In their stead, she left a one-page outline for a traditional three-act plot of a crime novel.

Mom held hostage not just the unfinished novel but Dad's beloved Rolex, a gift from the film studio after *Darkness, Behave* made one hundred million at the box office.

Dad had three months to write the draft, or both would be lost forever.

My parents fought well and they fought often. The fight after the great delete of 1992 was the kind of childhood memory that you can never erase. It wasn't a battle with airstrikes or grenades or even disciplined, well-choreographed domestic attacks. It was a cold war. The house had never been quieter. They plotted against and spied on each other; they played confidence games with their friends to gather information; they both thought I was their double agent. I saw myself more as a freelance mole, using my sway to both facilitate an endgame and recover whatever spoils I could.

In the midst of their deep freeze, my father wrote the crime novel my mother had outlined. *The Broken Kiss,* he called it. He left it outside my mother's door, almost three months to the day after the night of the delete. She read it in one sitting. The next morning, my mother returned the marked-up manuscript to my father.

"It is perfect," she said. "Other than the places that I marked up."

Leonard Witt now exclusively writes crime novels as Len Wilde. No matter how hard he tries, Dad will never duplicate the inexplicable success of his first novel. But Len Wilde makes a decent living when he doesn't blow his deadlines.

As for my parents: They divorced ten years ago, just a month after I left for college. It came as no surprise. How those two stayed married for more than twenty years is a greater mystery than anything in the Len Wilde canon.

NORMAN CROWLEY

MY ORIGIN STORY

By Norman Crowley

Freshman year I was invisible. I had one friend, Ephraim Wiener, and that was enough. Every month the ~~editors~~ seniors would throw a school party. The organizers and primary attendees were upperclassmen. But the entire student body was allowed access to the kegs, as long as they paid the cover charge, which was actually some kind of ~~fucked-up~~ balderdash pyramid scheme: $20 for freshmen, $15 for sophomores, $10 for juniors, $5 for seniors, and presumably a windfall for the ~~editors~~ organizers. After spending every Friday night in our room playing Warcraft, Ephraim and I decided to shake things up.

At the time, the ~~editor in chief~~ man of the hour, the one in charge, was Ty Givens. He was so ridiculously white and rich and privileged and stupid. I'd heard he'd gone to Warren and was kicked out for academic in-excellence–that was his joke. Probably his only good one.

Ephraim and I paid the cover charge and hovered near the keg, waiting for the tap to be free. We wanted to get our money's worth. It was the first time I'd had two beers in a row. I was solidly inebriated.

Ty and his crew were having a laugh about a senior named Tracy Schlitt. I used to see her around. She wore vintage dresses with flower designs and large buttons and horn-rimmed glasses with diamonds on the edge. I knew that she had won a scholarship to study engineering at MIT and she made this really cool robot for her senior thesis that would make coffee and tea and say good morning and keep track of your schedule. I went to her presentation in Mr. Collins's class when she showcased her project. She called it Bitterman, based on a butler in some movie I haven't seen. Tracy was one of the slummers.

Ty's friend Blake was calling her Tracy Shit; then some other guy said "slit" and added, "I heard she's ~~fucking~~ having relations with ~~Collins~~ that guy."

"I guess that guy needs to take it where he can get it, but I wouldn't get near that heifer if she were the last woman on earth," said Ty.

Then they said more crap about wearing a blindfold and stuff like that and Ty interrupted and said, "To quote my good friend Nietzsche, 'When a woman has a brain, there's usually something wrong with her ~~pussy~~ face.'"

"How would you know?" I said.

Ephraim elbowed me in the ribs. They were howling

like animals. I'm surprised they even heard me.

"What?" said one of Ty's cronies, as the group fell silent.

Emboldened by the beer and reckless because I didn't know the ramifications, I repeated my statement and added, "No woman with a brain would ever ~~fuck~~ give you the time of day."

"Dude, dude," I heard someone say, like a warning.

I saw them puffing out their chests, like peacocks, but I didn't stop. I remember the adrenaline. It was like a drug I hadn't taken. The best I'd felt in weeks.

"Only ~~douchebags~~ morons quote Nietzsche, and only ~~megadouchebags~~ megamorons quote Nietzsche wrong," I said.

I was only fourteen then. Considering what happened next, it was a mistake. And yet a mistake I wish I could make again. I had more courage in those few minutes than I've had in my entire life.

MS. WITT

The cottage felt like an icebox when I woke up early Wednesday morning. I dialed up the space heaters, filled the kettle, and turned on the electric hot plate. It wasn't until I flipped the switch on the nightstand lamp that I realized I had no power. I searched briefly for an electrical box, but my heart wasn't in it. I grabbed a duffel bag, stuffed it with a change of clothes and my shower kit, and left my blacked-out cabin.

Trudging through the woods, I held my phone up to the morning light, looking for reception. Once I had two bars, I hit the second number on my speed dial. I knew his phone would be off, so I left a message.

"Hey, asshole. Where do you get off making life decisions for me? Stay out of my business, Dad. And don't call me back."

I heard the sound of a grumpy engine, then spotted an ATV slicing through the woods. An old guy was driving the thing. He had a head of thick brown hair with specks of gray that blew back like wings. I waved because we were the only two people out there. He braked and quieted the throttle. His hair flopped flat on his forehead.

"Good morning. You must be the new one," he said.

"Yes. I'm Alex," I said.

"Rupert, at your service," he said. "I take care of things around here."

"What kind of things?" I asked.

"How much time do you have?" he replied, making a point to look at his watch.

"The power went out in the cabin," I said.

"Sure." He sighed. "That was inevitable."

I thought he would offer to handle it. I waited. He didn't.

Then Rupert started shaking his head and said, "I don't know. I don't know, Alex."

"I don't know either," I said, which was as true a statement as I've ever made.

Rupert nodded as if I'd said something wise, gunned the engine, and drove off.

The drawbacks of the cottage had begun to pile up. I suppose I knew about all of them when I made the deal, but you start to feel it when you're out of cellphone and Internet range and even local television is a prohibitive notion. I had just returned from three weeks at Sun Ra Monastery and Meditation Center with none of the above. I'd tricked myself into believing I was beyond all that. If only I were half as good at bullshitting other people.

I took Stoker Lane around Headquarters to Beckett Gym. I rushed down the stairs and entered the door marked NO STUDENTS ALLOWED, NO EXCEPTIONS. My second visit to the Wilde Bathhouse was decidedly less enticing. I hadn't fully considered the notion of communal bathing or the quarter-mile trek to do so.

Everything in Wilde was behind a layer of steam. It was like being in a fogbank that smelled of eucalyptus. One could glimpse a warren of shiny lockers through the haze. On the opposite wall was a row of vessel sinks. On the middle wall, you couldn't miss the decorative fountain backed by a tile portrait of Oscar Wilde himself. I think he might have approved of the gauzy filter the steam provided.

I thought I was alone, but it was hard to tell. I dropped off my duffel bag and grabbed a thick cotton towel near a metal stand by the shower stalls. As I was debating the appropriate location for disrobing, a man appeared—out of the mist. He wore a towel wrapped around his waist. He was lean and tan, like beef jerky. I hadn't been in a coed bathroom since college. I assumed the code of conduct for professional peers must be different, but the etiquette eluded me.

"You're the new teacher, right?" he said, as he dropped his towel.

I had never seen a sharper contrast in a tan line. In a way, I found it comforting to know that he was typically covered from his mid-thigh to his waist.

"Yes. That's me."

"I'm Keith," he said.

"Hi, I'm Alex," I said, averting my gaze. Then I caught the reflection of his bare ass in one of the mirrors above the sink. I turned my attention to the image of Oscar.

"How's that cabin treating you?" he said.

"It's—I don't know," I said.

I was too surprised by his casual nudity to elaborate.

"Those space heaters still working?"

"No."

"Huh."

"Do you know why?" I said.

"The generator must have run out of fuel."

"There's a generator?"

"Not much of one. I think it's only a thousand watts. That cabin was intended as a warming station or a place to recharge equipment for the groundskeeper. It wasn't meant for habitation."

"It looked like someone lived there once," I said.

"Maybe in summer," Keith said.

The next time I accidentally glanced over, he was wearing jeans.

"What do you do here?" I said.

"I coach most of the team sports. Speaking of, we've got a few kids interested in fencing, if you ever want to pitch in," Keith said. "I've watched some videos and try to offer some suggestions. But it's not my bag."

"It's not my bag either," I said, retreating to one of the shower stalls. "See you around, Keith."

Even though I was showering in an individual stall, it felt like someone was going to join me any second. I made it quick and, to avoid another awkward encounter, dressed behind the curtain. By the time I stepped out of Wilde, my clothes clung to my skin like I had just finished a long hike.

I rushed over to Headquarters and entered Agatha Christie Admin to collect my anonymous assignments. By then my damp clothes had cooled and I had the chills.

Ms. Pinsky, the secretary, sat alone at the front desk, nibbling on a Danish. As I collected a thick stack of papers from my box, I heard clomping behind me.

A high-pitched voice said, “Is that you?”

I always hated that question.

I turned around to find a woman standing just one foot away, popping up like the genie in that old sitcom I sometimes watched with my dad. A few pages slipped out of my arms and floated onto the floor.

“You’re Alex Witt. Who else could you be?” she said, as she picked up a wandering page.

She introduced herself as Martha Primm, guidance counselor and school psychologist. She said she’d heard all about me and was excited to finally make my acquaintance.

Martha Primm was like a human strobe light. There was just too much to take in. She wore her long, highlighted hair in perfect ringlets. Her kelly-green wrap dress was cinched at the waist with a sparkling gold rope belt. There were bracelets clanking and synthetic fabrics rustling. Her perfume seemed to camp out inside my nostrils. Even her footwear—blue clogs adorned with daisies—was aggressively cheery.

“My goodness, would you look at all of those papers. And so early in the year. The students were filing in all day long yesterday to turn in these assignments. A few of them started poking around and looking at each other’s work. I sent them on their merry way, I'll have you know. Let me get that for you," she said, bending down to pick up a few more wayward pages. "Most teachers use the Blackboard system for delivery of homework. If you would like a tutorial on Blackboard, please let me know. I'd be happy to arrange it."

"That's okay," I said. "We used something similar at—"

Primm glanced down at the paper she had retrieved.

"Now, this one didn't even write down their—" She broke off as she peered over the next page.

"This one also didn't put down—"

Primm's smile flatlined as her eyes tracked past the nonexistent name and down to the body of the paper. She cleared her throat and dropped the pages on the top of my stack. I glanced down and read the first few lines.

What do you love?
Pussy
What do you hate?
Dry pussy?
If you could live inside a book, what book?
The Kama Sutra

"Oh my," she said, returning the paper.

"Sorry," I said, feeling uneasy.

I had to admit, it looked bad. And who wants to read that shit first thing in the morning? I tried to explain.

"It's a word-association type of assignment. I try not to censor them," I said.

"Well, I don't know anything about creative writing, so I can't comment."

"See you around," I said.

"You will," Primm said, followed by a quick pivot and the sound of her clogs, like hooves, on the marble floor.

In class, while my students exchanged texts and pretended to write their origin stories, I began to annotate the Q&A's with tentative gender assignments. I've found a few telltale markers. For instance, if the answer to the hate question is a body part (other than abs or biceps), I promptly slip the sheet into the girl pile. If the answer to the hate question is a person, gender becomes irrelevant, although I see it as a solid marker for volatility and future conflict. Unless the object of hatred is Hitler, Stalin, Pol Pot, Chris Brown, or Kid Rock.

Likely male:

What do you love? The Darkroom
What do you hate? Snitches and douchebags
If you could live inside a book, what book?
The Picture of Dorian Gray
What do you want? Absolute power
Who are you? The boss man

Likely female:

What do you love? Neko Case, banana bread, the smell of Pine-Sol

What do you hate? BJs, editors, and agents of the Darkroom
If you could live inside a book, what book? The Girl with the Dragon Tattoo
What do you want? An invisibility cloak and cyanide
Who are you? I'm not who they think I am

Probably male:

What do you love? Bright Eyes, Reservoir Dogs, PB&J sandwiches, CS
What do you hate? The Darkroom
If you could live inside a book, what book? Tinker Tailor Soldier Spy
What do you want? For my real life to begin
Who are you? I'm a coward

I took note of the Darkroom reference. Whatever it was, my students either loved or hated it.

As a diagnostic tool, I've found the Q&A's to provide some valuable information. But it's not a lie detector or an X-ray machine. I'll never get the answer to the question that I'm ultimately trying to ask:

What are you capable of?

GEMMA RUSSO

It started last year. Every now and again, the showers in the boys' dorm would run hot or cold. Direct evidence of sabotage was never found, but the boys became convinced it was the act of some kind of vigilante. I was thrilled that the shower saboteur had struck again so early in the school year. Without fail, it ruins the boys' day and totally makes mine. I wish I'd thought of it.

There's a certain look they get, post–shower chaos: shoulders hunched, hair askew, with a vague aura of depression. Except Jonah, who would insist that the unpredictability of the temperature invigorated him.

In class, the boys huddled together in disgruntled knots, grumbling about their rough morning. I had to wonder if it was a salvo by an unknown comrade or comrades. I searched the room for a possible candidate. The obvious choice was Kate Bush, but I couldn't see her being that reckless so soon after her humiliation.

As the class settled in to first period, Witt paid us no mind. She sat at her desk, studying our Q&A's, sorting them in stacks. Her hand propped up her head, as if she'd collapse without it. She had the expression of someone who hates math trying to graph a quadratic equation.

Ms. Witt didn't look up until Carl Bloom blew his nose, making a sound like a poorly played trumpet. The poor guy has a buffet of allergies. Don't get him started.

Witt told us to work independently on our origin stories.

Sandra Polonsky immediately raised her hand: "I already have five hundred and fifty words and I'm only at age seven and that's with editing out my first day of kindergarten."

"I want you to write your origin story. Not your memoir . . . Sandra," Witt said, after consulting her seating chart. "Think about who you are, how you got to be you. Is there a single event that helped form your identity?"

"What if I don't have an origin story?" Sandra said.

"Everyone has at least one origin story," said Witt.

"What if mine hasn't happened yet?" Sandra said.

"This is a creative-writing class," Witt said, dipping into a whisper. "You're not beholden to the truth."

"So, our origin stories can be total bullshit?" Gabe asked.

"Don't be so hard on yourself. I'm sure your whole life hasn't been bullshit," said Devlin.

"Except for that one magical night with your mother," said Gabe.

Most of the class howled. It might have been funny if some variation of I-fucked-your-mother wasn't the *only* joke he ever told. Last year I found *Comedy for Dummies* at Mo's for two dollars. I left it in Gabe's mailbox, hoping to elevate the quality of his material. Two bucks, lost forever.

Okay, Witt said.

It was remarkable how efficiently she could quiet the class with a single word. I think she scared some students, especially the boys. Gabe, like a skittish dog, couldn't even look her in the eye. That dead rat really backfired on him.

ANNOUNCEMENTS

Good morning, students of Stone. Wainwright reporting on Friday, September 11, 2009.

Breaking news: Our plumber, Lester, has fixed the hot-water heater in Dickens House. We apologize to all of the boys who suffered the frigid waters again this morning. Other matters: If anyone is missing a half pack of grape bubble gum, come see me. Lunch today you have a choice of Hungarian goulash or vegetarian pad thai. We've got a beautiful sunny day ahead of us. A comfortable seventy-two degrees, dipping to a crisp fifty-nine at night. That's Fahrenheit, not Celsius. If it were Celsius we'd be dead. I remember the days we thought we'd switch over to the metric system. Didn't happen. . . . What? Okay. Today's news: The first meeting of the A/V Club will be in Milton Studio, Saturday, at 5:45 a.m. I repeat—5:15 a.m. Don't be late. [sound of a record scratching, static, music] This morning's tune. A little Charles Mingus to send you off into that dangerous world.

MS. WITT

"Who is Wainwright?" I asked my class. "A teacher or someone in admin?"

"Who isn't he? That is the question," said Mick Devlin.

"No. That isn't the question," I said. "Seriously, who is this guy?"

"He'd prefer we didn't know his true identity," said Adam Westlake.

"We've decided to respect his wishes," said Amy Logan.

"But don't rely on his weather reports. Ever," said Jonah.

My phone buzzed.

I glanced at the screen. It was a call from Annie, a friend and fellow teacher from my Warren Prep days. Annie never called. She said texting was the best thing that's happened in modern communication. I assumed it was important and stepped outside.

"Everything okay?" I said.

"Sorry to bother you," Annie said. "But I thought you should know. Barbara got a call yesterday from someone at Stonebridge. At first, the caller said that he was just confirming your references, but then he started asking about you, about what happened."

"What did she tell him?"

"Nothing. Don't worry."

"Did she get a name?" I asked.

"Yeah. Hang on. I got it here somewhere. Um . . . Jim Stark. Yes. Jim Stark. Why does that sound familiar?"

"Because he's a character in one of my father's books."

During my office hours, I swung by AA. There was a message slip in my inbox informing me that I had a message.

"I have a message," I said to Ms. Pinsky, dropping the slip onto the counter.

"Coach Keith would like to see you," Ms. Pinsky said.

"Did Coach Keith tell you why?" I said.

"Oh. I don't know. It's not really any of my business, is it?" Pinsky said.

Her message-delivery system was so impressively inefficient, I refrained from comment.

"Where could I find him?" I said.

Just then a woman in her forties, freckled and tan, entered the office.

"I'm not sure where Coach would be right now," said Pinsky.

"I'd check the gym," the freckled woman said.

"Maybe the gym?" Ms. Pinsky echoed, as if it were her own idea.

The woman to whom I hadn't yet been introduced smiled

and extended her hand. "You must be Alex. I'm Evelyn Lubovich. History, social studies, and welding."

"Welding?" I said, as we shook hands.

"Dean Stinson likes to call it 'metal arts.' Welcome," she said. "See you later. At Hemingway's."

"Yes," I said, remembering. "See you later."

I left Headquarters and followed the stone walkway to the gym.

Voices echoed throughout the corridor. I approached Keith's office and looked inside. It was empty. I followed the voices to the end of the hall.

"*How* is it possible you only have one ball?" said a young female voice.

"I don't know what to tell you, Linny," said Keith.

"This is ridiculous," said, I assumed, Linny.

"The person who loses the point gets the ball," Keith said, as if for the hundredth time.

I entered the gym. Inside, a Ping-Pong table stood in the center of a basketball court. The young girl, who bore a remarkable resemblance to Tatum O'Neal in *Paper Moon,* scowled aggressively and tossed the ball to Keith, who attacked the serve without any regard for the skill of his opponent. The ball whizzed past Linny, who threw her paddle into the air.

"I call bullshit," Linny said.

"Sorry to interrupt," I said. "Ms. Pinsky said you wanted to see me."

"Linny, grab the paper bag with the cat food from my office," Coach said.

As Linny slow-walked out of the gym, Keith said, "Pick up the pace, Matthews."

The girl sluggishly jogged away.

"Did you say cat food?" I said.

"Yes," said Keith.

"I don't have a cat."

"There's a feral cat that lives near the cottage. He'll leave mouse carcasses at your door if you don't feed him."

"I haven't seen any carcasses."

"I've been cleaning them up."

"Why?"

"I figured you had seen enough dead rodents since you arrived," he said.

"You heard?" I said.

"Got around fast. Kids think you're a badass."

Linny returned with the bag of cat food and delivered it to me.

"Well, thank you," I said.

"I'm going to take five," said Linny, departing once again.

"The generator working okay?" Keith said.

"Yes," I said. "I guess Rupert refilled the tank."

"That was me," he said.

"Why?"

"That cottage is barely habitable *with* power. Did you see the gas can?"

"No."

"There's about five gallons. That might cover a week if

the weather doesn't turn and you're really frugal. I wouldn't plan on an extended stay in—"

"Well, thank you," I said. "If there's any way that I can repay the favor."

"It would be great if we could start a fencing club," he said.

"I don't fence," I said. "I believe we already had that conversation."

"Did we? I don't remember."

"Have a nice day," I said, swiftly departing.

When I returned to Headquarters, I found Jonah Wagman sitting alone in my classroom, in his assigned seat. Fourth row, aisle three. There was a bright-red apple in the middle of my desk. I picked up the apple and checked my watch. It was one-thirty, technically office hours, but high school students rarely took advantage of the practice. I considered the time to be an extended lunch period.

"Can I help you with something, Jonah?"

Jonah finished chomping down on a jawbreaker. The classroom had a faint cherry odor.

"I was wondering if you'd be my faculty adviser."

"That's a thing here?"

"Yes."

"What happened to your old adviser? Did he die?"

"Nah. Mr. Ford's alive. But I'd like to switch to you. He was my adviser for like two years. Change is good. Adults are always saying that."

"You already have two classes with me and you want to spend even more time together. We just met, Jonah."

"I promise I won't come to your office hours every day. Just occasionally. And if, at any point, you are unhappy with the situation, I will seek advisement elsewhere."

"Who is Wainwright?" I asked.

"Please don't make that a condition for becoming my adviser."

"What are my job responsibilities as adviser?"

"To advise," Jonah said.

"What do I get in return?"

"I don't know. I can get more apples. Do you like other fruit?"

"I like bananas. But I can get my own."

"What is it that you want, Ms. Witt?"

"Tell me what happened to Kate."

MR. FORD

Witt was late.

Claude sat across from me in the booth, her leg jackrabbiting the floor. Her eyes toggled between her phone and the door, waiting for new blood to arrive, like a crack addict anticipating her fix.

Evelyn, next to her, leaned against the wood paneling, her eyelids hovering between open and closed, like a pair of broken garage doors. Always tired. I've noticed that the bags under her eyes have gotten worse. I saw a picture of her when she was younger and she was kind of hot. Two kids later, a lot of summers outdoors without sunblock, I think she's given up. Her husband travels for work, doesn't help with the kids, probably fucks other women on the road. Sometimes, during lunch, I give Evelyn the key to my quarters to take a nap. Invariably, when I return, she's made my bed and washed my dishes. I should stop giving her the key, but it's so goddamn nice to come home to a clean kitchen.

Primm was too close as usual and she reeked of Shalimar. I sat on the edge of the booth and she still managed to brush against me, to find some excuse to touch my hand, my arm, my leg, to engage in eye contact that resembled a staring contest. She must have unbuttoned her blouse before she walked into the bar, because her tits were hanging out. They're her best feature. Unfortunately, Primm thinks it's her hair. The sheer volume is extraordinary. Every time she turns her head, a ringlet grazes my neck. Claude and I used to play a game where we'd try to come up with something nice to say about the entire Stonebridge faculty. Claude would always get stumped on Primm. We used to joke about it, back when we used to joke about things. It's not funny anymore. Fuck, none of it's funny—Claude's anger, Primm's desperation, Evelyn's exhaustion. The day started wrong with the shower turning to ice. My apartment in Dickens has a private shower, but it is unfortunately connected to the same sketchy hot-water heater as the communal ones. I would make the trek to the Wilde Bathhouse, but the last thing I need is to see naked Keith before I've had coffee.

Primm inquired about Claude's home life. Claude, voice Antarctic, told her things were the same. Primm asked more questions about Claude's mother. Every week, we replay this loop, with Primm picking at scabs on a feral dog. I keep meaning to tell Evelyn to stop inviting Martha to drinks night.

I was bored. I looked at the time on my phone. I decided I'd leave if Witt didn't show in ten minutes. Claude made a crack about me checking to see if my agent called.

They never call, she said.

Sometimes I like Claude, but she's dangerous, which is

probably why. She's the woman who wraps her fingers around your neck and it feels rough and fun, but then she squeezes too hard and you can't breathe.

The three of them started talking about Witt, chopping her up into little pieces and reassembling her into a dummy they could play with. They dissected Witt's decision to live in the cottage. Claude thought it was austerity; Primm, bad judgment; and Evelyn, wise. Their opinions were more personally revealing than insightful.

The dirt-digging began after that. Primm brought it up, but in truth we were all deeply curious about Witt's move from plummy Warren Prep to mid-tiered Stonebridge. Primm had overheard Greg say that Witt spent the summer at a monastery.

"I should talk to her about leaving her Buddhism at the gates," Primm said.

Evelyn and Claude had a laugh. Primm didn't think it was funny. Claude then thought it was even funnier. She was just trying to rile Primm up. When Claude can't bear the feeling in her gut, she jabs at anything close enough to hit.

Most of the time I feel like I'm trapped in an elevator with Muzak playing.

For some reason that sentence caught in my head. Claude said it one day after we fucked. That's how she feels all of the time.

I clocked the door to make sure Witt hadn't arrived yet. Evelyn tried to toss some chum to distract Claude and Primm from their mutual hate by delivering the stale news that Witt is Len Wilde's child. Primm said she'd read one of his books—

Shadow Room, something room? She prefers Grisham. Primm looked at her watch and said that Alex wasn't coming. Evelyn still thought she'd show. Claude, impatient, sent a text.

Hugh, the tattooed guy who runs this joint, leaned over the booth and delivered a fresh whiskey to Claude and a chemical-green beverage to Evelyn. Evie is always ordering something ridiculous. I checked my watch again. Witt had four minutes to arrive before my self-imposed deadline. Primm tried to get table service from Hugh, holding the empty pitcher of beer over her head. He refused to look at her.

I went to the bar and ordered two pints. I didn't want to be stuck finishing a pitcher with Primm if Witt didn't show. Keith was sitting at the bar, watching an Orioles–Yankees game. We did that guy nod exchange and said *hey*. He had this smirk like he knew something about me. I wanted to punch that smirk off his face.

I gave Primm her pint, hoping it would take the edge off her desperation. I knew she'd mistake it for a chivalrous gesture, a note of attention.

The conversation had moved on to Witt's mother. Claude had a vague memory of reading an essay about Nastya Witt. She was trying to remember the title.

"Did you ever read that, Finn?"

"No," I said.

I don't know why I denied knowing about it. Shit, I practically knew the essay by heart.

"The Cruel Muse," it was called. Sometime after *Hidden Window* was released, Leonard Witt wrote a piece for *The New*

Yorker. The essay, which detailed the subversive ways his wife incentivized his writing, became legend.

Primm wasn't interested in discussing the lore of Witt's lineage. She just wanted to poke holes in her character until she was a human Wiffle ball.

"I don't know what, but I know something happened there," Primm said. "According to her employment records, Witt left halfway through the spring semester. Personal reasons."

"There are hundreds of non-scandalous reasons why someone leaves their job," I said.

"Just look at her, Finn; she's a mess. You know what I think? I think she had a nervous breakdown and that's why she left Warren. Let's just make a pact to keep an eye on her."

Claude, like a coiled snake, hissed, *"What the fuck is wrong with you?"*

Evelyn, words slurring, said, "Okay. Stop. You're both being mean girls."

Claude leveled her eyes at Primm and said, "At least I'm good at it."

I looked at the time. Alex was now two minutes past my deadline. I was trying to calculate whether the possibility of fucking Witt was worth the torture of this night. Claude slid out of the booth and said she had to use the bathroom. The time to leave would have been before Claude excused herself. I was trapped.

Evelyn then began this preposterous verbal debate with herself about whether she'd have another drink and what kind of drink. It was all noise, just so we wouldn't have to listen to

Primm talking anymore. But Evie was tired and soon ran out of steam. Primm gladly filled the vacuum by inquiring why Claude took so long in the bathroom.

One grasshopper too many and reliable, reasonable Evelyn becomes ornery.

"She's. Fucking. The. Bartender. In. The. Bathroom, you clueless, clueless woman. She fucks him every time we come here. How have you never noticed that?"

MS. WITT

I didn't know what I was walking into.

It looked like they were about to leave the bar. Then they froze, like in an action shot. I swear they looked blurry. Finn ushered me over and shoved me into the seat next to Martha Primm. He seemed hell-bent on having me act as a barricade between him and Primm. Across from us sat Claude and Evelyn, with so much room between them I felt a pang of jealousy.

"You've all met, right?" said Finn.

"We're so glad you could make it," Primm said.

She wasn't even trying to sound sincere.

The foursome traded uncertain glances. It was all so weird that it threw me off-balance. Finn got up and asked me if I wanted a drink. Of course I wanted a drink. Why else was I there?

I asked for whatever was on tap, because I didn't want to waste time with decision-making. I needed a drink.

Finn left us to order. I spotted Keith, sitting at the bar. I waved at him. I don't think he saw me. I asked why he wasn't part of the drinking club.

"I don't think he likes us," Primm said.

"Speak for yourself," Evelyn said. "Keith and I always sauna together."

"You're late," Claude said.

That was the first thing she said to me, come to think of it.

"Sorry. I lost track of time," I said.

I guess they took happy hour very seriously at Stonebridge.

"We almost left," Claude said.

"I'm glad you didn't," I said. "I have so many questions."

I recalled my conversation with Jonah earlier that day. In exchange for signing his adviser card, he told me what happened to Kate. When I asked a follow-up question, Jonah reminded me that follow-up questions were not part of the deal and he cautioned me against being too inquisitive. His exact words were: "*Curiosity killed the cat* could be the school motto." I heeded his warning without abiding by it.

"What kind of questions?" Primm said.

"Basic school dirt," I said. "I tried to get it out of Finn, but he wasn't giving it up."

"I'm surprised," Evelyn said. "He's always struck me as the kind of man who would last in a torture session no more than thirty seconds, maybe a minute. And we're talking light torture—minor sleep deprivation, no waterboarding or toenail disengagement."

"That's where I went wrong," I said. "I gave him no incentive to talk."

"Why are you thinking about Finn being tortured?" Primm said.

"Primm doesn't have a dark side," Evelyn explained.

"Or if she does," said Claude, "it's really dark. Like bodies-buried-in-her-yard dark."

The vibe at the table unsettled me. I wasn't clear on the dynamic. I asked how long all of them had been teaching at Stonebridge. Finn had clocked four years; Primm, five; Claude, seven; and Evelyn, nine.

"But Claude is a lifer," Evelyn said.

"Lifer?" I said.

"I went to school here," Claude said.

"Keith is also a lifer," said Evelyn. "In fact, he's done more time than anyone."

"How much time?" I asked.

Evelyn shouted over to the bar, "Hey, Keith, how long have you been teaching here?"

"Fifteen, next year," Keith said.

I watched Keith's cold gaze track Finn as he returned to the table with a pitcher of beer.

"Fifteen years," said Primm.

"I think she heard that," said Claude.

Finn delivered an extra pint glass for me. He huddled three glasses together and poured the beer in circles. Barely a drop hit the table. The librarian steered the conversation back to my original question.

"So. What do you want to know?" Claude said.

"Who are the predators and who are the prey?" I asked.

"Predators. Prey," said Primm dryly. "That seems a bit cynical."

"I get it," said Evelyn, ignoring Primm. "You want to know what you're dealing with."

"Just rattle off the primary lions and pumas and a few Bambis or bunnies, and I'll sort out the rest of the animal kingdom," I said.

Primm said she had to use the restroom. Finn and I cleared out of the booth. I started to sit back down, but Finn yanked my arm and switched places with me, taking the inside seat for himself. It was like an aggressive game of musical chairs. We shifted our three pint glasses, placing Primm's untouched beer in the outer seat.

"Very smooth," Claude said to Finn.

"Thank you," Finn said.

I had no idea what they were talking about. Claude slipped a notebook from her satchel, ripped out a blank page, and began jotting down names.

"Forget about your lions and bunnies and all of that. There's the Ten and there's everyone else."

"The Ten?" I said.

"Each class is roughly one hundred students," Claude said. "The popular club calls themselves the Ten because they're the top ten percent."

"Please don't mistake that for the top ten in academic performance. There is simply no correlation," Evelyn said.

"None at all," Finn echoed.

I looked over the list:

Emelia Laird
Tegan Brooks
Hannah Rexall

Rachel Rose
Gemma Russo
Adam Westlake
Mick Devlin
Jack Vandenberg
Jonah Wagman
Gabriel Smythe

"You're missing Amy Logan," Evelyn said to Claude.

"Then it's eleven," I said.

"The Ten aren't always ten," said Evelyn.

"But this year they are," said Finn. "Amy Logan isn't one of them. Although, arguably she's Ten-adjacent. None of them would mess with her."

"So, it is ten," I said.

"There's a new kid who just arrived. Nick Laughlin. From England. He vaguely resembles a young Mick Jagger. I have him for European history. I'd bet a week's salary that he'll be admitted to the club," Evelyn said. "Any takers?"

Primm returned as the table declined Evelyn's offer.

"Are you comfortable, Alex? I can take the middle, if you like."

Finn squeezed my arm, signaling that I should stay put. Things were beginning to make sense.

"I'm okay," I said.

Primm scowled and boxed me into the booth.

"What were we talking about?" she said.

"The new kid. Nick Laughlin," said Evelyn.

"Oh yes. I met with him today. I think he's transferring into your writing class," Primm said.

I really didn't want another student I had to see twice a day. I took the piece of paper with the list of the Ten and asked for their general opinions of each student. There was a shocking lack of consensus, with the exceptions of Adam Westlake, Emelia Laird, and Rachel Rose, who scored generally positive reviews, and Tegan Brooks and Jack Vandenberg, who drew negative ones. Their assessments of the rest of my class were all over the place. For instance, this was their take on Gemma:

Primm: Rude, no respect for authority.
Evelyn: Clever.
Finn: She's up to something. But I don't know what.
Claude: My interactions with her are limited. Can't comment.

On Jonah:

Primm: A very troubled boy.
Evelyn: Adorable and brilliant.
Finn: He's just a jock.
Claude: Smarter than he looks.

I asked about Kate and got the usual mixed bag of responses. Not one of my colleagues hinted at knowing what had happened to her.

Finn then inquired about my elective class, which ranged from freshmen to juniors. I showed him the roster and asked the table for any further insight. Again, there were inconsistent reports on the few students who had made an impression over the years. Alyson Mosby (junior, second period, row 2, aisle 3) came up because she was in a relationship with a notable attractiveness imbalance. Claude and Evelyn then took a deep dive, trying to discern what qualities the boy possessed to compensate for whatever was lacking.

Primm suggested he had a good personality. Claude and Evelyn had a laughing fit and I decided to shift my focus for the night from intelligence gathering to drinking.

Finn then inquired about cottage living. I mentioned the generator issues and he offered to do something I can't recall because right after that Primm's pint glass suddenly tipped over and a good eight ounces of beer landed on my lap. The rest splashed onto Finn.

"Oh my God. I'm so sorry," said Primm.

"Grow up, Primm," Claude snapped.

"Don't worry about it," I said. "It's just beer."

Rags from the bar were delivered. Evelyn and Primm began the cleanup. Claude ushered me into the bathroom and told me to take off my pants. While she flapped my jeans under the hand dryer, I tried to wrap my head around the tension at the table.

"I'm going to call it a night," I said.

"But I didn't get to ask you any of my questions."

"Lightning round," I said. "Go."

"Did you really spend your summer in a monastery?"

"Just three weeks. And I'll never go back. Next question."

"Why'd you leave Warren?"

"I needed a change. That's all," I said.

I could tell that Claude wasn't buying my answer.

"Why?" I said. "What did you hear?"

"Nervous breakdown," she said.

Nervous breakdown. I didn't like how it sounded, but I had to admit it sounded better than the truth.

I stopped at the corner service station and purchased a gallon of gas for my generator and a flashlight for the walk home. Then I crossed Hyde Street and hoofed it up the winding drive to the gates of Stonebridge. I signed in with the security guard and followed the fire road that ran to my cottage. As I strolled farther away from the center of campus, the lights of Stonebridge no longer illuminated my path. My new flashlight probed the ground in front of me as the sounds of my feet crunching on dirt and my own breath joined the complex orchestra of the woods. I heard a long howl. But the howl didn't sound right. It wasn't a coyote or a wolf. It sounded vaguely human.

As I approached my current home, my flashlight illuminated an S-shaped path edged with small stones that bridged the end of the dirt road and my doorstep.

Those stones hadn't been there when I left in the morning. My gut did a single flip and I took a breath to calm myself. I walked alongside the path to the front door. On top of a brand-new welcome mat sat a paper bag with a giant red happy face.

I shouted *hello* into the woods. I don't know why. If someone was lying in wait, it wasn't like he'd answer me. I dropped the gas can next to the door and reached for the knob. I found some comfort in finding the door still locked. I picked up the paper bag, unlocked the door, and entered my cottage, quickly securing the deadbolt behind me.

Inside, I said *hello* again, as I turned on the lamp. Then I searched every dark crevice, like a child hunting for monsters. Once I was satisfied that I was alone, I lay down on the mattress like a corpse and stared at the ceiling. I had that vague feeling of emptiness, where you know something is wrong but you can't name or fix it.

I remembered the bag. I retrieved it from the table and hesitantly peered inside. I found a single brownie wrapped in cellophane and a small square of paper with a note.

FIND WHITEHALL

As I contemplated the purpose of this note and the one before it, I ate the entire brownie. It had an odd aftertaste, but I was starving. Maybe you're asking yourself, *What kind of person eats food delivered by an anonymous stone-path-making lunatic?*

Now you know.

GEMMA RUSSO

Just one week into the school year and I felt like running again. It's like I'm a snake with a tight layer of skin that I need to shed. I sometimes imagine hitching a ride to a town that keeps its lights on all night long.

Instead, I headed to the nonstop celebration of life that is downtown Lowland.

At the end of Hyde Street was a brick box with a faded blue awning that read only MO'S. Outside was a sandwich-board sign that oversold Mo's interior. BOOKSTORE AND CAFÉ. There were bookshelves and books at Mo's, all used and not all available to buy—depending on Mo's mood. In the back of the shop there were a few old schoolhouse desks, a pot of coffee always on the burner, powdered creamer, packets of sugar, and a general assortment of store-bought cookies. It was an honor coffee/cookie bar. A Post-it stuck to an empty can suggested you should give whatever you could afford. Mo's coffee was usually burned and the cookies stale, but almost no one from Stonebridge frequented the store.

Mo generally closed at 8:00 p.m. Sometimes 9:00 or 10:00,

if he forgot to look at the clock. The place stank of cheap cigars and an odor I could never pin down—although I ruled out putrefying corpse. Mo's was the only place I could run to anymore. I couldn't risk expulsion. Stonebridge had to be my past, present, and future.

Sitting in one of those old-school desks—the kind where the seat and writing area are conjoined—I finished typing up the origin story for Ms. Witt. I worried that it hewed too closely to the truth, but I'd been keeping up my lies for so long, it felt good to be almost honest for once.

THE ORIGIN STORY OF GEMMA RUSSO

By Gemma Russo

[Ms. Witt: Don't ask me to read this aloud in class.]

I was born in Portsmouth, New Hampshire. I never met my father. My mother wasn't a bad mother, just a broke one who developed something of a drug habit. She cycled through a series of loser boyfriends until she met Homer–real name, I swear. Homer wasn't like the others. He was a grad student in philosophy when they met; he was also an addict. That was the main thing they had in common.

Homer's family was rich, and he went to boarding schools for his entire adolescence. Not just one boarding school. I think the final count was nine. Now, that's rich. Homer, at my prompting, would often regale me with stories of the antics he got up to back then. At night, in bed, I would imagine that one day Homer and my mom would get their shit together and send me to one of those schools.

They got married and clean, in that order. We moved to Springfield, Massachusetts, at some point. Homer couldn't find work and my mother wasn't good at keeping the work she got. They both had an entrepreneurial spirit and started a meth lab in our basement. Amazingly, they remained clean the whole time. At least I remember them being pretty normal and lucid that last year.

Everything was pretty good until the basement exploded. I was nine. I remember my social worker asking me if I knew what was going on down there. I said I didn't. Sometimes you don't know what you know.

I was at school when it happened. I remember it took a couple of weeks to track down my mom's mom. I had never met my Grandma Lucille, even though she only lived a few hours away in a suburb of Boston. She wasn't awful. But I think I reminded her too much of my mother, whom she liked to remind me I was no better than. I believed that for a while. Lucille died when I was thirteen. After that, I cycled through foster homes just like Homer and his boarding schools. I even tried to petition the court for emancipation, but they rarely let thirteen-year-olds do that, unless they're the star of a TV show.

I couldn't stop thinking about those schools Homer went to. My junior high school guidance counselor suggested I apply for a private school scholarship. Over the next three months, I researched schools on the sluggish IBM in the computer lab. I applied to every school that looked like it could double as a movie set. I got some kind of offer from five of those schools. But there was only one place, or person, who was willing to give me a home year-round.

Dean Stinson drove all the way to Boston to interview me. At least, I thought it was an interview. We met at the school library, talked for fifteen minutes. He shook my hand and offered me a scholarship.

Two months later, I was on a bus to Lowland, Vermont. Dean Stinson suggested a summer program might help me assimilate. I think he was just trying to get me out of the group home. That was the first time I saw the campus in real life. It looked so perfect, I felt like I shouldn't be there. The uniform only amplified my impostor syndrome.

Scratch that. You can't have impostor syndrome if you really are an impostor.

I didn't belong then. I don't belong now. The only difference is that I don't care anymore.

That was the end of my five hundred words for Ms. Witt, but there's more to the story.

That first summer at Stonebridge, I hung out exclusively with the orphans. In Stonebridge lingo, orphans are the students whose parents leave them on campus during school breaks. That first summer, I made fast friends with Mel Eastman, Amy Logan, and Jonah Wagman. I also remember Carl Bloom being around. We ate meals with him, but not much else. He was desperately trying to catch up on his science courses, all of which he'd failed freshman year.

I didn't even know about the Ten back then. None of us thought about status or popularity. We were just teenagers who had free rein among acres of land. During the day, we had about two hours of class, and then we'd hang out in Flem Square or Fielding Field or take a swim at Stevenson Falls. Mel made up scavenger hunts at least once a week. Half of them were a total bust. Mel liked to hide clues inside people's pockets or on the bottom of their shoes. But if someone didn't wear the right item of clothing that day, we'd get stalled out in the middle of the hunt. At night, Mario taught us how to make a few dishes for ourselves. We'd spend hours cooking feasts from the school's pantry. Jonah was the best cook, and he was always so thoughtful about each person's dietary concerns. Bloom was allergic to everything. He kept a piece of paper on him at all times because the list was so long even he'd forget. And Amy had this whole texture problem and Mel suddenly kept kosher, even though she was not Jewish. Sometimes Jonah and I would have a second dinner, late at night, so he could cook whatever he wanted.

When Jonah first kissed me, I felt a happiness so intense that it twisted into sadness. My life had become too perfect and I knew that it wouldn't last.

I heard about the Ten a week before the term started.

Apparently, every class had their Ten. According to Mel, there were a handful of promotions over the four years, to compensate for the statistical failure rate of approximately fifteen percent every year. Mathematically speaking, that meant by the time senior year rolled around, only six to seven of the original freshman Ten survived to the end.

The orphans started acting weird as more and more of the regular-term students began to arrive on campus. It was like the rain had washed away the fairy dust of summer. After the Ten of that year (which was actually nine) had arrived, I came into Dahl Dining one morning and saw the sudden divide. Mel and Amy sat with a group of girls I didn't know and Jonah lunched with the Ten of the sophomore class, which has mostly remained intact, plus Gabriel Smythe.

I didn't want to pick a side. Some days I hung out with Mel, Amy, and all of the non-Ten, and other days I sat with Jonah. There was a tension that I didn't understand. Even if Jonah invited me to sit with him, he was reluctant to talk to me in front of this new crowd. In fact, Adam Westlake was the only member of the Ten who gave me the time of day. Adam was a curious fellow. He asked more questions than any boy I had ever met. Also, there was something about his ridiculous outfits—those bright pastel shirts, and his assortment of bow ties. He was always scribbling something in his leather-bound notebook. I asked him once what he wrote in there.

"My to-do list," he said. "I wouldn't wake up unless this thing told me to."

Adam was kind of like an old man in a boy's body. I liked

him, as a friend. But the more Adam talked to me, the less Jonah did. I couldn't figure Jonah out. At first I thought he was jealous. Then I figured he'd lost interest.

Maybe a month after we'd quit hanging out, I was studying alone in Milton Studio. Jonah had the same idea. When he saw me, he apologized for interrupting me and started to leave. I didn't know what his deal was, but I was tired of guessing.

"What is wrong with you?" I said. "We used to—you know—and now you can't even be in the same room with me."

"That's not it," Jonah said.

"Then what is it?" I asked.

"It's better if we're not seen together," he said.

He kept glancing at the floor, like it contained crib notes for the conversation.

"Whatever," I said as I shoved my books into my bag.

"No. You don't understand. Look, I really like you," Jonah said.

"You just don't want to be seen with me?" I said.

"I don't know how to explain it," he said.

"Don't bother," I said, leaving the room.

That conversation predated my knowledge of the Dulcinea Award or the Darkroom. When Christine told me what was going on, Jonah's behavior finally made sense. He was protecting me.

I might have remained part of the proletariat through graduation. I might never have discovered my purpose here. But then one small thing, probably not unlike whatever it was that caused the basement explosion, sealed my fate.

Sometime during the second semester of sophomore year, I was returning to Woolf Hall from a long training run in the northwest woods. The trail end is just outside Milton Studio. Bent over, hands on knees, I was spitting up a piece of dirt or a bug that ended up in the back of my throat. I heard a few voices and then I saw Adam emerge from Keats Studio, which was just a few yards away. He saw me and then looked nervously over his shoulder. I waved. He didn't wave back. He turned around and walked briskly away.

The next day, I found a note from Adam in my mailbox in AA. It just said: *Please meet me at Mudhouse, 2:00 p.m.*

The Mudhouse was the only proper coffee shop/bakery in town. Adam was casually seated at a table when I arrived. He bought me a giant mocha with a tower of whipped cream, a chocolate croissant, and an éclair. Adam didn't eat. He just sipped green tea and asked softball questions, which I answered with softball lies.

After about an hour, Adam said, "What did you see?"

I finished chomping down on the éclair and said, "Huh? I didn't see anything."

Adam smiled. "I like you, Gemma Russo."

I laughed.

"Can I get you anything for the road?" he said. "I know you're on a tight budget."

Even though Adam was suggesting he knew my secret, he didn't say it like an asshole. The offer felt more like an old relative picking up the lunch tab.

"I'm good," I said.

"You should say yes to the next invitation you receive," Adam said.

A handwritten invitation came later that afternoon, delivered by none other than Emelia Laird. The sophomore Ten were having a soirée in Keats Studio, 8:00 p.m., black tie optional, which I was certain was a joke. It was not.

Emelia looked me up and down and said, "Come to my room in an hour so I can fix those horrid eyebrows."

My initiation into the Ten was thirty minutes of torture, as my thick eyebrows were shaped into a high arch one labored pluck at a time. I later learned that Adam had put a good word in for me with Emelia. I know he did that because he thought I was keeping his secret. It's strange how a small misunderstanding can turn your world upside down.

The weird thing is that I didn't see anything. I had nothing on Adam. Not then, anyway.

It was past nine when Mo woke up from his nap and kicked me out of the bookstore. I shoved my laptop into my bag and grabbed a couple of his stale Oreos for the road. I checked my phone on the way out and saw that Linny had sent a text.

Linny: KB alone on BB.

I walked briskly up the main drive to Flem Square, eyed the perimeter, where Byatt Bench stood. Kate Bush was sitting there, frozen, staring into space. Her profile was mostly hidden behind hair, which she always wore down, long, with bangs that hung curtain-like over her eyes. She wasn't not-pretty. But, as Emelia might say, she didn't do herself any favors. I took a seat next to her. The bench was damp—like really damp. She could have warned me.

"Hey," I said. Just to be sure she knew I was there.

"What do you want?" Kate asked.

"I think I want the same thing you want," I said.

"A cheeseburger?"

"You weren't responsible for the cold showers, were you?"

Kate smiled, a real smile.

"I wish."

I handed Kate my phone.

"Give me your number."

She typed in her digits and passed the phone back to me.

"We're on the same side," I said.

"Are we?" she said, getting to her feet.

"We could work together," I said.

"And do what?"

"Don't be afraid."

"I'm not afraid. *They* don't scare me anymore," Kate said.

"What does scare you?"

"I scare me."

MS. WITT

I woke up on top of the covers, still dressed in last night's clothes. My eyes were itchy and dry and my skull felt heavy, as if my brain matter were the consistency of taffy. I'd barely finished my drink last night before I was bathed in beer. I knew I wasn't hungover. I tried to piece together more details. I remembered the weird stone path and the happy-face bag. And the brownie.

It probably wasn't just a welcome brownie. I gulped a jar of water, then another. I opened the door to see if there were any more gift bags. A donut or a croissant would have been awesome. Instead, there was a dead mouse. I picked it up with the happy-face bag and tossed it into the woods. I opened a can of cat food, scooped it into a small bowl, and left it right outside the front door.

I shoved my bare feet into my boots and stepped outside into the fresh morning air. It smelled of pine, earth, and rancid fish. After I fed the generator with last night's fuel purchase, I wandered over to the pond to get downwind of the cat food. For the briefest moment, I couldn't imagine a more perfect place on earth. Then I heard my mother's voice.

"Alexandra. There you are," Mom said, circling the cottage.

She wore Levi's, running shoes, and a flannel shirt. She was never one for high-end clothing. My mother is still quite beautiful but does little to enhance or preserve her looks. I've often heard even strangers comment on that fact, as if it were a personal affront.

"What are you doing here, Mom?"

"I came for visit. I look for you last night. Cottage was dark. I stayed with Greg."

"Sorry I missed you. I was having drinks with some colleagues."

"Tonight I'm with you," my mother said, answering my next question.

"This isn't the most hospitable place for guests."

My mother gave me a sidelong glance. We weren't going to get started on the subject of hospitable accommodations. She shared a one-bedroom apartment with six other people for almost twenty years.

"Give me the grand tour," Mom said.

My mother followed me inside the cottage and began to investigate my modest dwelling. After completing an overall survey, she took inventory of my larder, which consisted of three apples, a box of crackers, and a jar of peanut butter.

Mom took the peanut butter, located a spoon, shoved both items in my hands, and said, "Eat something. We're going for hike in ten minutes."

"I don't feel like going for a hike," I said.

"That's when you need exercise most," she said.

* * *

My mother has always said that the point of taking exercise is to expel demons, to sweat, to breathe, to task your muscles, to reduce your mind to the basics—putting one foot in front of the other, not tripping over tree roots or shrubbery, acknowledging the small aches and twinges of your body and still moving forward. She also has an uncanny knack for finding the longest trail. We hiked for an hour until we reached a waterfall. We stopped there for a moment and regarded its beauty, waiting in vain for it to repair what was broken inside us.

"Okay. That's enough," my mother said.

We hiked downhill mostly in silence, Mom taking the lead. At fifty-three, she's more sure-footed than I am. As I chased after her, she finally admitted the reason for her visit.

"Your father told me what happened."

"He told you?"

"We don't have to talk about it," she said.

"Good. Because I don't really feel like it," I said.

I was, however, curious how my father chose to frame the story. The unvarnished truth: I walked in on my father while he was being fellated by his new assistant, Sloan. I should mention that Dad's last assistant, Greta, is his current wife and Sloan is younger than I am. It all happened just a couple of months ago. I had moved into my dad's house after I left Warren Prep. The incident with my dad was what prompted me to go to Sun Ra Monastery. I thought it would help erase the image from my mind. Unfortunately, with the vow of silence and the limited recreation options, my mind could focus on nothing else.

My accounting of the year thus far was that it fell well below average. I wrongly assumed it couldn't get any worse.

"Are you sure this place is what you want?" my mother said. "That was nasty business at Warren."

"I don't want to talk about that either."

We hiked back to the cottage in silence. Once inside, my mother pulled me into a tight embrace. Her physical strength is at once comforting and overwhelming.

"I love you more than anything," she said.

"I love you too."

"Remember what I always tell you," she said, taking my hand in hers and repeating the American saying that she misinterpreted so many years ago. "Warm hands, cold heart."

I've never told her she got it wrong, because she means it so deeply. Be tough, with good circulation: words Nastya lives by.

GEMMA RUSSO

Here's Stonebridge's dirty little secret: Behind the regal name, old-school architecture, the wrought-iron fence, the buildings named after dead writers, and the fifty acres of untamed land, Stonebridge is no better than any suburban high school. Maybe half of the student body will get into a mid-level state university or academically flexible private institution. But only a handful of Stoners ever make it to the Ivies. About ten percent of the graduating class will head off to Williams, Vassar, Colgate, Oberlin. Another ten percent will manage the competitive state schools. The rest of us will go elsewhere or nowhere at all.

Students land here because they either are too fucking weird to survive in cookie-cutter prep schools, have a deep history of insubordination, test poorly, or are unrepentantly lazy. There are outliers, of course, the brainiacs who inexplicably attend with the rest of us riffraff. Mel Eastman, Enid Cho, and Norman Crowley can be counted among the ranks of the slummers, as they are affectionately known.

What Stoners are truly known for is their infinite appetite

for revelry. A weekend without a party at Stonebridge would be like an ice cream parlor serving only sorbet.

BIOHAZARD
(keep out of Dick House lounge)
9/12/09
2130 hrs–last man standing

We use warning signs in lieu of invitations. *Biohazard* means cocktail attire, and *quarantine* is black tie optional. A *poison* sign suggests a more casual event, which is what I would have expected the first weekend of the year. My guess was that the editors were doing it up to impress the new kid.

Emelia had heard Nick was British and hot, so she decided she wanted him, sight unseen. I tried to finish my French homework as Tegan and Emelia thrashed in and out of half their wardrobes, trying to hit the right note of sexy but not desperate. I never join in this ritual, because I have only three options outside the school uniform. If Tegan knew how broke I was—how I stole the leather pants that I would wear that night and bought the sparkly tank for five bucks at a thrift store—she'd use it against me somehow. But she doesn't know shit, and I've managed to make her think I'm just too fucking cool to care.

In Dick House, the seniors live on the first floor, which they call "the basement" because they think it sounds cooler. They used to occupy the top floor, until some lazy Stoner, five or ten years ago, decided that seniors should climb fewer stairs than freshmen and inverted the hierarchy. This worked out best for the rule-bending upperclassmen because it put the faculty supervisor (currently Finn Ford) in an apartment three floors up.

Emelia, Tegan, and I arrived at the senior lounge before ten. The lounge is a massive study room on the north side of Dick House. A few streamers hung from the ceiling and there was an innocent spread on one of the study tables, including a giant punch bowl with un-spiked punch. The editors circulated with various flasks and bottles tucked away in hiding places. The subterfuge has little to do with the fear of being caught. It's part performance and part keeping the high-end liquor reserved for the high-end crew.

The editors scored a keg for the party. It's not clear which one is responsible for alcohol procurement, but Jack seems the obvious choice since he's the one most likely to have a plausible fake ID. The keg is hidden just beyond the tree line that abuts Woolf Hall. It remains a mystery how the fifteen-gallon barrel is delivered to campus undetected. Also a mystery: how the faculty never seems to be suspicious of the two-way traffic of students heading in and out of the woods with their Stonebridge commuter mugs.

Emelia figured she had the new guy in the bag—most Stonebridge boys worship at the altar of her ass. She wasn't banking on Hannah Rexall pulling out her showstopping move—side splits against the wall. God, she was predictable. When we arrived, a throng of male admirers was watching Hannah, closing around her in a tight semicircle, like an imminent gangbang.

New Nick slow-clapped his approval for Hannah's exhibition. Boys sure love bendy girls. Hannah released her leg, smiled, and leaned against the wall with a deep arch in her back. Her mangled feet (hidden in wool socks) rested in third position.

I heard New Nick say, "That was brilliant," in that stupid accent that all of these morons adore. He looked exactly like I thought he would. Shaggy blond hair, skinny, with Mr. Potato Head lips and a nose that should have been on a girl. He kept his brow in a constant furrow like a cheap James Dean imitation. He clocked Emelia for a moment but returned his attention to Hannah.

"It's actually really easy," Hannah said. "I mean, I've done ballet for ten years. It's just who I am."

Gabriel Smythe then attempted his own wall split and said, "I can totally relate. Dancing is my life."

In class, Gabe likes to wear his school tie around his head. That night, he had on a kung fu bandanna. I can't decide whether the purpose of his headgear is to hide the zits on his forehead or to act as a compression stocking for his brains. It may just be that he knows everyone needs a reminder that he's the "funny one."

Jack laughed because he really thinks Gabe is funny. Mick laughed because Gabe is so unfunny it's funny, and Adam shook his head, disappointed that the Ten hadn't managed to locate a true wit to bring into the fold.

Jack was the only one dressed down for the party. The guy really knows how to kick back. He took up half the couch, his legs spread wide, like he was about to give birth. I have no problem with casual wear, but Jack always goes commando in his sweats. I feel like every time I look at him, his junk is on display. Mick, as usual, was dressed like a pretentious filmmaker, and Adam was his perpetually preppy self. I think Adam truly believes that wearing pink is the ultimate expression of his manhood.

Jonah was nowhere to be found, which was annoying because he's the only one of the boys who walks, talks, and dresses like a regular human being. Rachel Rose asked the room where he was, although it was meant for me. Mick suggested he was hooking up with a freshman or sophomore. A few names of pretty young things were tossed around. Tegan just stared at me, smirking. The smirk turned to a scowl when she saw Rachel Rose take a seat on the couch next to Jack.

Make no mistake, Jack is a turd, but Rachel gets under my skin more than most Stoners. She's a different kind of traitor, a witting participant in the editors' game.

Adam Westlake strolled by. He nodded at me, ignored Tegan, and said, "Looking luscious as ever, Emelia."

I can't get his angle. Westlake parcels out flattery with an almost mathematical precision, but there's no follow-through. In fact, after Emelia's college boyfriend broke up with her, she chose Adam for her rebound fling, which he seemed to deflect without openly rejecting her. Maybe he really likes her, or maybe he's playing a long game. Adam's flattery shifted New Nick's attention to Emelia. Hannah did this ridiculous girl squeal, pretending like she'd just noticed our arrival.

"Love the dress, Emelia. You look hot," Hannah said.

Then she duckwalked over to us and pulled Emelia into an embrace that I think was supposed to turn on New Nick.

"You'll have to fight me for him," she whispered.

"I'll win," Emelia whispered back.

I'd had enough of the Ten for the night, so I ventured outside, in search of more beer. I wasn't paying attention and just made a beeline for the keg. Coach Keith, however, intercepted my path.

"The keg is dead. Time for bed, Russo," Coach Keith said.

Most of the girls and three of the boys have a thing for Finn Ford. I guess he's attractive, if you like eyebrows. A lot. I think he's a phony and totally vain. I'd take Coach Keith over that J.Crew–catalog reject any day. Coach is older, late thirties, maybe. He's lean and sunbaked and the lines on his face make him look like an actor in one of those old Westerns I used to watch with Homer. Coach recruited me for the cross-country team when he caught me going for a late-night run—I wasn't running for sport. I just had to be somewhere fast.

I'll never forget Coach Keith's cross-country recruitment speech: "You look strong and stubborn and I'm tired of losing. How about it?"

I still don't know whether I like running. What I do know is that when I train, when I cross the many winding trails at Stonebridge, every stride makes me feel more and more like it's mine.

I had just returned to Woolf Hall when I got a text from

Jonah. He wanted to meet in Milton. I said no. He said that he had something for me. He promised he'd leave me alone if I met with him. I agreed.

Our relationship had shape-shifted a number of times since that first fight in Milton Studio. For a while we just ignored each other. After Christine told me about all of the Darkroom/ Dulcinea bullshit, I sent him a text with instructions to meet me in Milton. I told him I knew about the contest and asked him if that's why he broke up with me.

"I never broke up with you," he said. "All I said was that I didn't want to be seen in public with you."

"Because then they'd start asking for my scores?"

"Yeah. Something like that," Jonah mumbled.

"You could have told me," I said.

"I didn't tell you because you would have done something about it. And I wasn't sure how they'd retaliate."

"Somebody ought to do something about your creepy friends," I said.

"No, Gemma. Don't underestimate them. Promise me."

I promised, which we both knew was bullshit. After that, Jonah and I agreed to be secret friends, cautiously meeting up at unpopular locations around campus, never entering or exiting a building at the same time. At first, the meet-ups were totally platonic. We'd just study together. Later, we fell back into our old habits.

We were a secret couple for about a year. I remember

because Jonah had marked the date in his calendar. He gave me a leather bracelet as an anniversary gift at the end of junior year. I felt bad when I broke up with him a week later. But it had to be done.

Senior year, I was going to destroy the editors. I couldn't have anyone standing in my way, even if it was just to protect me.

Inside, Jonah was juggling a stapler, a tape dispenser, and a three-hole punch.

"You're a talented man," I said.

Jonah replaced the office products on the teacher's desk and took a bow.

He reached into his pocket as he walked over to me.

"Hold out your hand," he said.

I extended my palm. Jonah dropped something small and hard into it. He flicked on a desk light so that I could see it more clearly. It was something metal attached to a silver chain. It looked like a goat or a bat or a rendering of a satanic image.

"What is this?"

"It has different names," Jonah said. "A devil pod. A bat nut. It comes from nature, an Asian plant; it looks evil and yet it's supposed to ward off evil. I made it in metal arts with Ms. Lubovich."

I dipped my head under the light and inspected the gift. I was impressed. I may have even been touched that he went to the trouble. I wasn't going to say that either.

"I'm not your girlfriend, Jonah. You shouldn't be giving me gifts."

"You don't like it?"

"No, I like it. But—"

"Just keep it," he said.

"Thanks," I said, shoving the chain into my pocket.

Jonah looked so sad, I kissed him. I shouldn't have. It just confused things.

"That doesn't change anything," I said.

"Do you like me?" Jonah said.

"I don't like the company you keep."

"But do you like *me*?"

"I like who I think you are," I said.

NORMAN CROWLEY

I'm not one of them.

I don't think like them. I don't approve of what they're doing. But I have to live with those guys, day and night, and I've seen what they do to the ones who refuse to toe the line. If you don't serve or follow the cult of the Stonebridge leaders, they won't just shun you; they'll put a target on your back and keep firing until your flesh looks like hamburger meat.

The Darkroom spun off from chat rooms in the Blackboard system. They were called "locker rooms" in the early days, but anyone could go in them. I wasn't around back then. The girls' and boys' locker rooms in Blackboard still exist, but only the clueless freshmen post anything there. Here's a brief history of the Darkroom: A guy named Wally Low, whose handle was MadMax, created the first iteration of the site, which was basically a primitive message board in the boys' locker room. MadMax's successor, the first Hef, who chose to remain anonymous, supposedly built the Darkroom after one of his classmates was suspended for posting a detailed description of his girlfriend's breasts on MadMax's original message board. The girlfriend somehow saw the post, recognized what I believe was a reference to a mole, and filed a formal complaint with the school. Hef expressed in his mission statement when the Darkroom was first launched that he wanted to create a safe place where guys could talk about their innermost desires. And post exploitative pictures of women.

When I returned to Stonebridge for my sophomore year, the Nietzsche dude and his henchmen were gone.

I was invisible again.

The Darkroom had changed guard with the new year. Oscar Chang, a junior, was tapped as the gatekeeper, the primary administrator and password protector. The senior class was woefully underpopulated with PHP-literate students in 2008. When Chang's mother got a job in Frankfurt, the editors began searching for a new gatekeeper.

The editors, as they like to be called, are members of the Ten who oversee the contents of the Darkroom, including the Dulcinea Award. They're the guys who determine who has access to the site and at what level. Adam, Jack, Gabriel, Mick, and Jonah are editors.

Mick is definitely the face and hair of the organization. I've heard it takes a full hour to get the volume and chaos that he's aiming for. Mick runs the board meetings and it always seems like he's in charge. He's certainly the one who gives me my marching orders. But there's an intense consigliere relationship between Mick and Adam, which makes me wonder who is really calling the shots. Jack is obviously the muscle. He's also weirdly obsessed with the security of the website. He's always inquiring about the health of the firewall. Gabe's the guy who makes everyone feel better about himself. I can't come up with another reason they keep him around.

And then there's Jonah, who is technically an editor. He has a password and a login, although I can't recall ever seeing him post content. Jonah tries to pretend he's just a jock, but I've had enough classes with him to know he's also a slummer.

My role in this organization started a few years ago, when Jonah's older brother, Jason, was on the editorial board.

Editorial board. I can't believe how stupid it all sounds. Anyway, Jason recommended me for the job because Jonah told him I could code. I wasn't being welcomed into the Ten or anything like that. But when they asked for my assistance in maintaining and protecting a secret portal for communications among the elite, I felt honored. And relieved.

I had only heard of the Darkroom back then. It was a nebulous idea that seemed harmless enough. Then I saw it.

I wish I'd had the courage to refuse the editors, to leave them scratching their heads trying to navigate the back end without crashing the system. I didn't just keep the Darkroom in operation, I rebuilt and refined it. I created the database for the Dulcinea Award; I designed portals for VIPs to post pictures and other materials; and I implemented the ciphers that identified each unwitting Dulcinea entrant.

I was not coerced, blackmailed, or cajoled into playing my role in this screwed-up game. I was a good soldier, at first. But, later, I was waiting for the smallest reason to become a turncoat.

MR. FORD

Must meet. Keats. 7:45 p.m.
You will not be disappointed.
MD

At 7:30 p.m. on Saturday, the note, inscribed on gray linen card stock, was slipped under my door.

They used to just knock, deliver information, make their requests, and leave. The cloak-and-dagger shit gets old fast. I could have blown off the meet. I'd planned to stay in that night and work on the latest notes from my agent.

I wanted to ignore Mick. But the kid rarely oversold his information. He's like a drug dealer who has reliably good shit. Still, I kept him waiting.

Inside, Mick Devlin sat on a large wooden desk, legs crossed, with an unlit cigarette poised in his hand. Only the front right corner of his white oxford shirt was tucked in; a tie hung around his neck more like a scarf, and his hair was so disheveled I began to wonder if he ever washed it. Lazy and rich was his brand, I suppose. He sure nailed it.

"Ford, good man. Always so prompt. One of my favorite things about you."

For fuck's sake. I've got to take *Gatsby* off the required-reading list.

"What is it?" I said.

Mick held out another square of artisanal paper. It contained a handwritten shopping list for the liquor store. He laid a hundred-dollar bill on top of the list.

"That was a one-time deal. I'm not making a habit of it," I said.

"Ford, good man, what if I told you I acquired some intelligence so sublime you would buy out an entire liquor store just for a glimpse of it?"

"I'm not in the market for information anymore," I said.

Mick fought back a sneer. Having a marginally intelligent teenager regard you with superiority can put a man into a deep psychological trough. I really needed to sell that goddamn book.

"Not even information on the mysterious and strangely fetching Ms. Witt?" he said.

"I know all about her family," I said.

"This is different. Something very unfortunate went down at Warren."

He got my attention. I agreed to get the booze and Mick coughed up his dirt. Was it worth it? Don't know. But I've found that you have better luck with women if you know their deepest shame.

* * *

I delivered the liquor stash to a spot by the Douglas fir marked with an X. You'd think someone in authority would have noticed the hiding place by now. It's only about ten feet into the woods.

I stood there for a long time, at the base of campus, debating whether to go home or go see Witt. I wanted to warn her, although I didn't know if there was a way to do that without incriminating myself. I used the dim glow from my phone and walked carefully along the fire road until the light from the cottage came into view. I remember hearing a faint ringing noise in the direction of campus. It sounded like a fire alarm. I didn't go back. There's always some dickhead setting off the alarm just for the hell of it.

I knocked on Witt's door. Inside, a voice, not Alex's voice, said, "It's open."

I debated walking away, but the voice had an accent and I knew at once who she was and I wasn't going to pass up my chance to meet her. I opened the door. There she was, on the floor, her back against the wall, wearing reading glasses and reviewing a sheaf of papers.

The cruel muse.

The essay itself was better than anything the man had written since his debut novel. After the Witts' divorce, Len claimed that he'd overstated her influence—that her methods had in fact sabotaged his work rather than enhanced it. But I ate it up. I've been looking for my own cruel muse ever since.

Nastya Witt. Even her name added color to his narrative.

She peered over her reading glasses and asked me if I was lost.

I said I was sorry; I don't know why.

"I'm Finn Ford. I teach here with Alex."

"Yes, I assumed so much. I did not think you were a man who wandered the forest at night," she said. "Alex is taking a shower."

"Sorry to bother you, Ms. . . ."

"I am Alex's mother. Nastya."

"Nice to meet you, uh, Nastya. Are you here for a visit?"

"I don't plan to move in permanently, if that's your question."

Write. Breathe. Fuck. That was her maxim to Mr. Witt. Or so he originally said.

In college, it was our mantra. I wanted to hear her say it. I couldn't ask; it was stupid. I wanted her to like me.

"Finn Ford. Finn Ford," she said. "Oh yes. You're the writer who made my daughter angry," she said.

"I am sorry about that," I said.

"You apologize often, like a girl," said Nastya.

I apologized again and left. Alas, the cruel muse was more fun on paper. She made me want to get drunk, not write.

MS. WITT

My mother has the energy of an Olympic athlete half her age. Post-hike, she insisted on a quick dip in the ice-cold pond, followed by a walk into town for lunch. After that, we strolled around Lowland for two hours or so. Then we had drinks at Hemingway's and discussed my father's latest manuscript, specifically where it went off the rails. The day ended with a late dinner in my cottage—sausage and broccoli cooked on an outdoor flame. As exhausted as I was by then, I needed a shower and maybe a break from my mother, since I knew she'd stay awake until at least 1:00 or 2:00 a.m.

I told my mother I was going to take a shower at the school gym. I didn't mention the bathhouse amenities. My mother declined, as I expected, citing the earlier pond bathing. She has more faith in the cleansing properties of groundwater than I do. Besides, she looked content, sitting on the stone floor, reviewing my father's manuscript.

It was after 10:00 when I trudged into the dark woods toward the distant constellation of lit dorm rooms. Armed only with my flashlight, I felt more on edge than usual. I had to wonder if autonomy was worth the cost.

The bathhouse was empty, which unnerved me more than I expected. I should have forced my mother to come with me. I took a shower and dried off in the dressing room. Already, I felt a slight dread about the walk back and wanted to get it over with. I wrapped a towel around my head for the journey. I cut through the first floor of Beckett and strolled down the hallway that led past the free weights and cardio rooms, which was dark at night.

The trip lights flickered on when I entered the corridor. As I passed the girls' locker room, I heard voices echo into the hall.

A boy first, harsh and cold: *No, not like that.*
A girl, pleading: *Can I stop?*
The boy: *No, keep going.*
The girl: *But I'm tired.*
Boy: *If you quit, it's a forfeit.*
Girl: *I'm trying.*
Boy: *I don't get off, you have no shot at dulls—*
Girl: *Okay. Okay. Give me a sec.*

They were quiet after that. I had a sick feeling in my gut. I couldn't be sure exactly what I'd overheard, but I do know that the girl didn't want to do whatever she was being asked to do.

I saw the red box out of the corner of my eye.

IN CASE OF FIRE, BREAK GLASS.

I smashed the heel of my hand against the—not glass—plastic. The fire alarm screamed, stabbing my eardrums. I raced down the hall, out of the building, and ducked under the bleachers by the field. I waited for a minute or two to see who exited the building, but there were at least three other ways out. I walked briskly toward the rear of Headquarters, planning to cut back on Waugh Way.

Headquarters was a dead zone on the weekend. No student was allowed inside. And yet I could see a light flickering on the second floor. I counted the windows from right to left and realized the flicker was coming from my classroom. I rushed to the side entrance of the building and unlocked the door. I climbed two flights of stairs, stopped at the top landing, and listened. My sneakers were squeaking on the marble. I removed my shoes and left them at the end of the hall, tiptoeing down the corridor. The light from my classroom escaped into the hall. I ducked under the window as I reached for the knob and swung open the door.

A fierce scream shook the room as I was blinded by light.

GEMMA RUSSO

After I left Jonah, I didn't feel like going back to the party or my dorm. I grabbed a flashlight and Rupert's spare keys—he shouldn't leave them on a hook in a utility closet if he doesn't want other people to use them—and headed up to the second floor of Headquarters. My intentions were pure. I wanted to see the Q&A's. I wanted to know who was on my side. I was in there only a few minutes before a figure with a giant, amorphous hairdo walked into the room. I didn't know what I was looking at.

I screamed and trained the flashlight on the weird figure. Then I realized it was Ms. Witt wearing a goddamn towel on her head. Witt screamed, then staggered backward, careening off the door and crashing to the floor. "Ouch," she said, as she got to her feet. She wasn't wearing shoes, which seemed odd.

I was so scared that I forgot I was trespassing, among other things.

"Ms. Witt?"

"Get that light out of my eyes."

"Sorry," I said.

Ms. Witt got up and searched the wall for the overhead-light switch. Eventually the bright fluorescents flickered on.

"Gemma? What the fuck are you doing in here?" Witt said.

That's when I realized I was caught and in trouble. Ms. Witt rubbed her back and took a seat on top of her desk.

"Are you injured?" I said.

"I'm fine," she said.

I saw her eyes clock the papers on the floor. The Q&A's. I had just found them in the bottom drawer of her desk when she lumbered down the hall.

Shit.

I didn't know what to do. It never occurred to me that she'd be in her classroom so late on a Saturday night. I gathered the papers for her and placed them in a neat stack on her desk, like it was no big deal.

"Sorry," I said. "They have detention here. Hardly anyone gets it. But that seems like a fitting punishment. I'll do however many days you think is appropriate."

"Sit down, Gemma. That's not how this is going to play out."

I went for my usual seat in back until she said *front row,* in a tone that reminded me of my court-appointed attorney. I took Sandra P's desk, since I'm pretty sure Carl sticks boogers under his. Then I waited as Witt looked over the papers I had been studying.

"Explain yourself," Witt said.

"Honestly, it was just run-of-the-mill snooping," I said.

"If you have to preface your sentence with *honestly,* you're not being honest," she said.

Usually I'm better at thinking on the fly, but it's hard to explain why you've broken into a classroom for any other reason besides stealing test answers. I went with that excuse.

"I was looking for test questions and maybe answers?" I said.

"What tests, Gemma? There are no tests in my classes. If you're going to lie to me, please do it with some flair."

"Once again, I accept whatever punishment you deem fitting."

Witt reached up and touched the towel on her head. She seemed surprised to find it there. She removed the towel and tossed it over her chair. Then she picked up the stack of Q&A's, looking them over thoughtfully. She didn't say anything for a while. It might have been one minute or twenty minutes. I lost track of time. Eventually she spoke.

"What do you love?" Witt said.

"I don't know."

"What do you hate?" she said, leafing through the stack.

I didn't answer.

"Do you hate the Darkroom?"

I guess my poker face isn't as good as I thought. I should probably play more poker.

Witt placed a Q&A on my desk. "Is this yours?" she said.

What do you love? I don't know
What do you hate? The Darkroom and Dulcinea
If you could live inside a book, what book? Great Expectations
What do you want? Revenge
Who are you? I'm a spy

I don't remember answering, but I guess that was another tell.

"So you're my spy," she said.

She had so many goddamn questions. It's not like I could plead the fifth. I had to tell her something but not everything. If I didn't give up some information, she would march me over to Dean Stinson's house. I wasn't sure what he'd do if there was another strike against me. It was impossible to say how punishable this crime was.

Witt asked me if I'd been leaving things at her door. I hadn't, but I wanted to know what things and who had left them. She wasn't giving me anything.

"I noticed something unusual about the Q&A's," Witt said. "Several of my students—presumably the female ones—gave the answer BJs or blowjobs to the question *What do you hate?* Weird, huh?"

"They don't call it a job for nothing," I said.

"If you hate something, you don't do it. If you don't do it, you don't hate it," said Witt.

"Is that an example of a tautology?" I asked.

Witt picked up the towel and twisted it back around her head. She walked over to the thermostat and adjusted the temperature. She looked cold and tired. Her eyes glazed over for a second and then snapped into focus, like those old cameras.

"Why would you break into my classroom just to see these anonymous Q&A's?"

I didn't have a good bluff for that question.

"Inspiration?" I said.

Her eyes searched the room; she was trying to find an angle, a way to get me to talk.

"Gemma, you've got to give me something here."

"I heard that Warren students take a blood oath by the statue of Samuel Warren, to pledge allegiance to the school. Is that true?" I said.

"Real blood has become passé," said Witt. "They decided that any bodily fluid would do. Most of them just spit on his placard. Some of them . . . It doesn't matter."

"They pee on it. I know," I said. "Anyway, Stonebridge has its own thing. Do you know what it is?"

"No."

"We close ranks. Cheating, fighting, bullying, stealing, anything. Stonebridge students will *never* rat each other out. Anyone who breaches this unspoken contract is not just shunned but destroyed. Teachers and faculty are no exception."

"You can't be serious," she said.

"What do you think happened to Ms. Whitehall?"

MS. WITT

My mother slept on the floor and woke me up at the crack of dawn. She had already rolled up her sleeping bag and made a pot of coffee. She served me a mug and sat down on the floor. She mentioned a man dropping by. She described Finn.

"Do I need to worry about you?" she said as she was leaving.

I told her she didn't.

I slept for another hour after she left.

Then I got dressed, grabbed a cup of coffee at Dahl, and returned to my classroom, where there was reliable Internet and phone reception. I called my father. It was early, but he answered.

"Are we talking now?" Dad said.

"I need the number of your PI. What's his name?"

"We call him Lucky. His name's Pierre."

"Okay. Can I have his number?"

"What do you need?"

"I need to track someone down."

"Give me the information and I'll call you back," he said.

"Why can't I have Lucky's number?" I said.

"Because that leaves me out of the equation."

I had only Whitehall's name, age range, and previous place of employment. Dad called back in an hour with the phone number and address for a Mary Whitehall, DOB 5/7/78. She lived just outside Bennington, Vermont.

"Are you sure this is the right one?" I said.

"She's the only Whitehall who ever lived in Lowland," Dad said. "What do you want from her?"

"Information," I said, ending the call.

Bennington was about a forty-minute drive from Lowland on a traffic-free Sunday morning. Whitehall's house was just outside the city limits. As I passed through a short stretch of retail, I stopped first at a liquor store and then ordered a dozen donuts and two cups of coffee at a drive-through window.

A few minutes later, I parked my car in front of a one-story clapboard house with a shaky porch and a paint job so ancient it was peeling rainbows. A patch of brown lawn and weeds surrounded the house. I looked at my watch. It was almost eleven. Even my father, with a hangover, doesn't sleep that late.

I grabbed my provisions and strode up the walkway. The front stairs squeaked and bent under my weight. I heard the mumble of a TV playing inside. I knocked. The TV quieted. I knocked again.

"Mary," I shouted. "You don't know me. I teach at Stonebridge. We need to talk."

Silence.

"I have coffee, donuts, and vodka. I'm going to wait on your porch until you open the door. Take your time. But the coffee is warm now," I said.

It took about ten minutes before she opened the door. My guess is that she was cleaning herself up, although it was hard to say.

Before I left Lowland, I had looked at Mary Whitehall's picture in the yearbook for the prior year. The woman before me was definitely the same person. Maybe after a three-year bender.

"What do you want?" Mary said.

I held up both cups of coffee. "How do you take your coffee?"

It took a while before she answered.

"Cream and sugar," she said.

I gave her the cup in my left hand and pulled two packets of sugar from my pocket. Mary turned around and walked back into the house, leaving the door open. I followed her inside.

I was expecting the inside to look like her outside, but Mary kept her home clean and uncluttered.

Whitehall took a seat at an old wooden table. She ticked her head to the side, silently inviting me to sit. I unloaded the booze and donuts from my backpack and placed them on the table. Whitehall chose an old-fashioned from the donut bag and split it in half, placing one side on a napkin and biting into the other.

"What happened at Stonebridge?" I said.

"No," she said, taking another bite of donut. "You came to my home without invitation. You talk. I'll listen. Then I'll decide if I'm going to answer any questions."

"Fair enough," I said.

I told her about my Q&A's and the ratios of specific answers, the repeated references to something called the Darkroom, and some kind of editors mentioned in one of the assignments.

Mary removed a chocolate glazed donut from the bag. "Go on," she said.

"Last night I was coming out of the bathhouse—"

"That's the only thing I miss about that place," she said.

"I was walking through the hallway of the gym and I heard a conversation between a boy and a girl. He was trying to make her do something she didn't want to do. In light of the Q&A's, I'm fairly certain it was a blowjob. She definitely wanted to stop. The boy said that if she stopped she didn't have a shot at—something I couldn't quite make out. It sounded like dull-something."

"Dulcinea," she said.

"Dulcinea? Like *Don Quixote*?"

"Yes," she said. "What did you do when you heard them?"

"I pulled the fire alarm."

Mary smiled and nodded her approval.

"What does it mean?" I said.

"It's an 'award' for the girl who gives the best blowjobs that year. There's some kind of scoring system that I never worked out."

"Jesus. How many girls participate?"

Whitehall shrugged and searched the donut bag, debating whether to indulge in another.

"Most of them didn't know they were being scored. Something has changed, if it's out in the open like that," she said.

"No one's tried to stop it?" I said.

"One or two, unsuccessfully. Like I said, it was a well-kept secret for some time."

"When did you figure it out?"

"I didn't know anything for the first four years. Your anonymous questionnaire gave you quite the head start. I'm not sure that's a good thing."

"Why do you say that?" I said.

"Because now you think you have to do something. But you haven't been there long enough to know what you're dealing with. Stonebridge may look like Green Gables, but it's the Bada Bing Club for the preppy set."

"Who told you about it?" I said.

"I was an adviser to a senior. Christine Cleary. I'd known her for three years. We were close. One day, something had changed. She was different. She looked defeated, I guess. I kept after her until she told me what was wrong. She said her boyfriend was scoring her blowjobs and sharing the data with his friends. She said there was some kind of website they maintained. I thought I had to do something. I reported the issue to Martha Primm, because that was the protocol. Is she still there?"

"She is. What did she do?"

"She made all of the girls meet in the auditorium on a Saturday for a 'female-empowerment seminar,' I think she called it. She told them that they had to take ownership of their sexual destiny and it was on them to control the situation."

"And there was no reciprocal seminar for the boys?" I asked.

"You're joking, right?"

"Has anyone spoken to the board about Martha?"

Mary laughed. "No. Her job title may be guidance counselor, but she's just another arm of the board. They hired her to make sure that the school's record stays clean, and they don't care how that's accomplished. Parents look at those statistics. No one will send their daughter or son to a school that has a shaky record on consent. Where were you before?"

"Warren Prep."

"You didn't have any problems there?" she said.

I conceded there were problems and returned to my original question.

"Back to Christine," I said.

"A day after the seminar, Christine dropped out of Stonebridge. I still don't know how they got to her. I tried to talk to some of her friends; they shut me out. It all happened so quickly after that."

"What happened?"

"The police came to campus and searched my apartment. They found a pound of weed, which was not mine. I was accused of dealing to the students. And then I was gone. I would have fought it if I wanted to keep teaching. But I didn't, and I didn't want to have hearings and hire a lawyer. They offered to drop the charges if I resigned. I just wanted to forget about the whole thing."

I had a queasy feeling. I ate a donut. It didn't help.

"Did you ever go to Dean Stinson?" I said.

"No. That's why Martha was hired. To deal with all non-academic problems. The culture there is locked in. Many private schools exist like a sovereign nation. They have their own customs and laws and are not easily swayed by outside influence."

"Are you telling me there's nothing I can do?"

"I'm telling you to watch your back."

I had to fight the urge to be bold and shine a light on the whole damn thing right away. I drove back to Lowland, parked my car, and headed straight to my classroom. I reviewed the Q&A's one more time. I pulled three papers that made the boldest statements against the status quo. Then I summoned Gemma to meet me.

As soon as she walked into the room, she said, "Please don't expel me. I have nowhere to go."

"You're not expelled," I said. "Sit down."

She was so relieved she practically collapsed into the chair.

"Last night, I couldn't figure out what you were after," I said. "I thought maybe you planned to screw with some of your classmates, get dirt on them. That wasn't it, was it?"

She shook her head. I placed the three Q&A's on her desk.

"You need allies," I said. "I think you'll find them here."

GEMMA RUSSO

Ally #1

What do you love? Neko Case, banana bread, the smell of Pine-Sol

What do you hate? BJs, editors, and agents of the Darkroom

If you could live inside a book, what book? The Girl with the Dragon Tattoo

What do you want? An invisibility cloak and cyanide

Who are you? I'm not who they think I am

Ally #2

What do you love? Vicks cough drops, rain, the Ramones

What do you hate? Dulcinea, shag rugs, obligatory BJs

If you could live inside a book, what book? The Maltese Falcon

What do you want? To buckle the patriarchy; a spork revival

Who are you? The enemy

Ally #3

What do you love? Waffles, Red Sox, sleeping in (and family, obv)

What do you hate? BJs, the Darkroom, Them
If you could live inside a book, what book? True Grit
What do you want? A revolution or a time machine
Who are you? A fool

Ms. Witt took a risk giving me those Q&A's, and I had to respect that. But she didn't give me three allies. She gave me two. The first Q&A was Kate Bush. I'd already begun my recruitment process. The second one, however, came as a bit of a surprise. Mel Eastman. The fact that she mentioned Dulcinea by name meant she had more skin in the game than I would have thought. If she'd heard of it, she was a victim of it. That's the general rule.

The third Q&A I couldn't figure out. I put that one on hold. My first order of business was getting Mel on my team. I sent her an anonymous message through the Blackboard system.

M,
I also hate Dulcinea.
If you want to discuss remedies, meet me at Burns trailhead.
3:00 p.m. sharp.
Signed,
A friend

When I arrived at the appointed time, no one was there. I noticed a piece of paper covered by a rock at the bottom of the wooden stake. I picked up the paper and unfolded it.

Friend

If this is the "friend" I used to know, meet where the slummers summer.

M

Mel and I rarely spoke during the school year, but I always wished I could hang out with her without sacrificing my social standing. She was legitimately one of a kind. I still remember our first *real* conversation, the summer before my first year at Stonebridge. Mel sat next to me at breakfast one day, regarded her cereal spoon, and said, “I feel like they’ve just given up on eating utensils, you know what I mean?”

She then launched into a whole speech about how no one is bothering to improve on an item that could very well be improved upon. Later, we had a long discussion about her idea for a compromise between hardwood floors and carpets. She understands that sometimes people want something soft under their feet but carpets are simply unsanitary. A few times I was worried Mel might need medication or something, but I later concluded that she just has a strange, fascinating, and rare mind and thinks aloud more than most people.

I hiked twenty minutes from the trailhead to Stevenson Falls, which is where I assumed Mel suggested we meet. That’s where we killed most summer afternoons. Mel was sitting on a rock, drinking out of a thermos.

“I thought I was being cautious with the trailhead meet,” I said.

“You can never be too cautious,” Mel said. “What if someone

happened to be near the trail or followed you? You wouldn't want to be caught talking to a second-class citizen. Coffee?"

"Sure," I said, sitting down on a rock next to her.

Mel had been hurt when I stopped talking to her. I would have been too.

"I'm sorry," I said. "I can't fight them unless I'm one of them."

"What are you fighting, exactly?" Mel said.

"The system," I said.

"You're being vague," she said.

"Okay. I'll be straight. I want to destroy the Darkroom. I want to end the Dulcinea Award. I want to bring the editors to their knees, begging for mercy."

"How do you plan to do that?" Mel asked.

"I don't know. Build an army, start a campaign of disinformation, fracture their union."

"How's that army coming along?"

"It's a work in progress," I said.

"It's an army of one," Mel said.

"Got to start somewhere. At least I have a plan."

"I have a plan," Mel said.

"Oh yeah? What is it?"

"I'm going to hack the Darkroom," Mel said.

That was a good plan.

"We can work together," I said. "Now we're an army of two."

"Right," Mel said dryly. "An army of two."

"There are others just like us," I said. "We can recruit."

"Who do you have in mind?" Mel asked.

"Kate Bush, for one."

"Is she in?"

"I think so. I don't know. I'm not sure that she trusts me."

"Because you're one of them," Mel said.

"But I'm not. Maybe you could talk to her."

"Maybe," Mel said.

"See, now we're an army of three," I said.

I was doing what Ms. Witt had asked me to do. She gave me allies so I could build an army. And you build an army so you can fight a war.

PART II
ALLIES

The whole secret lies in confusing the enemy,
so that he cannot fathom our real intent.
SUN TZU, *THE ART OF WAR*

ANNOUNCEMENTS

Good morning, students of Stone, on this Thursday, September 17, 2009. Friday is the last day to add or drop a class and switch advisers. Please be sure to have all your paperwork in order. Maintenance, once again, apologizes for the scorching showers in Dickens House. Rest assured, the situation has been remedied and a deadbolt installed in the engineering room. In today's lost and found, we have a pink cashmere scarf—this is very soft. If no one claims the scarf by the end of the day, I might keep it. Heh heh. Expect the weather to be in the mid-seventies with maybe one or two perfect, billowy clouds. Today's quote comes from Epictetus, the Greek Stoic philosopher, born A.D. *50. It is impossible for a man to learn what he thinks he already knows. That's all, folks. Be safe out there.*

MS. WITT

I was well into the second week of class before I truly accepted my fate as the creative-writing instructor. Jack Vandenberg dropped my class at the last minute, but I got New Nick in his stead. Even taking into account the unsettling Q&A I'd narrowed down to Jack, I considered the switch a net loss.

In class, I asked for volunteers to read aloud from their brief origin stories. New Nick read his, about the day when he, at age eleven, met the Dalai Lama. Mel Eastman, after some cajoling, shared her piece, called "A Portrait of Count Chocula." She recalled the time that she, age seven, threw an epic tantrum in a grocery store, demanding that her mother buy a box of Count Chocula cereal. Her mother relented. Mel, after consuming the product, cut out the front of the cardboard box and taped it on her wall as art. The next morning, her wall art was in the recycling bin. She retrieved it and hung it on her bedroom wall again. A standoff ensued, involving a hunger strike (on young Mel's part). In the end, Mel became an avid collector of and foremost authority on cereal-box art. Her collection, hung in her bedroom, included early pieces of Lucky Charms, Cocoa Puffs, Froot Loops, and Grape-Nuts.

I asked Mel if she deliberately modeled the style after any particular author. She smiled and said she was in a Dashiell Hammett mood. It was the kind of unselfconscious creativity that can only come from a brain still in wild flux.

"Well, that was *interesting,*" said Tegan.

"You're a nut, Mel. And I mean that in the best possible way," said Adam.

"I would rethink the Grape-Nuts," said Jonah. "You have all of the fun cereals and then Grape-Nuts. That seems out of place."

"I think the Grape-Nuts add depth and crunch to the story," Norman said.

Jonah seemed to be mulling over Norman's comment.

Nick, whose piece did not incite as much conversation, looked deeply disturbed, like he'd just moved into a halfway house for adolescents plagued by a rare form of early-onset dementia.

"Can I have a show of hands on who knows what their thesis project will be?" I said.

About a third of the hands rose, some only to half-mast.

"If you don't, you have a grace period of two weeks to figure it out," I said.

What I didn't say was that it was kind of weird that I had nineteen writing students and only a handful had any real interest in writing.

* * *

After my conversations with Gemma and Whitehall, I wondered whether I could teach effectively while seeing so many of the boys as potential villains. I knew that my bias was dangerous. That's why I worked so ardently on decoding those Q&A's. I needed to know that at least some of the boys were inherently good.

I got sloppy during my office hours. I left the papers splayed on my desk while I ran to the lounge for a crappy cup of coffee.

When I returned to my classroom, Jonah was sitting in his assigned seat. The papers that had covered my entire desk when I left were now stacked in the corner, facedown. Jonah had his journal open and a pen poised over a blank page. I picked up the stack and turned it over. On top was this Q&A:

What do you love? GR
What do you hate? The Darkroom
If you could live inside a book, what book? Sense and Sensibility
What do you want? Peace
Who are you? I don't know yet

I had scribbled *F* and the initials of three possible girls in my senior class. They were crossed out with a pencil. *M* and *JW* were printed right below. I didn't know what to say.

"You said they would remain anonymous," Jonah said, eyes focused on his notebook.

"I did, didn't I?"

I felt caught and guilty. I couldn't decide whether Jonah was scolding or disappointed. When he finally raised his chin, I caught a smirk.

"You thought I was a girl," he said, shaking his head in mock indignation.

"Sorry. It was *Sense and Sensibility.* It's rare for—"

"That's very sexist of you, Ms. Witt."

"You're right. I apologize."

"Apology accepted," Jonah said.

"Why that book?" I said. "It's a great book, but to live in it?"

"Nobody calls out the brother and his lame wife for taking the sisters' money. I kept waiting for it to happen and then it didn't. I get that it all worked out in the end, but—"

"You want to live in the book to fix it?"

"Exactly," said Jonah.

I put the Q&A's into the bottom drawer of my desk and diverted my attention to other classwork for the rest of the period. I wanted to respect Jonah's anonymity, yet I was compelled to notate this new piece of information.

I scribbled in my notebook. *GR = Gemma Russo.*

When the bell rang, Jonah packed up his bag.

"Ms. Witt?" he said. "Be more careful, will ya?"

NORMAN CROWLEY

What do you love?

Bright Eyes, Reservoir Dogs, PB&J sandwiches, CS

CS = Claudine Shepherd.

I love her more than any of those other things. It's not a pining, romantic-crush kind of love. It's the kind of love you feel for someone who sees you as you really are.

The part of my origin story that was missing was what happened after I dared to insult an editor. It didn't end with the humiliation of that night. I became the primary punching bag for every dickhead at Stonebridge. Every prank you think you've heard of, I lived. My clothes were burned; my dorm room ransacked; my locker welded shut; I couldn't take a shower in the gym without the risk of waterboarding or worse. I can't say I was surprised when they pissed on my bed. But it did leave me with few sleeping options. I'm not an expert on the average urine volume per piss or the absorbent qualities of the average cut-rate mattress, but my guess is that the fluid in question was not single malt, if you will, but a blend. I asked Rupert if he could change my locks and get me a new mattress. The mattress, Rupert said, would take a couple of days.

I thought about trying to go to a motel. I had some money stashed away, but I've heard they only book adults or people with credit cards. I went to the library after hours and hid under one of the large study desks until Ms. Shepherd left for the night. There's even a bathroom in the library, which made my sleepover not only convenient but civilized. I brushed my teeth and washed my face and went to sleep on this old couch that was probably pretty gross but not damp. It was the best night's sleep I'd had in weeks. I should have set an alarm, but I didn't have one. I didn't even have a phone back then.

Ms. Shepherd came in early the next morning and caught me. She asked me why I was sleeping in *her* library. I told the truth, that someone (not me) peed on my bed and it was too damp to sleep on.

"That's disgusting," she said.

"It is!" I said.

"Who peed on your bed?"

"I don't know," I said.

"I think you have an idea," she said.

"Maybe, but I can't prove it."

Shepherd sat down on the other end of the couch and said, "You don't have to name names, but tell me what happened."

I told her the Nietzsche story.

"Did you really call them knuckleheads?" she said.

"No," I said.

"What word did you use?" she said.

I didn't answer at first.

"Norman, I've heard *all* the words," she said.

"I said douchebags, then megadouchebags."

"Excellent," she said.

"Huh."

"I think that was the right word or words for your bed-wetters. Get ready for class, Norman."

"Am I in trouble?"

"No. But don't sleep in my library without consulting with me first."

I braced myself for more trouble from the megadouchebags, but then another day or two passed, and then a week, and nothing happened. I never found out what Ms. Shepherd did, but I know she did something.

These days, if I'm not in class, the dining hall, or asleep, I can usually be found in the library. Everyone has a story about Claudine Shepherd. The way she looks, the way she acts, it's like she doesn't belong here. People need to provide a narrative to explain her. I heard she used to date the drummer of Pearl Jam and that she briefly lived with a Colombian drug lord. I also heard she has a nipple ring. Another rumor involved a tattoo of butterfly wings across her entire back. What is true is that she lives in that big house that looks like a crumbling ski chalet on the east side, where all of the rich people live three months out of the year.

The true things I know about Ms. Shepherd are kind

of weird and at odds with how she comes across. She lives with her mother, who has some disease or dementia. I saw Ms. Shepherd off campus one day. This was before the whole library-sleeping incident. She was pushing an old woman in a wheelchair into the medical building where I see my shrink. Ms. Shepherd was dressed as always—the heels, the blouses that tie at the neck, and her shiny, shiny hair. The old lady wore a big flowered dress and so much jewelry, you got the feeling she never let it out of her sight.

That day was weird, though. I don't know how to explain it. It was like steam hovering over a cup of coffee, but over them instead. Ms. Shepherd never looked at me, didn't speak to the lady, and had this look on her face. It wasn't an expression but the absence of one, like it took everything in her power to stay in control.

We never spoke about that day. Sometimes I wonder if she even saw me. Shepherd likes to keep things light. She treats me like a girlfriend, which I really don't mind. She likes to gossip and talk trash, and, with a few exceptions, we like and dislike the same people.

I was in the library one day in late September, when I heard Shepherd's heels clicking closer. New Nick had just walked in, roamed the stacks briefly, and then left, looking disappointed or something.

"What do we think of the new kid?" Ms. Shepherd whispered as she sat down next to me.

I told her about the stupid origin story that he read in Witt's class.

"He said, '*His Holiness* had the softest hands I'd ever touched.'" Then I told her that Ms. Witt said, "Don't sell yourself short. I bet you have some pretty soft hands."

Shepherd let out this deep, throaty laugh. It's like the best laugh you've ever heard. Then she leaned in again, conspiratorially.

"And what do we think of Ms. Witt?"

"We like her," I said.

A minute later, Mel walked in. I guess I was looking at her for a while.

"Norman, quit staring. It's creepy. If you like her, you have to talk to her."

"It's not like that," I said.

"Just be cool," Claude said, as she returned to her desk.

I've known Mel since we were kids. We grew up in the same town. I think we even took some art class together when we were like five. Since coming to Stonebridge, we've barely exchanged a word. It's like we don't know each other. But I do know her. Her old nervous habit of looping her hair around her finger looked violent now. I wanted to ask if she was all right but knew that would seem weird.

I was about to leave when Gemma sauntered in. I saw Ms. Shepherd clock her arrival and scowl. Gemma sat down and talked to Mel, which was weird because I never saw them together. Also, the way they were talking was weird. They both looked like they had stiff necks or something. Gemma made me nervous. One time I saw her break into Byron Manor, where Dean Stinson lives. She entered through the back door empty-handed and left with a full backpack.

After Gemma and Mel were done talking, Gemma casually roamed the aisles, like she was browsing in a shopping mall. Then she pulled a book off the shelf and shoved it in her book bag and walked right out of the library. I glanced at Ms. Shepherd to see if she noticed the theft. She did, and she didn't say a thing.

Then I turned back to Mel. She was talking to Enid, which made me feel better. I guess I was worried about Mel. She'd seemed off lately, kind of jumpy. I thought maybe I knew why. When I saw Mel's scores posted in the Darkroom, I was gutted. I hated her for being so naïve. Or maybe I hated myself because of my role in this organization. I told myself I was a reluctant cog in the machine, and yet I was so vigilant about a breach that I assigned a new password every week, which was delivered to the editors in a self-destructing email. They all got off on the spycraft of our secret society and I was the gatekeeper of this douchebag regime.

But this time, when I saw the breach, I didn't batten the hatches; I opened the door.

GEMMA RUSSO

Almost a month had passed since the photo of Kate Bush was first unleashed, but Tegan's obsession with it had not diminished. Tegan couldn't stop gaping at the photo, nor could she stop talking about it.

"I didn't think it was possible for a girl to have *that* much hair down there. If I didn't know better, I'd swear she was wearing a merkin."

"What's that?" Emelia asked.

"It's a wig for pubic hair," Tegan said.

"Why would anyone wear a wig on their Sally May?"

I still haven't gotten the entire etymology behind Emelia's use of the southern name in lieu of *vagina,* but I think it vaguely relates to men naming their penises, even though I have never met a guy who does that.

Tegan was apparently an expert on the merkin:

"In the 1800s, prostitutes used to wear them. Sometimes they'd have to shave their pubes to control lice."

"Gross," said Emelia.

"Or they'd don a merkin to hide evidence of a venereal

disease. Now sometimes actors wear them if they're doing a period drama."

"Congratulations," I said.

"For what?" said Tegan.

"You've figured out your senior thesis project. Write what you know, they say."

Tegan ignored me and held up her phone with the picture on full display.

"How could she get to the age of seventeen without doing anything down there? I mean, she's on the verge of pubic dreads. Have you ever seen anything like that?"

"You're really being a dick," I said.

"Gemma's right. That picture never should have gotten out," said Emelia.

Tegan returned her attention to her phone, but I could see that snaky vein pulsing in her forehead. Sometimes I feel like Tegan and I are vying for Emelia's soul. It's rare but so satisfying when Emelia levels mean-girl charges against her other BFF.

My phone was buzzing. I didn't dare look at it while I was in such tight quarters. I laced up my running shoes and said I was going to run some wind sprints.

In case one of them was glancing out the window, I kicked it across the square a few times. It always eases the straitjacket feeling I get when I'm around Tegan too long. Coach Keith saw me from across the field and told me to relax my hands. I shook them loose and nodded at him. He started to shout more instructions about my form. I nodded agreeably. Then my phone buzzed again. When I retrieved it from my pocket, Coach scowled and walked away. He hates mobile phones. He says only Maxwell Smart should have a phone on him at all times. I have no idea who that is.

Mel had sent two messages asking me to meet her at Tolkien Library. I crossed the square and headed inside.

Shepherd was doing whatever it is that she does. She looked up at me and looked away. I could feel her eyes on my back as I strolled down the aisle. I found Mel ducked behind her computer in the reading nook. I was anticipating major progress. Mel looked up, annoyed. Her eyes were rimmed red and swollen into a double squint.

"Looks like you got maced," I said.

"Allergies," Mel said. "And, thank you."

"Have you talked to Kate?" I asked.

"She's not sure she can trust you," Mel said.

"Maybe you could vouch for me."

"Maybe," said Mel.

"Have you gotten anywhere with your assignment?" I said.

We were doing that thing people do in spy movies, where you're sitting next to someone, talking, but you never look at them. I think it works better on a park bench than on a library couch.

"Not yet. It's complicated," Mel said. "Have you figured out Waffles yet?"

"No," I said.

"How many waffle-loving Red Sox fans who hate blowjobs can there be in the senior class?" Mel said at full volume.

"Shhh," I said.

I noticed Norman watching us from that corner of his. And then Enid came over to talk to Mel about some physics question. I didn't linger, because Mel and I rarely talked during the school year and I was paranoid about looking conspiratorial. While Enid and Mel conversed about projectile something (not vomiting), I checked out the computer section. There was a book called *Hacking for Dummies.* It seemed like something Mel ought to have, although I hoped she wouldn't take offense. I shoved it in my backpack and left the library.

I decided that Mel and I needed to start meeting in private. The next day, I sent her a text with very specific instructions.

> **Gemma:** Meet today at 4:00 p.m. at top-secret location. Directions: Take the southeast entrance to Headquarters. Use the stairwell on your left and follow it to the basement. Listen for jangling keys and make sure you weren't followed. Abort plan if either is the case. Otherwise, walk to the end of the hall and knock on door B-43. Delete this message.

Last year, while snooping around Headquarters, I found myself a nice corner office in the basement. It was just an extra storage room, but it was *my* storage room. I found the key, tidied it up, and made it my own. This is where I go when I need to get away. No one knows about it. I'm vigilant whenever I enter or exit the basement, and I always have a story and then a backup story in case I'm questioned.

It's a pretty cool setup. A threadbare couch from an earlier generation's lounge sits next to a shelf that I've packed with books. There's a lamp I use for reading. I have an electric kettle and a drawer loaded with snacks, tea, and coffee. There's an old green chalkboard that I can slide in front of the door, in case any of the staff decides to take a glance inside. It's been over a year now and I've kept the place to myself. I would have preferred to keep it that way. But I couldn't risk being seen in public with Mel, especially since she wasn't particularly adept at subterfuge.

There was a knock just after four.

I opened the door to find Mel *and* Kate standing in the hallway. I wished Mel had given me a heads-up about the extra guest.

"What is this place?" Kate said as she entered, uninvited.

"My office," I said. "Please come in."

Mel followed Kate inside. I checked the hallway and locked the door behind me.

"I want an office," said Mel, looking around.

"This is our office, for now," I said with some effort.

I was already regretting the invitation.

"I'm hungry," said Mel.

I showed Mel the supply drawer.

"Help yourself. But check the halls before you come and go. And make sure the battery in your phone is charged. It's pitch-black down here after ten p.m. You'll need a light to find your way out."

As Mel perused my food stash, Kate casually walked around my office, opening drawers, looking things over, testing out the furniture, while giving me suspicious sidelong glances.

"So, Kate, are you with us?" I said.

"Don't know. What's the plan?" she said.

"Build an army, take down the Darkroom, and end Dulcinea," I said.

Mel shook her head, disappointed.

"If someone had told me a recruitment pitch was necessary, I might have prepared one," I said.

"Some army," said Kate. "How do I know I can trust you?"

"How do I know I can trust you?" I replied.

Kate shrugged.

"I'm vouching for both of you," said Mel. "Tell her."

Kate sat down on my couch and put her feet up on my coffee table.

"Tell me what?" I said.

"The photo was my punishment," Kate said.

"For what?"

"I warned my little sister and a few of her friends, firmly suggesting a moratorium on oral sex. One of them told her stupid boyfriend about it," said Kate.

"But how did they get that photo?" I said.

"Rachel," Kate said, looking away.

"Rachel Rose? Why did she have it?"

"The girls are as bad as the boys," Mel said. "Let's leave it at that."

I had many follow-up questions, but I let them slide.

"What's your angle?" said Kate, homing in on me.

"Christine Cleary was my big sister. She also talked. It got so bad she had to drop out," I said.

"Huh," said Kate, unimpressed.

"Mel, how's that hacking coming along?" I said.

Mel unloaded her laptop and fired it up.

"I was almost in last night. It was late. I was so close. And then I saw a maintenance notice and got immediately locked out. I could tell it was someone else kicking me out, but I think it maybe was just a coincidence—everyone got kicked out, not only me. To be safe, I didn't try to get back in right away. But when I did, it didn't work."

"So you're nowhere?" I said.

"Excuse me," Mel said. "Until three weeks ago my computer expertise was limited to building a basic website to feature vintage cereal-box art."

"I'd keep that hobby to myself," said Kate.

Mel ignored her. "If I said *angle-bracket curly-brace if-then-else,* would you have any idea what I was talking about?"

"No," I said.

"Right. So give me a break," said Mel. "I'm working as hard as I can."

"My apologies," I said. "I appreciate your efforts."

Kate returned to foraging through my supply drawer. She grabbed a package of licorice and offered a rope to Mel, then one to me.

"So, it's just the three of us?" Kate said, chomping down on a red vine.

"I think I have someone else. I just don't know who she is," I said.

Kate turned to Mel and said, "Did that make sense to you?"

"Show her," said Mel.

What's the point in having allies if you can't trust them? I handed Kate the anonymous Q&A.

"How did you get this?" Kate said.

"I searched Witt's office. I figured it was the best way to work out who was inclined to join the resistance."

Kate nodded her approval. "Good idea," she said.

"Do you know a senior who loves waffles and the Red Sox and hates blowjobs?"

Kate returned the Q&A and picked up her backpack.

"Why do you think it's a senior?" Kate said.

"Shit. I didn't even think of that," I said.

"You know who Waffles is?" said Mel.

"Yes. I'll be in touch," Kate said, departing.

"I have a gift for you," I said to Mel, delivering the book I'd stolen from the library.

"Did you read it?" she said.

"No. That's your job," I said.

"Thanks, boss," Mel said.

"I'm not the boss."

"Really? Because it feels like I'm doing all the hard work."

"That's because I'm doing all the dirty work," I said.

MR. FORD

Barely a month in and the school year was shaping up to be one for the record books. At least ten boys got stung by the scorching showers in Dickens. There was one unfortunate freshman with slow reflexes who suffered second-degree burns that required medical attention. His parents promptly pulled him out of school and contacted an attorney. Dean Stinson was slammed with lawyer meetings and consultations with the school's board of advisers.

Claude invited a few people over to her house on Friday afternoon for a small get-together. Her mother was in the hospital, which only Claude would think of as cause for entertaining. It was the usual suspects, minus Primm.

Lowland has two distinct neighborhoods. The south side, where most of the full-time residents live, is primarily composed of apartment complexes and modest single-family homes, as outdated as a turquoise refrigerator. The south-siders, for the most part, serve the east-siders.

Claude's family home was on the east side. When I first saw the house, four years ago, I was struck by its relative grandeur.

Resting atop a modest hill, 344 Crestview Drive looked like a ski chalet fallen from its former alpine heights. Reaching the front door required a climb up a steep stone walkway. A few years ago, someone installed a wheelchair elevator on the side of the house. Claude says it ruins the remote elegance of her home. For my money, the house is best on the inside anyway. The backyard overlooks acres of lush, rolling land with a shimmering pond and towering oak trees.

Claude answered the door in this rose print dress that was outdated but lovely in all the right places. She wore pearls around her neck and lipstick in a shade of mauve that made her appear younger and warmer than her usual blood-red war paint did. Sometimes I forget that she's hot because she's so severe.

"Finn, so glad you could make it," Claude said, looking past me. "You didn't bring Witt?"

"I assumed she'd come on her own," I said.

Evelyn, slicing limes in the open kitchen, said, "You were vague about the time, Claude. 'After school' can mean anything."

"What are we drinking?" I said.

"Vodka mojito," Evelyn said.

"Vodka?"

"Don't start," said Evelyn. "I drank a lifetime's worth of rum in college. The smell alone causes a gag reflex."

Evelyn served me a drink and Claude asked for another.

"Are you sure you don't want to eat something?" Evelyn said.

"Let's watch the sunset," Claude said, weaving her way onto the back deck.

She'd been at it a long time. There are three distinct phases to drunk Claude. The first few drinks sharpen her edges—take a paper cut and swap it out with a razor. After that, she gets nicer, more fun, but her guard remains intact. The third phase is sloppy, sweet, and sometimes very sexy. Phase three made a rare appearance.

"She was like this when I got here," Evelyn said, popping some frozen appetizers into the oven. "She needs to eat something."

The deck was covered in candles. It looked like a music video from the eighties. As night fell, the candlelight played that trick of making everyone look ten years younger. Claude appeared as she did when I first met her, when all I could see was a fuckable bookworm.

Witt arrived after dark with a bottle of cheap red.

"Shit. This place is incredible," Witt said.

"You're late again," Claude said.

"Am I?" Witt said.

"You said come anytime," Evelyn said. "You can't be late for anytime."

"Of course you can," Claude said with a slur.

"What's the occasion?" Witt asked, remarking on either the candlelight or the untouched spread of prosciutto-wrapped cantaloupe, cheese puffs, and an assortment of cured meats.

Evelyn poured Witt her dangerous concoction.

"I never get to entertain here," Claude said.

"Why not?" said Witt. "Seems perfect for it."

"It is perfect," Claude said.

"Where is your mother?" said Witt.

"In the hospital," said Claude, without a note of concern.

"I'm sorry to hear that," Witt said.

"Somebody needs to eat this food," said Claude.

"Yeah, you," Evelyn told Claude.

"Did you grow up in this place?" Witt said.

"We moved here when I was eleven. My mother's third husband was Frank Woolsey, the dean of Stonebridge before Stinson."

There's a fourth phase of Claude's inebriation. Sometimes you can bypass it if she passes out. If not, tread cautiously, because her dark side is like a black hole with a powerful magnetic force. Evelyn gave Claude a glass of ice water and changed the subject.

"Do any of you have an idea who the shower terrorist is? I heard there's a reward. I could use some extra cash. Any theories?"

"Gemma," mumbled Claude.

"Really? I thought perhaps Kate or Tegan," said Evelyn.

"It could just be a mechanical problem," said Witt.

We laughed at Witt's naïveté. Evelyn asked me if I had any ideas.

"No idea," I said.

I was pretty sure the asshole was Keith. I couldn't prove it. I only know that I saw him lock the door to the engineering room early one morning. He doesn't live in Dickens. Why else would he be there?

Claude demanded another drink. Witt tried to distract her by asking for a tour of the house.

Claude took Witt's arm to steady herself as the women walked down the long hall.

"Don't forget my drink," Claude called out.

I poured a glass of water and followed after them. I'd visited the house only once, a few years back, when her mother was out of town. I remember Claude briefly showing me the hallway. She pointed at her bedroom door but never let me inside. We had to fuck on a chaise longue by the pool.

I heard muted voices in the master bedroom, at the far end of the hall. I took a quick peek at Claude's bedroom while I had the chance.

Inside was a canopy bed with an ornate iron headboard. A gauzy curtain, festooned with holes, wrapped around the bed like a veil. The only other piece of furniture was a pink dresser. The room was unsettling, not just because it was stuck in the past. There was nothing about the room that signaled the Claude I had come to know. I closed the door and followed the voices down the hall.

"He was older," I overheard Claude say. "Sixty-six when he died."

"How old were you?" said Witt.

"Twenty-nine. He died two weeks before the wedding. If he'd hung on just a little bit longer, I could have been a widow."

Claude and Witt were lying on Mrs. Woolsey's round bed. If it weren't for the medicine bottles on the nightstand or the cloying antiseptic odor, you'd think it was a porn set from the seventies.

"Did you love him?" Witt said.

"Of course I loved him. I was going to marry him. God, it was awful when he died. His horrible children kicked me out of his house. I had nothing."

Claude's eyelids flickered like a child fighting sleep, until they were entirely drawn. Witt rolled to her left, until she reached the edge and dismounted clumsily.

I set the glass of water on the nightstand.

"Let's go," I whispered. "She needs to sleep."

When Witt and I returned to the deck, Evelyn had already made a dent in the cleanup. I cleared the glasses and reloaded the dishwasher, which prompted a brief spat with Evelyn, who pondered the possibility of a male conspiracy on dishwasher protocol. Her husband is apparently a Nazi about the loading configuration. Witt stayed out of the argument and kept busy packing the uneaten appetizers in a Tupperware container.

Then Evelyn poured herself a jumbo glass of wine and told us to leave. She'd handle the rest of the cleanup.

"I don't have to be home for another hour," Evelyn said. "I'm going to have some me time. You two get out of here. The night is still young."

As soon as we left Claude's place, Witt started in with the questions. She wanted to know if I was friends with Whitehall. We were friendly, I told her. Although I couldn't recall a single conversation. Witt asked if I'd observed any disturbing behavior among the students. I asked her to be more specific. *Never mind,* she said.

Then she wanted to talk about Claude. She got a hinky feeling in that bedroom. I didn't want to talk about Claude, although I had the same feeling. I asked Witt about life in the cottage. Witt insisted it was habitable but admitted that she missed television and electricity, in that order. I told her she was free to use my television or electricity anytime. She was checking her phone. It's such a vulgar habit. I don't know if she even heard my offer.

"Does Dulcinea mean anything to you? I mean, beyond *Don Quixote,*" Witt said, out of the blue.

"No, Detective Stark," I said. "Should it?"

Witt got weirdly silent after I referenced her father's books. I probably shouldn't have mentioned him. All women have daddy issues, I've come to learn. The quality of the fathering is ultimately irrelevant. A shitty dad means a needy woman who can't trust you to turn off a light switch. But for my money, the good dads fuck you up the most, because you'll always disappoint their daughters.

It was dark. I asked Witt if she wanted company back to her cottage.

"I can't do this tonight," she said, sounding annoyed.

I'd offered to walk her home, not fuck her.

MS. WITT

When you live and work in a small pond, like a boarding school, there's a slow and steady beer-goggle effect that takes place. Eventually all age-appropriate men appear more attractive than they would in the outside world. At least that was a theory an old colleague used to have. My point is, I didn't fully trust my attraction to Finn. (Although I think I was genuinely attracted to him, at the time.)

As we were walking back to campus, we briefly discussed the merits, or lack thereof, of a round mattress. I tried to pivot the conversation to the blowjob contest, but he didn't seem to know anything. I turned my phone on and was suddenly barraged by an insane influx of messages. I could feel the text vibrations as my father grew increasingly desperate to make contact. I was not in the mood to deal with him.

It was dark and those woods were kind of freaky and I'd forgotten to bring my flashlight. I was hoping Finn would offer to walk me home. He didn't. Maybe feminism killed chivalry. Or maybe my expectations were unrealistic. I didn't ask and Finn isn't a mind reader.

We parted ways at the main gate. I started along the fire trail, then stopped to read the messages before I lost reception..

Dad: Please call. Must talk.

Dad: Alex, where are you?

Dad: Urgent. SOS.

Dad: Six months of work down the drain.

Dad: Oh my Lord. What have I done?

I turned off my phone for the night and continued to my cabin. About ten feet from my front door, a bright light flashed into my eyes. I looked away and stepped out of the beam. A newly installed floodlight was responsible for my temporary blindness. I quickly unlocked the door, stepped inside, and snapped the deadbolt behind me. I turned on a lamp and inspected the cottage for disruption. A small square of paper had been slipped under the door.

NOW THAT YOU KNOW, WHAT ARE YOU GOING TO DO ABOUT IT?

The only thing I wanted in that moment was to track down the note-leaving lunatic and break his writing fingers. Or at the very least remove all ink and paper from his—or her—household.

Some people count sheep. What finally sent me to sleep was cycling through possible job alternatives in alphabetical order. For soporific purposes, you can't leave anything off the table. I fell asleep sometime after *carpet installer*.

* * *

The shorter days made it easy to sleep in. I can't say I was refreshed when I did finally wake up. There was a brief moment of elation when I realized that it was Saturday, but that sensation was quickly dethroned by the murky memory of Claude's house, followed by my father's desperate pleas, ending with that fucking note.

I crawled out of bed, opened the front door, and found another carcass waiting for me. I threw on my robe and slippers and proceeded to feed the cat and then the generator. After that I made a cup of coffee and returned to the brisk outdoors to drink it.

I heard a splashing sound right away, followed by a high-pitched voice shouting *ha,* like in a karate class. I walked past the clearing and a few feet into the woods. Linny, the young girl I'd seen shouting at Keith a few weeks back, was standing in my pond wearing waders. She gripped a long metal stick and repeatedly stabbed it into the water. The stabbing and the *ha* were in unison.

I had no idea what Linny was up to, but I admired her dedication. She didn't notice me until I spoke.

"What am I looking at?" I said.

Linny shifted her hold on the stick so it looked more like a rifle resting against her shoulder.

"Did I wake you?" she said. "I wasn't supposed to wake you. I'm here to deliver a message."

"Linny, right? What are you doing?"

"I was spearfishing."

"Are there fish worth fishing for in that pond?"

"I don't eat fish. I'm practicing against a moving target, that's all. This isn't even a proper spear."

"I see that. What is it?" I said.

"It's a golf club. I cut off the head and sharpened the shaft. Do you want to hear your message?" said Linny.

"Why not?"

"Dean Stinson wants you to come to his house. Whenever it's convenient in the next hour."

"Do you know what it's about?"

"Dean didn't say, but there was another old guy with him. I think the other old guy is your father."

"What did the other old guy look like?"

"Gray hair, goatee. Dressed like he's on a safari."

"That's him," I said. "I'm going to get dressed. You have five minutes to finish practicing. Then you'll walk me back to campus and promise not to spearfish unsupervised again."

After I dressed, I found Linny orbiting my cottage, taking photos of the dirt with her phone. Waders now off, she was wearing military fatigues. I didn't know they made them in that size.

"What are you doing now?"

"Have you noticed these footprints?" Linny said.

I felt a single thump in my chest. I studied the ground as I walked over to Linny. There were footprints surrounding my entire cottage.

"Do you have exceptionally large feet?" she said.

"No," I said. I put my foot next to the print that Linny was studying.

Linny nodded and then looked up at the sky, like she was doing some kind of internal calculation.

"I'd say this is the footprint of a male who wears between a size-eight and -eleven shoe," Linny said.

I continued around the cottage to the front, where I noticed another set of footprints. The second set was larger, grouped primarily around the front door.

Linny followed me to the threshold and made a show of studying the larger shoe prints.

"These shoes are bigger and have deep treads. The smaller prints look like loafers. That's what the boys wear. Two different individuals, I'd say," she said.

I would have been much more amused by the little girl playing detective if two men weren't casing my home.

"Let's go," I said.

She slung the waders over her shoulder as we headed onto Eliot Trail.

"You have any theories about the footprints?" Linny said.

"Someone has been leaving me notes," I said.

"Interesting. Where are the notes left?" she asked.

"Front door," I said.

"Hmm," said Linny. "If he leaves them at the front door, why are his prints all around the cottage?"

I didn't want to think too hard about the potential Peeping Tom.

"Why don't you tell me about your private PE classes.

Wouldn't joining a team be easier?" I said.

"Easier, sure. But I'm very dedicated to my independent-study curriculum. Speaking of, I know it's been asked before, but are you certain you wouldn't consider teaching a fencing workshop?"

"I don't fence."

Linny lunged forward and stabbed the air.

"Keith said it never hurts to ask," Linny said.

"Really? He said that?"

"He did. Is that bad advice?"

"Not at all. It's just that I've made it abundantly clear to him that I don't fence," I said.

"That's unfortunate," Linny said. "It would be nice to be able to wield some kind of weapon, just in case."

"In case what?" I said.

"In case I have to injure, maim, or kill someone. In self-defense, of course," Linny said.

"Your beheaded golf club looks like a weapon to me. Be careful with that, will you?"

"I'm very careful."

I realized that Linny might be an excellent source of information if I played my cards right.

"You don't know who has been leaving me notes, do you?"

I could have imagined it, but I think she paused before she answered.

"I don't," she said.

"Are you sure?" I said.

"I haven't seen anyone. But I'll keep my eyes peeled," she

said, as she continued across Fleming Square with her waders bouncing on her back.

I found Greg and my father sitting on his porch when I arrived. I spun around and started back in the direction I came. Linny had already warned me about my father, so the move was all for show. I was determined to keep my dad at a disadvantage for now. Maybe forever.

"Alex, please," Greg said. "Len drove more than two hours. He won't leave until he speaks to you."

Dad was walking the tightrope between irate and terrified.

"I need your help, Alex. Is it your plan to ignore me for the rest of your life?"

I turned around and debated whether to stay or go.

"I have a fresh pot of coffee," Greg said, retreating inside. "I'll get you a cup."

I pretended the offer of coffee was the tipping point in my decision. I strolled up to the porch, where my dad stood with his arms open for a hug. I wasn't there yet. I extended my hand. Dad rolled his eyes as we shook hands like business partners.

"It is wonderful to see you, dear."

Dad sat back down on one of Greg's Adirondack chairs. His manuscript was in a messy stack by his side.

"How bad is it?" I said, pointing at the manuscript and taking a seat next to my father.

"You know when you crash your car and it looks like it could be fixed and possibly restored to some semblance of its previous glory, but the cost of repairs is more than the car is worth?" Dad said.

"Are you saying you totaled your book?"

"Quite possibly," Dad said.

"Sticking with the car analogy, where did you make the wrong turn?"

"Right after the office is burned to the ground, erasing all evidence of Coburn's involvement in the '73 murder. Quinn comes down with the flu. His fever induces visions in which he relives his wife's death. He realizes she may be alive and he flies to Toledo, still in the throes of a virulent influenza, and he meets a wealthy real estate mogul and his wife. Robert and Marcella Mondavi take Quinn into their home, ostensibly to nurse him back to health. But, of course, they have other motives. Oh yes, and the wife, Marcella, is so beautiful that Quinn begins to doubt that she is real. When Quinn is under their spell, Robert and Marcella convince him that Sanchez is behind his wife's disappearance. Quinn vows—"

"Stop, Dad. Visions? Fires? Toledo? None of that was in the original plot. Why do you have to Quixote everything?"

"I love that book. And I hate writing to an outline," he said, sounding old and deflated.

It happens with every book. Dad tries to make it on his own (or Cervantes's) and he goes off the rails. The problem isn't that he lacks talent; the problem is that he's never figured out how to make the most of his talent. He has too many ideas and can't rein them in. He needs round-the-clock editing. That was my mother's job for many years, even after the divorce.

Unfortunately, the longer they worked together, the more hostile the relationship became. Every editorial note was like a razor slice on my dad's thin skin. At some point, we noticed that Dad's skin thickens in my company. So now we funnel all of my mother's notes through me. I am my father's primary critic in all areas of his life. It's one of my favorite things about our relationship; I doubt my dad shares that opinion.

"Send me the file, Dad. I'll locate the detour and get back to you in a few days," I said.

"Thank you, dear."

Greg returned to the porch with a cup of coffee.

I looked at Greg. "You wouldn't have a to-go cup, would you?"

"Well, I have a commuter mug you could borrow," Greg said.

"That would be awesome," I said.

"I wish you would stay," Dad said.

"I'm busy fixing your book," I said.

While Greg was playing barista, Dad pretended to drink out of an empty mug, just so he'd have something to do. His commitment to the charade was amazing.

Dad put down his mug and finally met my gaze straight on. "I like to think that my flaws helped shape the strong, stubborn woman you are today."

NORMAN CROWLEY

Editorial Board Meeting—Minutes

Present: Mick Devlin (chair), Jack Vandenberg, Adam Westlake, Gabriel Smythe, Norman Crowley (secretary), Jonah Wagman (absent)

Next meeting: TBD

Agenda

- New member vote
- Shower terrorist
- Dulcinea status report
- Other business

There's a board meeting at least once a month. I have to take the minutes because some knuckle-dragger two years back decided there should be official minutes. The editors never want to see them until they do, and if you don't have them, all hell breaks loose. I've tried everything to get out of the job—the meetings are like a porn-centric think tank—but my resistance is always met with a friendly arm around the shoulder and a veiled threat.

The first meeting of October had far more agenda points than usual. It began as it always does: Jack lumbered into the lounge and banished all non-board members. Mick sat at his table, with a gavel in hand.

"Who are we waiting on?" Adam said, knowing the answer already.

Jack started counting on his fingers. There are five editors, so he was trying to do the math on who was missing. Jack looks like a Viking and can get a keg at the drop of a hat. But he's not in the Ten for his intellectual gifts.

"I'll bet anyone a hundred rubles that Jonah is a no-show once again," said Gabe.

Then Gabe began to chuckle, because he's his own best audience. Sometimes I want to explain to him the basic structure of a joke, how it has to invert the expected. I don't think he'll ever get it. When he comes into his inheritance, he can pay people to laugh with him.

Adam opened the lounge door, where his little brother was parked outside.

"Smitty," Adam said. "Go fetch Jonah for me."

I can't remember the sophomore's name, but it's not Smitty. Whatever-his-name-is hopped to it. For the next five minutes, as the editors waited for Jonah, we watched Gabe perform a series of impressions that were so inept that it became something of a game, trying to figure out who he was imitating.

When Jonah finally arrived, he dipped his head into the room and said, "Sorry, guys. Can't make it. Gotta hit the books."

Adam stepped into the hallway and said, "Jonah, my man,

this is the third meeting in a row. We're having a vote tonight."

"You can have my proxy," Jonah said, sinking his hands into his pockets and staring at the ground.

Adam shook his head, disappointed.

"You're not living up to the Bagman rep," said Adam.

Jonah's brother, Jason, was one of the first editors. I think his nickname was Bagman because it rhymed with his last name and he bagged a lot of girls.

"That's a tall order. Why even try?" Jonah said. "Later, Adam."

Jonah left. I was jealous. It's ironic that the only thing that could safely extricate me from this exclusive club was status. Mick slammed his gavel and called the meeting to order.

New Nick, as predicted, was voted onto the board. New guys, the ones sanctioned by the Ten, are typically given only limited Darkroom access until the editors are sure they can be trusted. But I guess Nick was special or something. Only Gabe questioned his meteoric rise in the school hierarchy.

Earlier that day, I had met with Adam and New Nick and been instructed to create a Darkroom account for VicVega. That's the username Nick chose. At least he wasn't yet another numbered Hef. I had to walk Nick through the login process as he created his password. I watched him as he clicked his way through the Darkroom until he found the Dulcinea portal. I was hoping for some kind of reaction—alarm, horror, maybe those cartoon eyes that spring out and retract. But New Nick just looked bored, which was especially annoying for a guy with at least three hot girls vying for his attention.

The capture of the shower terrorist was next up on the

agenda. Adam brought out a stack of red flyers that read WANTED: SHOWER TERRORIST. REWARD: $500. Below that was a black-and-white illustration of a masked man in a striped outfit (like the Hamburglar). He was under a showerhead, framed inside the crosshairs of a rifle scope.

No one commented on the laughably lousy graphics.

"I've collected three hundred and fifty from the first floor alone," Adam said. "We'll start the reward at five hundred and if there's no action, we'll collect more."

"All in favor," Mick said.

Aye, they all said.

Adam handed off the flyers to "Smitty," with instructions for where to hang them.

As aggravating as the shower terrorist was, Dulcinea was the true headliner for the meeting. Apparently, the editors had noticed a decrease in overall Darkroom activity as well as a shortfall of Dulcinea entrants. It was like they were in the video-rental business, struggling to remain relevant.

"Do we want the Dulcinea tradition to end with the class of 2010?" said Mick.

"Fuck no," said Jack.

"You know what we need," said Gabe. "A really great ad campaign. What would Don Draper do?"

"Were you dropped on your head as a child?" Adam said to Gabe.

"Gabe, I think what Adam is trying to say is that an ad campaign is the last thing we need," said Mick. "The problem is that our secret society has lost some of the secret part. In the history of Dulcinea, there has always been a select group of girls in the know, and we appreciate their sense of competition. But the competition ultimately relies on the pretense of a traditional courtship."

"What?" said Jack.

Jack often spaces out if communication isn't limited to a single sentence.

"Your average girl won't suck you off if she knows she's being scored," said Adam.

"Riiiiight," said Jack.

I went dark for a minute, disappearing into a Bruce Lee fantasy in which I took them all out with my bare hands and feet. They were sprawled on the floor, bloodied and mangled. I felt sick.

I must have looked ill. Jack asked me if I was all right. I forgot I was still in the room. "I'm fine," I said. Jack told me to hydrate.

Mick turned to Adam and said, "How do we fix this? We can't put the genie back in the bottle."

"If the problem is the girls are talking to each other, you just have to get them to stop talking," said Jack.

"Good luck with that," said Gabe.

Adam scribbled something in his notebook, then stared thoughtfully at the ceiling.

"Okay. Well, that's enough for tonight. Thank you, Norman," said Adam.

Jack started to get up but then sat down after Adam made a subtle gesture with his hand.

"I can go?" I said.

Adam nodded. It became clear that I was being dispatched while the rest of them remained to strategize against the girls.

As I walked down the hallway to my room, I could feel the anger coming back. My hands started to shake. I unlocked my door, put the laptop on my desk, and logged onto Blackboard.

To: Mel Eastman
From: Bill Haydon
Re: Darkroom

Stop trying to scale the walls like a jewel thief. Just fake an invite and get inside like a regular guest. Now. Please.

Yours,
Bill

GEMMA RUSSO

Saturday morning, Kate sent a text to Mel and me.

Kate: I've found Waffles. Meet @ base. 11:00 a.m.?

I headed over to my office an hour early. I wanted to be there when my new recruit arrived. Not just because I was anxious to meet her but as a proprietary statement about my space. I unlocked the door to find Linny sprawled out on my couch, in military fatigues, reading some book about poisonous shrubs.

"Did I leave the door unlocked?" I said.

"You left the key on your desk. I assumed you made a copy for me."

I didn't. But couldn't see Linny relinquishing the key without a fight.

"Why are you dressed like that?" I said.

"I'm doing a survivalist segment in my independent-study PE. In Outward Bound, they drop you off in the wilderness somewhere with a can opener, flint, and salt, and you have to fend for yourself for three days. I'm trying to convince Coach Keith that if I do three full days in the Stonebridge backwoods, then I could cover my PE for the entire year. Or at least this semester."

"Coach will not agree to that," I said.

"We'll see," Linny said.

Two loud and two soft knocks interrupted our conversation.

I opened the door. Alyson Mosby, a junior I knew just by name and sight, stood in the hallway, flanked by Mel and Kate.

"Welcome," I said, sweeping my hand across the room, like a butler or something.

Linny sat up and looked eagerly at our new guest.

"And now we're an army of five," Linny said.

"Time to go, Linny."

"Why?"

"You know why," I said. "Out."

Linny tried to hold her ground, but we'd been through this before. She's small enough that I can physically remove her if necessary. I gave her a moment to decide whether she wanted to leave with her dignity or not.

"I have an appointment," Linny said, quickly departing.

After Linny was gone, Kate made introductions.

"Alyson Mosby, meet Gemma Russo."

"A pleasure," I said. "Did Kate tell you about our work?"

"She told me you had some plans. I'm unaware of any actual work being accomplished," Alyson said.

"We're still in the planning stages," I said.

Then I looked at Mel. "Where are we, by the way?"

"I'm working on it," Mel snapped.

I told Alyson to have a seat and asked if I could get her anything.

"Like what?" Alyson said.

Mel opened the supply drawer and listed off the sundry edibles.

"You're out of licorice, FYI," Mel said.

"I'll have a licorice," Alyson said.

It seemed like a good sign that she still had a sense of humor. I took a seat next to her on the couch while Kate took a position on the coffee table.

"A cup of tea," Kate said, "if it isn't too much trouble."

"Coming right up," said Mel.

This is all I could tell you about Alyson Mosby: She was a junior slummer. Science was her thing. Never part of the Ten, but Ten adjacent from what I could tell. Pretty, with giant brown eyes, a long neck and thin lips. She was a forward on the soccer team. She looked like a real athlete, with noticeably muscular legs. I once overheard three boys arguing about the relative attractiveness of those legs. Their conversation could be reduced to these three opinions.

Boy #1: a work of art.
Boy #2: too beefy.
Boy #3: I only care what's between them.

I gave Alyson my brief sales pitch and asked if she had any questions.

"I know what happened to Kate. I guess I'd like to hear your war stories," Alyson said.

Mel turned on the kettle and gave me this look.

"You mind going first, Mel?" I said.

Mel pulled up a chair.

"Okay. Long story short," Mel said. "Mick asked me out last year. My roommate was in complete shock. She acted like it was a miracle that someone like him even knew my name. He said all the right things. He acted like dating a girl with a brain was such a thrill and he was always complimenting me, which I'd never had before. But I see now how it was totally over the top. He said that I was the kind of girl that he could fall in love with and, like an idiot, I believed him. We started hooking up and stuff, just making out. Once I was convinced that he really liked me, we started to do more. And then he became weirdly fixated on oral sex—I mean, like on him. I realized later it was a long con. But at the time, I—God, I was stupid."

"How'd you learn about the contest?" Alyson said.

"He was a dumbass," said Mel. "I went to his room one day to meet him and his computer was open. I didn't know what I was looking at, I just knew it was about me and it was awful. I called my big sister, Madison, at college and she said she'd heard some stuff over the years. She told me what she knew. After that, I tried to ignore Mick. I couldn't even look at him. Eventually he sent me a text and asked me why I suddenly stopped liking him. I replied with a one-word text: *Dulcinea*. Then he wrote back: *Don't tell anyone. It's our secret.* It was so creepy."

I felt guilty knowing the details of Mel's humiliation without having my own depraved story to reciprocate. As I was debating whether I should make up a story, Mel asked Alyson about hers.

"Remember Mike Cage? He graduated last year?"

"Yeah, I remember him. Mike? Really?" said Mel.

Mike seemed like that guy that sensible girls date. He was smart but lacked looks or charisma. In theory, he was the nice guy you're supposed to want but never really do.

"We started going out middle of my freshman year," Alyson said.

"And you *liked* him?" Mel said, her face scrunched up in disbelief.

I was grateful Mel was asking the questions that we all were probably thinking.

"I know, I know," said Alyson. "But he *was* super nice at the start. And my mother always told me to date men who are grateful to be going out with you."

"If you guys were a legit couple, why would he submit your name to Dulcinea?"

"The editors got into his head. He was always an outsider, and suddenly members of the Ten were acting like he was one of them. It was more important to him than I thought it was."

"Were you ever suspicious?" said Kate.

"Yeah. I mean, at some point I definitely noticed Mike was weird about blowjobs. Like, he didn't seem to want to do anything else. I had a theory that he'd watched too much blowjob porn and got locked into a fetish," said Alyson.

"Huh?" said Mel. "Is that a thing?"

"My mom says that if boys fixate on a particular kind of porn, they lose their ability to ejaculate when not viewing their porn of preference," said Alyson.

"That's what happens with foot fetishists, right?" said Kate.

"Exactly," said Alyson.

Mel tilted her head to the side and gazed up at the ceiling. "You know of any double-blind studies on the subject?" Mel said.

"So," I said. "Mike became fixated on BJs. But when did you figure it out?"

"I didn't figure anything out," Alyson said. "Mike and I went to a basement party and Toby Givens—you know, Ty Givens's younger brother? Pervert runs in the family. Anyway, Toby walked right up to me and asked me to suck him off. I asked *why,* meaning, *Why would I do that?* He just said, 'I heard you're good, but I want to make sure your boyfriend isn't padding your scores.' "

"No way," said Mel.

"Yeah," said Alyson. "Toby was super drunk. Some of the editors heard and took him away. I asked what he was talking about and the guys played it off. But Mike was a bad liar. I kept asking him about it over and over again. Eventually he cracked and told me everything."

"Really, he just told you. Everything?" said Mel.

"I promised I wouldn't break up with him if he confessed. He confessed," Alyson said.

"And then what happened?" said Mel.

"I broke up with the piece of shit."

Kate and Alyson exchanged a high five.

"Well done," said Kate.

"Did you tell anyone?" I said.

"I talked about it with a few friends. When I got a little sister this year, I warned her about the boys. But . . . I don't know. I've been thinking there's more to be done."

"I'm glad to hear that," I said.

There was a weird pause after that. I had hoped that the conversation would shift to another topic and I'd be spared having to tell my own Dulcinea confession.

"What's your story?" Alyson said.

"It's not very interesting," I said.

"It was Jonah, wasn't it?" said Alyson.

I didn't look at Mel or Kate as I told the lie.

"Yes," I said.

"Too bad," said Alyson. "I always thought he was one of the good ones."

MS. WITT

Back inside my cottage, I took sheets of aluminum foil and molded them to the windows. I had chosen this place for the privacy and realized I was living in a fishbowl.

Keith jogged by as I was circling my cottage, confirming that the foil obstructed any view of the interior.

"Greg asked me to invite you to dinner," Keith said.

"He sent you here to invite me?"

"You don't have cell reception and he knew I was probably going for a run. He's making rabbit stew. Should I tell him you're coming?" he said, squinting at the foil reflection.

I wanted to talk to Greg about a few things, but I didn't want to have rabbit stew for dinner.

Reading my mind, Keith said, "Whenever Greg invites me to dinner, I either pregame or postgame in the kitchen at Dahl. And I always bring beer. But maybe you like mulled wine and sweet vermouth."

"Tell Greg I'll be there," I said. "And thanks for the advice."

"Cool," Keith said, turning back onto the trail.

That's when I noticed the tread on his footprints.

"Stop," I said.

"What's up?" he said, turning back around.

"Why are your footprints all over my cottage?" I said, pointing out the clear prints by my front door.

"I installed the floodlight," he said.

"Oh," I said.

I wasn't sure if I was supposed to thank him or not.

"Was it wise to connect another electrical device to a system that's already barely functioning?" I said.

"I didn't. It has a battery," Keith said.

"Have you been leaving notes for me?"

"Why would I leave notes when our conversations are so awesome?"

"Huh. Must be Loafers," I said.

"What?" Keith said.

I pointed out one of the prints with the smooth sole.

Keith studied the other footprints. He was staring at them for a really long time. Then he looked up and scanned the landscape. His expression darkened when he met my eye.

"You shouldn't be here," he said.

He jogged away before I could ask him what he meant. Only later did I think it was odd that he didn't comment on the aluminum foil.

The rabbit stew was intended as a peace offering, even though I considered it yet another layer to his debt.

Greg answered the door wearing a white apron that looked

more appropriate for a butcher shop than a kitchen. I delivered a bottle of dry red wine. Greg ushered me into his weird parlor room. I could smell rabbit stew cooking.

"In my defense, I wasn't fully cognizant of this imbroglio between you two," Greg said. "May I ask what happened?"

"Do you really want to know?" I said, unscrewing the wine cap.

"I suppose not," he said.

I knew that would be his answer. My father has male friends with whom he shares and exults in his misdeeds, and then there's Greg.

"How is the cabin working out?" Greg said, placing two cordial glasses on his bar.

"It's okay," I said, as I poured the wine. I took a sip from my glass and poured another finger. "You need bigger glasses."

"I would like you to consider other living options," Greg said. "There is another campus apartment that you might find—"

"No, thank you. I'm good for now. I have a few administrative questions for you."

"By all means," Greg said.

"Martha Primm. When did she arrive at Stonebridge and why?"

"Oh. I wasn't expecting a Martha question."

Greg took two sips and gazed down at the empty glass. I also finished my glass and poured another round.

"The school board made me hire her about five years ago after an unfortunate incident."

"Can you be more specific about the unfortunate incident?" I said.

"I was hoping for a more pleasant conversation this evening," Greg said.

"I'll make you a deal. You tell me about the unfortunate incident over drinks and we can talk about botany or whatever you want over dinner. Again, what happened?"

"A female student accused a male student of rape," Greg said.

"And how did you hear about this?"

"The young woman came to my office and told me. We only had a career counselor on staff back then," Greg said.

"Is something burning?" I said.

Greg turned and ran to the kitchen. I followed him. He switched off the burner and stirred the murky concoction.

"So this girl came to you. What was her name?"

"I can't provide names," Greg said.

Greg returned to the parlor. I'd poured six times and yet we'd only drunk half the bottle.

"You don't have to give me real names. Just use Jane and John. So Jane came to your office and told you that John had raped her. What did you do?"

"I didn't know what to do," Greg said. "There was no procedure that I was aware of. It was the first time anything of that nature happened on my watch. I didn't know if I needed to take . . . Jane to the hospital or call the police. I was utterly out of my depth. I contacted a female member of the board and she told me that she'd handle it. Then the board member showed up with Martha the next day. I thought it was a good thing. I also thought it was better that Jane talked to a woman."

"What was the result?" I said.

"Martha interviewed both parties and, after a day or so, um, Jane retracted her statement. She also decided to leave Stonebridge."

"All of this happened after Jane started talking to Martha Primm?" I said.

"Yes."

"And then Martha was hired full-time for her remarkable ability to squash testimony."

"I honestly don't know what happened. Once Martha took over I wasn't part of the process."

"So you did nothing?"

"What should I have done?"

The question was asked so earnestly, it was hard to be angry with him.

"I'm curious," I said. "When Jane came to you and told you her story, did you believe her?"

"I did. But I thought it was best to remove myself from the situation."

"Why?" I said.

"Young girls don't want to talk to old men about such things. Am I wrong?" Greg said.

"An old man who listens is better than a young woman who doesn't."

* * *

I followed Keith's postgame instructions and went to Dahl after my inedible meal with Greg. The kitchen was dark and quiet when I entered. While I was foraging through the industrial-sized refrigerator, I heard a crunching sound, then a crinkling sound, coming from the pantry.

"Who's there?" I said.

"Alex?" a male voice said.

I turned around and saw Finn standing at the mouth of the pantry, gently cradling a bag of potato chips in his left arm. I closed the freezer door and the room went dark.

"Where's the light?" I said.

Finn flicked on an overhead light. His eyes, rimmed red, squinted against the bright fluorescents. He extended the bag.

"Chip?"

I took a greedy handful.

"You okay, Finn?"

"I'm so thirsty," he said, just standing there.

"You should drink some water."

"That's a really good idea," he said.

I filled a glass of water from the tap and passed it to Finn. He gave me the bag of chips in exchange, downed the entire glass in one extended gulp, then gazed down at the empty glass.

"This reminds me of something," he said.

"Drinking water?" I said.

"No. I met your mother."

"*This* reminds you of meeting my mother?"

"The feeling is the same, you know?" he said.

"I don't. What feeling?"

"Being caught."

"What did my mother catch you doing?"

Finn expelled a long sigh. "Visiting you," he said. "I made a bad impression."

"Nah, you were fine," I said.

I wasn't going to tell him that only his eyebrows had drawn my mother's notice.

"Can I tell you something?" Finn said.

His tone suggested a dark secret was forthcoming.

"You can tell me anything," I said.

"I don't want to be in the pantry anymore."

"I was hoping for a meatier secret," I said.

"I want to hang out," Finn said.

"With me?"

"Yes. But not here."

I was enjoying stoned Finn and his peculiarly guileless conversation.

"So, where do you want to hang out?"

"My place is closer than your place," he said.

"That works for me," I said.

We raided the pantry for more provisions and made our way to his apartment. When we reached the front door to Dickens, Finn suggested I disguise myself, I assumed in case a student was roaming the halls. It seemed a bit unnecessary, but I played along. He gave me his coat, flicked up the collar, and wrapped his scarf around the bottom half of my face. I thought the sunglasses were overkill, but I managed.

"Follow me," he said in a whisper.

We traveled four flights up the north stairwell and into his apartment undetected.

Inside, I noticed a collection of shoes by his front door. I assumed it was a shoe-free home. I kicked off my sneakers. When I looked back at Finn, I noticed an urgent panic set in. I worried that de-shoeing suggested I was planning a long stay.

"I could put my shoes back on," I said. That might have sounded even stranger.

"Oh. No. The shoes should stay off."

He quickly ushered me into the living room and offered me a drink or weed. I'd already had several shots of wine, so I opted not to mix my intoxicants. Finn gulped two more tumblers of water and set out a grazing spread from our pantry theft.

As we indulged in an assortment of processed-food items, Finn's high took a nosedive.

"Have you been leaving things at my door?" I said.

"No. What kind of things? Gifts?" he said, intrigued.

"I don't think so. They're just cryptic notes."

"Do you have a secret admirer?" Finn said.

"It's not like that."

"Do you have a not-secret admirer?"

"A not-secret admirer?"

"That was my casual way of asking if you were seeing anyone," Finn said.

"Oh. I'm not," I said. "Did you hear anything about me before I came here?"

"Like what?"

"You tell me," I said.

MR. FORD

Saturday night I'm on dorm watch. Officially, I'm required to roam half of Dickens House every hour or so, making sure no one's passed out, shooting up, or having sex in public. I don't do any of those things. We have an understanding. I don't police them; they come to me if a student is injured or incapacitated.

I was trying to grade all of the Camus papers so I could have the rest of the weekend to finish revisions on my book. I got stoned to make the student essays more interesting. I was about halfway done when I got to Adam Westlake's essay, which was fascinatingly off point. Adam breezed past Meursault's behavior at his mother's funeral and suggested that his guilty verdict was a result of a mangled defense: *If Meursault had not been sentenced to death, he would have had an excellent case for legal malpractice, since clearly Meursault was suffering from heatstroke when he pulled the trigger.*

I got more stoned as I debated whether Adam was serious or just fucking around. Then people started knocking on my door.

Jonah came by to deliver his paper. I think he smelled

the weed. I got paranoid, ushered him out, and Febrezed my entire apartment.

Another knock, ten minutes later. I didn't answer for a while, thinking whoever it was would go away. I was wrong. Rapid knocking followed by the sound of Rachel Rose's voice.

"Mr. Ford. Finn Ford. I know you're in there," she said in a singsongy tone, which felt like something from a horror film.

I opened the door. She pushed past me and said impatiently, "It's about time." Then she kicked off her shoes and tossed her scarf on the coat rack.

"You can keep your shoes on," I said, worried that more clothing items were about to come off.

I left the door open. I thought it would be better that way. Then I wasn't sure if it was worse with the door open. Stonebridge has never had any set rules of propriety—boys, girls, male and female faculty are essentially allowed anywhere other than gender-specific restrooms and locker rooms.

Rachel settled onto my couch, comfortably tucking one foot underneath her other thigh. She was wearing a short black skirt with those fucking knee-highs that they all wear with their uniforms. She said she wanted to explain why her Camus paper was late. I offered an extension. She said she was confused by the book.

"Why doesn't the guy—" she said.

"Meursault?"

"Whatever. Why doesn't he just pretend to be sad about his mother's death, so he doesn't get convicted of murder?"

"That would be lying," I said.

"So what?" she said. "Are you going to sit down?"

"No. No. I need to stand. My back is bothering me."

I paced for effect.

"Do you want me to walk on it?" she said.

"Excuse me?"

"I walk on my dad's back all the time. It helps. I promise I won't hurt you."

"No. Thank you," I said. "Look, Rachel, take the weekend on the paper, if you're still having trouble. We'll talk after class on Monday."

"You used to like it when we talked," Rachel said.

"I still like talking to my students. I just have a lot of work to do this weekend."

"On your book?"

"Yes, and other stuff."

Rachel hugged her knees to her chest. I saw more skin than I should have and I started wondering whether she was wearing underwear, until I became aware that I shouldn't have been wondering those things. I focused my gaze on my bare feet. I have an unnaturally long second toe. Or maybe it's my hallux that's shorter than average. I was thinking about toes so I wouldn't think about Rachel and her possible lack of underwear.

"Who are you going to dedicate your book to?" she said.

"I'm not sure," I said. "Probably my parents."

"Will I at least get a thank-you in the acknowledgments?"

"I'll thank all of my students," I said.

"Whatever," Rachel said, sighing. She slowly removed herself from the couch, slipped on her loafers with the speed of an invalid, gave me a final forlorn expression, and departed.

An hour later, Norman Crowley came by to deliver a form that allows him to handle his own meds. There was an incident before my time that required all controlled substances be distributed by a staff member until the student reached the age of seventeen and had parental consent. I couldn't speak for Norman, but these daily visits had become a major drag. Sometimes I felt like he was looking right through me.

After Norman gave me the form, I relinquished the rest of his meds.

"Take care of yourself, Norman," I said.

Norman clocked Rachel Rose's pink scarf hanging from my coat rack.

"You too, Mr. Ford," he said, with this knowing sneer.

Fuck you, Norman, I thought. *You don't know anything.*

I got really hungry and decided to chance it at Dahl. That's where I ran into Witt. I don't remember how it happened, but we came back to my place. I don't know why I made her wear the Invisible Man disguise.

I came down fast when we entered my foyer. Rachel Rose's scarf was draped over the coat rack. Everyone knows she wears that pink scarf all the time, everywhere. Witt kicked off her shoes and asked me if I was all right. I don't remember what I said or did. Witt sat down on the couch. I think Witt asked to see a sample of my handwriting. Maybe not. That part is a bit fuzzy.

I do remember that she asked me if I knew what happened to her at Warren. I claimed I hadn't heard anything. It's better if they tell you.

I might have felt guilty for lying if I hadn't made a deal to play bootlegger in exchange for Mick's silence. I was hoping she'd be worth the effort.

It was late. I told her she could stay over and I'd take the couch. She said we could share the bed, which is what I was hoping she'd say. I gave her a T-shirt to wear and I had an extra toothbrush. For half an hour we pretended that we were just going to sleep. I knew better than to make the first move. I remember staring at the ceiling and thinking it was going to be a long night.

Finally, Witt switched on the bedside lamp and asked me if I wanted to have sex. She said it casually, like she was offering to make coffee.

I grabbed my shirt that she was wearing and tugged her toward me. I kissed her neck, and she pulled my T-shirt over my head. She rolled onto her back, slipped off her underwear, and climbed on top of me. I began to lick her nipples. She told me to get a condom. She savagely cut the wrapper with her teeth and slipped on the condom with remarkable speed. Then she closed her eyes and rode my dick like I wasn't there. I ran my nails over her body, grabbed her ass, and pressed into her.

When it was over, Alex rolled over to her side of the bed and drifted off. While I appreciate an autonomous sleeper, I wouldn't have minded some contact. The whole thing felt kind of cold.

* * *

I was in a deep sleep when I heard the knock. Witt didn't stir. I answered the door and got rid of Primm. I returned to bed and fell asleep.

In the morning, Alex was gone.

MS. WITT

There was this student at Warren. He was awkward, but I saw—or projected—something good in him. I still don't know. He used to eat lunch in my classroom every day. Sometimes I'd make an extra sandwich for him. I suppose I knew he had a crush. But I didn't see the harm. I let him drop by my apartment on campus. Other students, girls and boys, had done the same. I listened. I thought that was my job.

One night I brought home a stranger from a bar. I was drunk, feeling reckless. It was one of those nights you wish you could forget. I should have been more careful. I didn't close the blinds. I never worried about that kind of thing before. The boy saw us through the window. He was angry at me, I heard. He started filming us. Later, the boy showed the video to a friend. The friend showed a friend. I don't know how many students saw it before someone reported it to the school. I remember the smug, creepy way some of my students looked at me. The investigation was even worse. Then it was colleagues, peers, giving me that same look.

I rarely spoke of what happened at Warren. I don't know

why I felt the need to confess that night. Maybe I wanted absolution for being so goddamn stupid.

"What a piece of shit," Finn said.

I felt grateful that someone was angry on my behalf, because, during the entire investigation, everyone on that committee looked at me like a slut who had inadvertently encouraged the affections of a young boy. There was always some part of my brain that wondered if they were right.

Finn put his arm around me. I rested my head on his shoulder. It was comforting having human contact. I'd avoided it for so long. Since that night with the guy from the bar. God, what was his name? Finn said something about taking the couch, but I didn't want to sleep alone. I wasn't sure what I wanted. I wanted to erase the memory of the last time I had sex. It was nice. It wasn't mind-blowing. I fell asleep and then I woke up.

I heard Finn talking to someone outside his front door. He whispered, but it was late and the gist of the conversation was easy to decipher amid the silence. He was angry; she was desperate and pleading. I heard this.

—I told you not to come here anymore.

—Please let me in. We need to talk.

—No. We don't. It's not going to happen again. Go back to your room before somebody sees you.

—I've been good to you. I've kept your little secret.

—You want to blackmail me into having sex with you?

—Fuck you.

I pretended to be asleep when Finn slid back into bed. He wrapped his arm around me and nestled his head behind my neck.

I wished I were a snake, so I could crawl out of my skin.

GEMMA RUSSO

Sunday morning, I woke up to the gurgling sound of Tegan using her neti pot and Emelia grunting through her ab routine. When I checked my phone, I had five texts from Linny telling me to meet her at the office.

The final text read: *SOS!!!!!*

I threw on my training gear and told my roommates I was going for a run.

"Do you have a slow metabolism or something?" Tegan said.

I should have ignored her. I said, "Huh?"

"You'd think with all of that running you'd be wasting away," Tegan said.

"Tegan, that's rude," said Emelia.

"I didn't mean to be rude. You look healthy."

I left the dorm and jogged across Flem Square and around the gym, circling back to Headquarters. I decided that I ought to train at least half as often as I claimed to. Maybe all those hours in my windowless office, supplementing my school chow with packaged snack foods, were making me soft.

When I arrived, Linny was in the compact space, holding a dried-up rose.

"This better be good," I said.

Linny gave me the dead rose and reached into her pocket for a small envelope that was already sliced open.

"These were in your mail this morning," Linny said.

"Why would you open my mail?" I said.

"Checking for a suspicious white powder," Linny said. "And *you're welcome.*"

Inside the envelope was a square card on expensive-looking stock with a note written in a meticulous cursive. I read the note out loud.

"Silence is a true friend who never betrays. Confucius."

"Is that a threat?" Linny said.

"At the very least it's a warning."

I immediately sent a message to Mel, Kate, and Alyson, instructing them to pick up their mail and meet at my office. I tried to send Linny on a fake errand, but she was determined to stick around.

About fifteen minutes later, there were several knocks at my office door in an odd rhythmic pattern.

"Is there a new secret knock?" said Linny.

I opened the door. Mel and Kate each held a dead rose. Alyson, standing behind them, had her hands in her pockets.

"Some weird shit is going on," Kate said.

"Did you read the card?" said Linny.

Kate and Mel showed me their cards, which came with the same aphorism.

"Did you get anything, Alyson?" I said.

Alyson held a small velvet box in her palm. "I didn't get a flower," she said.

"Open the box," I said.

"What if it's a finger?" said Mel.

"It's always a finger," said Linny.

"You're freaking me out," said Alyson.

"It's not a finger," said Kate.

Alyson flipped open the box. Wedged where a ring (or finger) might be was a USB drive. Mel breathed an audible sigh of relief.

Alyson just stood there, frozen, gaping at her strange delivery.

"Did that come with a card?" said Mel.

Alyson reached into her pocket and pulled out a small card and passed it to Mel. Mel opened the card and read it.

"You keep our secrets; we'll keep yours," Mel said. "Gemma, get your computer. Let's see what's on the drive."

"What if it's a virus?" Kate said.

"If those dudes wanted to spread a virus, they'd go the STD route," said Mel.

"You're worried about a dismembered digit more than a computer virus?" Kate said to Mel.

"No," said Alyson as she pocketed the jewelry box. "I'll check later. I have to go."

MS. WITT

I slunk out of Finn's apartment and trudged back to my cottage so that I could grab a change of clothes. Then I walked another quarter mile back to campus. All before my first cup of coffee. I realized during one of those treks that I had been at Stonebridge five weeks. It felt like five months. I got a cup of coffee from Dahl and headed to Wilde Bathhouse for a good delousing. The only upside of sex with a creep is the upgrade in personal hygiene.

After my shower, sauna, shower, I didn't know what to do with myself. Returning to the cottage was about as enticing as Greg's rabbit stew. I had hated Sundays at Warren Prep, but my apartment was on an electrical grid and there was an art-house theater in town. Sometimes you could see a movie and not a student.

I roamed around Lowland for the next few hours, confirming my original opinion that there wasn't much to do in town besides consuming liquor at Hemingway's or coffee at the Mudhouse. Mo's Bookstore and Café held some promise until I surveyed his inventory, which looked like it was picked clean after a going-out-of-business sale. There was an old guy with dyed black hair sitting behind the counter. I figured that was Mo. He was reading a newspaper.

After I had killed about twenty minutes perusing his shelves, Mo said, "Can I help you?"

"I'm just looking," I said.

"Well, you won't find it here," he said.

He was right. I left and walked down Hyde Street, planning to return to campus, until I caught sight of Claude through the window of Hemingway's.

I had nothing else to do, so I went inside and took a seat next to her.

"Alex," she said. "What are you doing here?"

"Killing time," I said.

"Let me buy you a drink," she said, waving over the bartender.

I looked at the clock—1:00 p.m..

"I'll have a seltzer," I said.

"Don't be like that," she said. "If you can't day-drink on Sunday, then what's the point of—well, anything."

Claude checked her phone and sent a text, which prompted me to check my phone, even though I didn't want to.

There were two texts from Finn.

Finn: You left without saying goodbye.

Finn: Call me later, will you?

Claude ordered another drink and turned her phone facedown on the bar. It vibrated against the wood.

"What did you do last night?" Claude said.

"Not much," I said.

"Really?" she said with a sly smile.

She was testing me. She already knew about last night. I assumed from Finn.

"You talked to him?" I said.

"He talked; I listened. What's wrong?" she said.

I was going to have to tell someone eventually, if it was true. I thought Claude might have some advice.

"I think a student came by Finn's apartment in the middle of the night."

"In the middle of the night?" Claude said.

Then she picked up her phone and began texting.

"Please don't—"

"Relax," Claude said. "I'm confirming my own suspicion."

My phone buzzed. Finn again.

Finn: That was Martha.

Finn: Did you really think . . . ?

I wrote back.

Witt: Sorry.

"I wish you hadn't done that," I said to Claude.

"Now you know," said Claude. "Although being desperate enough to screw Primm isn't exactly a winning trait in a man."

The news did little to assuage my overall discomfort.

"What's the problem, Witt?" Claude said.

"I have a bad feeling. There's something going on at this school that isn't kosher."

"I think that's safe to say about any institution," Claude said.

"Do you know about the blowjob contest?"

"I suppose I've overheard some chatter," Claude said casually.

"It doesn't worry you?" I said.

"Inappropriate behavior, boundary pushing. Isn't that all part of adolescence?"

"The boys are ranking and reviewing the girls' sexual performance on a secret website," I said.

"Would you be surprised if they shared that same information in a locker room? The only difference is that they're writing it down."

"I think it's more problematic than—"

Claude stopped paying attention. She looked at her phone and her expression flattened. She took a sharp inhale.

"Everything okay?"

"My mother had another fall," Claude said. "I have to go."

"Anything I can do?" I said.

"Nothing that's legal."

As I walked up the main drive to campus, I spotted Alyson Mosby, a student from my second-period class, standing at the front gate with at least five pieces of luggage. Her head was down, and she was staring at her phone.

"Alyson. What are you doing?" I said. "Are you taking a holiday in the middle of term?"

When she looked up, her expression was stolid but her cheeks ruddy from crying.

"Hey, Ms. Witt. No. I'm going home."

"For how long?" I said.

"Forever," said Alyson. "I mean, until college."

"You're leaving Stonebridge?" I said.

A black sedan pulled in front of the security gate. A man in a suit circled the car and confirmed that Alyson was his passenger. He popped the trunk and began loading her luggage.

I heard a girl shouting from a distance, "Wait. Wait up, Alyson."

I turned and saw Linny hurtling toward us. She was carrying a paper bag in her right hand and something wrapped in a napkin in the other. Alyson shut the door and rolled down the window.

Linny delivered the napkin item first. "Here's a waffle for the road."

"Thank you," said Alyson.

Linny offered the next item, which had a neck and was contained in a paper bag. It was better if I didn't know.

"This is a goodbye gift from all of us," said Linny. *"Fac fortia et patere."*

"Huh?" said Alyson.

"Do brave deeds and endure," Linny said.

"Back atcha. Let's go," Alyson said to the driver.

The window rolled up. The car disappeared down the main drive.

"Why did you give Alyson a waffle?" I said.

"Because she loves waffles," said Linny.

Something tripped in my memory bank.

"Is she also a Red Sox fan?" I asked.

Linny gave me a sidelong glance.

"Yeah. Why?"

Waffles and Red Sox. I had been pulling allies only from my senior thesis class. A paper must have gotten misfiled. The ally I had mistakenly given Gemma appeared to be the next victim of the Darkroom. I asked Linny where I could find Gemma.

"How would I know?" Linny said.

There was an odd tough-guy cadence to her delivery, which confirmed that she was lying. I didn't have the energy to negotiate. I offered Linny five dollars.

"I need to talk to Gemma. Can you take me to her?"

"Follow me," Linny said, pocketing the cash.

GEMMA RUSSO

Three hours after Alyson opened the box, she sent a farewell text to Kate, saying that she was dropping out of Stonebridge. She wished us all the best on our mission.

We all sent a flurry of texts, begging for an explanation. When an hour passed with no reply, Kate was sent on a reconnaissance mission.

Mel and I waited impatiently for Kate's return.

Our waiting styles, I learned, are incompatible. Mel paced and chomped on things. I stretched out on my couch and tried to chill. I put my earbuds in and blasted Pinback.

"What are you listening to?" Mel said.

I pretended that the music was drowning out her voice, but she was too agitated to pick up on any social cues.

"Do you have speakers? Why don't you have an audio system?" Mel said.

I didn't remind Mel that we shouldn't be blasting music in a secret office, because I was still pretending I couldn't hear her. I really could have used some alone time right then.

Kate returned. The second she walked in the door, I knew

we'd lost. At least the Waffles/Red Sox battle.

"She's leaving. I can't talk her out of it," Kate said, shaking her head.

"What happened?" I said.

"What was on that drive?" said Mel. "Pictures?"

"Worse," said Kate. "Mike had made a video of them doing it. And then he bequeathed a file of the video to the editors upon graduation."

"Did Alyson know the file existed?" I said.

"No. He filmed her in secret," said Kate.

"Douchebag," said Mel.

"She could go to the police," I said. "She could destroy him. She was, what, fifteen when that tape was made? We could probably get the police to investigate. I mean, isn't there some law against distribution of child pornography?"

I was getting amped at the prospect of a takedown on a much larger scale.

"Gemma, get over yourself. No one is going to the police," said Kate.

"Why not?" I said.

"Because she doesn't want to," Kate said, in that slow-talking way you communicate with annoying children.

"Did you even try to convince her?" I said, picking up my phone. "Let me talk to her."

"Stop," Kate said. "Think. Think it all the way through. She goes to the cops. Wait—no. She has to go to her parents first and tell them. She has to show her parents the sex tape. Then, what, they go to the police? The police need to see the evidence. So then a bunch of *male* police officers are watching her have sex. Then the police have to consult with prosecutors about pressing charges. More people watch the tape. So, the only way to get justice is to endure one humiliation after the next. She's sixteen. Let her get on with her life."

"If everyone stayed silent—" I started.

"Shut up, Gemma. You don't know what it's like to have people look at you that way, like . . . like they have a piece of you. And what do you care, anyway? Why is this your fight?"

I shrugged. I didn't have a good answer. I could pretend that my quest to bring down the Darkroom was entirely born out of moral outrage, that I was defending my big sister, Christine, or the dignity of all women, but the truth was that I started this fight just to have a fight. But then it became something different. It's part of me now. I talk a lot of shit about Stonebridge, but I love this place. Stonebridge saved me. I wanted to save it.

"Do you have any alcohol or weed?" Mel said. "The tension is killing me."

"There's some vodka in my desk drawer," I said.

Mel rummaged through my desk. "There's no vodka. Where else could it be?"

"There's a pint of Absolut in a paper bag," I said.

Then Kate started looking through my desk.

"You must have misplaced it," said Kate.

"I don't misplace vodka," I said, as I began to search the drawers. "Where is it?"

I don't remember hearing a key in the door. The next thing

I knew, Linny entered the office, followed by Ms. Witt.

Mel, Kate, and I froze in place like we were in the middle of a larcenous act.

"Ms. Witt insisted on seeing you," Linny said casually.

"What is this place?" said Ms. Witt.

"Headquarters," said Linny.

"What's up?" I said.

It felt like everyone in the room needed an explanation for something, except maybe Linny.

"Why is Alyson leaving?" said Witt.

"Speaking of leaving," said Mel. "We have to be at the thing. Right, Kate?"

Mel was yanking Kate by her sweatshirt.

"Don't leave on my account," said Witt.

"She knows," I said to Mel and Kate.

"Knows what?" said Kate.

"I know about the Darkroom and the idiotic blowjob contest," Witt said. "And I just ran into Alyson. What happened?"

Ms. Witt settled in on the couch. Linny offered her a cup of coffee. Mel and Kate made to leave again, but Witt started talking about how she gave me the wrong Q&A. Mel and Kate wanted to know what Ms. Witt was talking about and then I had to tell them that I hadn't stolen the assignments; Witt had given them to me. I think I lost some street cred with that confession. Ms. Witt, on the other hand, gained some.

Mel and Kate ended up sticking around, giving Ms. Witt a rundown of the last twenty-four hours.

Ms. Witt closed her eyes and mumbled, "It really is the Bada Bing Club."

Linny said, "What's the Bada Bing Club?"

"The boys don't know about your conspiracy, right?" Witt said.

"Conspiracy," Mel said. "I love that word."

"I don't think so," I said. "The editors have noticed that the girls are more suspicious, that we've been talking. They're trying to quiet the ones they think are the most vocal against Dulcinea. But I don't think they know that we're working together."

I made that statement convincingly, though I wasn't one hundred percent sure. But unless we had a mole, I didn't see how the boys could've figured out there was a faction of girls working to bring them down.

"You know what I don't get," said Witt. "How are there enough blowjobs going on at this place to justify creating a contest around them?"

"Stonebridge didn't invent giving head," said Kate.

"I know. But it does seem weirdly pervasive," said Witt.

"Sometimes you just want to hook up. We can't all wait until we're in love," Mel said.

"But there are other sexual acts, and a blowjob only gives the guy pleasure. And if you're going to pleasure someone, they ought to be worthy of it. I would be far less baffled if everyone was just screwing. But it's so one-sided."

"They expect it," I said.

"Who cares what they expect?" Witt said.

"Sometimes it's easier than sex," said Kate. "Like you feel like you're in control."

"Does it really feel that way?" Witt said.

Kate shrugged.

"Well, if you're choosing to give oral, you don't have to have regular sex," Mel mumbled.

"You don't have to have any sex at all," Witt said loudly.

"We know that," I said.

"I'm sorry. I'm not judging. I just want to understand the logic of it, you know?" said Witt.

"Logic isn't really part of sex," said Mel.

"It could be," said Kate.

"You're right," Witt said, as her eyes darted about the room.

Witt approached the old green chalkboard. "Do you have any chalk?"

Linny found a couple of pieces in the desk and passed them to Witt.

"Turn around so you can see the board," Witt said.

Mel, Kate, Linny, and I reconfigured our space so we had a full view of the chalkboard. Witt scribbled the question *Should you blow him?* at the top. We laughed. I don't think Witt thought it was funny.

"Let's start with a very simple question," Witt said. "*Do you want to?* Is this something you really want to do? If not, then *no.*"

Witt wrote the question on the board along with a swooping arrow that led to a giant *NO* in the bottom-right corner.

"Second question," Witt said. *"Are you sure?"* The small *no* below the question led back to the giant end *NO.*

"What if the answer is yes?" said Linny.

"Okay," said Witt. "If yes, then let's ask another question. *Has he gone down on you?* If not, *no.* If the answer is yes, *how many times*?"

Sometimes Kate or Mel or I would add a question. Most answers led back to *NO.* Ms. Witt made sexual choices seem so simple, like basic math.

When she was done, she put down the chalk, dusted herself off, and said, "Any questions?"

We shook our heads.

"Lesson over," Witt said.

After Ms. Witt departed, Mel stood in front of the chalkboard, scrutinizing the flowchart.

"Can you read her writing?" Mel said.

"Not if I didn't already know what she'd written," Kate said.

"We should make a copy," I said.

Linny had already found a sketch pad and began redrawing the flowchart in a legible script. When she was done, she held up the sketch pad proudly.

"What should we call it?" said Kate.

"A blowchart," I said.

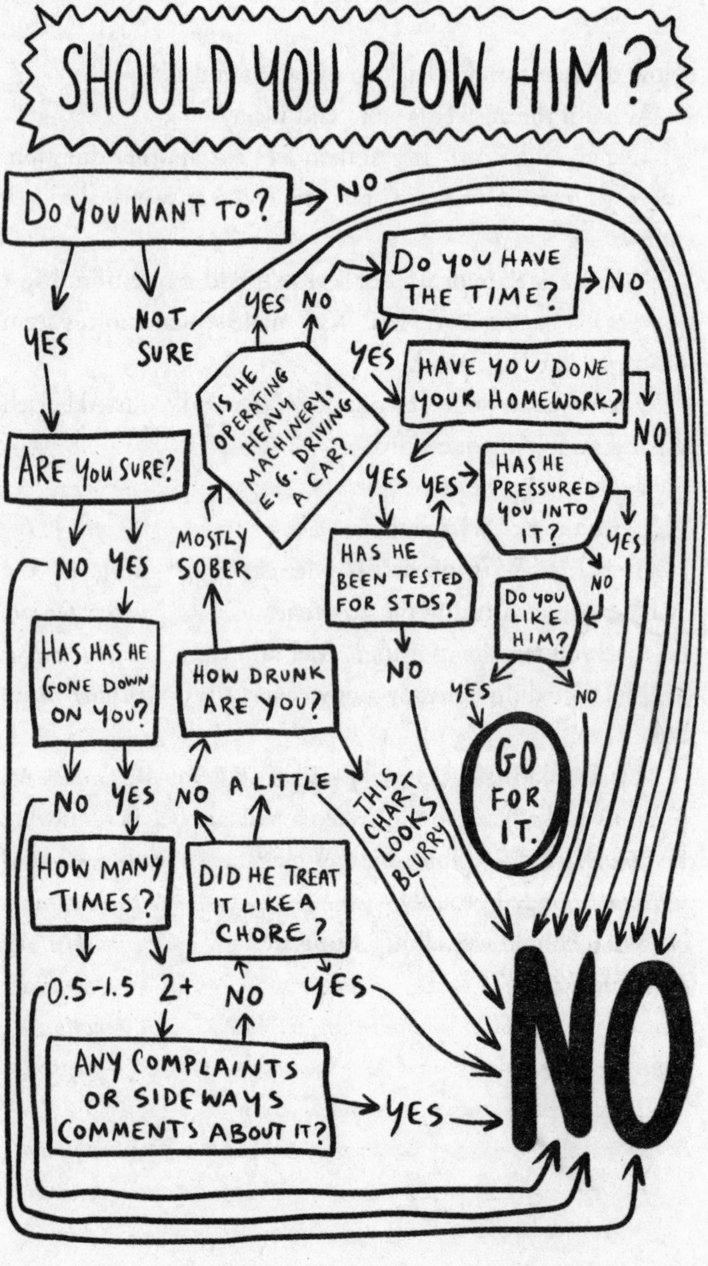
SHOULD YOU BLOW HIM?
Do You WANT TO?
NO
YES
NOT SURE
ARE You SURE?
NO
YES
HAS HAS HE GONE DOWN ON YOU?
NO
YES
HOW MANY TIMES?
0.5-1.5
2+
ANY COMPLAINTS OR SIDEWAYS COMMENTS ABOUT IT?
YES
NO
DID HE TREAT IT LIKE A CHORE?
YES
NO
A LITTLE
HOW DRUNK ARE YOU?
MOSTLY SOBER
THIS CHART LOOKS BLURRY
IS HE OPERATING HEAVY MACHINERY, E.G. DRIVING A CAR?
YES
NO
Do you HAVE THE TIME?
NO
YES
HAVE YOU DONE YOUR HOMEWORK?
NO
YES
HAS HE BEEN TESTED FOR STDS?
NO
YES
HAS HE PRESSURED YOU INTO IT?
YES
NO
Do you LIKE HIM?
YES
NO
GO FOR IT.
NO

ANNOUNCEMENTS

Good morning, students of Stone. Wainwright here to wish you a happy Monday, October 12, 2009. Today will be a breezy sixty degrees. Lunch today is a choice between mushroom-and-bulgur loaf or pasta Bolognese with a green salad on the side.

Is anyone here on Facebook? I have ten friends so far and counting. There's also a Wainwright fan page, where I will be posting the transcripts of announcements for those who missed them or for personal reference. What?

I have a note that I am supposed to read from our nurse, Ms. Hanning. Ahem.

There has been an unusual uptick in cases of poison oak. If you have a new rash, please wash all clothes that have come in contact with the rash and use soap and water on your skin. Ms. Hanning has extra bottles of calamine lotion if the commissary has run out. Should you have an extreme allergic reaction—if your eyes swell up or you have trouble breathing—please call 911. Calamine lotion is for topical use only.

That's all, folks; don't forget to check out my Facebook page. I have pictures of poison-oak rashes, for those who are interested.

One more thing. The suggestion box is for suggestions written on paper. It is not a trash can. That should be obvious, considering the slot is just a half-inch thick and the box doesn't look like a trash can and it says suggestion box right on it. The next time I find a banana peel inside, we'll eliminate our suggestion program.

GEMMA RUSSO

Ms. Witt, pacing in a pair of thick wool socks, was delivering one of her very rare lectures.

"When you write fiction, you're creating your own universe. There are no rules. Write whatever you want to write; structure it however you see fit. You live in a world where virtually everything is out of your control. You cannot predict anything that will come next. As you get older, you will see how often the universe can disappoint, alarm, or undermine you. Fiction can reflect all of that, but here's what's important: When you write, every word is of your choosing. You own that world. You can turn it upside down, send it into space, deliver it into the ice age. You are the god of the page. So enjoy the one thing in your life you can lord over."

"What happened to your shoes, Ms. Witt?" Adam Westlake said.

"Rupert confiscated them at the door because they were covered in mud."

"Maybe you should invest in a pair of rain boots," said Mick.

"Would you stop scratching?" Tegan said to Gabe, who,

along with a dozen or so boys in Dickens, had gotten a bad case of poison oak. We still had no idea about the identity of our avenger. But she was escalating.

Norman, Jonah, and Adam were spared. Was it by design or just luck? Ms. Witt walked over to the window and gazed outside. There was a steady flow of rain and the skies were gray.

"Wainwright said it would be clear and in the sixties today," she said.

"Gotta love that man," Adam said.

"Do you?" Witt said, returning her attention to the classroom.

She asked again about Wainwright's identity.

"You already know who he is," Adam said, trying to sound like a sage or Yoda.

Ms. Witt rolled her eyes and said, "I give up." Then she switched topics.

"Several of you are now more than three weeks late with your senior thesis proposal. I'm trying to be reasonable here, but if I don't have a thesis statement and an opening chapter, scene, stanza—but, please, no epic poems—by the end of the week, there will be a price to pay."

"Like what?" said Nick Laughlin. "Will you leave pebbles in our shoes or make us sleep on the floor?"

By now that essay about Witt's mother, "The Cruel Muse," had made the rounds on campus. I had read it a few months ago, when Greg first told me about her impending arrival.

It changed how everyone saw her, but in completely different ways. Come to think of it, Witt herself was like an inkblot test. Everyone saw something different. Tegan stood by her bitch label. Gabe stayed with bonkers, and Emelia said Witt was growing on her. She thought she was funny. Mick, on the other hand, kept wondering why Leonard Witt wouldn't shake out his shoes before he put them on, because Mick always does that, just in case.

"Will you steal all of our socks or put salt in the sugar dish?" Adam asked.

"Nope. I'll just pick the topic, the format, even the title," Witt said with a poker face.

Sandra Polonsky raised her hand. She didn't have a question about the assignment. She needed to pee. I swear, she can't go more than a half hour without a bathroom break.

Witt nodded her permission.

"Maybe you need antibiotics," Mick said.

Sandra ignored him and threw her tiny frame into the industrial door.

"Maybe you should keep your medical opinions to yourself," Mel said to Mick.

"I wouldn't want to step on any toes," said Mick. "If I remember correctly, you're the foremost UTI scholar at Stonebridge."

"But you're the authority on STDs, right?" said Mel.

Howls of laughter erupted, followed by more cross-talk. Witt rubbed her temples.

Mel was getting bolder. In theory, that was a good thing; in practice, I needed her to lock it down until we'd made more progress. I'd asked for another status update on the Darkroom. She said she was getting close. When I asked for specifics, she tossed out a bunch of words that sounded like tech-speak, but I wasn't entirely convinced. She was hiding something from me. I put Linny on her trail.

"Everyone clear your desks and close your eyes," Witt said. "For the next five minutes, I don't want you to do anything but concentrate on your breathing."

A couple of students asked what we were doing, and Witt told them to be quiet and follow her instructions. Then she told us to breathe. To inhale and count to seven, exhale and count to seven. It was kind of awful. Half the guys had cases of poison oak, so you heard more scratching than breathing. The sound of nails on dry, scaly skin is bad enough. If you add pervy mouth-breathing, it's an assault on the senses.

As we filed out of class that day, Mick said, "Good God, what was that in there?"

"I think we were meditating," Jonah replied.

MS. WITT

Stonebridge looked like a postcard in October. Like one of those photoshopped pictures with color-enhancing tints that aren't quite of this world. The moment was over almost as soon as it had begun. The landscape took on a brittle, haunted quality. It felt like the ground was constantly shifting beneath me, or sinking, considering all of the rain that Wainwright refused to acknowledge. Stonebridge was a mercurial home. I could be confused, inspired, and gutted all in the same day.

One predictably bright spot was Jonah Wagman. He reminded me that sometimes a person can surprise you, be more interesting or better than you originally believed. He took to spending office hours in my room. I got the sense that he was avoiding something. Sometimes he would try to meditate and ask for my advice. I'm not an expert, but I did tell him I thought he might be able to focus better if he weren't chomping on those red jawbreakers. Also, the constant crunching sound was starting to wear on me. Still, I admired his effort.

"Can I ask you a question?" Jonah asked, after a very brief attempt at meditation.

"That's a weird question to ask your teacher-slash-adviser."

"It's not that kind of question. It's a girl question," Jonah said.

"Shoot."

"What do they like?" Jonah said.

His tone was plaintive and his brow made a perfect W, and his big brown eyes gave me the most earnest look I had ever seen.

"What do *girls* like?" I said, trying not to laugh. "They like all kinds of things and not the same things. You know this, Jonah. They're like boys that way, like all people. The variety can astound you."

"That was a bad question," Jonah said.

"There are no bad questions. But that was sort of a bad question."

"There's a girl—one girl," he said.

"Okay, we're getting somewhere," I said.

"This girl. I want to show her that I like her, so I keep giving her things that I really think she'll like, but she doesn't like them."

"Why are you giving her things?"

"Because I want her to know that I like her. And sometimes I just want to give her things that will make her happy. How do I know what will make her happy?"

"Maybe you're thinking too narrowly," I said. "Maybe she doesn't like things. Don't ask what does she like. Ask yourself what does she *want*?"

Keith, on the other hand, consistently baffled me. I remember stopping by Dahl sometime after lunch one afternoon. Unbused plates remained scattered on the tables, and the floor was covered with detritus. Linny, that delightful spearfisher, was methodically going from table to table and cleaning the mess that students had left behind. I grabbed a coffee and was on my way out when I heard Coach Keith.

"Knock it off, Linny," he said, angry.

The severity in his tone seemed extreme, considering Linny's undertaking. I slipped behind the kitchen door and listened to the rest of their conversation.

"We talked about this, right?" Keith said.

"It makes me feel better," Linny said.

"I don't give a shit," he said.

I peered around the door and watched Keith toss a balled-up napkin toward the trash can. He missed. Linny looked at Keith, raised an eyebrow, and took a step closer to the trash.

"Don't," he said.

"Whatever," Linny said, as she stomped out of the room.

I knew my days at Stonebridge were numbered when I got the video. At the end of the day, I logged in to the Blackboard system. I had an email from Jonah Wagman, which seemed odd since I had just seen him during office hours. The subject line read: *Check this out.*

In the body of the message was a video icon. I clicked on it. A grainy image popped up on my screen. It was a tracking shot through the woods. I could hear the labored breath and the sound of the videographer's footsteps in the woods. After less than a minute, my cottage came into view. A light was on inside; no foil on the windows. The cameraperson approached the cottage and trained the lens through the window.

I wasn't doing anything remarkable. I was wearing pajamas, sitting on my bed, grading papers. The camera stayed on me for about five minutes. Then the screen went black.

It shouldn't have bothered me. It was nothing. I'd been through the same thing before, under far uglier circumstances.

I went back and checked the email address. It was a random Hotmail account. I didn't know why Jonah's name was used, but I knew it wasn't him. The person who took the video was calculating and sadistic. I have been disappointed by students, even hurt and humiliated. That was the first time I felt fear.

NORMAN CROWLEY

After the poison-oak outbreak in Dickens, Carl Bloom started burning sage in the hallways. I wanted to tell him that it wasn't a curse. It was karma. Whatever happened next, they had it coming.

We had another editorial meeting to arrange the Halloween party. Mick suggested a pimps 'n' hos party, like the seniors did last year and the year before that. Adam, weirdly, nixed that idea.

"It's bad messaging, Mick. We can't tell the ladies we respect them and then ask them to dress like prostitutes. Let's have a fancy-dress party instead. They'll love it."

Something was going on. It started sometime after the October board meeting, the one I got evicted from. The editors were all acting like gentlemen, holding doors and crap. I'd never seen so much hand-holding between pseudo couples at this school. Nick and Emelia looked full-on. He was always walking her to class and stuff—even carrying her books. But then I'd see him slipping out of the woods or into one of the studios with Hannah. I was dying to warn Emelia, but we've never had a conversation that got any deeper than *Hey, how was your summer?*

Even Jack Vandenberg managed to look legit with that freshman. Although he was more careful about being seen in public with her. He said Tegan would cut off his dick if she caught him with another girl.

At the end of the meeting, Jack took out a beat-up poster that I'd seen around campus. I'm not sure how to describe it. It was like a logic chart for when to give blowjobs. Each editor saw the poster as a personal affront. They were determined to identify and destroy its maker.

"I thought we handled the insurgents," Mick said.

"I have to wonder if Ms. Witt is behind this," said Adam.

"I thought we dealt with her," Gabe said.

I must have looked too interested, because Adam dismissed me again.

Whatever the editors were up to felt diabolical. There's no way Alyson left Stonebridge because she was homesick. I was worried about what they had done to Ms. Witt. I liked her. I didn't want her to leave.

The worst part was that they were getting away with it.

Later that night, I headed over to Milton Studio to study. The door was locked, which was unusual, so I walked around the side to peer through the window to see whether the room was occupied. I saw Nick, leaning against the wall, a girl on her knees before him. I wish I had the balls to take a picture and show Emelia. Nick looked up, but I'm not sure whether he saw me or not. I crouched down between Keats Studio and

Milton and waited. A few minutes later, I heard the door open and shut.

A girl's voice: "Now, remember, Nick, I want a perfect score on the trifecta."

I ducked down and walked to the edge of the wall and peered around the corner. Rachel Rose tossed an air kiss in Nick's direction as they parted ways. I don't know what Rachel's deal is. I get that she wants to win Dulcinea, but it doesn't explain half of the other stuff she does. Like, why did she give the editors that photo of Kate? And I still don't want to think about how her pink scarf turned up in Ford's apartment. I used to have to visit Ford every single day to get my meds. God, that was torture. The only upside was that I think it irked him more than it did me. For the longest time I couldn't figure out why I hated him so much. Then I realized why. He's the editors all grown up. Ford reminds me that I might never escape this place.

I checked the door to Keats Studio. It was unlocked. I sat down and opened my computer. I tried to work, but I couldn't stop thinking about Nick and Rachel and Nick and Hannah and Nick and Emelia.

I couldn't wait for Mel to earn a PhD in computer science before she got into the Darkroom. I sent another anonymous message to Mel with simple, straightforward instructions and prayed that she wouldn't overthink it.

To: Mel Eastman
From: Bill Haydon
Re: read this message

When you view source in the forum control panel, you can make any grayed-out option live by removing the word "disabled" from that line of code. It shouldn't be this simple, but this works on "log in as user." Pick Andre. Don't enter or alter data. I don't know how much more specific I can be.

Delete this message immediately.

Sincerely,
Bill

MS. WITT

I searched my cottage repeatedly for any type of video surveillance device. I inspected my classroom to the best of my ability. I was cautious in the Wilde Bathhouse, using the shower farthest from the light fixture. I couldn't see how a camera could be embedded in that wall of white tile. I looked at each of my students as suspects. I combed through the Q&A's one more time, trying to determine which one of them had sent me the video. I hadn't ruled out any of the senior boys, except Jonah. Although I had to wonder why anyone would try to implicate him.

I wasn't going to let it happen again. I was clear on that. I took every precautionary measure I could think of to preserve my sanity. What I didn't do was tell anyone. I wouldn't give that sociopath the satisfaction of knowing I gave it a second thought. I doubt any of them noticed how unhinged I felt day to day.

I focused on wrangling my seniors into making a final decision on their thesis proposals. I got most of them to commit.

Gemma and Mel were both working on revenge sagas.

Neither had turned in more than a few pages. Their method, they said, was to do a deep dive into research, then write. Adam Westlake was one hundred pages into an espionage novel about a fixer. Tegan intended to write a screenplay about a love triangle between a hit woman and two of her targets. Rachel Rose delivered a stack of faux gossip columns about the goings-on at a school called Woodbridge.

Ephraim Wiener planned to write a novella focused entirely on a doomed *Star Trek* training exercise, the Kobayashi Maru. He started to explain the no-win scenarios, but I told him it sounded fine and to write it. I didn't want any spoilers. Carl was going to serialize his Dungeons & Dragons games. Sandra and Bethany were working on *Twilight* fan fiction. Sandra intended to shift the focus onto the werewolves, and Bethany said she wanted to write a more adult version. With sex, she clarified. She asked me if I thought that was okay.

"That's a million-dollar idea," I said.

Norman remained cagey about his project, even after he dodged the first deadline. I heard he had been working on the same novel since last year. I saw him in class, editing pages, always scribbling notes. But when I inquired about the subject or whether I could see any work, he always demurred and said he wasn't sure. He might try to do a screenplay instead. I sent him a text on the day of the second extended deadline and told him to meet me in my office with pages.

I sat on the floor in the hallway and waited for Norman. After he sat down next to me, I extended my palm.

"Hand it over," I said.

Norman reluctantly handed me a stack of typewritten pages in prose form. I skimmed the text. It was about a male creative-writing teacher at a boarding school not unlike Stonebridge. The teacher was an aspiring novelist working on a book about a school not unlike the school where he worked. The teacher/novelist was plagued with writer's block and would give his students pointed assignments. One, in particular, was to record fellow students' conversations. The teacher, Mr. Fellows, claimed the point of the eavesdrop assignment was to learn the rhythm of dialogue, but he was really using it to flesh out his novel.

The narration was third person, omniscient, and intensely judgmental of the primary character of Mr. Fellows.

"I like it," I said.

"Thanks," Norman said, twisting a loose button on his jacket.

"It seems kind of meta."

Too quickly, Norman said, "Nah. I mean, isn't everything meta?"

Norman was so agitated by the meta remark that I didn't ask him if his novel was based on Mr. Ford.

After I'd reviewed all of my students' thesis proposals, and the added biographical details that they unintentionally provided, I finally nailed down the respective authors of my Q&A's. My calculations weren't one hundred percent, but I was pretty damn close.

SENIOR WRITING CLASSES

Q&As = solved

EPHRAIM WIENER

What do you love?	The Original Star Trek
What do you hate?	Flem
If you could live inside a book, what book?	Lord of the Rings
What do you want?	Ten thousand in unmarked bills
Who are you?	You said this was anonymous

KATE BUSH

What do you love?	Neko Case, banana bread, the smell of Pine Sol
What do you hate?	BJs, editors, and agents of the Darkroom
If you could live inside a book, what book?	The Girl with the Dragon Tattoo
What do you want?	An invisibility cloak and cyanide
Who are you?	I'm not who they think I am

ENID CHO

What do you love?	my parents, popcorn, Katy Perry
What do you hate?	Dahl Hall cuisine, BJs
If you could live inside a book, what book?	Harry Potter and the Order of the Phoenix
What do you want?	an early acceptance letter
Who are you?	the most likely valedictorian

NORMAN CROWLEY

What do you love?	Bright Eyes, Reservoir Dogs, PB&J sandwiches, CS
What do you hate?	The Darkroom
If you could live inside a book, what book?	Tinker, Tailor, Soldier, Spy
What do you want?	For my real life to begin
Who are you?	I'm a coward

RACHEL ROSE

What do you love?	FF, my pink scarf, power
What do you hate?	bad hygiene, two-faced bitches
If you could live inside a book, what book?	New Moon
What do you want?	to win
Who are you?	one of a kind

TEGAN BROOKS

What do you love?	myself
What do you hate?	stupid questions
If you could live inside a book, what book?	Alice in Wonderland
What do you want?	for you to go back to where you came from
Who are you?	I'm your worst nightmare.

JACK VANDENBERG

What do you love?	Money
What do you hate?	Snitches
If you could live inside a book, what book?	I wouldn't
What do you want?	A black Range Rover
Who are you?	The MAN

EMELIA LAIRD

What do you love?	Lucy (my dog), my family, Beyonce
What do you hate?	the head push, Whitney
If you could live inside a book, what book?	Paper Towns
What do you want?	A BMW M6
Who are you?	a good person

GEMMA RUSSO

What do you love?	I don't know
What do you hate?	the Darkroom and Dulcinea
If you could live inside a book, what book?	Great Expectations
What do you want?	Revenge
Who are you?	I'm a spy

CARL BLOOM

What do you love?	D&D, A warm shower, my parents
What do you hate?	dander, chemistry, nature walks
If you could live inside a book, what book?	the thesaurus, maybe? Is that weird?
What do you want?	to breathe through my nose
Who are you?	Undecided

SANDRA POLONSKY

What do you love?	Vampires
What do you hate?	my thighs, apple bobbing, Tofurky
If you could live inside a book, what book?	Twilight
What do you want?	World peace and to lose fifteen pounds
Who are you?	a good person

MELANIE EASTMAN

What do you love?	Vicks cough drops, rain, the Ramones
What do you hate?	Dulcinea, shag rugs, obligatory BJs
If you could live inside a book, what book?	The Maltese Falcon
What do you want?	To buckle the patriarchy; a spork revival
Who are you?	The enemy

BETHANY WISEMAN

What do you love?	vampires, people named Taylor, Rihanna, my sister
What do you hate?	the Darkroom, BJs
If you could live inside a book, what book?	Twilight, New Moon, Breaking Dawn
What do you want?	to be Bella
Who are you?	Not Bella

ADAM WESTLAKE

What do you love?	Information
What do you hate?	Disorder, weakness
If you could live inside a book, what book?	The Fountainhead
What do you want?	So many things
Who are you?	The puppetmaster

AMY LOGAN

What do you love?	snowboarding, music, sleep
What do you hate?	Chris Brown; the word yummy
If you could live inside a book, what book?	Harry Potter (any one)
What do you want?	freedom, an end to global warming
Who are you?	an enigma

JONAH WAGMAN

What do you love?	GR
What do you hate?	The Darkroom
If you could live inside a book, what book?	Sense and Sensibility
What do you want?	Peace
Who are you?	I don't know yet

HANNAH REXALL

What do you love?	ballet, modern dance, yoga
What do you hate?	my feet
If you could live inside a book, what book?	Dancing on My Grave
What do you want?	fame, fortune, and a hot husband
Who are you?	Everything

MICK DEVLIN

What do you love?	The Darkroom
What do you hate?	Snitches and douchebags
If you could live inside a book, what book?	The Picture of Dorian Gray
What do you want?	Absolute power
Who are you?	The boss man

GABRIEL SMYTHE

What do you love?	Pussy
What do you hate?	Dry pussy?
If you could live inside of a book, what book?	The Kama Sutra
What do you want?	What have you got?
Who are you?	Who are you?

GEMMA RUSSO

Every time Emelia debriefed Tegan and me on her hangouts with Nick, I would sit there and dig my nails into my palms until I came close to drawing blood. I like Emelia, but she has no idea how boring her fuckless dates are.

"After the party, I took him up to the roof. I was cold. He gave me his jacket. It smelled like him—that man smell that's so intoxicating. Nick and I gazed at the stars. He knows all of the constellations. He held my hand. Then I let him kiss me. His tongue is so smooth and gentle and he doesn't do that super-annoying thing of just shoving it in your mouth without a plan. He tasted like mint. He reached under my dress and I told him to slow down. He put my hand on his dick and he told me I had to put him out of his misery. I told him it was too soon. He said I was worth waiting for. Then he kissed me again and walked me home. He told me that he had to go back to his room to masturbate."

Or he summoned Hannah to swing by and blow him.

"And this morning, I found a rose and a poem in my mailbox," Emelia said.

It was a fresh rose, not a dead one, I should mention. Tegan read Nick's poem out loud.

> *"Escape me?*
> *Never—*
> *While I am I, and you are you,*
> *So long as the world contains us both,*
> *I must the other pursue."*

I plugged a few lines into my computer. It was Browning, sort of. I wanted to tell her I'd heard things about Nick. But the messenger always gets shot, and I knew I'd have to play that role eventually. When I had more evidence, or thought Emelia was actually ready to screw him, I'd step up.

Tegan and Emelia created an avalanche of clothes getting ready for the party. Emelia finally decided on a backless, high-collared satin dress cut just above the knee. She looked great, as usual. Tegan looked like she was wearing a giant sparkly compression bandage that stretched from just above her tits to just below her vagina. The inevitability of a wardrobe malfunction made me seriously consider bookmaking the over/under on that dress. I slipped into a pair of jeans, a silver top with spaghetti straps, and a black leather jacket. I reapplied the eyeliner and shadow that hadn't completely washed down the drain and painted my lips red.

"Is that what you're wearing?" Tegan said.

"I don't know," I said, making a point of looking at the garments on my body. "Is this what I'm wearing? I'm trying to remember that Kant shit from last year's philosophy class. Objectively, I think I'm wearing this, but my view of my clothes and your view are both subjective, so I'm not sure if there's wiggle room for consideration that maybe I'm not wearing what you think I'm wearing."

"I'm just trying to be helpful," Tegan said. "I thought you might want people to know that you own more than two pairs of jeans and a shoplifted dress."

"Thanks," I said. "I appreciate your concern."

Tegan got a call from Jack, although she pretended it was her mother like she always does. It had taken me a full year to realize that the secret-keeping was Jack's doing. I have few kind words for that girl, but I always thought she was better than that. Once Tegan was out of the room, Emelia pulled a black dress from her closet. It was plain but pretty, and it had a generous A-line cut that would skim over my more substantial ass.

"I know it's not really your style, but I'd love to see it on you. And I think it would look good with your black boots," Emelia said.

I love how Em tries to make her kindness sound like I'd be doing her a favor.

I wore the dress. Then I let Emelia fix my hair. As she was fussing over me, trying to twist my neck-length hair into something of an updo, an ancient memory of my mother came back to me. Mom was awake, braiding my hair. What sticks with me the most is how much it felt like a memory in that moment.

"Em? Be careful with Nick," I said.

"Don't worry about me," said Emelia. "I have him just where I want him."

I said nothing. Was that a lie of omission?

I was impressed by the restraint the editors showed by not having another pimps 'n' hos party. It was practically a Stonebridge tradition. The editors decided to bypass Halloween altogether and have a black-tie soirée.

There wasn't even a keg. Only hard alcohol, wine, and a few six-packs of beer, *for the philistines,* as Adam would say. Some people even drank out of real glasses. The usual suspects—the Ten—plus another ten or twenty to keep it interesting were in attendance. Freshmen and sophomores worked as unpaid labor, bribed by the promise of future club membership or the delusional belief that they were climbing another rung in the social hierarchy. It was a thankless job for those underclassman butlers and maids. I would have set them straight if I didn't have other priorities.

Most of the boys were just in regular suits, but Adam and Mick went full throttle. Mick wore a tux and Adam had on some ridiculous waistcoat with tails.

"Look at you, Gemma, all dolled up," Adam said.

"Look at you, Adam," I said.

I couldn't decide if Adam looked more manservant, symphony conductor, or penguin, but I so appreciated his whimsy in a room full of dicks in well-tailored designer suits that I refrained from insulting him.

Emelia ignored New Nick for the first thirty minutes or so of the party. She chatted with Westlake, believing she was playing the game with cold, hard calculation.

Tegan and Jack, as usual, pretended like they didn't know each other, even though they probably just screwed an hour before. Rachel Rose and Mick Devlin disappeared for a few minutes and returned. I sat on the filthy couch and let a freshman whom Westlake called Jeeves refill my drink.

Mel had just sent two emphatic, yet vague, texts. I was looking at the screen when Adam sat down next to me.

Mel: Oh my God.

Mel: Oh my fucking God.

Gemma: ??????

"Gems, quit looking at your phone and have a conversation with me," Adam said.

I started to say something. But then the third text rolled in.

Mel: I'm in the Darkroom!!!!

MR. FORD

To: Finn Ford
From: William Langston
Subject: good news!

Dear Finn,
While you were (hopefully) whittling down your manuscript to a more manageable word count, I took the liberty of allowing a young editor I know to take a look at your manuscript. I will leave all the details for our phone call, but I am thrilled to tell you that we have a preempt on *Mr. Finch*. Call me in the morning to discuss. It's a fair offer, all things considered. Not enough to quit your day job, but it'll get you back in the game.
Best,
Will

Evelyn and I were sitting in the lounge when I got the news. I said *fuck me,* because I hear from the guy so rarely. Evelyn said, *I have a headache. Maybe later.* Then I told her about the email. If there's one person here who won't undercut a good mood, it's her. Evelyn smiled, folded the newspaper, walked over to me, and kissed me on the cheek. She was so goddamn sweet. I kind of wanted to fuck her even though she's not really my type.

"We should celebrate," Evelyn said.

"Not yet," I said. "Let me make the call."

Of course, Will was in a meeting when I first rang his office. Then at a lunch for the second. He got back to me four long hours later while I was mid-lecture on Miller's *The Crucible.* I fumbled with the phone and stepped into the hallway.

The call itself was far less exciting than the anticipation that the email incited. Once Will gave me the lowdown, he started pushing for me to take the deal. I suggested he might be able to get an auction going. He actually laughed and then gave me that bird-in-the-hand lecture. He did a hard sell for Emily Parker from Hartford Press. He described her as young and crazy ambitious. Then, to derail my confidence, he said that Emily thought the book had potential but needed a lot of work. By the end of the conversation I felt less like an author with a newly minted publishing deal and more like a guy who'd paid the sticker price on a used car.

I ran into Dean Stinson later that afternoon. He congratulated me. I told him it wasn't a big deal and that I wasn't quitting my job. He asked me to come over to his house the next day. Around eight, he said.

There were already about a dozen teachers and staff at the dean's house when I arrived. I asked Evelyn what was up and she said that we were celebrating my book deal. Then she smiled sheepishly and apologized for the lack of cocktails at the cocktail party and suggested we hit Hemingway's after. Primm was hovering, lying in wait. I felt like a rabbit being hunted by a really fucking annoying coyote.

Stinson's home reminds me of a hunting lodge. The room he uses for drinking and standing around is called the parlor. It looks like a dining room, minus the table. There's one small couch, in the corner, a few old mahogany chairs, a chandelier, and an ornate Oriental rug with a large rust-colored stain. The stain has faded considerably, but it always makes me think that someone or something bled out on it.

"Finn, it's a *wine* stain," Claude said, suddenly appearing at my side.

Claude punched me in the arm and congratulated me. She was happy for me and jealous, she said. Not of getting published but of the cash influx. I liked her honesty. I told her it wasn't much money. That made her feel better.

Dean Stinson clinked his glass with a knife and told everyone to gather around. He was stumped after that. Stinson gazed at the ceiling, searching for something. Maybe the guy was going senile. Lost in thought, he turned to Alex.

"Alex, help me out here. What was that thing Nastya used to say?"

"Take the blank page by the throat and beat it to a pulp. Do not let it beat you," she said.

"To Finn, for winning that fight," said Greg.

There were two bottles of champagne for twelve people.

Fifteen minutes after I arrived, the toast was made and everyone stood around staring at the bottom of an empty glass.

A few other colleagues offered good wishes and all of that shit. I wanted to free everyone from the cocktail-less cocktail party. I was just about to say, *Well, this has been fun,* when Dean Stinson asked me what the book was about. Loudly, like it wasn't just a question for him and me but for the entire group.

"It's about a place not unlike this one," I said.

"I can't wait to read it," he said.

I really couldn't tell whether he was being snide or sincere. My glass was still empty. I watched Evelyn pour the dregs from the bottles into her mug. She caught my eye and made a sad face, like a child at the end of a birthday party.

"Well, this has been fun," I finally said. "Thank you all for coming."

Drinking a bottle of bourbon alone in my apartment would have been a more celebratory event.

The next time I saw Alex, she was standing outside, talking to Keith. At first I thought she was angry, but then as he spoke, I swear I caught a smile, a real one. I couldn't figure her out. She'd barely said a word since we slept together. If I weren't stuck in the Stonebridge bubble, I doubt I'd have given her the time of day.

MS. WITT

Even I felt bad for Finn. The whole thing would have been fine as an impromptu toast in the teachers' lounge. But when Greg committed to a formal celebration in his "parlor" and barely had enough sparkling wine for half a toast, it took on a sad shape. I asked Greg who'd done the math on the alcohol. Greg blamed Ms. Pinsky, who blamed Mario at Dahl. Mario said a case of champagne had simply vanished.

I didn't want to be there. The video was still making me twitchy and there was nothing to drink. As soon as I escaped through the back door, I found Keith loitering just under the kitchen window.

"What are you doing?" I said.

"Debating whether I should go inside or not."

"Don't," I said. "Save yourself."

"That bad?"

"There's nothing to drink or eat."

"Thanks for sparing me," Keith said. "I'll walk you back. I have to stop by the greenhouse."

Keith took a path directly through the woods. There was no trail to speak of.

"It's called Graham Greenehouse, right?" I said.

"Not that I know of."

"How disappointing," I said.

"We can call it the Graham Greenehouse from now on," Keith said.

"Thank you."

Since I had Keith alone, I decided to ask about the odd exchange I'd witnessed between him and Linny.

"She was cleaning up after other students," he said. "I told her to stop."

"It sounds to me like she was being considerate. If she doesn't clean, then it's left to the janitorial staff, right?"

"Last year, I was supervising lunch period and, uh, Linny started cleaning before anyone was done. It was a full lunchroom. She was acting like a maid. There was a table of senior boys. They were throwing napkins and silverware on the floor, waiting for her to pick it up. It was amusing to them, making her clean up after them. Linny is thinking that if she doesn't clean up the mess, then it's left for the cafeteria staff, who already have plenty to do. Cut to ten years later. Linny has a job. She works at some kind of corporation. She's at a meeting in a conference room. Food is served. Meeting adjourns. Linny stays to clean up. What does that say to the boss? Does it make him think, *That tidy woman deserves a promotion?* No. Because he doesn't respect her and he wants to keep her just where she is because he likes having someone who will clean up other people's shit."

My phone began to buzz. I looked down and saw two new texts.

Gemma: We did it!

Gemma: Oh my God. Come to my office. Now.

Keith was saying something about moving to higher ground. I told him I had to go. I made my way to Headquarters and down the stairs to the basement.

As I approached Gemma's office, I could hear feverish chatter from the other side of the door. I knocked. Kate swung open the door and ushered me over to the desk, where the girls were huddled around a laptop.

"Oh my God. What the fuck?" said Mel.

There were a few complete sentences spoken, but, for the most part, communication was in the form of repeated expletives.

"So, is this the Darkroom?" I said.

Gemma tilted the computer screen, showing me a page with pictures of breasts and comments I couldn't read from that distance.

"This is your evidence," I said. "You can do something now."

Kate slowly shook her head and said, "No. We're not there yet."

"Oh my God!" Mel said.

Then Gemma shut the laptop.

"We have to complete our research first," said Gemma.

"What research?" I said.

"If this were a bank robbery—we're putting on our ski masks," Kate said.

"No, that's not right," Mel said. "We're still looking at the blueprints for the dog-grooming business that shares a wall with the bank."

While Mel and Kate quibbled over the type of business next door and the description of the current phase in their plan, I turned to Gemma for insight.

"Right now we can only see one part of the Darkroom," she said. "Everything is codified, so there's no way to move forward until we break the codes and find where they keep the information on Dulcinea. But we're so close."

Horseshoes and hand grenades, I thought.

GEMMA RUSSO

No one had smoked anything, but we'd reached another stratosphere of emotional chaos when we finally got inside the Darkroom. It was the feeling of being on a roller coaster, including the rush of adrenaline and the part where your stomach flips and you think you might barf.

There were countless galleries and message boards and photos that looked like gynecological textbooks—if you ignored the commentary beneath the brightly lit close-ups. Mel had only been reviewing the evidence for a few hours. She had five years of unedited content to sift through.

There were photos one couldn't always interpret by the thumbnail pictures from my laptop screen. Mel clicked on one; when enlarged, it was clearly a close-up of a vagina. Beneath the photo was commentary by TonyStarx: *The protruding labia is the inverted nipple of vaginas. Avoid at all costs.*

Mel clicked on another thumbnail, another photo of female genitalia.

A perfect specimen, tight and wet, says mADSKILLz.

"What the fuck!" Mel said.

Angry Mel was my favorite Mel. We could have explored the photos and message boards and gained a more comprehensive understanding of our enemy, but we were after something more specific than this anonymous bullshit.

"Where's the Dulcinea Award?" I asked.

"We don't know," Mel said. "There are so many message boards in different sections, and it's hard to navigate. There are also codes, and we have to figure out the code names and if there are other codes."

Kate was already scribbling letters and numbers down on a pad of paper.

"I'll break the codes," Kate said. "It's kind of my thing."

"So how'd you hack the Darkroom, Mel? You never told me," I said.

"Unless you know how to navigate a LAMP stack, you wouldn't understand," she said. "No offense."

"None taken."

"But mostly it was luck. Yeah, luck," Mel said.

Ms. Witt came by. We told her about our progress. That we were close. She wanted to see the proof. I gave Mel a specific glance. I don't know how she managed to interpret it correctly, but she chose one of the tamer posts. There was a page devoted entirely to pictures of the "perfect" breasts, with a poll that was happening in real time.

Ms. Witt said something about hand grenades and left. Come to think of it, that was a good analogy for where we were at. We'd just pulled the pin on the first grenade.

Mel was a lunatic. She was clicking around the Darkroom,

shouting expletives and reading aloud from the screen. I looked over her shoulder as she enlarged an image of a woman's already ample buttocks and began to read the comments aloud.

"**dead_klown:** what make you of this trend for the ample ass?
DoomsDay: I'm old school. Small and tight.
mADSKILLz: You could serve a three-course meal on that thing.
LennyBro: That just nasty."

I was trying to get Mel's attention, but it didn't work. So I flicked her on the head.

"Ouch."

"Sorry," I said. "But this is important. We need to gather as much evidence as possible before someone sees that you're fishing around. Copy everything; save it to this jump drive."

"Okay, boss," Mel said.

Kate had been quiet for a while. When we looked over, she was stretched out on the couch, eyes closed, breathing deeply.

"Kate? What are you doing?" Mel said.

"I'm trying to meditate," Kate said.

"Now?" said Mel. "I thought you were code-breaking."

Kate sat up suddenly and opened her eyes. She swallowed like she was nauseous. She gripped the edge of the couch and a tear fell down her cheek.

"What's wrong?" I said.

"I'm so angry," Kate said. "All the time. Sometimes when

I want to feel better, I imagine burning this place to the ground. I picture myself holding a machine gun and mowing down all of the editors and a few of their enablers. Sometimes the only thing that gets me through the day is the thought of outliving some of those dickheads. I picture myself in twenty years, standing over their graves and spitting on them. Or something else. I don't know. But now, because there's nothing I can do with this, I start crying and then I feel weak and pathetic and I get angry all over again."

We've all felt that impotent anger. I tried to find words that might help. Mel reached into her pocket.

"I have half a donut left over from breakfast. You want it?"

MS. WITT

Since Martha Primm was the Ethics Czar of Stonebridge, I decided it was time I got her alone to see what she was really about. I found her in the teachers' lounge and invited her out for drinks that night.

"Just you and me?" she said.

"Just you and me."

"I'd love to," she said.

I arrived early at Hemingway's to fortify myself before Primm got there. I ordered a beer. As Hugh pulled my pint, he asked about Claude. He said she hadn't been around for a while and he was worried. I told him about her mother and he nodded.

I was halfway through a beer when Primm showed up. She took the seat next to mine and ordered a vodka cranberry.

"Well, this is nice," Primm said.

"Yes," I said, with effort.

We didn't say anything else until Hugh served her drink. Primm held up her glass for a toast.

"To new beginnings," Primm said.

We clinked glasses and drank. I finished my beer and ordered another.

"How are you liking Stonebridge?" Primm said.

"I . . . like it," I said.

I couldn't muster an enthusiastic response, but I doubt she noticed.

"I always wondered why you left Warren Prep. It has an impeccable reputation."

"Reputation isn't everything," I said.

"That is so true," Primm said.

"I wanted to ask you about something," I said.

"Happy to help in any way," Primm said, attempting an open smile.

"Hypothetically speaking, how would Stonebridge handle a claim of sexual assault or rape?"

"Oh. That's not how I expected to spend happy hour," Primm said.

"Maybe I should have warned you about what I wanted to discuss. I'm just trying to understand the protocol at Stonebridge. Do you mind?"

"Of course not," Primm said. "Hypothetically, we would take the matter very seriously, I assure you."

"How does *very seriously* translate into action?" I said.

"Um. Let's see. We would interview both parties."

I noticed Primm had a nervous habit of lightly touching her halo of hair, as if she were making sure it was still there.

"What if the two parties told a different story?" I said.

"I would have to use my best judgment," said Primm.

"You know what? This hypothetical thing isn't working. Can we talk about the incident that brought you to Stonebridge?"

"How would you know about that?" Primm said.

"I asked Dean Stinson."

"There's a gag order," Primm said.

"He didn't give me names."

"What is it that you want, Alex?"

"I want to know how things are done around here. That's all. I'm not trying to re-litigate anything."

"There were no lawyers involved, I'm happy to report," Primm said.

"How about the police?" I said.

"I feel like I'm talking to the police right now," said Primm. "You must have learned a thing or two from your father's detective novels."

"Not really. So, no rape kit, no police report?"

Primm cleared her throat. "It wasn't necessary. In that particular case, we interviewed both parties and determined whether disciplinary measures were necessary."

"Who is *we*?"

"I misspoke. *I* interviewed both parties and came to the conclusion that there was no misconduct."

"What did your report say?"

Primm finished her drink. I clutched my beer close, so she wouldn't have anything to spill on me.

"Alex, I assure you there was no sexual impropriety. The girl and the boy were dating. When he broke up with her, that's when she made the allegation," Primm said with aggressive impatience. "We spoke for a long time and came to the conclusion that it was a simple misunderstanding."

"Was the board of directors involved in your decision?" I said.

"They were informed after the fact. Look, Alex. The girl was confused. It was a misunderstanding. That's all."

"What was the crux of the misunderstanding?" I said.

"She didn't say no."

GEMMA RUSSO

Linny had managed to gain access to the school's mimeograph machine and generated fifty poster-sized copies of the blowchart. She'd been posting them throughout the campus in subtle and not-so-subtle locations. Meanwhile, the cheap WANTED posters for the shower terrorist kept getting a manual update. The $500 reward was now $1,500. Rachel Rose had started playing gumshoe. She even wore a trench coat over her uniform as she roamed the campus, interviewing suspects. If you didn't submit to an interview, she put you at the top of her list. Turns out, I was already up there.

Rachel caught up with me after lunch, as I was leaving Dahl. She asked if I would mind answering a few questions, as she flipped open her notebook and clicked her pen to attention. I told her I was taking a walk and she was free to come along. Rachel inquired about my whereabouts during specific attacks. She had trouble taking notes while keeping up with my brisk pace.

"Can we please sit down?" she said, pointing to the bleachers by Fielding Field.

We sat down in the first row. I answered Rachel's questions with polite indifference. When she was done and mostly satisfied that I could not have been the culprit, I had a few questions of my own.

"This whole charade can't be about the reward money," I said.

"No," said Rachel. "I don't even think there is an official fund. Every time something goes wrong, someone adds a couple hundred to the sign."

"Then why are you helping them?"

"I'm being neighborly. That's all."

"Seems like you're neighborly enough."

Rachel readjusted the scarf around her neck.

"How pedestrian," she said.

"Huh?"

"Your narrow-minded view of feminism," Rachel said.

"Well, damn," I said. "Wasn't expecting you to trot out the F word."

"My view of feminism is inclusive, not judgmental and alienating."

"Am I really getting a lecture on feminism from the class slut?"

I'd never seen Rachel angry before. She fidgeted with her scarf, like it was strangling her, and kept clearing her throat.

"You think a feminist can't use her sexuality to gain advantage. I think every woman has the right to do whatever she has to do to get by," Rachel said.

"So, it's okay to exploit another woman to get ahead?"

"What are you talking about?" Rachel said.

"I know you took those pictures of Kate," I said.

Rachel rolled her eyes and adjusted her scarf.

"I was trying to empower her."

"By blanketing the school with naked photos of her?"

"I was the photographer," Rachel said. "*Not* the distributor."

"And who was that?" I said.

"No idea. That's all for now. Thank you for your cooperation."

I hadn't realized how much anger I had tamped down until Rachel walked away. My nails had left red crescents on my palms. I felt my eyes begin to water. I knew exactly what Kate had been feeling. I fought hard to bring myself back to my cold, calculating normal.

Linny appeared like a wraith next to me. She must have crawled under the bleachers and wiggled through the metal scaffolding.

"Wow. That was intense," Linny said.

"Yeah."

"Should you have called her a slut?"

"What do you want, Linny?"

"Mel and Kate are looking for you. We have a problem."

I arrived at my office to find Mel pacing in an oddly diagonal formation, like she was following the pattern of an invisible pentagram on the floor. She marched back and forth, covering as much space as possible, chomping on licorice the entire time, the bulk of the work being done by her neck as she yanked pieces from the vine.

"Mel?" I said.

"Someone removed all the photos from the Darkroom. It's just words now."

"When did that happen?" I said.

"I don't know. Overnight," said Mel.

"You got copies, right?" I said.

"I got most of them," said Mel. "But why did they take them down?"

"You think they know?"

Mel gazed down at the end of her licorice rope.

"Maybe," Mel said. "I don't know. It doesn't change anything."

Kate, in her own world, stood in front of the chalkboard, scribbling things like *3Hawk27, 2Loon89,* and *1Sparrow526.* Below that she had the alphabet written out, with number equivalents beside them. *A=1; B=2; C=3,* et cetera.

"What's up with Beautiful Mind over there?" I said to Mel.

"She's code-breaking," Mel said.

"Care to explain?" I said.

"The guys go by random dumb-fuck nicknames, like Hef13, TonyStarx, and Doomsday," Kate said. "But I think they're using a cryptogram for the girls. Something with birds and numbers and letters. If I can figure out what girl they're talking about, then we should be able to figure out the boys' code names."

Linny picked up a sheaf of printouts on the coffee table and began reading aloud: "LennyBro says about 2Owl420: *Her tongue feels like a salamander when Frenching, but her suction is incredible. Advice: Limit foreplay.* Hef80 replies: *Why are you making out with 2Owl420?* LennyBro says: *Brah, someone needs to break her in.*"

I took the papers from Linny. Mel covered her eyes and began rocking back and forth.

"Fuck. Fuck. Fuck," Mel said.

"Relax, Mel. I promise we'll get there. We won't just knock the editors down a few pegs; we'll take them to the rooftop of a skyscraper and shove them off one by one."

NORMAN CROWLEY

After I gave Mel entry into the Darkroom, I started to get paranoid. Like so paranoid I almost went back to my shrink. Jonah noticed how jumpy I was one day and just slipped a joint in my pocket.

It was the photos that freaked me out. Not just because they were creepy, but because they might have been illegal. I had never posted a picture myself. But I'd shown them how. I coded the page and gave them the links to do whatever they wanted. I rarely looked at the pictures, I swear. And I suspect that they were shots of women, adult women, that they found online. But I really didn't know, because most of the pictures cut the woman's face out of frame, which also creeped me out.

Everyone who posts in the Darkroom has a unique screen name and password. I set them up; I know who most of them are. Last year a senior named Crosby Whitaker, I kid you not, asked me to create a "wild-card account," as he called it, under the username Bagman2. He said it was an homage to the original Bagman, Jonah's brother, Jason. I figured Whitaker retired that screen name when he graduated, but clearly he'd bequeathed the cyber identity to one of the editors. Bagman2 posted the picture of Kate.

Kate was younger than the rest of the class. She'd just turned sixteen. I told the editors to take the photos down. I suggested it was child pornography and could potentially get us in a load of legal trouble. Mick Devlin said he'd call his father and check. I really wish I had a recording of that phone call.

Mick got back to me right away and told me to cool my jets. Sixteen is legit and Vermont has notoriously lenient pornography laws. Yay, Vermont. Good for you. I went over his head and told Jack Vandenberg we were playing with fire. Jack instructed me to take down the photos. I got some backlash from some of the heavy Darkroom users—a few guys wrote *scrooge, prude, pussy,* on the message board outside my dorm room, but Adam and Jack came to my defense. I remember Adam patting me on my back like we were old chums and saying, "Don't worry, we got your back."

I smiled and said thanks. God, I was a pussy. If I could fight I would have punched him. But this was all I had.

It was decided. The photos came down. I really thought that the modification would put a dent in the Darkroom activity. I was wrong. Without pictures, those dickheads had to use their words. You'd think it would be less disgusting. You'd be wrong. It was basically a wash.

I don't think Mel saw it that way. It had been more than a week since I sent the second anonymous message, which was basically an instruction manual on how to break into the Darkroom. After the photos came down, Mel replied to Bill

Haydon's message, requesting a private meeting. I ignored her; Bill Haydon had done enough. A day later, Mel sent a message directly to me.

To: Norman Crowley
From: Mel Eastman
Re: we need to talk

Meet me at Mo's at 4:00 p.m. sharp. And please convey my gratitude to Bill.

Damn. I should have known Mel would figure it out. I also should have known that she wouldn't just accept the gift and move on. If you gave Mel an inch, she'd take a football field.

I skipped cross-country practice and went into town. Mel was alone in the back of Mo's. She offered me a fresh cup of coffee and placed a paper plate with Oreos between us. I sat in one of those old student desks. Mel looked tired and a little crazy. Like those gamers who stay up all night jacked on energy drinks and Adderall.

"How did you know?" I said.

"Bill Haydon? *Tinker Tailor Soldier Spy*? You were on a le Carré kick all last year."

I drank the coffee and remained silent. Anything I might say could be used against me somewhere, sometime.

"Why did you take the pictures down?" Mel said.

"I didn't put them up. I didn't even look at them."

"You looked at a few," she said.

I looked at my feet.

"You let me into the Darkroom," Mel said. "You wanted me to see it. Right, Norman?"

"Yes," I said.

"Thank you," she said.

She put her hand on my arm and said *thank you* again. I nodded.

"Why did the pictures come down? They don't know that I'm in, right?"

"No. They don't know anything yet. They've been paranoid lately. Technically some of the pictures are child porn."

"Right," said Mel. "So it's just a coincidence that they took down the photos a few days after I got in?"

"Yes," I said.

Mel reached into her backpack, pulled out a notebook, and leafed through it.

"Who are LennyBro, mADSKILLz, and TonyStarx? And why are there so many Hefs? I assume it's a Hugh Hefner reference?"

I nodded. She knew too much. I couldn't believe what I'd done. If Mel wanted to, she could ruin me.

"Let's talk about the birds," she said. "There are only four types of birds, right?"

"Mel, please don't tell them what I did."

"I'll never rat you out, Norman. Not ever."

"Really?"

"I promise. Back to the birds," she said.

"There are five birds," I said.

"Hawk, loon, sparrow, owl," Mel said, consulting her notes.

"There's another bird. Look for that one."

Mel searched through her notes.

"I don't see any other bird," she said.

"Keep looking."

I could have told her more, but if she found it on her own I had plausible deniability.

"Can I ask you something, Norman?"

"All you're doing is asking me things," I said.

"It's a different kind of question."

"Okay."

She started to say something but stopped. She removed her glasses and wiped the lens with the bottom of her shirt. She held them up to the light. They were still filthy. She sighed, gave up, and put them back on.

"When I look at what the editors have written about us, I have to wonder how they see us. Do you know what I mean?"

"I'm not sure," I said.

"Like, are we even human?"

ANNOUNCEMENTS

Good morning, students of Stone. It is Thursday, November 12, 2009, which means tomorrow is Friday the 13th.

Here's a little trivia for you: Triskaidekaphobia is the scientific term for fear of the number 13. It's all hogwash if you ask me.

We're expecting another sunny day, with a brisk breeze and maybe a few high clouds. For lunch today, you have a choice between pizza à la king or a bulgur-and-Tofurky meatloaf. Interesting.

Let's talk about the elephant in the school. We have a lice outbreak, I'm sad to report. Housekeeping asks that you put all your sheets in plastic bags. Laundry should also be put in tied plastic bags. I believe it suffocates the lice. Fresh sheets will be supplied once you confirm your delousing. You can pick up a supply of RID at the main office. Please check out my Facebook page for more information on lice eradication and prevention . . . Well, I am sorry to hear that. You know there's a suggestion box.

What was I saying before I was interrupted? You need to

suffocate the lice. Ah, okay. I'm being told to cut it short today.

Last business: All students who plan to remain on campus for the Thanksgiving holiday must give notice by next Monday to admin. That's all, folks.

MS. WITT

There wasn't just a light drizzle outside. It was biblical. It had been pouring rain for three days. I even went into town and bought a pair of rain boots.

When Wainwright started in on the lunch menu forecast, I raced out of my classroom, through the hall, and down the stairs to admin.

"Ms. Pinsky, where's Wainwright?"

"I have no idea," she said, refusing to make eye contact.

"You too?" I said.

I was done with this game. I stalked the first floor of admin, shouting at the top of my lungs.

"Wainwright. I need to talk to Wainwright!"

A few instructors opened their doors and asked me to keep it down, but I kept going until Greg emerged from his office.

"Where is Wainwright? I will not return to my classroom until I see him," I said.

Greg just ticked his head in the direction of a door behind the stairwell.

There was a placard that said ELECTRICITY ROOM, DO

NOT ENTER. I put my ear to the wall and heard Wainwright's distinct drone. I turned the knob and swung open the door.

Rupert, the groundskeeper, sat in a small room—more like a closet—behind a desk with a tube microphone just below his chin.

"... for more information on lice eradication and prevention ..."

He looked up and tried to shoo me away.

"You're Wainwright," I said.

"Excuse me," Rupert said, covering the mic. "Can I help you?"

"Look outside, Rupert. It's raining!"

The room had no windows, which undercut my argument.

"Is it?" he said.

"You always get the weather wrong."

"I am sorry to hear that," he said. Then he dropped into a whisper: "Got to get back to the show."

Rupert said something about a suggestion box and I left.

My class was in stitches when I returned.

"Ms. Witt," said Adam, "you look disappointed."

"When an entire institution manages to keep a secret, you kind of expect it to be earth-shattering."

"Come on," said Amy Logan. "You were a little surprised, right?"

I shrugged. "I still don't get it."

Later, during my office hours, Jonah gave me his take on the Wainwright conspiracy of silence.

"What you have to know is that just about everyone likes Rupert. Other than the two or three kids each year who want to join the A/V Club. Also, you want to stay on Rupert's good side, because if you lose your keys, you're screwed without him. Anyway, Rupert's secret identity is what he needs to feel special or something. Every year there's someone who doesn't know, and it's fun to let Rupert have that win. I like it because it's the only time I think we're all together on something, you know? There are so many bullshit secrets at this school. It feels like a good secret to keep. It makes someone happy."

It wouldn't stop raining. The mud was so thick it felt like I was walking on a giant piece of chewed-up gum. After my boggy commute home, I fed the generator one more time and left my boots right inside the front door. I performed my usual sweep of the cabin, searching for electronic devices and double-checking the foil seal on the windows. Once satisfied that I was safe from any observation, I changed into my pajamas and crawled under the covers. The rain on the tin roof was deafening, and a musty, moldy smell overpowered the cabin. I had to admit that living here was not a sustainable option. And yet I remained resolute about not residing in student housing.

That was the third or fourth time I thought about quitting.

That night, I graded papers. It was a two-part assignment. The first part was eavesdropping on a conversation and transcribing it. After that, my students would take the real dialogue and make it interesting. I have no idea what Gabriel Smythe was thinking. He took a scene from *The Dark Knight* as his "found" dialogue and rewrote it in pig Latin. *I'mway otnay away onstermay.* I fell asleep. I must have slept hard. The relentless rain had the effect of a white-noise machine, lulling me into a deeper and deeper slumber. I even slept through the sound of water as it breached the crack in the doorway and quickly flooded the room. But it wasn't the sound of my home becoming a river that woke me; it was several loud thuds on the door.

When I finally came to, I thought I was in a dream. Papers, shoes, and several pens floated around me.

"Alex! Alex! Wake up."

It was Coach Keith's voice. There was about a foot of brown water surrounding my bed, which was the only safe island in the room.

"I can't come to the door right now," I said.

"Are you okay?" Keith said through the door.

"I'm not drowning, if that's what you're getting at."

"Mind if I come in?"

"It's locked. And I don't know if I can get to the door."

"Not a problem."

Keith unlocked the door and entered the cottage, wearing Wellingtons and an anorak. He resembled a young Greg.

"You have a key," I said.

"Rupert is on his way with sandbags," he said, wading over to my bed.

"How'd you get a key?"

"I had a key," he said. "I used to stay here sometimes."

Coach Keith turned around, offered up his back, and said, "Hop on."

He gave me a piggyback ride out of the cabin, grabbing my rain boots on the way out. He carried me up a hill and set me down under the awning of a Douglas fir. The sun was rising as the rain was beginning to abate.

"Shit. My phone is inside," I said. "It's on the table. My clothes are in there too. And there might be a dry jacket in the closet."

"Be right back."

While Keith was salvaging my personal items, I had a sudden revelation.

"It was you, wasn't it? You are the note-leaving nutjob," I said, aggressively pointing at him when he returned with my belongings.

"I think *informant* might be a better term," Keith said, delivering my phone and the wrong jacket.

"Why?" I said.

"It sounds better than nutjob. Isn't that obvious?"

"No. Why have you been leaving me notes?"

"I wanted to point you in the right direction. There's something wrong with Stonebridge," Keith said.

"I figured that out already!" I said.

"Good. Now you can do something."

"Why don't *you* do something?" I said.

"Because I can't. The students here don't like it when you fuck with the status quo. Four teachers before you had to resign under questionable circumstances. Mason Roberts, computer science, went to the dean about a disturbing website he saw. The next thing I heard, he was accused of inappropriate physical contact by five different boys. Faith Cooke, calculus and carpentry, resigned after two years and never taught again. I don't know if anything happened there, but it did seem odd since she was only thirty-five. And I think you know about Mary Whitehall. And then there was a chem teacher four years ago—I can't remember his name; he walked out in the middle of class, drove away, and never came back."

"So, what am I supposed to do?" I said.

"I think you're on the right track, for what it's worth. The kids have to crumble this bullshit from the inside. If the girls revolt, the entire school culture will change."

I shoved my feet into my waterlogged boots. I cringed from the sensation.

"You should have warned me about the brownie. I ate it all in one sitting."

"Who gives *one* brownie as a housewarming gift? You give a plate of brownies. One brownie means it's special."

"That's not something everybody knows."

"I think it is," he said.

Keith hadn't been able to salvage anything else. My clothes were in cubbyholes under the flood line. Keith told me there was a room where they kept extra uniforms.

We crossed paths with Linny on our way back to campus.

"Go eat breakfast," Keith said. "And make sure you're in the gym for PE today. I think we'll do suicides."

Linny squinted, like a bad guy in a Western, and toggled her gaze between Keith and me.

"Your vacation is over," Keith said to Linny.

"Goddamn it," Linny said.

She stomped off toward Dahl.

"She knew you wrote the notes, didn't she?" I said.

"Yeah. She's been blackmailing me for two months."

Keith took me to a large room in the basement of Beckett Gym, which had a giant mound of mismatched clothes and two racks of boys' and girls' uniforms. Keith pulled a plaid skirt off the rack.

"This should fit," he said.

"Dream on," I said.

Keith left me to piece together an outfit for the day. I found a pair of boys' trousers that were too big in the waist and too tight in the ass. I belted them with a tie, threw on a large white shirt and a navy-blue cardigan. I kicked off my rain boots for fear of trench foot and plucked mismatched socks and sneakers from the lost and found.

I arrived early to room 203, which was preferable to making a grand entrance in my ridiculous ensemble. As my students filed in, I got a few sidelong glances. Once the entire class had arrived, they were in full-blown hysterics. I took a bow and explained my housing and clothing crisis.

"Call me crazy," Adam Westlake said. "But you're somehow making it work."

"Would you mind terribly if I took a picture?" Tegan said.

"No pictures," I said.

"You look like an escaped mental patient," Gemma said.

"Oh my God, it's Friday the thirteenth," Bethany Wiseman said. "You're lucky you didn't drown."

Jonah was laughing so hard, I thought he might be sick.

"If you don't stop laughing, I'm going to send you to the nurse's office," I said.

I felt like an exotic creature on display at the zoo. There were several random visitors that morning, all trying to get a glimpse of me. Keith, when he dropped by a few hours later, didn't say a thing about my look.

"I took some of your drowned clothes and sent them to the laundry. They should be ready at the end of the day," he said.

"Thank you," I said.

"No problem."

"We're done with the note business, right? If you have something to tell me, you'll just tell me," I said.

"Yep."

"I don't understand why you've stayed here so long."

"It's home," he said.

"There are other homes," I said. "This one isn't so great."

"Now you're insulting my home," he said.

"That was not my intention."

"I know this place is messed up, but I think it's worth trying to salvage."

"Okay," I said.

"Greg wants to see you at lunch. You need to discuss alternative living arrangements."

As instructed, I dropped by Greg's office shortly after noon. Greg sat down behind his desk and gestured for me to take a seat.

"I feared something like this would happen," Greg said.

"My God, was the space heater on?"

"I think I'd be dead if that were the case."

"I've taken the liberty of making other living arrangements."

"What is that motel in town called?" I said.

"Motel," he said. "No. Not that. We have other quarters. Not in the dormitories, have no fear, but on the top floor of Beckett Gym, far away from the students. You'd be just two flights away from our exquisite bathhouse. Even though it has a full bath. It's the chambers we reserve for special guests and alumni."

As Greg and I strolled over to Beckett Gym, I thanked him for not mocking my outfit, to which he replied, "Why would I? You look the same as you always do."

The apartment on the top floor of Beckett was actually kind of swank, nicer than the teachers' quarters in Dickens or Woolf. It even had a flat-screen TV and was wired for cable and Internet. Greg referred to it as "Godot's Place." I let that detail slide, because I could not have pictured anything more enticing after waking up in the middle of a swamp.

"I'll take it," I said.

"Oh, good. I should mention that it comes with a tithe."

"A tithe?"

"I need another adult supervisor over Thanksgiving break. I hope that's all right?"

The tithe was more than reasonable, to my mind. Plus, it saved me the complications of choosing between my parents for the holiday.

"You drive a hard bargain," I said, eyeing my pristine new home.

GEMMA RUSSO

Mel and Kate were toiling away in my office, hopped up on sugar, caffeine, and wrath. And yet there was something blissful in their joint code-breaking. They'd left the door open, which pissed me off, and I gave them a stern lecture.

"You done?" Mel said when I was not done.

"We broke the code," said Kate.

"Not entirely," said Mel, "but we found distinct patterns that we can extrapolate from."

Mel approached the chalkboard and pointed to a list of four birds:

Sparrow, Loon, Owl, Hawk

Let me condense a twenty-minute code-breaking lecture down to the basics. Each girl's code was a number, one through four, followed by one of those birds, with numbers tacked on to the end. The first number was the year in school. They still didn't know exactly what the birds meant. The addendum numbers were simple numeric swaps for the specific girl's initials. For example, my code would be 4, some kind of bird (hawk, I assume), 718 (G being the seventh letter and R the eighteenth).

The boys, on the other hand, used screen names. Once we parsed some of the Darkroom chatter, it was no wonder they kept their real names under wraps. Kate and Mel had collected some of the sleaziest commentary for my perusal.

Dead_klown: Steer clear of 3Loon12: Bad breath, smelly pussy, and clingy.

Hef47: No reason to get near pussy, brah.

I knew instinctually what they were like, and I'd heard bits and pieces over the years, but it was the first time I'd seen the depth of their contempt for us. I had been too distracted by breaking into the Dulcinea contest to grasp how sad it all was. Mel put her hand on my shoulder and offered me a licorice vine, as if it weren't from my own stash.

"Have a licorice. It'll make you feel better."

"I was sick too for the first few hours," said Kate. "It fades, and then what's left is an unquenchable thirst for revenge, which is quite invigorating."

"What's up with the birds?" I said.

"The bird designation seems to be fluid," said Kate. "I saw a reference to a sparrow turning into a loon and an owl into a hawk."

"The bird references have something to do with traits or behavior," Mel said. "And there's supposed to be a fifth bird, but I don't see it anywhere."

"Let's not get stuck on this bird shit," I said. "Why aren't there any references to Dulcinea? That's the whole point of this, right?"

"It's not here," said Kate.

Mel gave her comrade a sharp glance.

"What do you mean it's not here?" I said.

"There's another room inside this one. We don't know how to get in yet," said Mel.

"How do you know there's someplace else?" I asked.

"I just know," said Mel.

She was hiding something. I didn't have time to think about it. I studied the printouts in front of me and noticed a few common threads.

"LennyBro and Hef21 were both talking about 3Sparrow12. If we know even one of these three, then we might be able to deduce the rest," I said.

Mel lay flat on the floor, gazing at the ceiling. She held her chomped-down licorice rope between her index and middle finger and pretended to smoke it.

"LennyBro, Lenny Bruce," Mel said.

"That's got to be Gabriel Smythe, right?" Kate said.

"Has to be," said Mel.

"That narrows down the options for 3Sparrow12," I said.

When I returned to my dorm room, Emelia was out with Nick, and Tegan was studying with her earbuds on.

"You've been gone a lot lately," Tegan said.

"Are you complaining?" I said.

"Nope. Where do you go?"

"Nowhere, everywhere."

My phone buzzed.

Linny: I have information

Gemma: Greenhouse? 5 minutes.

"You're up to something," Tegan said.

"Isn't everyone up to something?" I said.

"Sure," she said. "Piece of advice? Respond to a text now and again. At least pretend you're one of us."

I had muted the text thread a while back. I was so enjoying the silence, I forgot. Shit. The odd thing was that Tegan wasn't taunting me with this information. If I didn't know better, I would have thought she was genuinely concerned.

"You should be careful too," I said.

I wasn't trying to be an asshole. I didn't like her, but I didn't want Tegan to be made a fool of.

"About what?" Tegan said.

"Watch yourself with Jack."

"There's nothing going on with Jack and me," she said.

"That's good, because I see him all over school with other girls."

"Good for him," Tegan said, giving away nothing.

When I arrived at the greenhouse, Rupert was astride his ATV, having a loud conversation with Linny. The conversation was loud mostly because his engine was still running.

"No, no," said Rupert. "I said I'd meet you at seven-thirty. I waited until seven forty-five."

"No," said Linny. "You told me to meet you at eight-ten, which is a stupid time, anyway. I arrived at eight and stayed until eight-thirty. You never showed."

"Sounds like a simple miscommunication," Rupert said.

"You may have fleeced the rest of the school, but I'm on to you."

"If you have any issues about how things are run here, feel free to use the suggestion box," said Rupert.

"Oh, I will," Linny said.

Rupert gunned the engine on his ATV and disappeared into the woods. Linny stood there, fuming.

"Let it go," I said.

"You can't pretend there's an A/V club if there's no A/V club," she said. "That's bullshit. My brother gets to do the morning announcements at his school. That job isn't for the groundskeeper. It should be up for grabs. Plus, he gets the weather wrong *Every. Single. Day.* How hard is it to read the newspaper?"

Everyone has their own war. But Linny seemed to be fighting many wars. I started to feel like I didn't know her anymore.

"What have you got for me?" I said.

"I saw Mel leave campus in the middle of the day. I followed her."

"You're not allowed off campus, Linny."

"Do you want to know who she met with?" Linny said.

"I do."

"Norman Crowley."

MS. WITT

My birthday is on November 16 and my father's is on November 14. My mother used to throw us combined parties on November 15. I found the whole thing unfair and infuriating, and my father found the abundance of children at his celebrations unseemly. No matter how much we protested, my mom could not wrap her head around the excess of two parties in three days. But later, in the years AD (After the Delete), my father and I ended up continuing the tradition and meeting in the middle.

For a while we attempted birthday-like activities, the things people do at a children's party. But my father dismissed them one at a time.

On bowling: *Well, this is simply unsanitary.*

On miniature golf: *Wait, where did it go? Oh, I give up!*

On the arcade: *Why do you have so many more tickets than I do?*

After a purgative roller-coaster ride on my sixteenth birthday from which I may never recover, I suggested that a simple meal followed by no physically jarring activity was the best option. From year seventeen on, Dad and I would have a fancy meal at a location of my father's choosing. We hadn't missed a year yet, but I assumed this would be the one. Unfortunately, he wasn't taking no for an answer. He'd made a reservation at a place called Manger. It was the finest restaurant within thirty miles of Stonebridge. Dad said he'd pick me up at six.

I've told my father on many occasions that I would rather have one thing I love than one thing I like, one thing I'm ambivalent about, and seven things that don't resemble regular food at all. He conveniently forgets my tastes. When we arrived at Manger (which I purposefully and repeatedly pronounced with a hard g and r), the waiter said we could choose from a four-, seven-, nine-, or twelve-course menu.

I made a preemptive strike on the twelve-course meal, threatening to eat alone at the diner down the road. Dad suggested nine. I said two and he reminded me that four was the lowest option. Four, then. Dad told the waiter that we'd do the seven-course meal—"splitting the difference," he said, giving me a dad-wink.

After we ate our deconstructed Waldorf salad, my father suggested we exchange presents. I handed him a plain brown box wrapped in a bow. He handed me an envelope filled with cash.

"You're light this year," I said, feeling the thinness of the envelope.

"Not my best year," he said, opening the box.

"Why don't drug dealers do this?" I said. "That box could

be filled with drugs and we just made this exchange in a public place. No one would think anything of it."

"Hmm . . . I could use that," he said, taking out his notebook and scribbling.

Dad returned his attention to his gift. Inside the box were several pieces of paper filled with solid three-act story outlines, on which he could hang the next Len Wilde novel.

"Plots," Dad said wistfully. "You shouldn't have."

We do this every year. The pretense is that I conceived most of the story lines, with a minor contribution from my mother.

"Which one is Nastya's?" he said.

The real question, however, is: *Which one didn't she write?*

"I can't remember, Dad. Just pick the one that speaks to you most."

The third or fourth course was a reinterpretation of surf and turf. It had sea urchin and mushrooms. Dad took the sea urchin off my plate because he knows it makes me angry. He tried to make small talk about his work in progress, *Bitter Prayer.*

"I had to scrap a hundred pages, but Sloan thinks it's coming together quite nicely."

"I'm surprised you have the balls to say her name."

"You will be hearing her name again, so it's time you got used to it."

"You're getting divorced again, aren't you?"

"Yes."

"How old is Sloan?" I asked.

I already knew she was younger than me. Dad didn't answer.

"We had a deal," I said.

I was twenty-two when my father was hooking up with Greta, age twenty-seven, his then assistant, soon-to-be ex-wife. I made my dad promise never to date a woman younger than his daughter. He promised.

"It's not exactly a binding contract," Dad said.

"How would you feel if I brought home a sixty-six-year-old lover?"

"Stop it, Alex. That's a grotesque notion."

"Isn't that what Sloan's father would think?"

"Sloan doesn't know her father," my dad said. "And I think it's important to note that you've never brought home a louse. You've always been quite savvy with men. I'd like to think I've had a hand in that."

"No. No," I said, feeling my face flush with heat. "You don't get to pat yourself on the back for my choices. And I'm never going to let you think that the way you behave is okay."

Dad put down his fork and knife and looked me in the eye.

"I'm sixty-two years old—"

"Sixty-six," I said.

"If I'm lucky, I have ten good years, and maybe ten mediocre years. Not a day goes by where I don't feel like the best is behind me. Everything good has already happened. Even the once reliable pleasure of sex is not what it once was. So, if I meet someone who makes me feel alive and capable of—"

"If you finish that sentence," I said, "I'll stab you with the sea-urchin fork."

"My point is," Dad said, "I'd rather be happy and fulfilled than adhere to some nebulous moral standard. Do you understand?"

"What if I gave you an ultimatum?" I said.

"Alex, please. That's absurd."

"If I told you I wouldn't see you again if you continued with this relationship, what would you do?"

"You don't even have a relationship with Greta. What do you care if I leave her?"

"Answer the question," I said.

"I would choose you, Alex. Of course. And I would be miserable. Is that what you want?"

"Works for me," I said.

"Fine. I will call off the engagement."

"Excellent."

"I assume you will take responsibility for my care once I become infirm."

"Forget it," I said. "Marry her. But I'm not going to the wedding."

"Understood," Dad said.

The waiter asked if we wanted another bottle of wine. I ordered the most expensive one, as retribution.

My father sighed and said, "I would much rather spend that money on dental work."

"Don't be an asshole," I said.

"Please, Alex, please let me pay to fix that tooth."

"No," I said. "And you're only bringing it up to change the subject."

"Nonsense," my father said.

My teeth used to be quite a point of contention between my parents. I was teased some in primary school, and several dentists advocated for braces. But one honest orthodontist admitted that the fix would be purely cosmetic.

My parents got into one of their great fights when I made the decision to leave the tooth alone. Dad was convinced that my mother's anti-orthodontia stance was anti-American. It wasn't. It was practical. Dad thought my decision meant that my identity aligned more with hers. It wasn't that complicated. I liked having one rebel tooth. Besides, it cuts food just the same.

I arranged to stay in Greg's guest room and delivered Dad to my new quarters at Beckett Gym. Dad surveyed his accommodations, restlessly meandering about the room. Eventually I realized he was searching for the minibar.

"I hope Greg isn't offended that I'm not staying with him," Dad said.

"He's not," I said.

He really wasn't. My father is a notoriously demanding houseguest. Greg accepted the exchange of me for my father without question.

"I'm going to go now," I said. "Are you clear on your assignment?"

"I am."

I sent Finn a text.

"Tell him to bring booze," Dad said.

I sent another text.

"Do you still love me?" Dad said.

I paused for a moment, just to fuck with him.

"I guess so," I said.

I kissed him on the cheek and left.

MR. FORD

Witt: Come to my new apartment. I have a surprise.

Witt: Could you bring some bourbon?

I thought I was getting laid. I got Len.

In real life, he looked like the mug-shot version of his author photo. He shook my hand with a domineering grip, but he was pleasant enough, drunk, and clearly in need of more booze and company. Maybe he just needed the booze. He eyed my bottle of Maker's with brazen lust. I handed him the bottle. He had a heavy pour.

I told him I was a fan because I was (of his first three books). He was my hero after I read *Darkness, Behave*. And I think his first two crime novels transcend the genre, to use a hackneyed phrase. I read one or one and a half of his later works and gave up when I realized he'd given up. Len asked what my favorite book was.

"*Darkness, Behave,*" I said.

He looked disappointed. Then I mentioned the next two, both written at least fifteen years ago. It was a rookie move. No man wants to be reminded that his best work is behind him. Then I told him how impressed I was with *Hidden Window,* which might have been his worst. His language had lost its ease. It had a heavy-handed, molasses-thick quality about it. I remember reading a line that referred to a Post-it as a *devil square backed with glue.*

Then I added *The Last Short* and *Shadow Room* to the list of books I'd read, since I recalled those specific titles. Len appeared to be waiting for me to mention more. I improvised.

"Forgive me," I said. "My memory is not what it used to be. I read the one with the widow and the one that came out two years ago?"

"Oh, yes, *Mortal Alley* and *The Ninth Station.*"

"Yes, *The Ninth Station,*" I said. "That was intense."

"Most of my readers didn't respond to that one."

"I'm an outlier," I said.

"Did you get the Dante references?"

"Who the fuck wouldn't?"

I felt like how my students must feel when they haven't studied for their exams. I poured Len another finger of bourbon, hoping he wouldn't probe me for more details.

"Young man, how long have you been at this strange school?"

"Four years now."

"You're a writer, I am told."

"Yes," I said, relieved I no longer had to improvise. "About five years ago my first novel was published. *Tethered.* Didn't sell very well."

"I think I read it," Len said. "It was an audacious undertaking."

"Thank you, sir."

The old man was bullshitting me. Now I wanted to make him dance.

"I got a lot of shit about the scene where the wife gives her husband a shave with a straight razor and deliberately cuts him," I said.

"Utterly gripping," Len said.

Yep. Bullshit artist, just like me. There's an unsettling moment when Avalene ties Wade's necktie, but it could not be mistaken for a close shave.

"What are you working on now, son?"

Well played.

"I just sold my second novel. My agent is negotiating the deal now."

"Congratulations," Len said, refilling my glass.

"Thank you."

"What's it about?"

"It's about the dark secrets behind an elite boarding school."

"Intriguing," Len said with a forced smile. "I'd love to read it sometime. Send it to me, will you?"

"I'd be honored," I said.

We raised our glasses.

"This is the toast I used to give my students before they embarked on their next great work," Len said, clearing his throat. "Take the blank page by the throat and beat it to a pulp. Do not let it beat you."

We clinked glasses and drank. Len casually studied the room, leaned back on the couch, and crossed his ankle over his knee.

"Let me ask you a question, son. How do you concentrate on your writing with all of this fresh pussy around?"

ANNOUNCEMENTS

Happy Monday, students of Stone. This is the final week of class before the Thanksgiving holiday. A friendly reminder to the majority of students who will be going home for break: Please do not leave any perishable food in your dorm room. That message is for you, room 307, Dickens House. The weather forecast is an overcast but dry fifty-two degrees. It looks like we have a few days' reprieve from rain, so please make sure to get some fresh air and vitamin D, and go smell the pines. It's November 16, a slow day in history. But before I sign off, let's give a warm happy birthday to our very own Alex Witt.

MS. WITT

Before class the next morning, I dropped by my new apartment to say goodbye to my father. He was too hungover to work out the coffeemaker, so I brewed it for him while he showered.

After he dressed, Dad dragged himself to the kitchen table and waited for me to serve him. We sat and drank for a while in silence. I like Dad best this way, with the pomp beaten out of him. Sometimes, on bleary mornings like this one, he even looks serene.

"Happy birthday, Alexandra."

"Thanks, Dad. Did you enjoy your company last night?"

"He served his purpose, and the bourbon was decent enough," Dad said.

"And?"

"He's going to send me that book of his."

"Excellent. So what did you really think of him?"

"He's an amiable drinking companion. But I'm sure you've already figured out he's a lecherous S.O.B."

* * *

My students sang "Happy Birthday."

Jonah gave me a perfect lily from Graham Greenehouse.

Sandra Polonsky got me a latte from the Mudroom.

Mel gifted me with a spork she made in metal arts.

And Gemma gave me a promise that she'd bring down the Darkroom by the end of the year.

Claude wasn't at school that day, but she sent a quick birthday text and gave me an IOU for drinks. We had a quick exchange.

Alex: Everything okay?

Claude: Of course. Why wouldn't it be?

After class, I went back to my old cottage. Sandbags still hugged the perimeter, but the water had receded. Inside, I found my mother and Coach Keith, packing up my belongings. I got the feeling that Keith just happened by and Mom had shanghaied him into service.

She hadn't mentioned a trip to Stonebridge, but I wasn't surprised. Even though their child had reached the ripe old age of twenty-nine, my parents still acted like joint custodians. Dad got to see me two days in a row, so Mom's arrival was right on cue.

"Hi, Mom."

"Happy birthday, darling. I came to help you move."

"Keith, are you here of your own free will?" I said.

"Yes," Keith said.

It was a quick move. Perhaps the quickest of my life. Keith

double-timed us up and down the stairs of Beckett with the few boxes of personal items that I owned. My mother tried to tip him, but he waved away the cash and said he had to go.

Greg knocked on the door a few hours later. My mother was in the bedroom, refolding my clothes.

"Looks like you're settling in," Greg said.

"Can I offer you some water or hot tea?" I said.

"No thank you. Have you heard from Claude?" Greg asked.

"Yes. She texted this afternoon."

"Good," Greg said. "She's having a wake Friday evening at her house."

"What wake?" I said.

"Her mother died," said Greg.

"When?"

"Last night," Greg said.

I checked the message from Claude, trying to make sense of it.

My mother entered the room. She and Greg were talking about a bag.

"No. I left it in my car," my mother said.

"Just give me your keys, Nastya. I'll grab it and put it in the guest room," Greg said.

I couldn't figure out what my mother and Greg were discussing.

"What's going on?" I said.

"I invited your mother to stay on for Thanksgiving break," Greg said. "Isn't that wonderful?"

NORMAN CROWLEY

Mick called an emergency board meeting soon after the lice outbreak. Gabe suggested a remote meeting for the purposes of containment. Jack said something like, "Don't be gay and it won't spread."

Adam arrived at the lounge wearing a shower cap.

Jack doubled over in hysterics.

"Laugh all you want," Adam said. "This scalp will remain vermin-free."

"It's like a condom for your head," said Nick thoughtfully.

Mick thought it was a grand idea. "You got another?"

Adam pulled a fresh shower cap from his pocket. Mick unfurled the plastic and placed it like a crown on his head.

"How do I look?" Mick said to Adam.

"You look as good as a man can look wearing a shower cap," Adam said.

"You too, good man," Mick said.

"Grandmas," Jack said. "Let's get this meeting started. I have to do another round of RID."

Mick scanned the room and sighed. "Jonah's a no-show again?"

"It's time to vote him out," Jack said.

"All in favor," said Mick.

There were three ayes, and one abstention—Adam. Jonah was officially out. This seemed to piss off Adam, but I couldn't say why. My best guess is that Adam liked Jonah better than these other buffoons. But maybe there was something I was missing.

The meeting, however, wasn't about Jonah, the Darkroom, or Dulcinea. It was about the plague on Dickens, of which the lice outbreak was just the latest wave. I could see how someone might have managed the poison-oak attack, but wrangling lice seemed risky. And none of the girls had it yet, even though they've got a lot more hair. As always, I didn't share my opinion with the board.

"My source thinks it's Gemma," Adam said.

His source was Rachel Rose. We'd all seen her Veronica Mars-ing around school, demanding alibis.

"Is your source hazarding a guess, or does she have proof?" I asked.

I never speak, so they all looked stunned and suspicious.

"I mean, you want to be careful leveling accusations," I added. "That's how you let the real perp slip away."

"Good point," Mick said. "In the meantime, I think we'll have to go to our backup plan."

The backup plan was to use the little brothers as sentries during all non-school hours. They created six four-hour shifts. I was glad I didn't have to put a sophomore through forced insomnia—my little brother had dropped out of Stonebridge after two weeks. I was never assigned another. I was kind of bummed about it at the time. Now I consider it a bonus. Besides, what great wisdom could I impart to an underclassman? *Keep your head down and don't make trouble.*

As soon as the meeting was up, I texted Jonah to warn him. He asked me to meet him out on Fielding.

I found him kicking a soccer ball around by himself. He kicked the ball in my direction, I think expecting me to trap it, but it breezed on by. He should know better. I ran after the ball and picked it up.

"Congratulations. You've been officially made redundant," I said.

Jonah pumped his fist in the air. "Fuck, yeah."

He legit looked happy—like, happier than I'd seen him in weeks.

"Are you sure that was the right move?"

"I don't know. I was deadwood anyway," Jonah said.

He jogged backward, waiting for me to pass him the ball. I tossed it in front of me, kicked out, and completely missed. It would have looked cooler if I rolled it on the ground two-handed, like a bad bowler. Jonah didn't bother kicking it back to me after that.

"Stay cool, Norman. You're now the only inside man. We need you."

Jonah was going to toss me the ball as some kind of jock handshake. I flinched. He was kind enough to pretend he didn't notice.

I was walking back to Dickens when I ran into Enid Cho.

We're not friends, exactly, but we talk about class stuff and I see her in the library.

"Hey, Norman. Did you hear about Shepherd's mom?"

I didn't have a plan exactly. I walked off campus and strolled down Hyde Street to see what was open at eight-thirty on a Thursday night. It was dead in town, other than Hemingway's and a small grocery store called Otto's.

I don't know that I'd ever been there before. And I won't go back, because someone—maybe Otto—kept following me around the store, asking me if I needed help. I told him I was browsing. I couldn't tell if Otto was giving me a hard sell or thought I was shoplifting, but I could not shake that green-apron-wearing old man.

"What are you looking for?" he said for like the third time.

"I don't know!" I said.

"You should always go to the store with a list."

Otto had a small selection of flowers. But they looked pretty beat up, and flowers had taken on a sinister vibe lately.

"You got the munchies or something?" Otto said.

I opened the freezer and picked the first two pints of ice cream I could find. Then I went to the juice section and got one of those green juices in case Ms. Shepherd wanted something healthy. And for a reason I will never be able to articulate, I got a bag of prewashed spinach. I assembled all my items on the conveyor belt. You would think that Otto would have been pleased I'd made a decision and was getting out of his store, but no.

"You should get a steak to round out the meal."

"I don't want a steak, thank you."

Otto rang up my order, giving me shit for not bringing my own bag. I paid and got out of there. My one small act of revolt was refusing to say goodbye.

I almost never went into Lowland at night. No one does. Now I know why. It's a ghost town. I had been to Ms. Shepherd's house once, ages ago. She had to stay home, taking care of her mother, but she'd left her book bag at school. She sent me a message and asked me to bring it to her. She was nice that day. But she didn't invite me inside or even let me past the front door. I gave her the bag and left.

Her house is on the east side, maybe half a mile off Hyde Street. When I arrived on the front steps of 344 Crestview Drive, I stalled outside the front door, trying to decide what I should do. It seemed really stupid, going to a teacher's house with ice cream and spinach right after her mother had died. I kept thinking of that day I saw her at the doctor's office.

Ms. Shepherd opened the door before I had a chance to make a run for it.

"Norman, what are you doing here?"

"I, uh . . . didn't know if you needed anything," I said, holding out the bag.

Shepherd took the bag and invited me inside.

"You got me ice cream and spinach!"

She was smiling, but her eyes were watering.

"I'm sorry," I said. "I just found out and I went into town and then I went into Otto's."

"You went to Otto's for me? You're so sweet," she said.

"I wasn't able to make a more thoughtful purchase, because he was such a jerk," I said.

"Oh, I hate Otto," Ms. Shepherd said. "He's always following me around, staring at my ass."

"He followed me too. You think he was staring at my ass?" I said.

Ms. Shepherd laughed and unpacked the groceries, leaving the pints of ice cream on the counter.

"Mint chip and chocolate fudge. Excellent choices," she said.

Shepherd asked me if I'd had dinner. I told her about the overcooked roast beef and she insisted on heating up a plate of lasagna that her next-door neighbor had dropped off. People kept bringing her food. She made it seem like I was doing her a favor by eating it. She drank something with gin while I devoured the lasagna. It was really good. We never have lasagna, even though a guy named Mario cooks our food. I started to ask Shepherd how she was doing and all of that stuff, but Shepherd switched subjects immediately, explaining that she wanted to talk about anything but her mother.

Ms. Shepherd wanted to know if I'd asked Mel out yet. I told her I hadn't, that I wasn't even sure that Mel liked me. Shepherd asked if Mel had given me any signs. I don't know about signs, but she gave me a spork as a gift. I didn't tell Shepherd that the spork was a thank-you for helping her hack a pornographic website I helped create.

"She gave you a spork?" Ms. Shepherd said. "Like the things you get at those fried-chicken places?"

I keep it my backpack, so I showed it to Shepherd. She held the metal object up to the light and ran her fingers over the edges.

"She made it in metal arts," I said. "There's some good craftsmanship in there."

"It's a most unusual gift," said Shepherd, handing it back to me. "Is it practical?"

"I like it as a piece of art," I said. "But I think Mel really wants to bring it back into the mainstream and, honestly, I tried to eat with it the other day. The tines aren't really long enough for a good grip on solid food. Ultimately, it's inefficient as a fork, and who wants to be stabbed by a spoon?"

"I don't," said Shepherd. "But here's the good news. She likes you."

"I'm not so sure," I said.

Shepherd shook her head and went to the kitchen to make another drink.

"You don't make a spork for a guy you're not into," Shepherd said. "Oh, Norman, I wish you could see into the future. It would make everything you've been through worthwhile. But you'll see one day. It's kids like you who have a real life, a good life. The ones who thrive in high school, they're not the ones who rule the world. Just wait a few years; that's when your real life will begin. Promise me you won't become a rich asshole."

"I promise."

We ate ice cream and then it was time for me to leave. Shepherd was tipsy by then. I thought it was kind of beautiful, the way her eyes were half open and the loose sway of her walk. I walked down the steep hill and looked up at Shepherd, who waved from the door. I hoped that she was free now, that her real life had begun.

MS. WITT

Friday night, my mother, Greg, and I arrived together at Crestview Drive for the wake of Candace Woolsey, Claude's mother. I asked Greg about the late Frank Woolsey. He recalled a warm and inclusive school leader who regarded every student as a member of his family.

I searched the spacious room for familiar faces. Finn and Evelyn were sitting together on a divan, drinks in hand, whispering conspiratorially. Rupert was by the buffet, along with a few other faculty that I only knew by sight. It didn't come as a surprise that neither Martha or Keith scored an invite.

"I brought ice," I said.

"Ice," Claude said. "How incredibly thoughtful. People should bring ice more often." She accepted the cold bag and held it like a small child.

I introduced my mother, and Claude pointed out the table with drinks and refreshments. I followed her into the kitchen and helped her refill ice buckets and gather more bottles of booze. Claude was tipsy but in good spirits. She looked serene, in fact—a word I never would have applied to her before.

Hugh the bartender arrived. He and Claude exchanged a familiar glance. I left them alone and wandered the mid-century living room. A few guests introduced themselves as we plucked food from the deli spread. Most were neighbors. None of them seemed to know the deceased all that well.

Finn walked over to me as I was serving myself a mysterious cocktail from a pitcher. I wasn't trying to avoid him. I had come to accept that you can't really avoid people at Stonebridge.

"Hey," Finn said.

"Hey," I said. "Claude seems okay, I think. Is she?"

"Not sure. She never talked about it much, but it was a difficult relationship, and the final years were hard on her. Happy belated birthday, by the way."

"Thanks," I said. "And thank you for entertaining my father the other night."

Finn half-smiled, sank his hands into his pockets, and looked at the floor.

"When you invited me over, I thought *you* were inviting me over," he said.

"Did you?"

"It's wasn't an absurd conclusion, since you sent the text," Finn said, glancing up.

"I'm sorry," I said. "I didn't think about that."

"It's okay," Finn said. "Sometimes you want to know what you're walking into."

He made a good point.

"Hope he wasn't too obnoxious," I said.

"Nah, he was fine," Finn said.

Maybe Finn was a good liar after all.

"Dad said you were an excellent drinking companion."

I left Finn with an apology and roamed the room, looking for something to tell me about the woman who had just died. There were a few photos on the mantel but none of Candace. I spotted a few pictures of adolescent Claude and her stepfather, but nothing more recent. As I walked down the hallway to the bathroom, I noticed that the white walls had squares of bright paint, marking the recent removal of pictures.

Other than a toast made by a neighbor, it was a wake without a nod to the dead. There were no speeches or stories about Claude's mother. Not a single tear was shed that evening. I heard that Mrs. Woolsey had been cremated immediately, but no urn was on display. It felt more like a muted retirement party than a wake.

Claude was sloshed by the time we left. A statement of fact without any judgment. Everyone grieves in their own way, I reminded myself when I saw her retreat with the bartender to one of the bedrooms, where they remained for at least an hour.

I thought maybe I was the only one who'd noticed Claude's griefless behavior. But as we were leaving, my mother took my arm and whispered, "When I die, you better cry like the Danube. And then you get over it and move on."

GEMMA RUSSO

"Freedom smells like a keg of cold beer," Adam Westlake said, as the Ten gathered in the woods around the metallic drum of Pabst Blue Ribbon.

I'm not sure you can actually smell the beer when the keg hasn't yet been tapped, but there was something in the air that Friday before break. It felt like the end of a really long family dinner, where everyone is sick of one another and yet they can't quite bring themselves to leave.

When a holiday approached, Stonebridge students liked to play a game of chicken, waiting until the last second to decide whether to stay and be orphans over the break or go home. The decision was always based on the quality of the other orphans. When Emelia heard that Nick might stay, she canceled her trip home and contrived a story about her parents opting for a last-minute holiday to Copenhagen. Then, when Nick's itinerary changed, Emelia's parents suddenly abandoned their *Oslo* vacation and Emelia returned home to Manhattan, like she always does. Not one person called her on the discrepancy.

The only game I played was keeping my plans as secret as possible, because not having a home to go to on Thanksgiving isn't something you advertise. But I felt different about it this year, when I heard Ms. Witt was staying on and that Mel, deep in her Darkroom obsession, couldn't bring herself to go home until her work was done.

Norman was also on the orphan list, which I found odd, since I'd heard his mother lived in nearby Dover. I decided my chat with him could wait until the school cleared out. He might speak more freely if no one was around. There were also a few freshmen, sophomores, and juniors lingering behind, to whom I would pay absolutely no attention. Linny was going home to Maine. She asked me to feed her fish in her absence. I didn't even know she had a fish.

The Ten and their minions were having one final party before the student body dispersed across the globe. It was my hope that I'd have Dulcinea cracked wide open before anyone returned.

Adam had reserved Milton Studio because it was close to a good spot for the keg. Mick made the rounds, patting guys on the back and kissing girls' hands. Adam played attentive host, always asking if someone needed to have their drink refreshed. Although he never refreshed it himself. Nick smoked and practiced furrowing his brow. Hannah did the splits against the wall. Rachel Rose kept scribbling shit down in her notebook. Jack scratched himself, everywhere, with utter abandon. And Jonah and I delivered brilliant performances of two very casual acquaintances.

It was a crap party. Everyone started to feel like fellow

inmates rather than schoolmates. The room had thinned out by eleven. I don't know why I stayed. Maybe I was hoping that one of the drunk dickheads would accidentally spill some intel. When Gabe turned popping a zit into a performance piece, Mick decided we'd all had enough.

He flicked the lights on and off and said, "I'm calling it. Time of death: twelve-fourteen a.m. See you all after the break."

Tegan was back in our dorm already. I found her on her bed, laptop splayed, her earbuds drowning out her aggressive stabs at the keyboard. I figured she was messaging one of her second-tier friends. She still, however, managed to take note of my arrival.

"Did I miss anything?" she said.

"Nope. Where's Em?"

"With Nick," Tegan said.

"Of course," I said. "Remind me how long it's been?"

"If you count their first hookup," said Tegan, "and Em can't decide if she should count it or not, almost seven weeks."

Unlike some of her friends, Emelia doesn't offer blowjobs to members of the editorial board. She believes in romance and wants to fall in love. She doesn't kiss on the first date and has claimed that she waits three months before intercourse. But Nick was playing to win and Emelia couldn't see that he was playing at all.

"Seven weeks," I said. "So still at least five more to go?"

"I think Em's reassessing her timeline," Tegan said. "No one waits even two months anymore, let alone three."

Shit.

"I think I left something in the . . . uh—"

I couldn't be bothered finishing the lie. I had to at least try to throw a wrench in Emelia's date with Nick. I needed her to wait until after the break. By then we'd have the editors in the crosshairs.

I left Woolf Hall and followed the tree line back to Milton Studio, Nick's preferred hookup location. On the way, I heard hushed voices near the keg. I turned and walked deeper into the woods, following the voices. As I ducked behind a tree, I saw an odd group huddled around the barrel and soon realized that it was the dean, Ms. Witt, Coach Keith, and a woman I'd never seen before.

"I feel a little guilty," said Witt. "But Mick and Adam were just guzzling beer right in front of me. They weren't even pretending to drink coffee."

"We have to crack down every now and again," said the dean.

Keith tested the weight of the keg. "You want me to pour it out?"

"That would be the responsible thing to do," said the dean.

"That is very wasteful," said the other woman. She had a slight accent.

The other woman—older than Witt, but not old-old—picked up a plastic cup and filled it. I think it was the only cup left. She took a long sip and passed the cup to Keith, who drank and passed it to Witt. The woman with the accent refilled the cup and offered it to the dean. He hesitated and then took the cup.

The strange woman said, "Don't be pussy, Gregory. Drink."

I didn't know who she was, but I wanted to be her when I grew up.

Then I remembered why I'd gone out again. I thought maybe I could rescue Emelia before she boned New Nick. It was a stupid idea, I know. It's not like I had a plan for what I'd do when I reached them. I checked Milton Studio. It was empty. I headed over to Dick House, where the slick Brit had nabbed a single on the sophomore floor. There's always an extra room kept as a reserve in case of a roommate blowout that can't be managed or a new student who requires the privacy. There was once this kid with a deviated septum. On a summer night, you could hear him snore all the way to the north woods, some said.

I climbed the stairs to the third floor and strolled down the hallway. I paused outside Nick's door, listening. Then I heard the whine of door hinges behind me. I started to walk away, since I had no idea who was behind me. Cock-blockers are frowned upon at Stonebridge. I couldn't risk being cut from the Ten.

As I tried to make a quick escape, a male voice said my name. It was late and he was quiet enough to avoid waking the sleeping gents, so I figured it was plausible to pretend I didn't hear him.

I kept walking until I reached the north stairwell and opened the fire door. I heard the quick patter of feet behind me just before the door slammed shut. I remember being scared, which didn't make sense. I jogged up the stairs, thinking that wasn't the obvious move and that I'd elude my tail. I heard my name again. I recognized the voice.

Adam Westlake. That time I couldn't pretend.

"Where's the fire?" Adam said.

I stood on the landing and looked down at him.

"Hey, Adam. Didn't hear you."

"Where are you going? Got some freshman on the fourth you need to rough up?"

"I thought maybe the rooftop would be clear. I wanted to look at the stars."

"Great idea," said Adam, as he climbed the stairs.

I was committed now. It was a good lie. Dick House has roof access because someone paid for safety fencing after a student tried to fly sometime in the eighties.

"Can't sleep either?" Adam said.

"No," I said. "Tegan snores."

"Yeah," he said, like he had secondhand information on the subject. Maybe firsthand.

Adam gallantly opened the door for me. We stepped out into the cold air and took seats in the cheap lounge chairs they leave up there. I looked at the sky; it was an unusually clear night. There was a picture-perfect crescent moon surrounded by gleaming stars. It would have been lovely if Adam hadn't been there.

"I should come up here more often," he said. "This is nice."

Adam leaned over and bumped my shoulder like we were old, old friends.

"We don't talk anymore. Why is that?" he said.

"I don't know. You tell me."

"When you first came to Stonebridge, man, I thought we were going to be great pals. And then . . . did we grow apart, like an old married couple?"

"Maybe we don't have enough in common. You like khaki; I don't like khaki," I said.

"Bullshit," said Adam. "The problem is we have too much in common."

"No. I don't think so," I said, getting to my feet.

I was tired of playing his game, pretending I was his friend, his ally, his secret-keeper. That time Adam thought I saw something, I saw nothing. But later, I saw everything and I kept quiet about it. Maybe he wouldn't be acting so smug if I reminded him of his secret.

"Leaving so soon?" Adam said.

"Got to go; wouldn't want to be caught roaming Dick House after hours."

"I better get some shut-eye myself," Adam said, following me to the door of the stairwell.

I jogged down a flight ahead of him and said, "Later, Adam."

Before I hit the second landing, Adam said, "Hey, Gemma?"

I should have kept walking. But I didn't. I looked back.

"I was glad to see you threw your hat into the ring," Adam said.

He was practically radioactive with self-satisfaction.

"What ring?"

"You know, Gemma."

"I don't."

He whispered: *"Dulcinea."*

I could feel my heart pounding in my chest, my blood on fire. It took everything I had to keep my shell from cracking. I didn't move; I said nothing. I let one eyebrow slide up, just enough to express confusion.

"Your scores were excellent, by the way," he said.

"Good night, Adam," I said.

I felt like one of those bomb technicians who's called in to deactivate an explosive device on countdown mode. Only the device was me. I walked down the steps slowly and carefully as I heard Adam call out from above.

"Congratulations."

PART III
THE ARMY

It is fatal to enter any war without the will to win it.
GENERAL DOUGLAS MACARTHUR

MS. WITT

Memory and reality are like cousins. Best-case scenario, they're first cousins. But sometimes they're the kind of cousins who can marry.

Thanksgiving at Stonebridge might be my one solidly good memory of my short tenure there. It's telling that my fondest recollection occurred when most of the student body was absent.

In retrospect, it was the calm before the category 5 hurricane.

It was the last week before everything went to shit.

From the south-facing window of my new apartment, I watched the students file through Fleming Square, limping sideways with the weight of their suitcases. Some students were accompanied by parents, a few met cabs at the security gate, and others wheeled their own luggage off to destinations unknown.

I remember waiting around on Saturday morning for my mother to spontaneously arrive and force me on a three-to-eight-mile hike. By noon she hadn't shown up, so I got dressed and took a leisurely stroll around the deserted campus.

When I reached the entry to the trail system, I stood at the three-pronged fork, trying to decide between Austen, Burns, or Hardy Trail. I wasn't even sure I wanted to go for a hike. As I attempted to decipher my own inclination, I heard the rumble of Rupert's ATV. Before I knew it, he was idling next to me.

"Alex, Alex."

"Hi, Rupert."

I hadn't seen Rupert since I'd discovered his secret identity.

"Good to see you, Ms. Witt. I heard you got flooded out of the cottage."

"I did. But I'm settled now," I said.

I remember looking at the trailheads, trying to decide whether I wanted to go for a hike at all.

"You look lost, Ms. Witt," he said.

"I'm not lost. I just can't decide which trail to take."

"Indecision plagues all of us. What do I want, what do I need, what do I hope for out of life?"

"Right," I said. "Something like that."

Rupert nodded knowingly and said, "Which trail is speaking to you?"

I considered the three trailheads.

"None of them," I said.

Then I felt sad and aimless.

"What do you want to do right this second?" Rupert said. "Don't think. Just answer the question."

"I want to take that thing for a spin," I said, pointing at his ATV.

Rupert tilted his head, considered the request, and promptly dismounted.

"Hop on," he said.

I climbed on board. Rupert showed me the throttle and the brake and made sure the belt buckle was secure.

"I got three rules for you. You take the Burns loop, stay on the dirt the whole time, and never go more than twenty miles an hour. Got it? Got it?"

"I got it," I said, thrumming the engine.

I hit the gas pedal. It was sensitive. The vehicle lurched and slowed until I got the feel for it. The terrain was bumpy and disorienting and far more satisfying than any predictably thrilling ride at an amusement park. I followed the loop around once and circled back to Rupert. *One more time,* I asked with pleading eyes and a raised index finger. I saw Keith jog over to Rupert. They were talking during my second loop. Then Keith jogged away.

When I closed the second loop, Rupert was giving me one of those two-armed waves off the road like you see at NASCAR events. This time I slowed without giving myself whiplash. Rupert leaned over the gears and turned off the engine.

"Coach Keith just gave me a talking-to. He thinks you should be wearing a helmet."

"He should mind his own business," I said.

"Nah. He made a good point. I have a nephew. Many years ago he fell off his bike, got a head injury. Every time I see him he keeps talking about the Lynn Swann catch in Super Bowl Ten. I'm glad he gets to live a great moment over and over, but that's his only moment. You're young. You should have many moments. Now, an old fart like me, I like feeling the wind in my hair."

I climbed off the ATV and thanked Rupert for the experience.

"My pleasure," Rupert said. "Enjoy the good weather while it lasts. Snow will be here before you know it. Like, maybe this weekend."

There was no chance of snow that weekend. But I did admire Rupert's ability to bend the concrete world to his will.

I followed Stoker Lane back to the square. As far as I looked, I couldn't see another soul. The unpopulated campus looked as incongruous as a deserted shopping mall. Back at my apartment, I took a shower and then a nap.

It was sunset when I was finally awakened by someone knocking on the door. I staggered over groggily and opened it, expecting to see my mother.

Coach Keith walked past me without a word and drew open the curtain covering the window facing east into the woods. The light inside turned the glass into a mirror, making it impossible to see the landscape. He flicked off the closest lamp; our reflections vanished.

Keith pointed to a location in the distance.

Far off, I could see a dark figure in motion. It looked like someone swinging a baseball bat, only the bat was hitting a tree. It wasn't until the tree began to list that I realized the bat was an ax. I looked closer, framing my eyes up against the glass. The person wielding the ax was Gemma.

"I liked that tree," Keith said.

I stepped into my slippers and coat and ran down the stairs, out the back door, and across the field. As I approached, I could hear the hard labor of Gemma's breaths and the thwack of her final swing. The tree sagged beyond repair; Gemma gave it the killing blow with one final side kick. She let the ax fall at her feet, spent from exhaustion.

I said her name.

Gemma turned to me, but her gaze remained unfocused.

"Why did you do that?" I said.

"Because I had to kill something."

GEMMA RUSSO

My anger felt immense and mythical. It felt like I could breathe fire and torch the school, or at least burn a few of the editors to a crisp. It was the kind of anger that makes the world look like an ugly kaleidoscope, splintered into so many pieces you don't know what you're looking at anymore.

Ms. Witt took the ax away, after I was done, when the tree lay dead on the ground.

Later I remembered that it was Witt's mother who gave me the ax. Nastya was her name. I saw her last night drinking from our keg and figured out who she was. She was the cruel muse the boys had been talking about.

I had been running wind sprints up Scott Hill, trying to purge my rage or at least quiet it enough to make clear, calculated decisions. Running didn't help. I slowed down at the end of the trailhead. I felt the choke of impending tears in my throat. I let out a scream. It felt like sandpaper on my vocal cords. I thought I was alone. Then I saw her.

I should have been embarrassed. If it were anyone else, I would have been. But she looked at me as if my wails were a perfectly normal mode of expression, like a smile or a laugh.

"Follow me," she said.

I followed her around the back of campus to Rupert's toolshed. She opened the door, removed an ax, and trudged through the grounds until she found a small birch tree and regarded the haggard branches. She picked at the bark and nodded with satisfaction. Then she gave me the ax.

"Here. This tree is whatever makes you scream. Chop it down and then you will feel better."

She left me to it.

When I was done, Alex brought me into her apartment and made me a cup of tea. I told her what had happened. I left out Adam's name. I can't say why. I wasn't protecting him. Maybe I was protecting myself; maybe I had envisioned a silent counterattack and wanted to maintain plausible deniability.

"Why do I feel this way? I didn't do anything and I feel . . . ashamed."

"Shame is cunning," Ms. Witt said. "Even if the feeling doesn't come from a rational place, it sticks. But that doesn't mean it's real."

I was so angry I started crying. And then I got angrier because I was crying.

"This is so embarrassing," I said.

"Why?"

"Because crying is weak," I said.

"Why? Because girls cry more than boys?"

I wasn't in the mood for a lecture on gender stereotypes. I closed my eyes and took a few breaths until the tears stopped.

"I'm fine now," I said. "All done."

"You keep tamping down emotions, they'll find another way to get out," Witt said. "Be careful. Don't make any impulsive moves. Be clear on what you want."

What did I want? I wanted to know why someone had entered my name in the contest. Was it a warning to me or to Jonah? I knew it wasn't him. He had no motive, nothing to prove, and nothing to gain. His standing at Stonebridge was cemented early on by the sexual legend of his older brother, Jason, the Wilt Chamberlain of Stonebridge. He had been with so many girls, rumor had it, he kept a spreadsheet of them, ranking their looks, evaluating their sexual performance, checking off the number of encounters, and highlighting areas that needed improvement. He could take an entire human being and reduce her to five columns.

But Jonah was not his brother. Jonah had a girlfriend at Wiley Academy for his first year at Stonebridge, while he rose up the social hierarchy under the auspices of his sibling. Jonah and what'shername broke up before sophomore year, which he kept to himself. He found it easier to stay out of the fray if he could use his relationship as a foil. By the time Jason graduated, Jonah was fully embedded as an editor, even though it was common knowledge that he never contributed to the vile union that was the Darkroom posse.

Jonah had it easy. He was good at things—just about every team sport, academics, even metal arts. And he knew how to get along with everyone without distancing himself from the power players. I always figured he was a mediocre student until I accidentally saw his report card. When I accused him of being a secret slummer, he just shrugged. That was the one time I realized he had a game, his own game. He was like the player who always suited up but never got on the field. No one could ever blame him for losing.

I refused to be honest with myself about how he made me feel. I never wore that devil pod, but I kept it in my pocket. I would sometimes feel comforted by the sharp wings and let the hollowed-out back leave a stamp on my thumb.

Jonah and I used to have a "don't ask, don't tell" policy when it came to the Darkroom. I never asked him to snitch on his friends, and he'd never tell anyone about us. That was fine for a while. But the lines were now drawn. Anyone who peacefully coexisted with the editors was an enemy of mine. It was time for Jonah to pick a side. I went to Jonah's room and knocked on the door. I can't remember the last time I'd done that. It must have been summer.

It was late. I'd woken him. Jonah was so alarmed by my sudden appearance, all he could manage was *hey.* I entered the room and shut the door behind me.

"What's up?" he said.

"I want to know everything there is to know about the Dulcinea contest. I want to see how it's scored. Is it like a tournament with brackets, girls going literally 'head to head,' or are there score sheets? Are we graded on a bell curve or with a point system? And I want to know who entered my name."

Jonah's jaw clenched and his eyes narrowed in anger. He was more surprised than I was and almost as angry.

"I never look at the Darkroom anymore. Fuck, I will kill him."

"Kill who?"

"I don't know! Whoever put your name up," he said.

"Will you get me the information?"

"I'll find out what I can and—"

"I just want information. Don't defend my honor. Don't tip them off. It needs to be business as usual. Got it?"

"Yeah. Got it."

"You haven't told anyone about us, right?"

"What would I tell them? That I'm your bitch? Yeah, I'd just as soon keep that to myself."

I moved toward him. It was the first time he'd ever retreated from me. But it was a small room; there wasn't far to go. He looked sad and sweet. And I had always liked him. But I had my own game, my own set of rules that I needed in order to survive. In that moment, when the rules seemed more important than ever, I threw them out the window. I backed Jonah against the wall and kissed him on the lips. Even then he had the faint taste of those stupid cherry jawbreakers.

NORMAN CROWLEY

My mother wasn't even a little bit sad when I told her I wasn't coming home for Thanksgiving. She'd met a guy online. His name was Ron. Things were getting serious. She said something about me meeting him sometime but it was too soon. After she started fishing around about my plans, asking whether I'd want to go to Dad's or not, I knew I could stay at Stonebridge. Without Ron, she'd have had an aneurysm if I'd chosen to spend Thanksgiving with my father and his new girlfriend.

I'd only spent a holiday at Stonebridge once before, during spring break my sophomore year. It was in the middle of my parents' divorce, when they were contemplating a reconciliation and going to therapy three times a week. My mother thought they needed "alone time." I think sex, or not having sex, was a big reason for their breakup—at least that's what my dad said. I was happy to stay away that week. I was even happier that my father never mentioned their sex troubles again.

I expected to be lonely Thanksgiving week, but I wasn't.

It was kind of great, other than that really awful dinner. And most people hate Thanksgiving anyway. My point is, I wasn't lonely. Come to think of it, I hardly had any time to myself.

Monday morning, I'd found a folded scrap of paper slipped under my door.

MILTON STUDIO. 9:00 A.M. SHARP.

It was eight-forty. I only had time for a quick shower and to grab a bite from Dahl. Jonah was sitting alone, eating cereal. He looked up and beckoned me with a nod.

"I've got to go," I said, separating a banana from its bunch. "I have a—uh . . ."

I'm not a good liar.

"Hoops, later?" Jonah said.

I'm not a hoops player.

"Tennis and we're on," I said.

I'm not a tennis player either, but I've found I get less beat up in games that don't involve personal contact. Jonah and I agreed to meet at two. I was now late for whatever was happening at Milton. Mel shouldn't have expected me to show up at a specific time without prior warning. Yeah, I deduced it was Mel when I read the note. There weren't any other credible options. I finished the banana on my way to the studio. I was still hungry.

Mel sat at a drafting table, papers splayed out in front of her.

"You're late," she said.

"If you wanted me to be here earlier, you should have given me more warning."

"You would have been here earlier if you didn't stop to get that banana from the dining hall."

I was still holding the peel. Mel isn't Big Brother. Not yet, at least.

"I was hungry," I said.

"I made you breakfast," Mel said, pointing at a cup of coffee and a paper bag sitting atop a file cabinet.

The coffee was lukewarm, but I definitely needed coffee for this. Inside the bag were a sandwich, an apple, and a bag of Mario's Mix, which is an ever-changing "trail mix" based on dry to semidry pantry items that are about to expire.

"Have a seat," Mel said, pointing at the chair facing her on the right side of the desk. It looked like the seat where witnesses give their statements in a police station.

I removed the sandwich from the bag. It was cut in quarters. I always cut my sandwich in quarters. I smelled peanut butter. I took a bite. Something chewy and sweet got stuck in my teeth. I asked Mel what kind of sandwich it was. Mel told me it was a peanut butter and prune sandwich. I asked her why she didn't just use jelly, like a normal person, and she said that there were too many different jelly/jam varieties and she had no idea what I liked. Peanut butter and prune was something her grandmother made, and she thought I should have a more open mind.

"Mel, what do you want?"

"Right," she said. "Let's get straight to business. Gabriel Smythe is a douchebag and, for a guy who fancies himself a class clown, decidedly unfunny. Don't you agree?"

"I would agree," I said, removing the smashed prune from my sandwich.

"So why would Jenna Trevor and Naomi Klein ever hook up with him? Plus, they're best friends. Isn't that gross?"

Mel had certainly made the most of her time inside the Darkroom.

"Gabe's dad runs Lofton Arena. He can get tickets to any show there," I said.

"Right. Fucking Jonas Brothers were there last year," Mel said, shaking her head in disbelief. "Little-known fact: I actually threw up the first time I heard them."

"Because of their music?" I said.

"I also had the flu, but still," Mel said.

"Got it," I said. "So you cracked the code?"

Mel snorted/laughed.

"It's hardly rocket science. The first number is the school level, and the last digits are a numeric representation of the alphabet. To be honest, Norman, I was hoping it would be more complicated. Not even a Caesar cipher?"

"I had to keep it simple for those pinheads. You wouldn't believe how challenging they found that numeric cipher."

I should have kept my mouth shut instead of defending my codes.

Mel gave me one of those suspicious sidelong looks.

"I don't even look inside the Darkroom, if I can help it," I said.

"No," Mel said. "You just keep it operational. Let's talk about the birds. I think I've got it, but let me run it by you just to be sure. You can start out as one kind of bird and turn into another. I've seen sparrows turn into loons and owls turn into hawks. What's that about?"

"A sparrow is young and pretty, or that's what they think at first, before they hook up. Then something happens and they see another side."

"So the loons are the crazy ones and the hawks are mean? And owls are nerds or something?"

I had just taken a bite of the sandwich, so I nodded my reply. She was close enough. Owls could be nerds. Or sometimes they were virgin hawks. I wasn't prepared to scrutinize the nomenclature with her. Answering her questions took enough out of me.

Mel consulted the vast array of documents in front of her. She had that puzzled look she gets, which is a combo of anger and confusion. But it's really adorable. Then I felt guilty because I had to question whether I was helping her because I liked her or because I thought it was the right thing to do. And then I felt uncomfortable because I remembered reading something that Mick wrote about her last year.

"I better get back," I said, standing up.

"Sit down," Mel said.

I sat down. Maybe I sat down because I wanted to help. Or I sat down because I'm always doing what other people tell me to do. I really don't know.

"First of all," Mel said, chewing on the end of her pen, "most of the really popular girls, the girls you'd think would be plastered all over the Darkroom, are nowhere in sight.

Where are Rachel Rose, Hannah Rexall, Emelia Laird? Rachel, I'm guessing, would be 4Loon1818. Hannah may be 4Hawk818, and Emelia would have to be 4Sparrow512. But they're not here."

"You can't tell anyone I'm helping you."

"I won't, Norman. You have my word. The site has a lot of portals, just numbered doors, password protected. What's behind those doors?"

"Most of them are dummies. If you try to break in, they'll kick you out of the system."

"Why?"

"It was practice, that's all," I said. "I was just working on cybersecurity measures."

"So there's nothing behind any of the doors?"

"They're all dead ends, except thirteen," I said.

"Thirteen? Why that number?"

"I don't know. It was always behind door thirteen. It's an old reference that I've never figured out," I said.

"Everything I'm looking for is behind that door?"

"Are you sure you want to see it?" I said.

"That's the whole point, Norman. The Dulcinea Award. So it's door number thirteen I need to get into, right?"

I nodded.

"What kind of bird am I?" she said. "An owl? I think I'm an owl."

"No," I said. "There's only one kind of bird behind that door."

MS. WITT

On the Tuesday before Thanksgiving, Greg had a cocktail/mocktail party at his home for the senior orphans and the few members of staff who couldn't find an excuse not to attend. Claude was out for obvious reasons; Finn was bogged down with revisions; Rupert and Mario were in charge of the freshman, sophomore, and junior orphans; and Primm was on vacation.

It was a motley crew that night. Greg in his tweed, my mother in a red cheongsam that never fails to spark flattery by anyone who has seen her in it fewer than five times. *Buy another dress* is generally what I say to my mother when I see her. Coach Keith wore his best corduroy trousers and a stretched-out brown cardigan with visible moth holes.

"Duuude," Gemma said, sticking her finger through one of the holes, "the moths have won."

The seniors took full advantage of the relaxed dress code to wear whatever suited their whim. Gemma wore leather pants and a black top with spaghetti straps, revealing the edge of a snake tattoo just below her shoulder blade. Mel had on a black skirt, boots, and a Ramones T-shirt, with a navy-blue velvet blazer. Norman wore regular clothes but tucked in his shirt for once. Jonah was in a well-tailored blue suit, no tie.

I heard Mel ask Jonah if he was going to a bar mitzvah later. Jonah responded with *thank you.*

That night, Gemma, Mel, Norman, and Jonah—a configuration I had never seen before—huddled together like they'd been friends their entire lives.

My mother and Greg had a similar ease with each other. A small part of me wished it were more than a friendship, but I knew that wasn't the case.

I began hunting through Greg's cupboards looking for wine that wasn't mulled. Eventually, I located a jug of generic vodka that had my mother's name written on it. Literally. I suspect it was from an abundant liquor stash that my folks had divvied up after the divorce. As I was pouring a shot, Coach Keith walked in and asked if he could use my kitchen the next morning. I asked why he didn't use his own kitchen and he explained that he didn't have a kitchen or a home, which was news to me. He apparently makes his home wherever it's most convenient and cheap. He hadn't had a permanent residence in ten years. When I asked why, he explained that he saves a lot of money on rent. I asked where that money went.

"You're getting really hung up on this," he said.

"It's unusual," I said. "How long do you think you can sustain this semi-nomadic existence?"

"Hey, Alex. I've answered about ten questions so far. Will you answer my *one* question?" he said.

"Sure. What was it again?"

"Can I use your kitchen?"

"Of course," I said. "As long as I can take half credit for whatever you're making."

The students left the cocktail/mocktail party early because it was filled with boring adults and they had a better shot at real booze back at their dorms. Even I began to eye my jacket on the coat rack. I looked at the clock and decided that two hours was a proper showing and planned my escape.

The next thing I knew, my mother, Greg, and Coach Keith had surrounded me. I don't remember how the conversation had begun, but Greg was rattling off Coach Keith's varied school responsibilities for my mother's benefit: football, basketball, lacrosse, wrestling, baking (I didn't even know there was a baking class), botany—

"I water the plants," said Keith. "And I have two students who help me water the plants. I don't have a degree in botany or even an above-average green thumb."

Greg ignored Keith and continued: "I had hoped we would be able to add fencing to our extracurricular activities. You can't imagine how disappointed I was when Alex told me she never learned. I could have sworn I saw a photo of you in uniform years ago."

"It was probably a Halloween costume," I said.

"I'm surprised that you didn't insist, Nastya. That's so unlike you," Greg said.

My mother smiled and frowned simultaneously. She paused long enough to set my nerves on edge.

"I tried," my mother said. "But the weapons scared her so much. She would cry and cry before every lesson. I make her watch Errol Flynn, thinking he will teach her to love swordplay. I mean, who doesn't like Errol Flynn?"

Mentioning Errol Flynn was an overt challenge. My mother *loathed* Flynn. If an old swashbuckling film was on TV, she'd slander his image until you changed the channel.

Fucking fraud, asshole, she'd shout at the set.

Her hate was feral, but she never hinted at its origin.

Greg laughed and said, "Who doesn't love Errol Flynn?"

"Errol Flynn was a piece of shit," said Keith.

My mother kept quiet, but I could tell that Keith had shot up a few rungs in my mother's estimation.

Greg ignored Keith's hostile remark about the beloved swashbuckler and said, "Well, we're glad to have Alex, whether she fences or not. Sometimes the apple falls off the tree and rolls down a very steep hill."

"Yes, that apple has mind of its own," my mother said with a smile that suggested I was her bitch for the rest of the week.

GEMMA RUSSO

Sparrows, loons, hawks, and owls.

It was like the Hogwarts Sorting Hat. Each girl who had the honor of a Darkroom mention was first thrown into one of those four categories. The rough equivalents were virgin, crazy, bitch, and nerd. But the moment a girl blew one of the guys with access to the Darkroom, she became a swallow and was entered into the Dulcinea contest, all details hidden behind door number thirteen. Just about any male Stoner had access to the main Darkroom. But not just anyone could enter a name in the Dulcinea contest. The judges were carefully vetted by the editors.

Maybe if Mel had had more time, she could have broken past the Dulcinea firewall on her own, but there wasn't time. I'd told Mel that I knew she was working with Norman and that it was time we set up a meet. At first Mel denied even knowing Norman. I asked her why she was hanging with him at Mo's. That really freaked her out. I told her that Linny had been doing some amateur spying. She relaxed. Then I told Mel that I had my own double agent. I didn't think Jonah would like that moniker, but I took a gamble that no one would bring it up.

We'd arranged for the four of us to meet in Milton Studio on Tuesday afternoon, before the dean's thing. We all sat around the desk, in silence. Like an international summit without the translators. Mel took the initiative to break the ice.

"Do you want to be on the right side of history or the wrong side?" Mel said.

"The right side, I guess," Jonah said. "Does anybody say, *Yeah, I'll take the wrong side*?"

"Hitler, Stalin, Pol Pot," Mel flatly replied.

"I'm sure Hitler thought he was on the right side of history," Jonah said.

I should have had a brief conference with Mel before the meeting. It's unwise to alienate new recruits. Norman, I noticed, remained quiet, picking at a hangnail.

"It's weird how easily you can relate to mass murderers," Mel said to Jonah.

"I don't relate to them. I'm just saying—" Jonah said.

"Okay," I said, invoking Witt's standard conversation ender. "We need your help."

"More help?" Norman said sheepishly.

His hangnail was now bleeding.

"I told you to leave it, Norman. You need to put some Neosporin on that," Mel said.

"Give us Dulcinea—all of the material related to it. I promise it won't come back to you," I said.

"Do you know what they'll do to him if they find out?" Jonah said.

"They won't find out," I said. "And if they do, we'll say I hacked it. It'll all be on me."

"Like anyone is going to believe that," Mel mumbled.

I looked at Norman and waited.

"Norman?"

"I'll do it," Norman said, shoulders slumping.

It looked like he was melting in front of my eyes.

"When?" asked Mel.

"After the party," he said, checking his watch. "We have to go."

I was jumping out of my skin at that stupid cocktail party. We were only allowed mocktails, and I was terrified Norman might change his mind while we were not imbibing.

"If you ask Norman one more time if *he's still cool,* he's going to have a nervous breakdown," Jonah said.

We got out of Byron Manor as soon as we could. Mel and I waited impatiently in my office for word from Norman.

Two very long hours later, I received an email with a large file attachment from some guy named Magnus Pym. Mel told me it was Norman. I asked her why the hell Norman was going by the name Magnus Pym, and Mel said that Magnus was a double agent in a book and not to worry about it. Mel opened the file.

We were both huddled over the screen, reading through the entries at the same time. I didn't see it at first: 4Swallow135. Mel gasped and said a lot of cuss words, kind of like she was listing every one she knew from memory.

"Do you need to see a doctor?" I said.

"No—4Swallow135 is me," Mel said.

I'd seen angry Mel before. This Mel was about to turn green and split out of her clothes. I stepped aside and let her have some privacy as she went over the material.

"Swallow, swallow, swallow," Mel said. "Oh my God. It's so disgusting. And obvious, and stupid. And—disgusting. Oh, and I didn't swallow, I'll have you know."

"Breathe, Mel. Breathe. Please," I said.

"I understand murderers now. I never understood them before. I one hundred percent get it," she said.

I took Mel outside. We found a runty tree that looked like it had some kind of root rot. I gave her an ax and told her to chop it down.

It was almost 11:00 p.m. when Mel and I finished examining five years' worth of Dulcinea entrants. I even found my own scorecard, the one Adam had mentioned.

Bagman2 submits 4Swallow718 for consideration:
Technique: 7 (Excellent, but inconsistent, suction)
Artistry: 8 (Interesting assist with hands. Has had some practice)
Effort: 7 (Got the feeling she wasn't using her full potential)
Finish: 8 (Satisfying and professional)

I thought I'd be angrier, but having the evidence there, knowing that now I could take action, made it so much easier. It also helped that my entry was fake. I knew Bagman was the nickname for Jonah's brother. Bagman2, I suspected, was intended to point the finger at Jonah.

"If mine is fake, maybe some of the others are," I said, hoping to offer Mel a lie she could tell herself.

"No," Mel said. "Mine is real."

"How do you know?"

"I did accidentally bite him."

I didn't probe for details, even though I wouldn't have minded some. Breaking into the Darkroom was a cheap thrill. But this was different. It was private. It was ugly. It made you look at everyone you thought you knew in a different light.

"This is bigger than I thought it was," I said. "I see forty-seven unique entrants and one hundred thirty-four score sheets. I don't even want to think about the math on that."

Mel curled up into a ball on the couch and covered her eyes with her hoodie.

"There are fewer than two hundred girls at Stonebridge, which means around twenty-five percent of us are participating in this thing. And it's probably over fifty percent in the senior class alone," said Mel. "I feel sick."

"Me too."

"I'm too tired to chop down another tree," she said.

I gathered all of the paperwork and threw Mel's laptop into her bag.

"Let's go," I said, kicking her foot. "We need help."

MS. WITT

My father left a message while I was at Greg's house. Dad insisted that I return his call that night, no matter how late I got in. I called. Dad had obviously figured out that my mother was at Stonebridge with me. He wouldn't have minded, if Greta hadn't left him after discovering his new mistress, or his mistress hadn't gone home to her mommy for Thanksgiving.

There was dead silence as my father waited for me to proffer an invitation.

"Did you get that book yet?" I said.

"I did."

"Can you send it to me?" I said.

Silence.

"Yes. I will put it in the mail posthaste."

"Thanks, Dad. And, if I don't talk to you before then, happy Thanksgiving."

It was 9:00 p.m. when Mom dropped by my apartment. She made tea and poured brandy in it. I was already drunk from the neat vodka at the cocktail party. But we kept going.

"I was good at keeping your secret, no?" said my mother.

"Very good. Thank you."

She cradled my face in her hands and smiled.

"I love you," she said.

"I love you too," I said.

"You know who I just saw in the bathhouse?" said my mom. "The tan man. You should have sex with him."

"The only reason you approve of him is because he hates Errol Flynn."

"No. Other reasons. Besides, if you don't have sex with right person, you will have sex with wrong one."

Too late, I thought.

My doorbell rang. It was a welcome interruption to the conversation.

Mel and Gemma stood outside. Mel carried her laptop and Gemma had a stack of papers spilling out of a large file folder. They both looked frazzled and furious.

"What's going on?" I said.

"We've seen it all," said Gemma.

"I've seen too much," said Mel.

It was surprising how quickly the girls opened up to my mother. Gemma told her the entire story of the Darkroom and the Dulcinea Award. She also reviewed the complete bird lexicon.

My mother was as baffled as I was by the ubiquity of blowjobs as an introductory sexual act.

"I don't understand," said Mom. "Don't girls give hand jobs anymore? Much less effort required."

"The blowjob is the new hand job," I said.

"Really?" said Mom. "How many girls are entered in the contest? And what do they get—money?"

"Most girls don't even know there is a contest," Gemma said.

"If you don't want to do something, why do you do it?" said my mom.

"There's this thing the boys do," Mel said. "They make it seem like there's something wrong with you if you don't do it. So, you're hanging out with some guy you like. You're kissing and stuff and the next thing you know, he's unzipped his fly. And you're like, what happened? But you don't say that because it's awkward and—and you're already not thinking clearly, because you like the person and everything you've done so far feels good. You don't want to ruin the mood, so you do it. And while you're doing it, you're not feeling anything at all, and you're telling yourself it's not a big deal. But then, later, you feel something. You feel wrong, like dirty and used, and stupid. And you wonder what happened to you, the *you* who has a backbone."

"I need another drink," I said.

"Me too," said my mother.

Me too, said Gemma and Mel. My mother would have given them both a shot of bourbon, but I nixed that idea when I saw her pull two more glasses from the cabinet. Gemma showed us a few samples of the scoring system but wouldn't relinquish the entire stack of entrants.

"Swallows were spies, right?" said my mother, as she gazed down at the page.

"Spies? What do you mean?" Mel said, perking up.

"The Russians called female spies 'swallows' and male spies 'ravens' in the Cold War," I said.

"See, Mel. You're a spy. That's all," said Gemma.

"I would cut off the penis of any man who talk about me like this," said my mother, as she gazed down at a score sheet. "You know what I would like to see? A *bad*-blowjob contest. That would teach them."

Gemma and Mel, who had seemed so lost, suddenly looked up at Mom like she was their new queen.

GEMMA RUSSO

Ms. Witt made us promise not to castrate anyone.

They were drunk, Witt and her mother. And they were laughing—like, really laughing. I wondered if that was what happy families looked like. Witt rolled her eyes and looked embarrassed, often. But there was so much love there it was hard not to feel jealous. I'm sure I saw my mother laugh now and again, but I couldn't remember the sound of it.

Mel was so ashamed. I just wanted to take her mind off things.

I kept asking Nastya for advice. Whatever she suggested, Ms. Witt objected to it.

"You must have bad-blowjob contest," said Nastya.

"I heartily discourage oral sex outside of a committed, mutually respectful relationship," Witt said. "Even if the goal is to subvert the desire."

Nastya waved her hand dismissively. "Of course, of course. We had long talk about blowjobs, remember?"

"I remember," Witt said, blushing. Her eyes time-traveled back to the memory. "I think it was around the time of the Monica

Lewinsky scandal. Do you remember Monica Lewinsky?"

"Yes," said Mel. "She had relations with President Clinton. Also, something about her dress?"

Mel was finally emerging from her dark place; I could feel her cloud of shame lifting.

"It was a vicious public shaming," said Witt.

"She never had intercourse with him," my mother said. "She just give him blowjobs. I try to explain to my daughter that a blowjob-only relationship is not healthy relationship, and so Alex asks me when, in the relationship, you give a blowjob."

"Did you give your daughter the blowchart?" I asked.

Nastya turned to Witt for translation.

"I made a flowchart to help them decide whether they should perform oral sex or not," said Witt.

"Why do you need a chart?" Nastya said.

"It's really cool. You need to see it," Mel said.

Mel showed Nastya the picture of the blowchart on her phone, but the image was too small to make out the details. I asked for a pen and paper and we duplicated it for Witt's mom. When we were done, Nastya nodded.

"I see now. Okay, I get it.

"This is good, but you are missing a few questions," Nastya said, as she grabbed a red pen.

MR. FORD

I regretted staying at Stonebridge over break. It was so goddamn lonely. I'd thought I might hear from Alex, but it seemed like whenever I looked out my window or ventured into the common areas, she was with *Keith*. Claude was completely AWOL. She hadn't responded to a single one of my texts since the wake. I figured she was rolling around in her mother's jewels. I left her a voicemail to see if she wanted to grab dinner or if she needed anything. Mostly I wanted to be sure she hadn't fallen down a rabbit hole of unexpected grief. When I hadn't heard from her by Wednesday night, I sent another text.

Finn: u okay?

Claude: No.

I drove straight to her house. I knocked a few times and rang the bell. I tried the door; it was open.

The house had been trashed, ransacked like in a police search. Every cabinet ajar, drawers on the floor, clothes, knickknacks, the detritus of life spilling out everywhere. There was hardly a path to walk from the entry through the hallway to the kitchen without stepping on a garment or a toppled piece of furniture. The kitchen stank of trash and open bottles of booze. The rotting hors d'oeuvres trays from the wake rested on the island.

I called out her name. She didn't answer. I walked down the hallway, peering in bedrooms that were in comparable states of disarray. I briefly checked Claude's bedroom, even though I knew she would take ownership of the master as soon as she could. I continued down the hall. I didn't bother to knock. The door was open.

The room was dark, but the moon shone a bright light through the wall-to-wall windows. Claude lay under the gold duvet of that absurd bed. Her eyes were open with a disturbingly fixed gaze on the night sky. I don't think she blinked once. If it weren't for the soft billow of the bedding, I might have thought she was dead.

I sat down next to her.

"Claude?" I said.

She began to cry.

"Tell me what's wrong."

The words came slowly, between sobs and hiccups, weighed down by whatever drugs or booze she had recently consumed.

"She . . . gave . . . me . . . nothing. Nothing."

"I'm so sorry," I said, stroking her hair, trying to calm her.

I knew she had been counting on the house. But her reaction felt intemperate.

"No. No. You don't understand," she said.

"What don't I understand?"

"This house was *mine,*" she said. "My stepfather would have wanted me to have it."

She cried and then let out a terrifying wail.

"Claude, stop," I shouted.

"You don't understand," she repeated. "I earned this house. I worked for this house. I was more of a wife to him than my mother ever was."

I knew Claude was fucked up. I had no idea how fucked up. Even as I felt the cold chill of her confession, I wondered if I still had time to get this detail into my book.

I was fucked up too.

NORMAN CROWLEY

Jonah had a bunch of stale weed his brother had given him. He decided that the perfect time to smoke it was an hour before the dean's Thanksgiving dinner. He was certain it would make the food taste good or at least better. I still don't understand why we went to the dean's house. The orphans usually eat separately in Dahl. I figured it had something to do with Gemma's weird thing with Stinson, but I didn't ask. I had other problems.

I was jacked up on nerves. We had given Gemma and Mel the keys to the depraved kingdom. One false step and they could destroy us. No, not us, not Jonah; he'd somehow make it through. But I'd be finished, filleted like a fresh sardine and spread on a cracker. I don't like sardines, but I suddenly wanted to have one. Jonah told me to chill out when I couldn't stop biting my nails. I smoked more weed, forgetting that weed makes me paranoid and hyperaware.

On the way to Byron Manor, I could have sworn this bird was following us. I kept looking over my shoulder. I think I told it to shut up.

"Who are you talking to, Norman?"

"The bird," I said.

I couldn't believe how calm Jonah was.

"Talk as little as possible in there, okay?" he said.

Dean Stinson shook my hand extra hard. And Ms. Witt kept glancing at me with this weird look, like she knew everything written in the Darkroom and thought I was a disgusting pervert. The refrigerator was making a gurgling sound. First I thought it was Jonah's stomach. Then I thought it was the oven, and I went into the kitchen to investigate.

I was thirsty. I filled a glass with tap water. I drank it and then another. It seemed impossible to consume enough water to quench my thirst. Coach Keith came up behind me, carrying a bunch of pies. He put them on the counter and looked my way.

"Relax, Norman," he said. "No one knows."

No one knows what? I thought.

Ms. Witt's parents were there. I don't know why. Her mom's name was Nastya. Her dad was that famous writer who had two names and I couldn't remember which one was real. I heard a really weird conversation between Witt's mom and dad. It was just a few whispers as Nastya left the sitting room.

"How are things working out with your new assistant?" Nastya said.

"You are a deeply cruel woman," the dad said.

"Not so good, I take it."

Then Ford showed up, and all I could think about was Rachel Rose's scarf on his coat rack. Then Mel and Gemma arrived, giddy and intoxicated on something. Oh yeah: *power.*

They looked like they owned the world. Mel was wearing a deep-purple dress and black boots that laced up to her knees. She had on a lot of eyeliner. She looked like a beautiful villain. Gemma was Gemma, with lipstick on. Jonah told her she looked pretty. She told him to shut up. Gemma looked at me and nodded, saying, "Norman."

I think I said hello. I said something. And then she told me to chill out.

I walked across the room, where there was some kind of appetizer. A ball of something with bread and a wet, crunchy item inside. Celery? I don't know.

Dean Stinson gave Gemma something to drink, and he had his hand on her back and she called him Greg. Nobody calls him Greg. It looked wrong.

I heard someone say something about Ms. Shepherd. It was Mr. Ford. Why was he there? He said she was *shattered.* Yes, that was the word he used. I tried to push it out of my head. Who cares what Ford thinks about anything? Ms. Shepherd was tough. She was fine.

The food was weird, not like at my mom's house. The turkey was shaped all wrong and didn't taste like turkey. I didn't know how to describe the taste. People kept saying it was gamey. The word came up a lot. *Gamey. Game.* It sounds weird if you say it a lot. Maybe all words sound weird if you say them over and over again.

Dean Stinson got really annoyed with all of the *game* talk.

He said, "It tastes gamey because it *is* game. Would you eat beef and say it tastes beefy?"

Everything but the mashed potatoes tasted gamey. But there was only one tiny bowl of mashed potatoes and all I wanted to do was eat the whole thing myself. When I asked Jonah to pass me the dish, he took a giant helping first. There were almost no mashed potatoes left for me.

I went into the kitchen to get water and look for more mashed potatoes. Mel showed up as I was drinking. Water cascaded down my chin. I bet I looked like a crazy person.

"You okay, Norman?"

"No. No. I'm not okay. Not okay at all."

"You're really baked, aren't you?"

I nodded.

"Relax," Mel said. "Focus on your breathing."

My breathing was so loud, it sounded like I was scuba diving.

"They know. They all know," I said.

Even I didn't know what I was talking about just then.

"Norman, try to say something normal."

It took me a long time to understand Mel's instructions.

"I can't let you back in the dining room unless you say something normal."

"I like your outfit," I said, maybe five minutes later.

"Good job, Norman."

I searched the countertops for more mashed potatoes, lifted the lids on a few pots and pans. It was disappointing. Someone should have made enough mashed potatoes.

"What are you looking for?" Mel said.

"More mashed potatoes."

Mel told me to save room for the pies. I asked her if they

would be gamey. She said they would not. She took my glass and filled it in the sink. We returned to the dining room. Witt's father was talking.

"I only read the first few pages, but I thought they were charming," he said.

Finn looked sour or paranoid or both. I thought maybe he'd also gotten high before coming here. I was really sad that Ms. Shepherd wasn't there.

Then Dean Stinson was talking: "I, for one, am ecstatic. Another published novel from our esteemed staff is always good for business. So glad you could make it tonight, Finn."

Coach Keith asked what the novel was about.

"An elite boarding school," Ford said.

I really wished that my head was straight so I could follow the conversation. My senior-thesis thing was like a parody of Ford's novel, even though I wasn't completely sure what his novel was about. But I was pretty sure. It would have been good information to have, is my point.

"You can do better than that," said Witt's dad.

Wait, his name is Leonard Witt; his fake name is Len Wilde. Witt/Wilde was drinking a lot. At least, every time I looked at him he was refilling his glass with red wine. I wasn't judging him.

"There's nothing more narcissistic than talking about your work in progress," Ford said.

"Do you agree with that assertion?" the dean said to Witt/Wilde.

"Are you fucking my wife?" Witt/Wilde said.

"Your ex-wife," Dean Stinson said. "And, no, I am not, and may I ask you to refrain from using such language in front of my students."

"We don't mind," Gemma said.

"They've heard it all," Witt/Wilde said.

Ms. Witt told her father to chill out, which I think Gemma thought was hilarious. Gemma pretended to look for her napkin under the table, because she couldn't stop laughing.

"I just want to know what the book is about," Coach Keith said.

I don't think he wanted to know at all. He just wanted to change the conversation.

"Yeah," said Witt. "I wouldn't mind hearing a little more about the story."

"The venison is wonderful," said Ford.

Somebody whispered, "Bambi." Maybe it was me.

I thought I was eating turkey. I was so confused.

"I hunted it myself, in the true tradition of an American Thanksgiving," said Dean Stinson.

"Did you murder a few Indians while you were at it?" said Witt/Wilde.

"Indigenous people," I said.

My mashed potatoes had vanished again and my glass was empty. Everyone in the room was staring at me.

MS. WITT

I couldn't begin to unpack the layers of dysfunction at that Thanksgiving dinner. I wish I could claim it was the worst one of my life, but that's far from the truth.

I arrived, got a drink, ate an appetizer that I have never had before and hope never to have again. Greg gave me a glass of mulled wine. Keith approached and offered to switch glasses with me.

"Not mulled," Keith said.

"I think I love you," I said.

"Drink it first," he said.

I took a sip. It was the wine you use to make mulled wine.

"I like you," I said.

My father turned up soon after. Uninvited, of course.

"Why are you here?" I said, cornering Dad in the foyer.

"The post office isn't open today," Dad said.

He opened his satchel and delivered a thick manuscript. I glanced at the title page. *Mr. Finch* by Finn Ford.

"And I wanted to see my daughter on Thanksgiving," said Dad.

"Did you read it?"

"About fifty pages," he said, shrugging off his coat. "I was hoping it was awful."

"Well?"

"No. It's a competent piece of fiction. A little too scandalous if you ask me. Kids today are screwed up, no doubt. They're not *that* screwed up."

I didn't have the energy to argue with him. There was a knock. I shoved the manuscript back in my father's bag and opened the door. Finn was standing there. He appeared confused when he noticed my father.

"I believe you two have met," I said.

They shook hands.

Finn started to tell me something about Claude, but then my father interrupted us to congratulate Finn on his *brilliant* novel. My father tosses that word around like birdseed. Then Dad asked Finn if he wanted a drink, because Dad really wanted a drink.

We sat down for dinner. Greg took the seat right between my parents.

Norman was so baked he could barely lift his fork to his mouth without getting lost along the way. Jonah kept whispering instructions to him. Mel was complaining to Gemma about the silverware. At least I think that's what she was talking about.

"Why not three or five? It's *always* four," Mel said.

The dinner conversation got weird when my Dad inquired about sexual relations between Greg and my mother. The main course was horrendous. And, no matter how much Greg didn't want to hear it, gamey. Keith's pies were excellent, and the bottomless pot of mashed potatoes was prescient.

Once the desserts were consumed, I told everyone under the age of twenty-five to get out while the going was good. Greg invited all of the "adults" into the sitting room, where we sipped sweet vermouth on top of vodka and mulled wine. We were grown-ups and we still didn't see how that was a bad idea.

Keith asked Finn again what the book was about.

"It's about a teacher at a private school, navigating the tumultuous terrain of adolescent angst," Finn said, his nostrils flaring.

My father poured another glass of sweet vermouth and interrupted.

"Son, you'll never get anywhere if you can't do a proper elevator pitch. You're burying the lead. It's a twisted noir about a bizarre sexual competition that has become the backbone of the social hierarchy at a long-standing boarding school."

I choked on the vermouth and had a coughing fit. It sure sounded like Finn's book was a novelization of Stonebridge life. I must have been giving him some weird looks. Finn quickly made his excuses and left.

Keith headed into the kitchen to do the dishes. I followed him and offered to dry. The task gave me the opportunity to check in on the sitting room and make sure no one was saying anything that couldn't be unsaid.

"Did you hear that?" I said.

"What?" Keith said.

"Finn's book. It sounds just like Stonebridge."

"Write what you know," Keith said.

"Are there any men who can come up with an original plot?" I said.

Keith shrugged. "Dunno. Don't write."

"You're growing on me," I said.

After dinner, Keith helped me relocate my deeply inebriated father to my apartment. Then we did rounds, confirming all of the orphans were safely tucked in their dorms.

Keith said he had to put some equipment away in the gym and asked for my assistance. I followed him back across the desolate campus into Beckett Gym. As we walked along the first-floor corridor, I spotted a blowchart on the wall. It was ripped and wrinkled, like it had been taken down and put back up. Keith removed a pushpin and smoothed it out again.

"Found that in the trash. Martha was on a tear that day," Keith said.

"You put that back up?"

"It seems like sound advice," he said. "And I'm not even your target audience."

Other than the bathhouse, the gym was foreign territory for me. Keith led me into a large echo chamber with a slick wooden floor and clean white walls, where they held basketball, wrestling, dance practice, and independent-study Ping-Pong. The space was immaculate. I didn't see a single piece of equipment out of place. I followed Keith to the supply closet. He opened the door and turned on the light. Again, all of the supplies—basketballs, baseball bats, mitts, and lacrosse sticks—were neatly tucked away.

"Catch," Keith said, as a fencing foil swirled in the air above me.

I caught the handle mid-flight, my left foot instinctually stepped back, and my right arm froze into position. I caught myself *en garde* before I let my fighting arm drop to my side.

"I knew it," Keith said, shaking his head.

"Not a word," I said.

"Sure," Keith said. "How good are you?"

"Just okay," I said.

It's all relative, I suppose. I went to college on a fencing scholarship. I didn't win a bronze medal.

GEMMA RUSSO

Mel began to get paranoid about leaks. The talk of swallows and spies made her think she actually was a spy and, overnight, she became consumed by notions of every double-cross scenario she could imagine. Mel's brain fixated on moles, double agents, stool pigeons, poisoned umbrella tips.

Kate returned to campus Friday night. I told her that we'd gotten into the Dulcinea portal, and she couldn't wait until the end of break to see it. Mel, in her paranoid state, found Kate's early return highly suspicious. Mel began to wonder whether Kate was a mole, even though we had no evidence to suggest there was one. Kate, sensing Mel's distrust, offered to take a blood oath and pulled a safety pin from her skirt. I spat on my hand and suggested that saliva was as good and unsanitary a contract as anything.

After we solidified our spit sisterhood, we got back to work.

Now that we had the intelligence to destroy our enemy, we needed to design a strategy. Mel wanted to go "full nuclear," as she called it, which involved lifting the curtain on the Darkroom, door thirteen, and every voting grid in the Dulcinea contest.

Kate favored the idea of gaslighting the editors—she wanted to destroy their sanity long before we razed the Darkroom and everything it fed. I liked both ideas; each course of action could present different levels of satisfaction.

While we were debating the merits of each plan, I got a text from Linny.

Linny: How's Edgar?

Gemma: Who's Edgar?

Linny: My fish. You fed him, right?

Gemma: Sorry. I didn't know its name.

Shit. I left Mel and Kate to strategize, while I raced over to Woolf Hall, hoping to find a live goldfish. Edgar was still swimming. There was a Post-it on the outside of Linny's desk drawer that said *fish food.* I opened the drawer and found the shaker bottle on top of a file folder. I gave Edgar a few extra shakes. He swam to the surface and chomped on the confetti grub.

I was about to return the fish food to the drawer when I noticed a box of latex gloves shoved in the corner next to the file. The gloves made no sense. Everything in that drawer suddenly became suspicious. I picked up the file and opened it. Inside was a large Ziploc bag containing a little stack of pretty leaves, three to a stem. Not the kind of plant you typically keep in a baggie. Beneath the poison oak were computer printouts of water-heater manuals. I couldn't believe how blind I had been. Linny was the shower terrorist, the poison-oak perp, and presumably the lice wrangler. I got my phone and called her.

"Is Edgar alive?" Linny said when she answered.

"Yes. He's fine."

I had so much to say that I said nothing for a long while. Linny broke the silence.

"I thought you'd figure it out sooner," she said.

"Did you have help?"

"Not really. I mean, Keith knew and didn't rat me out. And Rupert had to lend me his keys so I could make a copy."

"Why would he do that?"

"I promised not to join the A/V Club or make any trouble for him and his fake club."

I didn't say anything for a while as I contemplated how well she had orchestrated the plan.

"The poison oak, how did you . . . ?"

"Housekeeping works floor by floor. I contaminated the sheets when they came out of the dryer. The housekeepers wear gloves, so they were mostly spared."

"But the lice," I said. "How did you manage that?"

"That was just an amazing bit of good fortune," Linny said. "They got lice all on their own."

"Linny. You have to stop. They'll kill you if they find out," I said. "Let me take it from here."

"But I've had the blackout on my schedule for weeks. And my test run went beautifully."

A part of me was proud of Linny's initiative; I was also rattled, because it reminded me that you can never really know anyone, what's going on in their head and what they're capable of. We would have to move quickly to shine a bright light on Dulcinea before someone foiled our plans—or before anyone really got hurt.

I went to Ms. Witt's apartment and told her about our strategy session. I asked her what she would do—gaslight or bomb.

"Gaslighting is just revenge," she said. "Will it stop the Dulcinea bullshit?"

"Eventually," I said.

"No," Witt said. "This isn't a game of cat and mouse. You're trying to end something that should have never existed. That's your priority."

"Okay," I said. "So we go big. We bomb the entire school with Dulcinea scorecards. That should put the whole thing to bed, right?"

Witt shook her head, got up from the couch, and began to pace.

"If you widely distribute the scorecards, then everyone can see everyone else's card," Witt said, thinking aloud.

"Right. But the names are all codified," I said.

"And it'll take less than an hour for someone to figure it out. That means you expose every girl who's participated. You turn the whole thing into a public shaming. Can you imagine what that would feel like? Two humiliations for the price of one."

I hadn't thought about it that way.

"What do you suggest?" I said.

"Keep it individual. Show each girl what was written

about her. Privately, so as not to embarrass her. I guarantee when the girls see those score sheets, blowjobs will become virtually obsolete."

It took some time for us to hash out our plan. Mel, Kate, and I debated for hours about how to disseminate our information. We eventually decided to go old school, delivering handwritten cards containing each recipient's score sheet for the Dulcinea Award to her private mailbox in Brontë Mailroom.

We composed the form letter to be deliberately cold and precise.

> Dear Swallow,
>
> Congratulations! You have earned entry into the Dulcinea Award, whether that was your intention or not. Below you will find your scorecard or scorecards.
>
> We realize that your evaluation may come as a shock. Perhaps you thought you were in love or in like. For a few of you, the existence of this contest may come as no surprise.
>
> Take a moment to look at your review and think about how you feel.
>
> Are you angry? Do you feel duped? Do you want an explanation or perhaps revenge? If so, please bring this invitation to Keats Studio at 8:00 this evening.
>
> If you don't care, if your dignity hasn't been diminished, all we ask is that you destroy this card and

refrain from mentioning it to anyone. If you do not abide by our request, there will be dire repercussions. We are everywhere; we see everything.

Please do not underestimate us.

Signed,

La Resistance

The rest of the weekend, Mel, Kate, and I hid out in my office and compiled data on each swallow. We placed her scoring sheet (or sheets) in an envelope with her code name on top.

When we were done, there was nothing left to do but celebrate. I was out of weed, but we knew that Adam had a stash of fine liquor in his room. Mel would have no part of my B&E, but Kate, crazy Kate, was game for anything these days.

We stole Rupert's extra set of keys from Milton and began to case Dick House. Once Kate had cleared the first floor, I entered and approached Adam's door. I had to go through the keys one by one.

"Someone's coming," Kate said.

With my finger, I marked the location on the key ring where I'd left off and shoved my hand and the keys into the canvas bag. I leaned against the wall, trying to look like I was casually waiting for someone. It was just Norman. I said *hey.*

Norman opened his door and said, "Carry on. I'm taking a nap. Won't be out here for a while."

After Norman was inside his room and had plausible deniability, I tried six more keys until I reached the one that opened Adam's door.

I swear, we were only looking for booze. I opened his closet. On the top shelf were several bottles of champagne and a few bottles of hard alcohol. I had to stand on a chair to see all the way back. There were sixteen bottles total. I pulled bottles of bourbon and vodka from the back shelf. I could have taken more, but there was no reason to be greedy.

Most of the school's walk-in closets had two rows for clothes. Adam used only the front row, where he packed in his shirts, trousers, blazers, trademark pastel oxford shirts, even his gym clothes. Adam's closet was very un-Adam-like, which is why I explored further. I parted his clothes, like I was doing a breaststroke. That's when I saw the gray file cabinet. I grabbed a handful of hangers and started moving them to his bed. Kate was keeping watch.

"Make sure the door is locked," I said, clearing enough space to access the file drawers.

Kate regarded the file cabinet and reached in to open a drawer. It rattled as she pulled.

"Locked," she said.

"If the booze isn't worth locking up, what the hell is in that cabinet?" I said.

My phone buzzed with a text from Mel.

Mel: Abort mission. Too risky.

NORMAN CROWLEY

Aside from my paranoid, mashed-potato-deficient Thanksgiving dinner, I was happy that week. Happy that I didn't have to watch my mother cry through another holiday; happy that there were girls who talked to me without looking over my shoulder, searching for someone better to come along; happy that Jonah made me play tennis with him even though I really don't like tennis.

It wouldn't last, the happiness. I knew that. But I figured I should enjoy it, that feeling of being someone who mattered, who had cool friends. I wanted to stretch it out as long as I could. I felt nostalgic before it was even over. It might have been the best week of my life. I know how lame that sounds now.

On Saturday night, Jonah, Mel, Gemma, Kate, and I hung out on the rooftop of Dick House. I didn't worry about overstaying my welcome and I didn't have to think about being invited. We were all just there, being whoever it was that we were when no one was watching. It would have been weird if I left. We drank really good bourbon. At least that's what Jonah kept telling me. I pretended not to know whose bourbon it was.

"Plausible deniability. Yeah, yeah, we get it, Norman," Gemma said.

"Don't worry," said Mel. "We'll never tell anyone you're our Deep Throat."

I was even happy the next day, when my head was pounding from that *good* bourbon hangover.

Monday morning, everything was back to normal. I ate breakfast with my roommate, Calvin. Over the holiday, he had played Guitar Hero with his cousins for four days straight. He was convinced he had carpal tunnel. He asked me three times in an hour if his left wrist looked swollen. I said, three times, "I don't know, dude, I'm not a doctor."

In Witt's class, the Thanksgiving orphans pretended we hadn't just spent a week together. Jonah didn't even look at me. I did get a text from Mel. I thought it was a brush-off, like something you say on the last day of school when you know you won't see the person over the summer.

Mel: stay cool

Calvin was studying for a chem lab, so I was alone in Dahl at lunch. I didn't feel sorry for myself, exactly. I wasn't sure I had the right to have a steady circle of friends when I had no character, no backbone, no balls. It didn't bother me much before, but this time was different, because I knew what I had lost.

Gemma, Tegan, and Emelia were back in their circle, sitting with the Ten; Mel, Kate, and Enid were at the nerd table, heads in books, not acknowledging the others' existence. When Jonah strolled into Dahl Hall, I looked away.

Fifteen minutes after lunch began, Gemma stood up and bused her tray. At the door, she locked eyes with Mel and Kate. Gemma nodded, like she was giving a signal, and walked out of the dining room. A minute later, Mel walked out, followed by Kate. I was done with my whatever casserole and wanted to see what they were up to. I cleared my tray and followed them.

Once outside, I spotted the three of them walking separately toward Headquarters. Gemma, then Kate, took the nearest entrance, and Mel circled around to the other side. I followed a minute or so after Kate. In the first-floor hallway, I saw Gemma standing next to the entrance to Brontë Mailroom, her back flat against the wall. Mel and Kate took their stations by the two distant exit doors.

Gemma peered inside the mailroom, then took cover. They all looked like cops doing some tactical maneuver. Kate looked over her shoulder and saw me.

"Hey, Norman," Kate said.

"Hi, Kate."

I toggled my gaze between Kate and where Mel was stationed at the other end of the hall.

"What's going on?" I said.

"Nothing," said Kate.

A few seconds later, my phone buzzed. A text from Mel.

Mel: We need to keep Brontë Mail clear for 5.

When I looked up, I saw Ms. Primm coming out of AA. Kate muttered, *"Shit."* Mel looked at me with wild eyes. I didn't know what any of them were up to, but it appeared that Primm was going to foil their plan. I had chosen a side, so I fell in line. I quickly intercepted Primm in the hallway before she reached the mailroom.

"Hey, Ms. Primm. I was just looking for you."

"Hello, Norman, is everything all right?" Primm said.

"Oh yeah. Definitely. But I would like to have a chat—"

"Why don't you make an appointment with Ms. Pinsky and we can talk later on?"

I walked backward in front of her, forcing Primm to slow her pace.

"You wouldn't have time right now? In—in your office?"

Primm sighed, but she so rarely gets requests for her counsel, she couldn't resist.

"Okay," she said, turning around. "I have a few minutes."

Primm returned in the direction she'd come. Mel bent down to tie her shoelaces. She looked up at me as I passed her and mouthed *thank you.* I felt like I'd just thrown myself on a grenade.

I thought I could stall Primm. Sit there for a while worrying my hands, and then maybe her phone would ring, or my phone would ring. Who was I kidding? Nobody calls anybody anymore.

"Norman?" Ms. Primm said. "What's troubling you?"

She was smiling. I think it was supposed to be one of those comforting smiles, but it was all teeth and weirdly geometrical. It wasn't the smile of someone actually smiling. Her hair looked so much bigger when the light hit it. It was kind of hard to concentrate.

I wondered if the coast was clear. I couldn't exactly check my phone. I racked my brain for something I could give Primm. A secret that wasn't so awful. It came to me as I gazed down at the nervous motion of my hands.

"I can't stop washing my hands," I said.

Come to think of it, they did look a little dry, and I was perhaps overly conscious of hygiene and the general filthiness of doorknobs.

"Why do you think that is?" Primm said.

"I don't know," I said. "There are germs everywhere. Even soap dispensers carry potentially harmful bacteria. How are you supposed to be clean if the thing you need to get clean is filthy?"

Nothing I said was a lie. It occurred to me, I might actually have a problem.

"Norman, are you sure that germs are what you're really trying to clean?"

"Um, I think so?" I said.

I couldn't remember the last time I was in Primm's office. If I ever had anything real to talk to anyone about, like maybe a cleaning fixation, Primm was the last person I'd go to.

"Do you think it's possible that your handwashing is a physical manifestation of a psychological need?"

"Uhhhh," I said. I was going to let Primm run the clock on this.

"Perhaps you're trying to clean your soul," she said.

Who wasn't? I shrugged and looked out the window.

"It's okay, Norman," Primm said.

I nodded.

"There's nothing to be ashamed of," she said.

"You're right," I said.

I didn't know what we were talking about anymore. I pretended to have a bit of a coughing fit as I reached into my pocket and typed a text to Mel behind the cover of Primm's desk.

Norman: SOS.

I sat up and cleared my throat.

"I think I'm feeling better now."

"Are you really, Norman? Because I'm not feeling that, intuitively," Primm said.

"No. No. Really, I am. I feel fine. I feel like I could go days without washing my hands. You know what I mean. I mean, not really. But not as often. Just enough to not be disgusting or become ill."

"Norman, it's okay. This is how God made you. You are free to love whoever you want."

Primm did that concerned-adult look, but with a weird cartoon precision. I used to feel sorry for her because everyone hated her, but now I got it. I also got what she was getting at.

"I'm gay," I said.

Primm beamed.

"I'm so proud of you, Norman," she said.

"Thanks," I said.

The truth was, if I could do it all over again, I would have come out as gay freshman year. The straight guys would have left me alone and I'd have way more friends who are girls. Stonebridge Academy was not a healthy place for heterosexuals.

There were three loud bangs on the door. Then I heard Mel's voice shouting from the other side.

"Norman! *Norman!* I need your econ notes. Norman, are you in there?"

Mel opened the door and flew into the room. Primm got to her feet and gave Mel a stern reprimand for intruding on a private conversation. Mel apologized. I thanked Primm for her time. Mel grabbed my arm and we made a run for it down the long hallway, through the stairwell, and out of the building, where we collapsed on the grass, heaving with laughter.

"That was awesome," I said. "Wait, do you even take econ?"

"No. But I read a biography of John Maynard Keynes last year."

"You are amazing," I said.

"No, Norman. You're amazing."

It was and is my highest high.

GEMMA RUSSO

We choreographed the whole thing the night before. Brontë Mailroom is generally deserted during lunch hour. Mel and Kate kept watch in the hallway of Headquarters while I delivered each personalized invitation to its recipient's mailbox. Just their swallow handle was inscribed on the outside of the envelope. The only person who saw me in Brontë was the mailroom guy. He barely registered my existence.

Then we waited.

I texted Linny to meet me at the Mudhouse during one of her independent-study classes. Linny's Dick House subterfuge, while misguided and dangerous, was worthy of some acknowledgment or reward. I had her favorite chocolate cupcake waiting for her when she arrived.

"What's this?" Linny said.

"A token of my appreciation for your impressive work as the shower terrorist."

"A cupcake?"

"It's your favorite, right?"

"Thanks," she said, deadpan.

What did she want, a parade? We were busy. We had a mission that was time sensitive. If I had been smart, I would have dispatched Linny with various duties just to keep her occupied. Instead, I told her to keep her head down. I didn't want her association with me on the editors' radar. I told her to keep her distance from my team until we'd finished phase one of our plan.

"But I'm on your team," Linny said.

"You're right. But your job is to pretend you're not."

Back on campus, I crossed paths with Tegan, aka 4Swallow202. She looked like she'd been hit with the flu. It was the first time I felt sorry for her. Really sorry.

One hour until summit, I was back in the dorm with Emelia. Tegan was AWOL. Em had changed into street clothes. I asked her where she was going. She said that she and Nick were hanging out. She said they had texted throughout the entire holiday. Things were getting serious, she said, as she reapplied lip gloss, the color of watered-down blood. I asked Emelia whether she had any plans to screw Nick in the next week or so. She said no. I asked her to keep me posted. She asked me why I was being weird. I said no reason. I wanted to tell her that Nick Laughlin had entered scorecards for Hannah Rexall and Rachel Rose, but it went against Ms. Witt's no-shaming directive. If I'd thought Emelia was actually going to blow Nick, I would have intervened.

I left early for the summit at Keats. When I arrived, Mel and Kate were already there, biting their nails in anticipation.

It wasn't how we thought it would be, standing in front of our classmates, watching, as they adjusted to this new version of a world they thought they understood. To see their intimate acts judged and criticized, like a gymnastics routine, went far beyond your average betrayal. The game screwed with how you saw yourself. You weren't just a patsy; you were a slut.

Their reactions were as varied as their scores.

Sandra: Is this a joke?
Amy: I don't know what I'm looking at.
Tegan: Where did you get this?
Hannah: What are the other scores like?

After the first flurry of questions, there was chaos, like at a hostile city-council meeting, everyone shouting over everyone else. And no one understanding a single word. I stood on top of the teacher's desk, trying to quiet the frenzy.

Mel pulled out a whistle from her pocket and blew hard. The fact that she had the foresight to bring a whistle impressed me. The sharp sound pierced the fury and everyone quieted down.

"We didn't do this to humiliate anyone," I said, feeling like a street preacher on an impromptu soapbox. "We thought you had a right to know what was being said about you. If you think it's love, affection, or even respect, you're a fool. The winner of the Dulcinea Award wins nothing. She is celebrated for one thing and one thing only. At least a prostitute gets some money when it's over. What does the winner of the Dulcinea Award get? If you're okay with this sad Stonebridge tradition, we won't judge you. If you want to fight back, if you want to help us shut down not just the Dulcinea contest but the Darkroom and the culture at this school that objectifies, uses, and exploits us, then stay. Because we have some ideas."

I sat down on the desk as Mel, Kate, and I waited to see what they would do. They murmured in clusters, occasionally parting with one assembly and entering another. At some point, Amy Logan made her way over to me; it looked like she was cutting out.

She handed over her card: 4Swallow112.

"I admire what you're doing here, but this isn't me. 4Swallow112 is someone else."

"Are you sure?"

"I've never sucked dick in my life, and I don't plan on it," Amy said.

I thought about my fake entry. "Some of them are fake," I said. "They're just the guys being—"

"Maybe, but I'd think one of those assholes would be a little more accurate with his details. Whoever wrote this shit references a long, shiny ponytail, see?" she said, holding up the card. "He likes to grab it when . . . you know."

"You're right," I said, taking the card.

We were so busy decoding names and copying data that

we forgot that the coded names were human beings. Just like the guys did.

"Good luck here," Amy said. "It's about time. If you need anything, within reason, let me know."

"Just don't tell anyone," I said.

"Not a word," Amy said.

The chatter quieted down. I saw a few tears slide down pale cheeks and some hands close into white-knuckled fists. Tegan stepped forward, keeping her composure as cold and as solid as a frozen steak.

"What's the plan?" she said.

"I'm glad you asked," I said. "Phase one: business as usual."

"With a twist," Mel added.

MS. WITT

The girls took their time. They were cautious. They had a plan. I thought it was a good one. What other choice did they have? Another misguided seminar on sexual harassment or an "investigation" by Ms. Primm? Dulcinea and the Darkroom and all the other bullshit had to be brought to light.

"When the word gets out, I won't just have a few allies anymore. I'll have an army," Gemma said.

An *army.* The word sticks out now. Back then it sounded like bravado, something girls her age appeared to be lacking.

Gemma said they would empower their classmates with the truth. If every girl knew the gritty details of the contest, how could they go on being unwitting participants? Gemma, Kate, and Mel had done their job. I began to question whether I had done mine.

I read Finn's book. *Mr. Finch.* He mangled the truth just enough to call it fiction, but there was no way he could claim plausible deniability. His imaginary school, Wingate Academy, had its own sex games, code names, and wildly inappropriate teacher-student relationships. The novel indulged in Zodiac-like cryptology, which was how the illicit paramours communicated with one another. To his credit, he much improved upon the Stonebridge ciphers.

One of the novel's main characters was a befuddled headmaster who could walk into a sex den and remain utterly clueless as coeds screwed beneath the sheets. The primary conflict in *Mr. Finch* revolved around the murder of a PE teacher. And the Finn stand-in, the titular Mr. Finch, was so busy fending off the advances of sexually adventurous girls that he went slightly mad at the end.

While Finn's book had many departures from the Stonebridge story, one thing was clear: He knew. And if Finn knew, others did too. I just had to find out who.

A week had passed since the end of Thanksgiving break, and Claude hadn't yet returned to Stonebridge. I sent her a text to check in and she suggested I meet her at Hemingway's.

I locked up my classroom and headed into town.

Hemingway's was empty except for an old man at a table and Claude at the bar with Hugh. I greeted her with a quick hug. She had the sweet-and-sour odor of someone in the midst of drinking who's still metabolizing her last hangover.

"I've had a head start. You should catch up," Claude said.

I ordered a beer. Claude tipped back the rest of her bourbon and tapped the bar for another.

"Maybe you want to slow down," Hugh said.

"Maybe you want to pour faster," Claude said.

It had only been two weeks since I last saw her, but something was different. I couldn't place it. Everything was as impeccable as usual. But I had the sense that her clothes and makeup were more camouflage than an expression of style.

"How've you been?" I said.

"Alex, I don't need another human sympathy card. Just drink your beer and relax."

I chugged a third of the pint and started to talk. Claude pointed to my beer and said, "Finish it."

Claude wouldn't speak another word until I did. With one beer down, Hugh delivered another pint. Claude raised an eyebrow, as if she were waiting for me to demolish the second beer.

"No, Claude. I'm drinking this one on my own time."

"You're not as fun as I'd hoped you'd be," Claude said.

"I'm sorry," I said.

"That's okay," she said. "No one is."

"So, are you coming back to Stonebridge?"

"Of course," Claude said. "What else would I do?"

"I thought maybe you'd sell the house and take a long vacation."

Claude smiled. At least the mechanics of the expression looked like a smile. It didn't feel like one.

"Maybe later. I need to finish out the year," she said.

She slid her empty glass forward and tapped it lightly. Hugh poured a stingy shot.

"So, Witt, what have you been up to?" she said. "Did you and Finn ever hook up again?"

"No. But I did read his book."

"You get that there's no equivalency to those two acts, right?" Claude said.

"I do," I said.

"So, how was it?"

"It was derivative."

"We're talking about the book, right?"

"Yes."

"Aren't most novels?" Claude said.

"In the broadest sense, sure. But Finn's novel borrows extensively from Stonebridge. There's a whole story line about a contest just like the Dulcinea Award."

"Dulcinea?" said Claude. "What's that?"

"You know. The blowjob contest."

"It's called Dulcinea? That's so odd," Claude said.

She seemed more disturbed by the name than the nature of the award.

"Why hasn't anyone tried to stop it?" I said.

"How? News flash: Teenagers have sex with each other," Claude said.

"It's not normal, Claude. It's so . . . organized. The boys manufacture relationships in order to enroll unwitting participants."

"Look, Alex, I get it. You're a feminist and it looks bad," Claude said. "But they're still better off than we were at their age."

"I disagree," I said. "But I won't belabor the subject."

"Are you sure this isn't about your stalker last year?" Claude asked.

I knew the information was out there. But Claude's reminder wasn't just about what happened at Warren. I wondered again who made the video of me.

"Who told you?" I said.

"Finn. He has a gift for getting information out of people."

Finn got that information from me. I didn't bother correcting her.

"Were we this fucked up at their age?" I asked.

Claude laughed. "Being fucked up isn't cured by age."

The half-mile walk back to campus felt endless. I was so tired, I didn't notice Keith sitting in the stairwell of Beckett. I practically tripped over him on my way to the apartment.

"What are you doing here?" I said, stepping around his rangy frame and continuing up the stairs. Keith followed after me. There was a paper bag on the floor in front of my door. I picked it up, looked inside.

"I had to guard the brownie and provide clear instructions," he said. "Don't eat the whole thing."

"You want half?" I said, unlocking the door.

Keith followed me inside the apartment.

"You really shouldn't even eat half of that," he said. "It's not a regular brownie. I feel like you're not entirely grasping that concept."

"No, I get it. I just think you should be able to eat a whole brownie and also get appropriately high."

I turned on the overhead light and kicked off my shoes. Keith turned off the light and walked over to the window.

"The trees," he said. "The girls keep cutting down the trees. Look."

It was dusk. There was still enough light to see a stretch of woods with five felled trees.

"All the shit that's going on here and you're worried about the trees?"

"I'm not worried about the trees," Keith said. "I mean, I kind of liked that young oak at ten o'clock. But it takes a lot of work for a grown man to chop down a tree. I'm worried someone is going to get hurt. Linny has been going at that maple for almost a week. Her hand is covered in blisters. Even the blisters are a badge of honor. I'm scared for her. For all of them."

I stretched out on the couch and closed my eyes. I was so tired. I could have slept for days. Keith brought me a glass of water.

"Were you drinking?" he said.

"With Claude."

"Oh," he said.

"Did you sleep with her or something?"

I hugged my knees to my chest, giving Keith a place to sit.

"No. Why do you ask?" he said.

"Because you've known each other about twenty years and you don't speak. That usually means something has happened."

"She makes me uncomfortable," he said.

"You make her uncomfortable. Why do you make each other uncomfortable?"

"When I was a student here, there was some weird shit going on between a few of the teachers and students. Mr. Goode, history. I saw him flirting all the time. At first it didn't seem like that big a deal. I see now how—anyway, it wasn't just flirting. Junior year, maybe, I saw him in the classroom one night. He was with Claude. They were—"

"Having sex?" I said.

"Yes. I didn't know what to do. It was different then. I thought I should talk to Claude and see if she was okay. She was furious that I said anything to her. She said if I told anyone, she'd say I raped her."

"Fuck. So that was it. You never told anyone?"

"No. I didn't. I mean, I was a kid."

"Was it just him?" I said.

"No. The English teacher, Mr. Walters. I would see him with this senior. I can't remember her name. What was really weird was that everyone knew. They didn't hide it. No one seemed to care. I didn't understand much back then; I just knew it wasn't normal. I tried to talk about it once to Dean Woolsey. He was Claude's stepdad. I figured he'd want to know. He told me that I must have misinterpreted what I saw. Then I graduated."

"You don't think that's still going on? Teachers and students?"

"I've never seen it. I think the problem is mostly the Darkroom shit."

We sat there for a while, saying nothing.

"Do you know what happened at my last school? It seems to have gotten around," I said.

"Does it have something to do with the aluminum foil?" he said.

"So you did hear?"

"No," Keith said. "But aluminum foil on windows requires

some motivation. I'm just pleased to know that it wasn't aliens or the government. It wasn't, right?"

"It wasn't," I said.

"Do you want to tell me?" he said.

"Not right now."

"Okay. Do you want me to make you some tea?" Keith said.

"No, I'm fine."

"Is there anything else you need?"

I stretched out my legs. And closed my eyes again. Keith took my foot in his hands and began kneading the arches. It felt too good. I couldn't decide whether I wanted him to stop or stay the night.

"What are you doing, Keith?"

"I'm trying to make you feel better. Don't be so suspicious."

"It's this place," I said.

"Full disclosure: I, um—well, you know. I have other motives."

"You want to have sex with me?"

"Sure. But I'd like to do other things as well."

"Like what?"

"Okay, bowling was what first came to mind. And I have no idea why," he said.

"I think I'd rather have sex with you than go bowling."

"It's not an either/or kind of thing," Keith said.

I asked Keith where he was staying these days. He was back in a vacation home about two miles from the school. I told him he could stay over if he wanted. He told me to get off his bed, then. And gently kicked me off the couch. I appreciated his lack of presumption. I kissed him. Or maybe he kissed me. I told him he could sleep in my bed. He asked me if I was sober. I told him I was sober enough, but if he wanted to administer a field sobriety test . . . He asked me to close my eyes and touch my nose. I must have passed.

He kissed me again and we stumbled into my bedroom, removing each other's clothes. I had no regrets.

When I woke up the next morning, I saw a text from Gemma.

Gemma: Dulcinea is dead. The war has begun.

PART IV
THE WAR

I trust no one, not even myself.

JOSEPH STALIN

GEMMA RUSSO

A few of the swallows wanted to shoot the messenger. Seeing their scorecards was like catching a reflection of their worst selves.

We swore them all to secrecy, emphasizing the importance of restraint. Showing our hand at this point would give the editors leverage. The first mission for the swallows was to go back to their rooms and live their lives for the next twenty-four hours without letting on.

Kate had been reading *The Art of War.* She climbed up onto the desk and took her turn preaching.

"In all fighting," she recited, *"the direct method may be used for joining battle, but indirect methods will be needed for securing victory."*

The girls gaped at Kate. They weren't ready for wisdom. They were still absorbing the news that the recipients of their blowjobs were not only ungrateful but heartless.

"Tough crowd," Kate said, climbing down from her pulpit.

I gave them parting instructions: "Meet back here tomorrow and we'll start then. In the meantime, get your heads straight and keep your mouths shut."

I gave Linny strict instructions to quit it with her plague campaign. I told her the boys needed to get comfortable, believe it was business as usual. She reluctantly agreed but insisted on coming to the strategy meetings. I asked why she was so invested in a war that wasn't hers. And then I found out it was hers. Last year, a senior named Connor Pitts courted her until she gave in. He never spoke to her again. I asked Linny why she never told me.

"Because you'd warned me what they were like. I felt stupid."

Tegan masked her feelings well. Back in our dorm room, with Emelia prattling on about Nick, Tegan didn't crack. She even managed to parcel out enough small talk to avoid suspicion. Then she snapped on her earbuds and drowned out the world.

Later, Emelia left us to see Nick. When the door shut, the earbuds came out and Tegan leveled her gaze at me.

"You know who Doomsday is, right?"

Doomsday was Jack Vandenberg.

"I have a hunch," I said.

"How many other scorecards did he enter?"

"I don't know the exact number," I said.

It was twelve.

"More than three?" she said.

"I don't remember."

"Fewer than five?" Tegan asked.

"Yes," I said. It was the last lie I would tell her.

* * *

At the next swallows meeting, we began to talk strategy:

"We want to gaslight them first," I said. "We want to confuse them, throw them off-balance. When it's time to play our cards, we'll go all in. For now it's a long game. We ask for your loyalty, not your service. You don't have to fight; you can stay on the sidelines and we will respect your wishes. What we won't respect or tolerate is a traitor."

"Do you want to explain what *gaslight* means?" Hannah said.

"It's in reference to a 1944 film starring Ingrid Bergman—" Kate began.

"Make them think they're going crazy," I said. "Well, I guess it's 'light gaslighting' for now. Refusing to participate in the contest is one way. Don't tell them why. You have a headache or you're busy. But if you do choose to have relations, I encourage you to be less enthusiastic."

Mel whispered in my ear, "Remember Nastya? She said she wanted to see a bad-blowjob contest."

A bad blowjob was still a blowjob. I wasn't comfortable advocating that.

"Maybe we change the aim of the game. We can have our own winner of the contest. Our winner gives the worst blowjob ever," Kate said.

"Or none," I said.

"We should blue-ball them," Tegan said.

Some girls laughed, some cheered at the notion. There were also dissenters.

Sandra Polonsky said, "Why would I get near anyone's junk after reading this?"

"Play it however you want," I said. "Just don't tell them anything."

"Any questions?" Mel asked.

"Where's Rachel? Why isn't she here?" Sandra P asked.

Hannah looked at me and then at Mel, awaiting a response. When we didn't answer straightaway, Hannah did for us.

"Rachel was going to win, wasn't she?"

"Meeting adjourned," I said.

Hannah approached me on the way out.

"I'm right, aren't I?" she said.

I couldn't decide what hurt Hannah more: her low score or Rachel's high marks.

"We weren't sure we could trust her. We weren't sure we could trust you either," I said.

What I didn't say was that we took a calculated risk. We needed one of the girls who was playing to win on our side. We figured Hannah would be the easiest to flip.

"*We*—you say *we* a lot," Hannah said.

"I'm not working alone," I said.

"Makes it sound kinda Big Brother–like."

"I prefer to think of us more as a gang. A gang that will have your back if you have ours. Are you in or are you out?"

"I'm in, I guess," Hannah said.

She sounded defeated. I hoped it was the recognition of what she had played a part in—that it was all the Dulcinea shit that crushed her spirit, not us.

We—the original three—met later in my office for a quick debriefing.

Mel picked up the Amy Logan scorecard. "This one is bugging me."

"It might help if we knew who TonyStarx was," I said.

"What other senior girls have the initials AL?" Kate asked.

"Aileen Leach?" I said, looking down at our class roster.

"Aileen has had the same boyfriend since like sixth grade," I said.

"Maybe he misspelled it," Mel said. "Could be EL. Maybe he thought Emelia spelled her name with an A."

You could feel the energy shift on campus. I often saw the editors consorting in hushed tones, casting sidelong glances at the girls. They knew the tide had turned but couldn't figure out how. The swallows kept them off-balance, with our strict orders to tamp down open hostility until we were ready to don war paint and run at them with spears and savage wails.

The plan—Operation Blue Balls, as it was baptized—was working. You could see the effect on the boys. They were cranky, distracted, their spirits dulled. They were so confused. It was a challenge to keep myself from looking smug. Jonah would catch me relishing our success. He sent me a text.

Jonah: Quit smiling. They'll know it's u

But that was just the opening salvo. Leaving the boys

unsatisfied only sharpened my comrades' thirst for revenge. To quench it required something else altogether. We had been holding back so much energy, we needed to release it. We needed to fight.

"It's time to up the ante," Tegan said at our next meeting.

It was time. Only I wasn't quite sure what the next step should be. I opened the floor to ideas.

Let's build our own Darkroom, expose all their embarrassing secrets.

Ghost them.

Steal their shoes.

Linny raised her hand. "My sister told me about this friend of hers: She liked spicy food a lot. She could eat a whole jalapeño pepper with seeds and all, right? So she had been eating really spicy salsa and her boyfriend came over and asked her to blow him and she did. I heard he was in so much pain, he cried, like *real* tears. No permanent damage was done. But he never asked her to go down on him again."

Linny had come prepared. She handed me a paper bag.

"I tried to eat one earlier. But I don't think I can do it," Linny said.

"And I wouldn't let you," I said. "But I like the way you're thinking."

The room was quiet. Like that moment during a standoff right after all the guns are drawn. I could tell the girls liked the plan. But I didn't know if we'd have any takers.

Then Tegan walked over to me and took the paper bag.

"I got this," Tegan said. "But I think we need at least two

more soldiers for the message to be heard."

Tegan pocketed a pepper and waited for other volunteers to claim their ammunition. After a pause, Hannah and Sandra stepped up.

"You need to coordinate the timing of your attacks," I said.

"Make sure you have a glass of milk handy when it's over," said Mel. "Or some bread."

"Carbs? Really?" Hannah said.

After hanging out on Thanksgiving break, Jonah had some trouble snapping back into our old, unfamiliar ways. Sometimes he'd ask to see me, promising to be careful, but I said no out of caution, a warped sense of loyalty. But then, in the middle of our soft offensive, Jonah made contact again and insisted that we meet. He didn't wait for an answer. He just showed up at my office.

"This better be good," I said when he arrived.

"Norman and I have been checking thirteen to see if anyone has gotten wind of whatever it is you're doing," Jonah said.

"And?"

"There was a new entrant in Dulcinea, just a few hours ago," he said.

"Show me," I said.

"I took a screenshot," he said, removing his phone from his pocket.

I read the top line.

VicVega enters 4Swallow512.

"Fuck," I said. VicVega was Nick. 512 was EL: Emelia Laird.

Overall score: 5
Technique: 5
Artistry: 6
Effort: 5
Finish: 4
Comments: Put in a lot of hours on that one. S512 proves the tenet that pretty girls can't blow.

"Norman says Nick is VicVega. He's submitted other girls, but—"

I found the TonyStarx card for 4Swallow112 and showed it to Jonah.

"TonyStarx is Adam, isn't it?"

"Yeah," Jonah said.

I looked at the TonyStarx card that we had errantly delivered. It had to be Emelia. I didn't relish the job of telling her.

"Are you done now?" Jonah said.

"Of course not," I said.

He looked really serious right then. His arms were folded, brow furrowed. It was funny. I could see what he would look like as an old guy.

"Something on your mind?" I said.

"You're taking this too far. Call them out, expose them, and end the stupid contest. If you get them to take down the

Darkroom and maybe apologize, you've won. Right?"

"Exposing the truth isn't enough anymore. They have to learn from their mistakes; they need to pay for what they've done," I said.

"So it's revenge you want?" Jonah said.

"A day of reckoning, that's all."

"That's just a fancy way of saying revenge," Jonah said.

My phone was buzzing like crazy. I checked the screen.

Tegan: It's time. We're locked and loaded.

I texted back.

Gemma: Cool your jets. Back in ten.

I looked at Jonah. "Anything else?"

"Do you even like me, or am I just part of your *reckoning*?"

The answer should have been obvious to him. But we lived in a place where sexual deception was commonplace. Hell, it was expected.

"I like you," I said.

I kissed him again.

"I love you," he said.

No guy had ever said that to me before. I won't pretend it meant nothing. But I couldn't offer anything back. Not while we were in the thick of it. Every time I looked at Jonah, in those blue trousers, oxford shirt, blue-and-red tie, I saw his comrades, his brothers, his friends. He was wearing the uniform of my enemy. I couldn't get past that.

"I have to go," I said.

I returned to our dorm room. Emelia was out. Tegan stood rigid in front of the mirror, eyeing her jalapeño pepper, taking deep cleansing breaths, working up the courage.

"It's about time," she said. "Hannah and Sandra are ready to go. We only have one shot."

She opened the refrigerator and broke the seal on a carton of milk.

"Have that ready for me when I come back."

"Are you sure?" I said.

Tegan nodded. "After this goes down, it's war. We're not playing games anymore."

She wrapped her pepper in a tissue and shoved it in her pocket.

"Good luck," I said.

"I don't need luck," Tegan said.

She was seething with fury and bloodlust. She had never looked more beautiful.

NORMAN CROWLEY

I heard the first howl from the other end of the hall. It sounded like an animal caught in a snare. It gave me the chills. When I opened my door, Tegan rushed past me. She was crying and smiling at the same time. It was so weird. I didn't know what she had done to Jack, but I figured he had it coming.

And then I heard another wail, coming from Nick's room. Hannah emerged from his doorway and ran down the hall. Her eyes were red and watery, like Tegan's. Then Gabriel Smythe screamed and Sandra ran out of his room. I called her name. She said *milk* and ran past me.

All three of the guys were baying like wolves.

Adam stormed into the hallway, looked at me, and said, "What the fuck is going on?"

"I don't know," I said, retreating into my room.

I heard a stampede through the hallway, more shouting for milk, someone mentioning a doctor. I had no idea what had caused the pain, but I knew why. I stood behind my door, listening intently, hoping to figure it out. Later, I texted Jonah and he told me what the girls had done. I felt good. It seemed like the perfect dose of justice.

The next day Adam came to me in a rage. He blamed me for the breach, saying I'd been sloppy. He called me all kinds of names, like I still cared what he thought of me.

"Take it down, take it all down. Make sure there's not a trace of it left," he said.

"Yeah, boss," I said, like a good soldier.

I didn't destroy it. I moved the data to a secret server and cleared out all of their code names and passwords. I was now the keeper of the Darkroom, the only person who could shed a light on five years of douchebags airing their souls.

I'd known the girls were fighting mad. But after the jalapeño blowjobs, all uncertainty was lost. It was war. The editors were thrown off-balance at first, but after they recovered, Adam, Jack, Mick, Gabe, and Nick began to have secret meetings in the lounge. Sometimes, if I stood in the right spot on the stairwell, I could hear them.

"All of this shit started when Witt came to town," Adam said.

Jonah had warned me that things were going to get ugly. Everything was going to change, he said. I hoped he was right.

MR. FORD

I don't get paid enough for this shit.

Every time Rachel Rose dropped by my apartment, she left her pink scarf behind. Eventually I realized she did it on purpose—that she wanted her classmates to think something was going on between us. I can't even begin to unwrap the daddy issues with that one. I delivered it to the lost and found every time, but she'd still drop by. The last time she came over, I told her that she wasn't allowed inside anymore. She started to fake-cry, but then I heard the real deal. A keening wail from the first floor.

I locked my door behind me and rushed down three flights.

I met Adam at the base of the stairs.

"What the hell is going on?" I said.

"Their dicks are on fire," Adam said.

It sounded like a joke, but Adam, who never loses his cool, had this unhinged look in his eyes. I followed him down the hallway to the communal bathroom, the door of which was being guarded by Mick Devlin.

Adam said that Jack Vandenberg, Gabriel Smythe, and

Nick Laughlin had been attacked and were in excruciating pain. The girls did something to their dicks while giving them oral. What they did, Adam didn't know. He told the guys to take a shower, to wash it off, whatever it was.

All three boys were behind the shower curtains, still in agony, offering up palliative suggestions.

I think the soap helps. You got to wash it off.

Do you think we should go to the emergency room?

I'm not going to a fucking hospital.

Bloody 'ell. Those fucking cunts.

"Can someone tell me what happened?" I said.

One shower went silent and Gabriel Smythe emerged with a towel wrapped around his waist. His eyes were red, like he'd been crying. He opened his towel and showed me his bright-red penis.

"Jesus," I said, looking away.

"I think she ate a hot pepper right before she gave me head," said Gabe. "It was weird. We got started, she told me to close my eyes, and then I heard something, like chewing, I think. Then she, you know, and that's when I felt it. It was like she set my dick on fire. I pushed her off of me—"

"Dude," Jack said, "mine did the exact same thing."

I noticed that they never said the girls' names.

Nick and Jack appeared from the showers, towels wrapped around their waists. Adam shook his head.

"Three at the same time? That was a coordinated attack," Adam said.

"Fucking bitches," said Jack.

Nick grabbed his crotch and doubled over. "Fuck. Second wave."

He got back into the shower.

"You should get some milk," I said.

Mick shouted at a random kid in the hall and ordered him to pick up a gallon from Dahl.

"They know," said Gabe. "They have to know. They must have hacked into the Darkroom. Too much weird shit has been happening."

"We have to do something," said Mick.

"Do I need to call in a doctor?" I said. "We might be able to find someone who does house calls. Otherwise it's EMTs."

"I don't think that will be necessary," Adam said, pulling out his phone. "Let me do some research."

"Goddamn it," said Gabriel, returning to the shower. "The soap didn't work."

"What's our play here?" Mick said.

"You want to tell me what's going on?" I said.

All of the victims retreated to the showers.

Adam looked up from his phone. "Let's get some yogurt up here," he said to no one in particular. Although a few boys did begin running down the hall.

"Thanks, Ford," said Mick. "We've got it from here."

There's nothing quite like being summarily dismissed by a student. I left. What was I supposed to do, wash their dicks for them?

I was back in my apartment maybe five minutes when Witt showed up.

"Was that screaming or celebrating?" she said.

"Don't worry about it," I said. "It's over now."

Witt delivered a large envelope.

"My father asked me to return this to you."

I looked inside. It was my manuscript, with comments scribbled in the margins. I glanced at the first note.

PHYSICAL DESCRIPTION A BIT PAT, NO?

I'd asked Leonard Witt for his thoughts; I thought he might send me an encouraging email, maybe a blurb, not a marked-up manuscript, like I was back in an MFA program.

"Notes from the great Len Wilde," I said. "How thoughtful."

"Those are my notes," Witt said, cold and smug.

I couldn't figure out why she was looking at me like I'd just committed a felony or installed a hidden camera in her room.

"You read it?" I said.

"Yes."

"What did you think?" I stupidly asked.

"Your story bears some uncanny similarities to Stonebridge."

"All writers are thieves of reality. You know that."

"I don't care that you can't come up with a plot on your own. Okay, I care a little. But my main gripe is that the boys trusted you enough to tell you what was going on. Did it ever occur to you to say something?"

"Say what, exactly? Stop getting blowjobs? I don't think that advice would have gone over very well."

"Fuck you, Finn," Witt said.

Her father was the wordsmith, not her. She left after that. I was glad to see her go.

I must have been blinded by the aura surrounding the cruel muse, or the celebrity of her father, or the mere fact that there aren't many options for a grown man at Stonebridge.

Alex Witt was predictable, prudish, and a complete bore.

And she looked like a backwoods hick with that hideous tooth.

GEMMA RUSSO

Tegan really took one for the team. She'd scarfed down half a loaf of bread before Mel suggested she drink a glass of milk.

"I've always hated spicy food," Tegan said when her mouth finally cooled off.

Tegan and I decided to tell Emelia that night. We showed her Adam and Nick's Dulcinea scorecards, rating her "performance." She didn't cry, which surprised me. Tegan told her what Hannah had done to Nick.

"It should have been me," Emelia said.

Emelia didn't say anything for the rest of the night. She went to bed. In the morning, when I woke up, she was taking scissors to her beautiful hair. She chopped her long tresses right to the scalp. I asked her why.

It made her sick reading what Adam had written about grabbing her ponytail.

Tegan said that rapists often look for victims with long hair. It makes them easier to control. Tegan took the scissors next.

I knocked on Amy Logan's door and asked to borrow her

clippers. She always has a clean buzz on the left side of her scalp.

I had Emelia shave my head. I loved the feeling of running my hand over my buzzed scalp. I felt so clean and so free. Emelia asked me to do the same to her. Then Tegan did. We couldn't stop touching each other's scalps.

"I feel amazing," said Tegan.

Kate and Mel dropped by the room after that.

"Oh my God," said Mel, gaping.

I thought she was going to tell us we'd gone crazy. But she sat down in the chair.

"My turn," Mel said.

Mel had more hair than any of us. It was thick and wavy and so shiny.

"Are you sure?"

"Fuck yeah," she said. "Do it."

"May I?" Tegan said, taking hold of the clippers. "I haven't had my turn yet."

I can't remember the last time Tegan and Mel had a direct conversation.

"I'd be honored," Mel said.

Tegan turned on the razor and made a clean stripe down the center of Mel's scalp.

"No turning back now," I said.

"I'm next," said Kate.

It was an awesome moment of solidarity. Although, in retrospect, I wish we'd put down a sheet or done it outside, because we never, ever could clean up all of that hair.

But nothing could beat that morning. I remember feeling so

powerful when we walked down the hallway of Headquarters. Five furious women with buzz cuts.

We could feel their fear.

No one felt like a victim anymore.

MS. WITT

Gemma, Mel, Kate, Emelia, and Tegan walked into my class with shaved heads. The other girls huddled together, touching the scalps of their leaders. My first thought was that they were deliberately desexualizing themselves, demonstrating their opposition to the contest. It also just looked badass.

I asked to speak with Gemma in the hall. I told everyone else to take a seat.

"You want to feel it?" Gemma said proudly.

I felt her soft-sandpaper scalp.

"Wow."

"It feels amazing in the shower," she said.

It was the happiest I'd ever seen her.

She told me about the comments on Emelia's scorecard and that Emelia was the first to chop off her locks.

"People can surprise you," she said.

I agreed.

Keith had asked me to meet him after class at the greenhouse. He'd carved a sign out of reclaimed wood. It read

GRAHAM GREENEHOUSE. He hung it above the door.

"All is right with the world," I said.

God, I'd never been more wrong.

Keith was watering plants that already looked dead. I told him that the girls had broken down the Darkroom and exposed the contest. I told him that the worst was over. He asked, "So why are the girls still chopping down trees?"

He showed me a map of the woods where the bulk of the arboreal assault had taken place. He said Linny had made it. Next to each felled tree, she'd put the name of the responsible girl. She thought they'd want it memorialized.

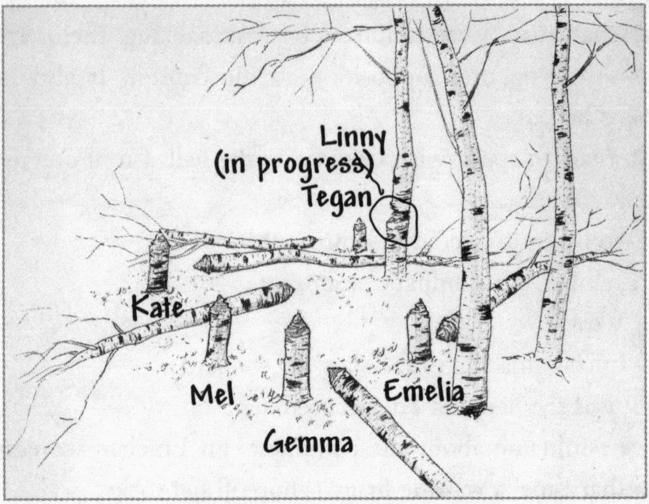

"Please talk to them," Keith said. "There are least ten downed trees. Ignoring the environmental angle, they're using an ax. Someone will eventually get hurt."

Later, when I asked Gemma about it, she said that it was either the tree or someone's head.

I remember those last two weeks before winter break with disturbing clarity.

In my classroom, the girls and boys now sat on different sides. No one even whispered, for fear that the other side might hear them. Gemma told me they were done fighting; they'd won. She said it was over. It wasn't over.

I let the class work independently, knowing they would use that time to text or scheme. I remember, at some point, Adam Westlake raising his hand.

"Why'd you leave your last school, Ms. Witt?"

"I was ready to move on," I said.

"Funny," Adam said, "I heard it had something to do with a cinema project."

It felt like spiders were crawling all over my body. I never could make my mind up about him. But then I knew. He took the video or, at the very least, he ordered it.

Later that day I received an email from Primm:

To: Alex Witt
From: Martha Primm
Re: meeting

I have a question for you. Please come see me at your earliest convenience.

Messages like that get under my skin. Ask the question

in the message; don't present a future conversation as a cliff-hanger. I didn't go to Primm when summoned. She found me cleaning out my classroom in preparation for the break.

"There you are," she said.

"Yes, I'm here."

"Did you get my email?" she said.

"No," I lied.

I don't know why, but it felt right.

She walked over to my desk and perched on one butt cheek. Then she sighed and looked at the ceiling. I was tempted to walk out of the room during her dramatic pause.

"What's on your mind, Primm?"

"Something has been brought to my attention. I know you've been teaching for a few years. And I'm sure you've learned many lessons of your own. But, as a counselor, I would be remiss if I did not remind you that students, especially at this age, are so easily influenced by authority figures. Things we say can be misinterpreted. Therefore, we have to be the adults in this relationship. We must be unimpeachable."

"If there's a point to this lecture, you need to get to it in the next thirty seconds," I said.

Primm's lips pursed, taking the shape of a rotting piece of fruit. I kept telling myself to breathe, which I did in spurts.

Primm opened up her bag and pulled out a folded piece of craft paper. She laid the blowchart on my desk.

"This was brought to my attention recently. It's my understanding that you are the original author."

"What about it?" I said.

"Decisions about sexual behavior should be discussed between students and their parents. I think we need to have a dialogue about appropriate conduct with students."

"*Dialogue* is code for *lecture.* And you'd have to pay me at least a year's salary to listen to you talk."

I grabbed my coat and bag and walked to the door.

"If you refuse," Primm said, "I'll have to write you up."

"For what? Discouraging blowjobs? Or telling you to go fuck yourself?"

To my deep satisfaction, Primm was speechless. Unfortunately, she was also motionless.

"You can leave or I can lock you inside. Up to you," I said, jangling my keys.

Eventually Primm got to her feet.

"To be continued," Primm said, as she made her ridiculously slow exit.

NORMAN CROWLEY

I remember the first time I saw them. They were walking down the hall together. Bald, proud, angry. The boys didn't laugh when they saw them. They'd never been quieter. You could feel their fear.

The girls didn't look like girls anymore. They looked like warriors.

At first the editors just seemed kind of stunned. Gabe thought things had gone awry starting with Adam's whole courtship strategy. Nick, on the other hand, behaved like the Englishman he was and took a step back.

"I don't want to get involved in your bollocks. It's all before my time," Nick said.

Jack kept going on about all the girls' menstrual cycles being in sync and how we had to wait them out.

Usually it's Mick and Adam who are in sync. Mick was the face of the operation, but Adam was the one behind the scenes, greasing the wheels. Adam liked to play the nice guy, to make the others be the brutish ones. I was always curious why Adam entered so few names in the Darkroom or Dulcinea. But now things were different. The girls had taken a sledgehammer (or an ax) to his entire world, and they showed no signs of letting up.

Adam wasn't hiding behind his dimples and pink shirts anymore. He couldn't prove I'd helped the girls, but I saw how he looked at me. He was waiting for me to fuck up. What he'd do after that, I didn't know. I was still helping Gemma and Mel. I changed their identities in my phone to Tom (Gemma) and Jerry (Mel). It wasn't a great cover, especially since I'd often forget which was which. "Tom" wasn't satisfied with just shutting down the Darkroom or exposing the Dulcinea Award—she wanted to know where it all began. She asked me to see if I could identify the original Hef. MadMax may have inspired the Darkroom, but the first Hef created the Dulcinea Award. I was able to access old chat-room data and discovered the very first reference to Dulcinea was associated with Hef's previous screen name. I didn't tell Gemma right away. I texted Jonah and asked him to meet me at the greenhouse.

When I arrived, I saw Ms. Primm circling the building, peeking inside. The last thing I needed was another Primm intervention. I took cover. When Jonah showed up, I threw a rock at his feet to get his attention. He casually walked over to me.

"Dude, why are you crouched in the bushes?"

"I don't want Primm to see me," I said.

"Why?"

"Because the last time I saw her, I had to tell her I was gay."

Jonah rolled his eyes, like that was no big deal.

"Who hasn't?"

We continued our conversation under the cover of the

trees. It was dangerous for Jonah to be seen with me. Up until now all he'd done was quit the editorial board. No one knew he was a true dissenter.

Besides, I didn't see Jonah taking any of those guys on. At least not yet. Jonah avoided confrontation whenever possible. We were the same that way, really. We just wore it differently. On me it looked like a pair of parachute pants.

I opened my laptop and brought up a screenshot of a message thread between Jonah's brother, "Bagman," and "LongJohn" where Bagman first mentions Dulcinea and suggests they start an unofficial contest and build it into the Darkroom site.

"What is this?" Jonah said, glancing at the screenshot.

"Your brother started the Dulcinea Award," I said.

"No," said Jonah. "The original Hef was Edwin Silver. He and Jason were tight, but . . ."

"I looked at the archives from the locker room site," I said. "LongJohn was Edwin Silver. It looks like your brother and Edwin started the Darkroom together, but Dulcinea was Jason's idea. This is the first mention of it anywhere."

"Nah. Really?" Jonah said, like I'd just told him his cat had died.

"Was Jason super into that book *Don Quixote* or something?"

"Jason read the sports sections and that's all I remember."

Jonah sat down on the dirt and rested his head in his hands. He didn't know. Or maybe he kind of knew but wouldn't let himself know for sure.

"I just want all of this shit to end," he said.

"Me too."

ANNOUNCEMENTS

Good morning, students of Stone. It is Monday, December 14, 2009.

So, this is a first: I just put my own suggestion in the suggestion box. Let me read it to you: There are an alarming number of trees being chopped down for sport. Look, if you were making paper or in dire need of firewood, I'd get it. But you're just chopping the trees down and leaving them there. Someone could trip over one. I consulted with Coach Keith and he insists that lumberjacking is not a new PE elective. Any student caught assaulting campus vegetation will be expelled, no questions asked. And please, please return all of the axes. Anyone caught with a Stonebridge-issued tool will be charged with grand larceny. I am very serious. *What? Hold on.*

[inaudible]

Correction: Expulsion and arrest are not necessarily inevitable; however, there will be repercussions. Okay? [inaudible] Dean Stinson concurs with that last statement.

Once again, the use of axes and the assault on trees will not be tolerated. Looks like it'll be a warm eighty-two degrees with no shortage of sun.

GEMMA RUSSO

We all had our own tipping point, when what we thought we had known, the rules we'd bought into, changed. When angry turned to feral.

For Tegan it was a list, a computerized printout of all the other girls who had been with her guy.

For Emelia, it was being duped. Believing that someone had held her in esteem, only to discover what he really thought of her.

For Hannah, it was her bad marks and knowing she was going to lose.

For Mel, it was all about the data, the massive effort involved in turning us girls into letters, numbers, ranks, and codes.

For Kate, it was the photo seen around the school. Her punishment for trusting a friend.

And for Linny, it was the loss of her innocence. But Linny was ahead of the curve, a savage and warrior long before the rest of us.

But the other girls, they weren't done. Taking an ax to a frail tree was merely a Band-Aid, incapable of stanching their ever-increasing rage. They needed more. They needed to spackle the craters that each humiliation carved out of their souls.

My trajectory took a different route. It was more like a light switch toggling on and off until the circuit blew.

NORMAN CROWLEY

There will be blood.

Adam Westlake actually used those words. I never noticed what a drama queen he was, not until the girls started laying siege to his kingdom.

Maybe Adam always knew I was a turncoat. I have a lousy poker face. Maybe he finally got proof; maybe he didn't. By the time everything blew up, proof didn't matter. Someone had to pay.

It was late when Adam, Jack, and Mick burst into my room. We keep the door locked, and I didn't hear anyone messing with the bolt. They got a key somehow. Mick shook Calvin awake and told him to sleep in the lounge. My roommate staggered out, bleary-eyed. Later, I heard that Calvin knocked on Jonah's door and told him something was going down. I always meant to thank him for that.

At first, Adam was friendly, in that sinister mobbed-up kind of way. Maybe he'd re-watched *Scarface* to get into character. He sat down on my bed, put his arm around my shoulder, and asked me what I'd done.

I denied everything. I told him that the girls had hacked the Darkroom, all of it, on their own. He shook his head in disappointment, like the way your father does when you tell him you don't want to go hunting over the weekend.

Mick sat down on the other side. Both of those buffoons had their arms around me and they were smiling. If you took a snapshot and published it in the yearbook, everyone would think we were the best of friends.

"Good man," Mick said. "Confession will cleanse your soul."

"I've got nothing to confess," I said.

I really wanted to confess. I just didn't want to get beat up or have my mattress turned into a urinal. I said nothing.

"I know why you did it," Adam said. "You thought if you helped out the girls, played the white knight, it might finally get you some pussy."

"And what man could blame you for that?" Mick said.

"Yeah," said Jack. "Pussy is everything."

Jack was standing right in front of me, playing the goon.

"But it didn't work out that way, did it?" Adam said. "You're just their girlfriend now, one of them. Don't despair. I'm sure you'll get lucky by the end of college. She may have a unibrow, an ass the size of Kentucky, and a wandering eye, but you'll love her all the same."

These meatheads were laughing their asses off.

"At least the girls like me," I said. "You should hear the way they talk about you dickheads when you're not around. You know they have their own Darkroom."

I was just riffing at that point. I realized I would get a

beatdown no matter what, and I wanted the pain to be worth it.

"They gave up ranking sexual performance because no one was ever satisfied. Mostly they just make fun of how bad you all are in bed, and sometimes they compare dick notes—"

I don't remember what I said after that. It was Jack who landed the first punch to my gut. I doubled over and curled up on the floor. Mick did a karate chop to my ribs. I thought I heard something crack. The pain wasn't as bad as the anticipation of the next blow.

I heard Jonah tell them to stop.

"It was me," Jonah said. "I let them in. I gave them my password. I told Gemma everything she wanted to know."

I remember it went really quiet. I opened my eyes and saw Jonah in the doorway, his hands balled into fists, ready to fight. Adam stood up and faced Jonah.

"Let me take this one, boys," Adam said.

In a fair fight, Jonah would destroy Adam, but Mick and Jack gripped Jonah's arms so Adam could kick him in the balls. Jonah doubled over. Jack and Mick dragged him into the hallway to finish the job.

I texted Tom and Jerry. I don't know what I thought they'd do.

The editors were tucked away in their rooms when Gemma, Mel, Kate, Emelia, and Tegan showed up. I still couldn't get used to their shaved heads. If that wasn't scary enough, both Gemma and Emelia carried axes over their shoulders. Emelia swung her weapon against Adam's door, leaving a giant gaping crevice.

The girls took Jonah to the infirmary, where he wouldn't tell anyone what happened. After that, Mel came into my room. I was still in a lot of pain, but I didn't want to answer any questions. I just wanted to sleep. I told Mel to go home. She closed the door, locked it, and shoved Calvin's desk in front of the door. She was stronger than she looked.

"Go to sleep, Norman. I'll protect you," she said, sliding into bed next to me.

I know I should have felt like a wuss having a girl come to my rescue.

I didn't care.

MS. WITT

Norman limped into class, head down, holding his side. He took a seat in row 3, aisle 2, still on the boys' side, but adjacent to Mel. And yet, the class divide seemed more pronounced. The silence had a strange simmering quality to it. I heard only one conversation between the warring parties.

Nick: Don't be like that, sweetheart.
Emelia: You're lucky I didn't burn your dick off.

Jonah was notably absent. I asked the class if he was sick.

"He's in the infirmary," Gemma said, holding her gaze on Adam.

There was endless tapping. I would have confiscated their phones if I didn't think it would cause a mutiny.

There was no point in starting a lecture or a class discussion. Everyone had shut down. I told them to work on their projects in silence. It occurred to me, not for the first time, that I wasn't doing much teaching. I think my longest lecture at Stonebridge was on the blowchart. The idea of quitting returned with a vengeance.

I asked Gemma to hang back after class.

"The situation looks dire," I said.

"It's a long-overdue reckoning. It will take the boys some time to adjust to their new world. It might even get worse before it gets better."

"Please don't say that. What can I do?"

"Nothing."

During my free period, I went to the infirmary to visit Jonah.

By the look of him, it wasn't a fair fight. The nurse informed me that Jonah had spent the night in the hospital as a precaution against a concussion. He had a black eye and a split lip and other injuries that I couldn't see.

I didn't bother to ask what happened. He wouldn't have answered.

"Are you going to tell me what the other guy looks like?" I said.

"Abbreviated forehead, beady eyes, can't breathe with a closed mouth. Not a scratch on him, I'm afraid to say."

I reached into my bag and brought out a jar of peanut butter and a large block of chocolate.

"The chocolate and PB are from the teachers' larder. We get better stuff than you," I said.

"Thanks," he said, putting the food on the end table.

"I heard you were on the right side," I said. "I'm proud of you."

"Don't be," he said. "I'm not sure I helped because it was right. I did it for a girl."

"Maybe it was for both reasons," I said.

"Maybe."

"If you need anything, you know where to find me."

"Thanks, Ms. Witt."

I visited Greg's office after that. The discord between the boys and girls was impossible to miss. When I told him about the Darkroom and the contest, he listened intently, as if I were delivering a thorny philosophical lecture. When I was done, Greg closed his eyes and rubbed his temples.

"I had no idea there were so many . . . what's the word I'm looking for?" Greg said.

"Douchebags," I said.

"Yes. That's it," Greg said. "We'll need a contingency plan if the tension doesn't deescalate. I suppose we could separate the classes between boys and girls. It would require a massive restructuring of the schedule and there would be some academic casualties, but it's better than having students try to learn in an overtly hostile environment."

Greg looked tired and older, and I couldn't help but feel guilty.

"There's only a few days until break," I said. "Then they'll have two weeks to cool down."

I figured the new year would be a fresh start. Teenagers were resilient, right?

I hadn't seen Claude since our afternoon at Hemingway's. I was surprised when I saw her text on Wednesday evening.

Claude: Meet me inside Keats Studio in 15. There's something important I need to show you.
Claude: Be quiet when you enter.

I was in bed reading, about to turn off the light. Curiosity got the best of me. And, frankly, I hoped to talk with her about the current state of affairs. I didn't bother getting dressed. I just threw on a coat over my pajamas and slipped into my rain boots. I strode across Fleming Square. There was virtually no sound coming from Woolf and Dickens. And only a few lights shone from inside. The campus felt eerily deserted. I followed the unlit path to the studios.

I entered Keats without a word, as instructed. I didn't consider the oddness of the request until later. The lights were out. I couldn't see much. As my eyes adjusted to the dark, I realized there was someone against the far wall. I couldn't tell what I was looking at. I searched for the light switch by the door. As the fluorescent bulbs ignited, I saw them. It was all too bright. I would have done almost anything to never see what I saw.

Adam stood in the corner of the room, staring right at me, his mouth twisted in a sneer. On her knees in front of him was Claude. She was—

"Oh my God, oh my God," she said, shielding her face from the light.

I didn't say anything. I turned around and ran. I felt sick, dizzy, and my head began to throb. As I climbed the stairs to my apartment, I could barely catch my breath.

I remembered my first meeting with Claude. How perfect I thought she was. What great friends I thought we'd become.

Back in the apartment, I took a glass and a bottle of bourbon to bed. I knew I wouldn't sleep that night. I poured one drink after the next. I didn't care how I would feel the next day. I just wanted to take the edge off the entire world. It was my drunken mind that kept coming back to that first introduction.

Hi. I'm Claudine Shepherd.

Claudine. It's not a name you hear very often. Claudine.

I was never a great Scrabble player, even though I was raised in a house of words. But sometimes your brain tells you things your unconscious mind doesn't want to see.

Claudine. Dulcinea. Claudine. Dulcinea.

Fuck. How did I miss that?

MR. FORD

I saw Alex in the hallway as she left Dean Stinson's office. Her eyes were open, but I doubt she saw me. It was like she was in a trance. Martha walked out after her, and Greg shut his door.

"What's going on?" I said.

"This isn't a hallway conversation," said Martha.

It was one of those rare occasions when she got me curious enough to follow her alone into her office. Martha was delighted to tell me the sordid tale. I sat down in one of the chairs across from her desk. She pulled her chair right next to mine, so we could have a close, intimate chat.

"Early this morning, before class, Adam Westlake came to my office. He said he needed to talk to someone, a professional," Martha said.

I knew right then that Adam was playing her. Unfortunately, Martha didn't.

"What did he want to talk about?" I said.

Martha took a deep breath, had her dramatic pause.

"Adam Westlake and Alex Witt have been having a sexual relationship since the third week of school."

I laughed.

"It's not funny, Finn."

"Martha, that's bullshit and you know it."

"God, Finn, you're pathetic. I can't believe you still like that . . . woman. There is irrefutable evidence. She did it. It's that simple. Dean Stinson just suspended her. He's called the board of advisers. She was ordered to leave campus. There will be an immediate investigation. I'm sure the board will want to interview you. Everyone."

"Did Alex admit anything?" I said.

"Of course not," said Primm.

"What's the evidence?"

"There was a witness," Primm said. "Someone—not a student, mind you; an *adult*—saw them together."

"Who?" I said.

"I knew right from the day I met her that she was bad news," said Primm.

"Who was the witness?"

"Our friend Claude."

I wouldn't have minded if Alex left Stonebridge of her own volition. But this wasn't right.

I went straight to the library. Claude's desk was vacant. I asked the students if anyone had seen her. A few kids pointed to the storage room in the far back corner of the library. I walked over and knocked on the door. There was no answer. I reached for the knob. It was locked.

"Open up, Claude. We need to talk."

I waited. Nothing. I knocked again and told her I wasn't

leaving. She unlocked the door. Claude was sitting in the dark on a stepladder. I turned on the light. She had been crying for so long, her tears had scrubbed her face clean.

"Why are you doing this, Claude?"

She wouldn't look at me.

"I have to," she whispered.

I had only suspected until that point. But then I knew that there was only one way Adam could convince Claude to tell such a lie.

"How long has it been going on?" I said.

She held up her hand to stop me.

"Don't look at me like that. You're not exactly a model citizen yourself," Claude said.

"I never fucked a student," I whispered.

"That's not the word on the street."

I never should have confided in Claude. It was a close call with Rachel, but that's all it was. But Claude made a good point. Appearances were everything.

NORMAN CROWLEY

There were two days left before break. We really needed to get away from each other. The teachers were done teaching. They'd just play movies in class or tell us to work independently. There was nothing else to do but sit on the sidelines while the feud festered like an infected wound.

Adam skipped class, but Ms. Witt pretended like she didn't notice. Then Witt was summoned to Dean Stinson's office and never came back. Adam left early for break. No one knew what was going on.

Coach Keith still made us run. The running felt like a punishment. On the cross-country loop, Gabriel Smythe slowed down and shoved me while I tried to pass him. I fell into a ravine and cut my knee. When Gemma ran past, she gave me a hand up.

She asked if it was Gabe. I nodded.

She took off after him. By the time I'd finished the loop, Gabriel was sitting on the field and Coach was wrapping his leg. I asked Gemma what happened. He tripped, she said. They took him to the hospital after that. He returned that night on crutches.

Adam's crew had secret meetings in the lounge. I thought about setting up audio surveillance, but I wasn't sure I could take another beating. Calvin was scared. He filed paperwork for a new roommate. Primm made me come to her office. She wanted to know if Calvin's request had something to do with my sexual orientation.

"Maybe," I said.

The truth doesn't matter here.

MS. WITT

I was so disturbed by what I had seen that I had no idea I was being set up.

I didn't know what to do when I saw Claude with Adam. I needed the night to think about it. But Adam's plan was already in motion. By the time the shock wore off and reasoning kicked in, it was the next morning. I went to Greg's office to tell him, but he spoke first.

He spoke in halting sentences, like he does when he's uncomfortable.

"Some very serious allegations have been brought—"

It felt like the outside world had slowed down while my thoughts had sped up. At first I thought that Greg was talking about Adam and Claude. I wondered who had told him.

"—to my attention. Obviously, I don't believe it. But I have to follow protocol, since an adult and a student have made the same allegation. Your employment is suspended until further notice. I'm sorry, Alex. I don't understand what's happening here."

"My employment?"

"Yes," Greg said. "I'm sorry—my hands are tied. Evelyn Lubovich will accompany you to your apartment. You have fifteen minutes to gather any necessities. We'll have the rest of your possessions packed and sent at a later date. I need you off campus within the hour."

"I don't understand. What did I do?"

"You have been accused of having sexual relations with a student, which is cause for immediate dismissal," Greg said.

"*I've* been accused?"

Greg's eyes searched his office, like he'd lost something. I think he just didn't want to look at me.

"Adam told Martha that you and he—and Ms. Shepherd confirmed the allegation. She said she walked in on the two of you."

"No. No. He didn't—she didn't—"

"If it were just his word . . . but with Shepherd's corroboration, you see how it looks?"

"That's not what happened," I said.

But I didn't say it with the power or the rage I felt inside. I felt hollowed out, like a scraped-clean avocado skin. My voice was thin and tinny.

"It was Claude and Adam. I don't know why he would say that—"

Then I did know.

My hands were shaking. I could feel hot tears on my face. I couldn't move.

"There will be an investigation and we'll sort this out," Greg said.

Primm walked in. She made me sign something. I don't know what it was.

"Until the investigation is complete, you must cease all contact with students. Stay at least a hundred yards from the campus at all times. Do you understand me?" Primm said.

"I will never understand you," I said.

"Do you understand my instructions?" she said. "No contact with students. No texting, no talking, and—"

"Walk away, Martha. I can't look at you," I said.

"Martha, please," Greg said. "Leave."

Primm walked out.

"I'll find you a lawyer, Alex. I'm sorry," said Greg.

I remember Evelyn accompanying me to the apartment. Inside, I forgot why I was there, what I was supposed to do. I sat down on the couch and stared at the TV screen.

Evelyn packed a bag for me. She walked me to the front gate.

"It didn't happen," I said. "I would never do that."

"Alex, we all make mistakes."

"You believe them?" I said.

"I don't know. But why would they lie?" Evelyn said.

Her eyes were cold. She looked at me as if I were a monster. I felt guilty for something I hadn't done.

GEMMA RUSSO

Witt didn't show up for class. Rupert rolled in a TV and DVD player and screened *Dr. Strangelove,* which is apparently his favorite film.

I asked Rupert what happened to Witt.

"A family emergency or maybe the flu," he said.

I sent Witt a couple of texts and I never heard back. I didn't think much of it. There were only two days left. People often skipped out early.

Jonah was still pretty beat up, but he said he was fine. We met secretly in Witt's old cottage. It smelled like mold, but it was private. I kissed Jonah's bruises and we had sex. Like, regular sex. It was really nice, even though he winced a lot from his injuries. He was sweet about it all, maybe too sweet. I told him that. He said that it was hard to know how to be a guy. He said that he was always confused.

I felt the same way.

Jonah's parents arrived a day early to pick him up from school. He wanted to introduce me to them, but I was afraid he'd break up with me if they didn't approve. They can't disapprove of someone they've never met. Jonah asked me when my parents were going to collect me. I told him that I was taking the train to New Jersey on Saturday morning.

"I thought you lived in Connecticut," he said.

"My parents live in Connecticut. My grandmother lives in Hoboken," I said, thinking fast.

"Write that down so you don't forget next time," Jonah said.

"I'll do that."

We kissed goodbye like regular boyfriend and girlfriend, although we didn't let anyone see us, because Jonah was already labeled a traitor and I didn't want him to get any more bruises.

I didn't keep up the pretense that I had a home anywhere else. I watched friends and allies pack and said my goodbyes.

Tegan and I hugged for the first time. She tried to put a positive spin on my two weeks under Greg's roof.

"Think of all the weight you'll lose eating his food. I'm just going to get fat at home. Wanna trade places?"

Linny's mother drove from Portland, Maine, to pick her up. In the past I would walk Linny to the front gate, but there was no way I was going to be present when her mother saw her hair. She'd chopped it off with a pair of scissors. She wanted the full buzz effect, but I talked her out of it. The Joan of Arc look kind of suited her. But I knew her mother wouldn't see it that way.

Mel and Emelia both invited me to spend the holidays with their families. I declined. Greg and I have a system. It works. Besides, Kate reminded me of our interrupted mission.

"While we're gone, maybe you'll find the time to see what's in Adam's locked cabinet," she said.

There would be plenty of time for that.

There are a couple of weeks in winter and summer when the school is entirely vacated. I'm not allowed to stay in the dorms those weeks, so I move into Greg's guest room. I don't call him Dean Stinson when I'm staying in his home.

We eat all of our meals together and watch a lot of BBC mysteries. Greg sure loves that Hercule Poirot. During the day, we go for ridiculously long walks where Greg tries to teach me about every goddamn weed on the Stonebridge grounds. You'd think with all of those weeds there might actually be some weed.

We've been doing this for almost two and a half years. Greg had to apply years ago to be my foster parent so I wouldn't have to move in with a stranger twice a year during Stonebridge breaks.

I was eating cereal in the kitchen of Byron Manor, which is not as fancy as it sounds. Greg sat down at the table. He looked like he had something on his mind.

"What's up?" I said.

"I'll never get used to that hair," Greg said. "I can't believe you girls thought you had to shave your heads to get rid of lice."

"I know. Stupid, huh?" I said, shaking my head.

It was easier telling him the lice story. Sometimes I just want to protect him from the truth. I know how he wants the world to be, and if I can move his perception just an inch closer to that, why not?

"I want to talk to you . . . Huh. Well, I'll just say it. You'll be eighteen in four months," Greg said.

"I know," I said.

"We're running out of time," Greg said.

"I'm not following," I said.

"If I were to adopt you, I would need to do it before you turned eighteen."

It hadn't occurred to me that he was even thinking of that. "Adopt me?"

"It's just an idea. And it doesn't have to change anything. My home is your home, no matter what. I know you plan to go to college. But over holidays and summer you can stay here, like we do now. I just thought it might be nice to make it official. It would make some things easier. I could put you on my health plan and deduct some of your expenses."

I started crying, and I couldn't stop for like twenty minutes. I didn't know what was wrong with me. Greg just sat there handing me one tissue after the next.

When I finally stopped crying, Greg said, "You wouldn't have to call me Dad or anything."

Then I couldn't stop laughing. We filled out the paperwork together. I didn't think it would change things, but it did.

During one of Greg's afternoon naps, I headed over to Dick House. I used Greg's master key and broke into Adam's room.

Then I picked the lock on his file cabinet. It's not a talent of mine or anything. I watched a video online. The guy in the video cracked the lock in thirty seconds; it took me forty minutes. I collected the files and a small box of USB drives, and confiscated three bottles of his stolen champagne. Back in my office, I stored the champagne and reviewed the stolen material.

I always had a gut feeling that Adam was running the show. It wasn't until I saw his files that I understood the breadth of his operation. Adam had dossiers of disgrace on just about anyone who was anyone at Stonebridge. Gathering dirt on people was basically Adam's life's work.

I wasn't surprised at all when I saw the compromising photos of Ms. Shepherd. When Adam first brought me into the fold, he thought I'd caught them together. That's why he invited me out for coffee and was acting all nice. When I said that I didn't see anything, Adam thought I was pledging my allegiance. It was almost a year later when I caught them screwing in the library. That time Adam didn't see me. I didn't tell anyone for all kinds of reasons. I already saw what happened to snitches at Stonebridge. And I didn't perceive Adam as a victim. The blackmail photos of Ms. Shepherd confirmed that theory. Adults can debate that one. It wasn't my problem.

As I continued reviewing Adam's files, I found a folder on Ms. Witt. There were cryptic handwritten notations that suggested he was looking for a sex tape. Since there was a flash drive inside Witt's file, I assumed he found it. I didn't want to look at it, but I had to. I had to know.

I'd never been so happy to see such a dull movie. It was just a video of Witt sitting around grading papers.

Still, I had a feeling that something wasn't right. Adam doesn't give up. And Witt never responded to my text.

While Greg took his nap the following afternoon, I found his phone on the kitchen table. I sent Witt a text. I even remembered to spell out all of the words and use complete sentences.

Greg Stinson: Dear Alex, Please remind me where you are staying over break. Warmest regards, Gregory.

I waited impatiently, hoping that Ms. Witt would reply before Greg woke up. She did.

Alex: I'm with Keith. I thought he told you.

"Greg" asked for the address. Alex replied a few minutes later with 2865 Mountain Road.

I deleted the text thread and ventured out.

I never figured out how Keith knew so many rich people with second homes in Lowland. But, damn, he had one hell of a racket going on. The house on Mountain Road was one of those new, modern houses that's all window. I could see Witt and Coach Keith sitting around day-drinking or something. Neither of them noticed me until I was standing in front of the glass door.

Witt looked panicked. Keith said something I couldn't hear and Witt disappeared behind an actual wall.

"Gemma," Coach said when he opened the door. "You can't be here. Go home."

"Let me talk to Ms. Witt," I said.

Keith stepped outside and closed the door.

"Gemma, you have to leave. Alex can't have any contact with students."

"What happened. What did Adam do?" I knew Adam was behind it. I didn't know how.

"Ask Greg," Keith said. "You need to leave."

I ran back to campus. Greg was waiting for me in the kitchen. Coach had texted him as soon as I left.

Greg told me to stay out of it. That wasn't going to happen. It took about an hour to get Greg to spill the dirt. The first part of the story, Greg gave up pretty easily. Adam had made an allegation against Witt for inappropriate conduct. How Adam got that allegation to stick was what took some time. Greg kept trying to say it in a way that didn't sound gross.

I told Greg what I knew about Adam and Ms. Shepherd. He was angry at me—like, really angry—for not telling him sooner.

I figured that would be the end of the investigation. Ms. Witt could come back to Stonebridge after the break. Greg said it wasn't that simple. The accusation had been made. The investigation would have to continue.

Greg sent me to my room. He told me I was grounded.

I sent Witt a text.

Gemma: You told me to fight. Why didn't you fight?

MS. WITT

After Evelyn packed my bag, I walked to Motel and checked in. I pulled the blinds, crawled into bed, and fell asleep. When I woke up, sometime in the afternoon, Keith was at the door, knocking. I don't know who told him. He drove me to his current residence—a three-story monolith on the east side of town. It was run-down but well appointed, with a swimming pool, Jacuzzi, and fully stocked bar. Behind the pool was a dense patch of woods.

I went outside and chopped down a tree, a white spruce. Swinging an ax, slowly chipping away at the trunk, the exhaustion of throwing your whole body into something, it made sense. How was that the first time I'd ever felled a tree?

We talked about the school as if it were an infection. Keith wondered whether the cycle of abuse began with Claude's teacher. If so, would it end with her? He was trying to figure out how to save this place he loved. I would have to take out another tree if we were going to keep talking about it. He never brought it up again. But I could tell it was always on his mind.

My mother drove up in the morning. Keith left us alone to talk.

"Why are you staying here?" she said.

"I have to clear my name."

"Greg says the board won't meet until after the new year. You could come home for a couple of weeks," she said.

"I'm going to stay," I said.

"You like him," she said.

"I do. But it won't last."

"Why is that?" she said.

"Because Stonebridge is his home. It'll never be mine."

"So don't fall in love."

"I'll do my best," I said.

My mother is of the opinion that one can control such emotions. She asked me if I would be all right without her, because she had to go back. My father had blown through his second deadline and, for the first time in years, Dad asked my mother directly for her help, since Sloan was now gone and I was unavailable. Because my mother still receives royalties for the Len Wilde canon, she was happy to assist. If I hadn't been so occupied with my own concerns, I would have derailed their inevitably fraught collaboration. My parents still had many years of being old and at odds. I needed to pace myself.

After my mother left, Gemma dropped by. I don't know how she found me. I hid in one of the bedrooms. I was trying to do everything right, so I could clear my name. That was naïve. My name would never be cleared.

I knew I wouldn't teach again. It was the only thing I was sure of.

NORMAN CROWLEY

I hated Christmas break. Ron, my mom's new guy, was around constantly. He kept pestering me to go outside and throw a football with him. I finally did, to make my mother happy. Ron was showing off, tossing bullets at me. One hit me in the rib that was probably cracked.

"Got to toughen you up," he said, when I doubled over in pain.

The only bright spots were the iPhone my dad got me and the daily texts from Mel.

It was Mel who told me what happened to Ms. Witt, what Ms. Shepherd had done to her. I know Ms. Shepherd was supposed to be the responsible adult, but I hung all the blame on Adam. I didn't forgive Ms. Shepherd, exactly, but I couldn't bring myself to hate her. I wished that I could have talked to her and gotten her side. I still feel like there's some part of the story that I don't understand.

Mel said Gemma had a plan, that we'd get revenge on Adam in the new year. As much as I wanted Adam to pay for all the shit he'd done, I didn't want things to get any worse.

Mom and I were alone on New Year's Eve. We watched that lame special with Ryan Seacrest and waited two hours for a disco ball to drop a hundred feet. I don't get it. What does that have to do with anything? If the ball dropped and then exploded with money, like a cash piñata, it would make sense for thousands of people to endure hours upon hours of crowds and cold and not peeing.

Mom let me have a flute of champagne, which she thought was an enormous privilege. I didn't mention all the quality bourbon I'd had at Stonebridge. At least my mom seemed happy. She mussed my hair a lot and kissed me on the cheek. And sometimes I'd catch her looking at me like I was a puzzle.

"What, Mom?" I'd say.

"Nothing," she'd say. "You look different, older. I can't put my finger on it. Maybe you're just growing up."

I couldn't sleep that last night I was home. I kept thinking about Dulcinea. It was an odd name for an odd tradition, especially one whose founder didn't read books, like Jonah said. Mel had told me about Adam and Ms. Shepherd. I had heard things over the years. I figured they were lies. The editors told so many, why would I believe one that I didn't want to be true? I couldn't bear to think of Ms. Shepherd and Adam together. Mel said she hated Shepherd. I hated what she had done. But—and I know I'm not supposed to feel this way—I still loved her.

I was supposed to head back to Stonebridge on Sunday morning. The night before, I was barfing. I could have stayed home indefinitely. My mother had never wanted me in a boarding school to begin with. I thought about never going back. But I didn't want to be a coward. I didn't want Mel to think I was a coward. Besides, I thought they needed me. For the first time, I felt like I was a part of something.

GEMMA RUSSO

Winter break at Stonebridge has always been remarkably dull. Maybe Greg thought that was punishment enough. He did insist on one hike a day and I had to eat venison twice. But that probably would have been the case no matter what I had done. Eventually, I realized that I could come and go as I pleased. It's not like there was any more trouble I could get into.

We had a white Christmas. Greg was elated. He just stood on the porch, gazing out into the glittering layer of white powder. Without hundreds of boots pummeling the fresh snow, Stonebridge looked so pristine, like something you'd see in a children's book.

I made a snowman behind Byron Manor. I dressed him in one of Greg's tweed jackets and the deerstalker cap he always wears on hikes. Since I didn't have a proper present for Greg, the kind you wrap in paper, I thought it would be nice to stick a bottle of champagne into the snowman's base. It was one of the bottles I'd stolen back from Adam.

"Merry Christmas," I said, when I took Greg out back.

"Now, that's delightful," Greg said.

He promptly removed the coat and hat and shook off the snow. Then Greg noticed the champagne.

"Where did this come from?" Greg said.

"Don't worry. I didn't steal it from a store or anything. I stole it from the thief who stole it from the school."

"I see," Greg said. "And may I ask the identity of the first thief?"

If I mentioned Adam's name it would take some of the shine off the day.

"You're welcome," I said.

I could tell that Greg was debating whether he wanted to get into it or not. But we had a nice tree and a table full of hot food—I'd convinced him to roast a regular chicken—and he'd already signed the adoption papers.

"Thank you, Gemma. That is a handsome snowman."

I asked Greg if I could have a glass of champagne as my Christmas present. He gave me three pairs of wool socks, a fifty-dollar bill, and snowshoes. The next day, I trekked through the fresh powder, spelling out my name in giant loops.

Coach Keith dropped by sometime. The days between Christmas and New Year's blurred together. There was a brief thaw and the snow lost its sheen. I remember Keith stomping his muddy boots at the door. While Greg was getting him coffee, I told Keith that I had physical evidence that might prove Adam's relationship with Shepherd. If my word wasn't enough.

"He'll be taken care of. Don't worry," I said.

"Gemma, you sound like a mobster. Please don't *take care* of anyone."

I told Keith to relax. He did not relax. He made me promise not to do anything.

"I won't do anything. I promise," I said.

Sometimes you have to lie to adults for their own good.

After two weeks of nature walks and PBS, I was ready for 2010. I missed my friends and allies. And, honestly, I missed the thrill of the fight. I was ready to finish this thing.

Jonah came back to Stonebridge a day early so we could be together. With all of Dick House vacated, we could hook up in his room. We tried to get comfortable in that twin bed, but we fit together like pieces from two different puzzles. Jonah got a cramp in his shoulder, and my leg started falling asleep. I got up and dressed.

"How was your Connecticut-slash-Hoboken holiday?" he said.

"Nothing special," I said.

I was trying to keep my lies to a minimum.

"I know, Gemma. I know you were here over the holidays. I know you're an orphan."

"Actually, not an orphan anymore," I said.

Jonah was the first person I told about the adoption. I think he was happier for me than I was. I felt so good in that moment that it scared me. It never lasts, that feeling. Never. It wouldn't last more than five minutes.

Since I was being all confessional, I told Jonah about stealing Adam's files. Well, I started to tell him. But then Jonah got all weird. He wasn't happy anymore. He said he didn't care. He didn't want to talk about it.

"Adam has to pay for what he's done. They all have to pay," I said.

"An eye for an eye will only make the whole world blind," Jonah said.

"Where'd you get that gem?"

"Gandhi."

"Oh my God," I said. "I hate quoters. If you have something to say, say it in your own words."

"Okay," Jonah said. "You're like a cartoon villain. Get over yourself."

"When you were home over the holidays, did you ask your brother why he started Dulcinea?"

Jonah didn't react. He wasn't surprised by the information or the fact that I had learned of it.

"You knew," I said.

"Norman told me a few weeks ago," Jonah said.

"He named it after Claudine Shepherd," I said. "Did you know that?"

He didn't know that part. Though he wasn't all that surprised.

"Gemma—"

"Were you ever going to tell me?" I said.

"I found out when you did," Jonah said. "Look, my brother was a complete douche. But he's my brother and he's not at Stonebridge anymore. There's nothing I can do."

"You could help extinguish his legacy."

"I did that already. No one else needs to get hurt," Jonah said.

"That's where we disagree," I said.

I gathered my things and left. I didn't even know if Jonah and I were together. If we were, we had just broken up.

Greg had left that afternoon for Manchester. The board of advisers scheduled an emergency meeting to discuss the case against Witt and my written testimony about Shepherd. I told Greg I could get pictures if he needed them.

"You have pictures of Adam and Ms. Shepherd together?" Greg asked.

"No. I have naked pictures of Shepherd that Adam took," I said.

"Photos that you are now in possession of?" Greg said.

"They're on a USB drive," I said.

Greg didn't look well. I was worried that I was causing him too much stress.

"I'm not sure what that would prove and I certainly do not feel comfortable presenting such material at a board meeting," Greg said.

"You believe me, right?"

"Of course I believe you," Greg said. "But I am concerned about your methods."

I asked Greg what was going to happen to Ms. Witt.

"I'll make sure we clear her name," he said.

"So, you think she'll come back?" I asked.

Greg shook his head. "No matter what happens, she won't come back."

While Greg was meeting with the board, I summoned the group—the new group, the five—into my office to orchestrate a plan.

Everyone was distracted. Emelia had just learned that New Nick would not be returning.

"I wanted to show him my ax," Em said, swinging her shiny new weapon. Her mother had apparently given her one for Christmas. Then Mel grabbed Kate's wrist and said, "Did you get a tattoo?"

Then everyone huddled around Kate as she showed off her ink. It was just a simple line drawing of an ax, but everyone wanted one after that. If Lowland had a tattoo parlor, everything might have gone differently. Instead, Emelia drew axes on everyone's wrist. Linny showed up uninvited. I told her she had to leave. She had two more years at this school. If there was any fallout from our actions, I wanted to keep her out of it.

I opened my desk drawer and removed a thick folder. It contained a compilation of Adam's secret files. I shared them with my allies.

Tegan wanted to know how long Adam and Shepherd had been fucking.

Mel asked how many other boys the librarian had been with.

Emelia couldn't take her eyes off the pictures of Ms.

Shepherd. She was naked, looking into the camera. The photos weren't taken on a whim. It was like Adam knew this day would come.

"He's just like J. Edgar Hoover," said Mel.

"Who?" said Tegan.

"He's sick," Emelia said.

"She's sick," Kate said.

"They're both sick," Mel said.

"Adam was abused. Something with his stepmother," said Emelia.

"Oh my God," said Tegan.

"We can use that," said Kate.

"No," said Emelia. "He told me in confidence."

"Who gives a shit," said Kate.

"We're not letting him get away with what he did to Witt," I said.

"Agreed," said Emelia. "But that part stays with us."

We didn't need that detail anyway. The files themselves were all we needed to destroy Adam's role as King Dickhead.

Kate, fully engrossed in the files, was in the first stage of shock. I remember it well. She would turn one page after the next, saying, *Oh my God.* Repeat.

It was an impressive collection for a guy who was only seventeen. Anything you might want to keep hidden, Adam would add to your file. His muckraking ran the gamut from inconsequential to darkest shame. Carl Bloom suffered from hemorrhoids; Sandra Polonsky had a third nipple; Bethany Wiseman took lithium; Hannah Rexall had been arrested four times for shoplifting; Norman Crowley attempted suicide at age fourteen. Rachel Rose, despite her claims to the contrary, never fucked Finn. Although there was a grainy shot of them kissing.

The list goes on.

Adam's cohorts, the editors, his so-called friends, were spared the least. Smythe had a micropenis; the browser history on his computer was positively hysterical. Mick was molested by a priest when he was eleven. He even testified against that priest in court a few years later. Nick's file contained love letters between Nick and his stepsister Chloe. In fact, Nick's arrival at Stonebridge was his parents' attempt to separate the two. Jack Vandenberg's file was no surprise at all. Two girls, ages eleven and twelve, had accused Jack of sexual assault when he worked as a camp counselor in upstate New York two summers ago. Mr. and Mrs. Vandenberg somehow managed to quash any official police report.

Some of the information that Adam had amassed was in the form of a memo from a private investigator named Gus Moody. Even without Moody, Adam had an aptitude for investigation way beyond his years.

I should also mention that I was not spared. Adam's PI had assembled a report on me not long after I arrived at Stonebridge. It might have been one of his meatier files.

I wasn't all that surprised Adam had figured out where I came from. Some of it is public record. He also had a newspaper clipping from eight years ago when our house exploded. There were a few copies of reports from my social worker. He had one thing that might have derailed my resolve at another time.

Handwritten in the margin of one of the memos, I saw this: *11/5/06. Prost Arrest. MA.*

It was only the second time I'd tried to make some extra cash. After the arrest, I found other ways. I didn't like the reminder of things I'd rather forget, but I was done keeping secrets.

We had a plan. It was a good one, I thought. We'd destroy Adam's credibility and hobble every single editor with one solid swing of the proverbial ax.

But before we could release the information, Adam discovered that his files were missing. I had considered putting them back before he returned to campus. But then I changed my mind. I wanted Adam to know they were gone; I wanted him to experience that moment when you feel like the earth beneath you isn't solid anymore.

I couldn't have anticipated his retaliatory move. And I still don't know how he convinced the editors to go along with it. It's not like they knew about the files.

Maybe if Ms. Witt had stayed, she could have helped us see a peaceful way out. But she wasn't there, and we didn't want peace anymore.

NORMAN CROWLEY

Jonah got a text from Carl Bloom, whose room is next door to the lounge. I was impressed that Carl decided to rat on Adam and his mates. Jonah and I found Carl holding a glass to the wall. I didn't bother telling Carl that you could hear everything without the glass.

We all leaned against the wall, listening in.

"Tell us what you know about the Darkroom breach," Adam said.

"The darkroom?" Linny said. "Isn't that a place where you develop photographs?"

It was surprising how cool and calm she sounded. I sent Mel a text.

Norman: Editors have Linny in lounge. What's going on?

Mel: Hostage sitch. Gemma took something from Adam. So A took from G.

"Linny, we know you know. Just tell us and we'll let you go," Adam said.

"I have no idea what you're talking about."

"Dude," said Jack, "just hold her hand over a candle or something. I promise you, she'll talk."

"Jack, my friend, we shall treat this prisoner of war according to the Geneva Conventions. Understood?" Adam said.

"Most appreciated," Linny said.

"Get the girl something to drink," said Adam.

"No thank you," said Linny. "I never drink beverages served by sketchy men."

"What is she even doing here?" Gabe said. "I mean, all the Darkroom stuff was Gemma and her crew."

"There's more information to be had," Adam said.

Adam was stalling. I didn't know what Gemma had, but it must have been important to him.

"Right," said Jack. "Like who fucked with the showers. We never caught that bitch."

"You wouldn't consider untying my wrists, would you?" Linny said.

Jonah closed his eyes and rested his head against Carl's wall when he heard that part. He looked beat. I texted Mel again.

"Don't rile them up," Jonah said. "That'll make it worse."

Carl Bloom, meanwhile, was trying to track down Finn or whatever adult was supposedly supervising this house of miscreants.

"Finn's phone is off," Carl said. "Dean Stinson isn't answering his home line. Should I contact Ms. Primm?"

Jonah and I shouted in unison: "No."

"Quid pro quo," I heard Mick say from the other side of

the wall. "Give up the shower terrorist—if you know who it is—and we'll untie your wrists."

"Untie my wrists and then I'll tell you," Linny said.

Jonah stepped out of Carl's room and tried to open the doors to the lounge. They were secured from the inside. They'd probably stuck something through the thick chrome handles. Jonah banged with his fist. "Let me in, guys. I need to tell you something."

"Get lost, Jonah," shouted Adam from the other side.

"I'm listening," said Mick—to Linny, I think. "Who did it?"

"It was me, you dimwitted degenerates," Linny said.

"Fuck," said Jonah.

Jonah and I returned to Carl's room and continued listening in through the thin walls.

"Who put you up to it?" Adam said.

"Non ducor, duco," Linny said. I think.

"What?" said one of the guys.

"*Non ducor, duco.* I am not led. I lead," Linny said.

"Fuck me," said Jack.

Then there was silence. I felt sick.

Suddenly, Jack burst through the doors with Linny tossed over his shoulder like a rag doll. She was screaming something. In Latin.

"Come on, dude, let her go. I'll get your stuff back," Jonah said, exiting Carl's room, chasing Jack down the hall.

"What are you going on about?" Mick said to Jonah.

"Linny is the shower terrorist. She needs to be punished," Adam said, before Jonah could respond.

I heard a rush of water, then Linny's screams. Jonah started running down the hall. Gabe tripped Jonah with his crutch. Then Mick and Adam restrained him. Linny finally stopped screaming, which was so much worse.

I looked at my phone. I texted Finn. Then I called Dean Stinson's house and then I texted Ms. Witt. I started to back away, thinking I could slip into the stairwell undetected and track down any person of authority who could get this mess under control.

"Where the fuck are you going?" Adam said.

He was different, this Adam. His weird, too-pleasant armor was gone. Before I knew it, he sucker-punched me. Although any punch from Adam is a sucker punch. My neck snapped back and I lost the grip on my phone. I felt woozy and crumbled to the floor. Adam seized my phone and shoved it in his pocket. My forehead felt like someone was holding a torch to it. Carl Bloom quietly shut the door to his room, securing the deadbolt.

"Norman, you're such a little snitch," Adam said.

I heard Linny screaming again.

Aut neca aut necare.

GEMMA RUSSO

Adam sent me a text with a picture of Linny gagged and tied to a chair.

Adam: My files for your girl.

Adam's files were his superpower. Without them, he was Clark Kent standing next to a stockpile of kryptonite. Maybe even dumber than taking Adam's files had been stealing the champagne. One look in his closet and he knew that there was a breach. He might not have looked in the file cabinet for days or weeks. But when he saw the missing champagne, he checked. And then he knew what I had done.

I honestly didn't think he'd take it so far.

"Norman says they got Linny tied up," Mel said, looking up from her phone.

"I know," I said, showing her the photo.

"So let's get her back," said Mel.

"Yeah, let's go," Emelia said.

Then I received a text from Jonah.

Jonah: Don't escalate.

Gemma: I won't.

Jonah was right, this time. My priority was getting Linny out.

"This is between Adam and me," I said. "He wants his files back. That's all."

"What can we do?" Emelia said.

"Go back to Woolf and keep watch from the room. Text if you see Linny."

Emelia and Tegan took off. I began loading the files and flash drives into a paper shopping bag.

Kate stood by the door, checking that the hallway was clear.

"I think I should go to the library and send an email, don't you?" said Kate.

Mel and I exchanged a nod.

"Yes. It's time," I said.

"See you on the other side," Kate said on her way out.

While Mel double-bagged my files, rambling about a handle breakage being a sign of weakness, I sent Adam a message.

Gemma: I have your files. Release Linny.

Adam: 5 min. Bench across from Dickens. Files first.

Gemma: Same time.

"Ready?" Mel said, handing me the bag.

"Ready," I said.

"Once we get Linny back, we stop. Okay?"

"Okay," I said.

"I'm tired," Mel said.

I was tired too.

Mel and I left Headquarters and parted ways at the edge of Flem Square. Mel took watch inside Tolkien Library while I waited on the bench outside of Dick House with the paper bag by my side.

Within a minute, I saw Adam walking toward me. He was bundled in a high-tech down jacket, like he was about to scale a mountaintop. What a pussy. He sat down next to me, but we spoke like spies, staring straight ahead.

"Gems," Adam said, in that light, friendly way he had. "You've been a naughty girl, haven't you?"

"And you've been a sociopath," I said.

"We used to be such good friends. What happened?"

"We realized that we wanted different things," I said.

He smiled. "We grew apart. That doesn't mean we can't be friends."

"Nice play, throwing me into the contest," I said.

"I was just having a little fun, Gems. Lighten up."

I placed the bag on the bench next to Adam.

"If Linny doesn't come outside in five minutes, I'll send an email with the highlights from your files to the entire student body," I said.

"That's one hell of a threat. Will you include your own

biographical details? I have to say, Gemma, most orphans with your history struggle to stay out of juvie. Landing at Stonebridge was quite an impressive feat."

"The email is ready to go," I said. "Do you really want your friends to know your hobby is collecting dirt on them?"

That was a lie. Kate had just sent a draft to a select list of recipients.

"Linny," I repeated. "Give her back."

Adam looked inside the bag. He sent a text and clocked the north exit of his dormitory. Linny and Jack emerged from the boys' dorm. Adam nodded. Jack let go of Linny. She ran toward me. Adam picked up the bag and gave me a salute.

"It's been fun, Russo," Adam said, as he returned to Dick House.

MR. FORD

The new year didn't feel new. It felt like an old pair of shoes, the soles worn so thin you might as well walk barefoot.

I clocked out of all things Stonebridge during winter break. I didn't check Blackboard, respond to emails, or grade a single paper. Primm, however, was relentless with her text updates, so I was more informed than I would have liked. I phoned Claude once, after I learned that Greg had suspended her, pending an investigation for misconduct. I didn't know if someone told on her or she had confessed. I was just glad that I could stay out of it. When I spoke to Claude she was drunk and seemed unconcerned with the allegations.

"The age of consent in Vermont is sixteen. He's seventeen," Claude said.

"Well, then it's okay," I said.

"Fuck you, Finn," she said.

I'll never forget that.

I returned to campus the Sunday evening before classes were to resume. I poured a drink, opened my laptop, and braced myself for the influx of messages on the Blackboard system.

There were about thirty student messages that could wait and the usual administrative shit, including five missives from Primm that I didn't bother reading. There was also a message from Claudine Shepherd, which was odd. If Claude was suspended, why would she use Stonebridge's communication portal to send me a message? Anything she wrote would now be under extreme scrutiny.

I clicked on the header.

To: Finn Ford
From: Claude Shepherd
Re: Important. Read immediately

Dear Finn,
I don't like how we left things. I was being an asshole. I apologize. My mistakes are my own. And you've always been a good friend to me.

Please come to my house as soon as you're back.

Yours,
Claude

I texted Claude, telling her I was on my way. I grabbed my coat and keys and walked to the parking lot behind Dickens. I got into my car and took the main road off campus. As I was leaving, I saw Gemma and Adam sitting on a bench together. They looked like two spies in an old movie, trying to act like strangers.

I drove straight over to 344 Crestview Drive. I remember

being relieved when I saw Claude's car in the driveway. I don't know why. In retrospect, I wish she had run, dyed her hair, changed her name, and found an old man she could swindle out of every last penny.

I knocked on the door and waited. I knocked again. I knew she kept a spare key under a dead plant—at least she had two years ago. It was still there. I unlocked the door. I entered the house and I called her name. I called her name again. I don't know why.

I sat on the couch in the living room, debating whether to call the police and let them make the discovery. I didn't because there was a reason Claude wanted me to find her. I walked down the long hallway, opening one door after the other.

I think I was stalling. I knew I'd find her in the master bedroom. She was wearing a black cocktail dress. She'd even donned a pair of strappy red sandals, one barely hanging on from the tip of her toe. A plastic bag was cinched around her head and an open bottle of pills lay by her side.

There was a note scribbled on the nightstand.

REMOVE THE BAG.

She was so goddamn vain.

As I pulled the plastic over her head, it smudged her lipstick and eye makeup. I took a tissue and tried to fix it.

My phone rang. It scared the shit out of me. I felt like I might have been having a heart attack.

I looked at the screen. It was Alex. I sent her to voicemail and called 911.

GEMMA RUSSO

Linny was dripping wet and shivering when Jack released her. I put my arm around her and rushed her back to Woolf Hall.

"What the hell happened in there?" I said.

"The showers," Linny said. "Hot and cold. Hot and cold."

"Were you hurt?"

"No. Keith fixed the water heater after that kid got burned. I'm just cold."

"How did they find out?" I said.

"I told them."

"You moron. Why did you do that?"

Linny's eyes narrowed; her tone was seething.

"Because I wanted them to know. No one sees the contribution I made to the cause. You all get to walk around with your shaved heads, swinging an ax, and everyone knows who you are and what you stand for. They should know who I am and what I'm capable of."

Linny and I were in the hallway outside the lounge. Amy had seen us from the window and brought a blanket to wrap around Linny.

"Let's get you in a hot shower," Amy said.

"No more showers!" Linny shouted.

"No more showers," I said.

"Change of clothes, then," said Amy.

"Where is everyone?" I said.

"Your friends are in the lounge," Amy said. "You might want to talk them down."

Behind the door, I found the four of them sitting around one of the study desks. Kate had researched online how to make Molotov cocktails and raided the art department for supplies. The tabletop was covered with old T-shirts, scissors, and bottles.

"Make sure to wipe down the outside of the bottle," said Kate. "And, Tegan, that's too much fuel."

"I love the smell of turpentine in the evening," said Tegan.

"Is this necessary?" I said. "We got Linny. It's over."

"It doesn't hurt to have a backup plan," said Kate.

"You should make one," Emelia said. "I find it therapeutic."

I sat down and cut a long swath of fabric, poured the combustible solvent into the bottle, and shoved one end of the cloth down with a chopstick. I looked at my handiwork for a moment. The revenge it symbolized offered no comfort. Not then, at least. I remember feeling empty, deflated. I thought I'd have a sense of completion when it was all over. But it was a nothing feeling. There was no satisfaction.

Then Amy showed up at the doorway to the lounge. She beckoned me over.

"What's up?" I said.

"Linny said that they stripped her naked in the shower. They took pictures. She wants to know if you can get the pictures back."

The nothing feeling was gone.

MS. WITT

It was the last day of winter break. Keith wanted to stay in and watch a movie. I kept looking at my watch. Greg was supposed to call me at around nine, after his meeting with the board of advisers.

"Where's my phone?" I said.

"The meeting isn't over yet."

Keith had confiscated my phone earlier in the evening.

"The cultural apocalypse will be traced back to these things," he said.

"I'm pretty sure it'll be the Kardashians," I said.

I had a bad feeling. I thought it was about my fate. Not anything else. I demanded that Keith return my phone. He had hidden it outside in a planter, which struck me as a very odd hiding place for a phone. When he returned it, the home screen was ablaze with messages. I read the text story in reverse time, trying to make sense of it.

Jonah: BTW, I locked the editors in the lounge.

Gemma: We need you. You have to come back. No

one is here.

Jonah: Don't respond to his text.

Jonah: Norman wants me to tell you they took his phone.

Norman: Linny was taken hostage. I don't know what they're doing to her.

"Shit," I said. "We have to go back to campus."

"Alex, it's better if you—"

I showed Keith the message about Linny.

"I'll fucking kill them," he said. "Who's on watch tonight?"

We grabbed our coats and got into Keith's car, doing fifty in mostly thirty-mile zones to campus. As he drove, I left desperate messages for Greg, Finn, and Evelyn.

I didn't know what we were racing toward or what we might find. I didn't think it could get any worse. I was so naïve back then.

GEMMA RUSSO

I can't recall every detail. I sent Jonah a text. I thought he should know about the pictures.

Then I told my bomb-making comrades what they had done to Linny.

We discussed strategy.

We implemented a plan.

We said that we had to fight back, that it was our moral imperative. We topped off the bottles with turpentine. I remember the smell stinging my nose.

I remember circling Dick House. We spotted the editors in the first-floor lounge. We tried to open a window, but it was either locked or stuck.

We took our axes and smashed out three windowpanes.

We lit three Coke-bottle torches. We all ducked for cover after launching them into the lounge, like soldiers do in movies after they pull the pin from the grenade. It was a bit of a letdown at first. There was a small flash of light inside, but it took a while to build. But then the fire lit up, big and wild, and it matched the feeling we had inside. Once the room was ablaze, we ran back to Woolf Hall and got rid of the evidence.

We were breathing so hard it sounded like a windstorm.

We heard the alarm. Then the sirens from the fire truck, then the ambulances, then the police. We didn't know that the editors were trapped in the lounge.

We looked outside from our top-floor perch and saw boys running out of Dickens. Then someone pulled the alarm in Woolf. There was no orderly evacuation. Everyone was running for their lives.

We knew we weren't on fire, so we waited until most of our dorm had cleared out before we evacuated. Tegan thought we should stay inside and hide. She said they would be coming for us, that we stood out with our shaved heads. Mel said it was more suspicious if we took cover. Kate seemed surprised that the fire had taken hold.

"Did we do that?" Kate said.

Outside, we stood in plain view and watched the flames. They were the color of a sunrise I once saw.

We weren't thinking clearly. I know that. I couldn't remember the last time we were.

We watched and waited, like everyone else. We were scared and we were proud.

The adults finally showed up. Ms. Witt, Keith, Finn. Primm finally showed up. She was on duty that night, but she always goes to the bathhouse. Without knowing what had gone down, Primm pointed the finger at us. Ms. Witt shoved her. Primm fell on her ass. Mr. Ford had to physically restrain Witt. I was glad she'd come back. I wanted her to see what we had done.

We didn't know the boys were trapped in the lounge.

The fire was extinguished. The paramedics took someone out on a stretcher. I thought that was the only injury.

A uniformed police officer started walking toward us.

We didn't run. We stayed. We cooperated.

NORMAN CROWLEY

Adam had been stashing away dirt on his cohorts for years. According to Mel, it was his insurance policy in case of disloyalty. It was brilliant how the girls used his insurance to undermine his authority. While Adam was busy with the exchange, Mel or Kate or all of them had sent an email to Adam's "friends," detailing some disturbing shit that he'd gathered. I never saw the email. I just knew I wasn't mentioned in it.

Whatever information the email contained had the desired effect. After Linny was released, the guys returned to their rooms and discovered who Adam really was. Mick, Jack, and Gabe then confronted Adam when he returned to the lounge.

I could hear him pleading his case: "Dudes, come on. Those swallows are setting me up. You can't believe those bitches."

Jonah came to my room and showed me a text from Gemma.

Gemma: They took pictures of Linny in the shower.

I felt sick. I'd heard her screaming. But I just thought it was the cold water.

"Any sign of Finn?" Jonah said.

I shook my head. Jonah banged on Carl Bloom's door.

"I need your bike lock. Now," Jonah said.

Carl just handed over his U-lock, no questions asked. Jonah used it to secure the double doors to the lounge.

"What are you doing?" I said.

"We need to keep them contained."

Bloom had his phone to his ear. "Ford's not answering."

"Where's a fucking adult when you need one? You can't escape them the rest of time," Jonah said.

Jonah handed me his phone.

"Keep texting or calling until you get someone. Does anyone have Coach Keith's number?" Jonah said.

"He doesn't believe in cellphones," said Carl.

I looked at Jonah's phone and saw that he had already texted Witt. I sent her a few more messages.

The editors started banging on the lounge doors. They had only just realized that they were locked in. Jack was growling threats. The entire floor was vibrating. I didn't know what they would do if they got out. I was scared. We needed help.

"Linny is fifteen," I said. "It's—it's child pornography."

"Fuck it," Jonah said. "Call 911."

"Are you sure that's wise?" Carl said.

We were beyond knowing what was wise or not.

"I have a bad feeling," Jonah said. "Make the call."

I dialed 911 while Jonah moved a bureau out of Carl's room and used it as a second line of defense against the lounge doors. I didn't know what to tell the operator. I just gave her the address and hung up.

Jonah's phone buzzed with two more texts from Gemma.

Gemma: Get out of there.

Gemma: Get the good ones out.

I heard glass break. I figured the guys were busting out the windows since Jonah had locked them in. Then the fire alarm sounded and we ran outside. We thought one of the girls had set it off to screw with us. I didn't know about the fire until I smelled the smoke.

MS. WITT

I don't remember the exact order of events. The sirens were deafening and there were so many lights, from the emergency vehicles and flashlights and the fire. Students were spilling out of Woolf and Dickens and congregating around the square. A girl was shouting that people were trapped in the lounge. Then three boys seemed to jump through fire, right out of the window. Gabe first, then Mick and Jack.

Keith and I ran over to the boys.

I asked the boys if everyone was out. They said yes. I believed them.

"Where is Linny? Is Linny in there?" Keith asked.

Keith was holding Mick by the collar of his shirt and shaking him. A fireman pulled him off.

"We don't have her anymore," Mick said. "She's with the girls."

"Find her," Keith said to me. "I have to clear the floors."

Keith ran inside the building.

A squad car arrived, followed by a fire truck and then an ambulance.

More and more students spilled onto the square. The boys were escaping, rushing out of the building, fighting through the crowds; the girls slowly walked outside to regard the spectacle.

I spotted Linny on the square, watching the fire. She was wearing a bathrobe with a towel wrapped around her head, shivering. I asked her if she was okay. She just nodded and stared at the flames.

Two firemen aimed hoses through the broken windows. Jets of water eventually turned the fire into smoke. Another two firemen entered Dickens. A police officer approached and asked who was in charge. I said I didn't know.

I overheard a fireman talking to a policeman. He said something about a homemade explosive.

Then I saw Gemma and the other four girls, huddled together by Keats Studio.

After that, Martha turned up. Where had she been? She delivered a piece of paper to one of the officers and then she pointed at the girls. The school was on fire and she was playing snitch.

I thought the girls were going to run, but they didn't. I wanted to talk to them, to remind them not to say anything. But then Martha got in my way.

"What did you do?" I said.

"I gave the officer a list of girls to arrest. You shouldn't be here. I thought I was clear on that," Primm said.

My nails were digging into my palms. I had never wanted to hit anyone so badly.

Someone stopped me. I don't remember who it was.

* * *

When the fire was extinguished, the campus smelled like the end of a barbecue. The girls had been transported to the Lowland police precinct. Keith opened the gym while the fire marshal inspected the building. No one knew when or if the boys would be allowed back in their dorm.

I waited alone in the Lowland precinct for three hours while Greg was at the hospital, awaiting news of the injured and communicating with their families. There was a desk officer behind a glass partition. Behind him was a metal door. Every time someone opened the door, I could see the girls, handcuffed to a bench.

When Greg finally arrived, he approached the duty officer and identified himself.

"I'm the dean of students at Stonebridge Academy. May I see the girls?" he said.

"Only parents or guardians right now," the officer said.

"I see. Well, I'm Gemma Russo's father," he said.

"Ten minutes," the officer said, retreating behind the metal door.

Greg finally noticed me. He walked over and took a seat on the bench next to me. When he closed his eyes, I saw a single tear slide down his cheek.

"Is Jonah all right?" I said.

"He's in surgery. Something happened with an ax and his leg. I've been assured that he'll be okay," Greg said. "Eventually."

A middle-aged man in a rumpled suit entered. He was

the first of four lawyers to arrive that night.

"Adam didn't make it," Greg said.

I wasn't prepared for that. It never occurred to me that anyone would have died that night. I tried to summon sympathy. I'm sure that many factors led to the disturbed young man he became. But at that moment, I couldn't feel much of anything. Then I felt guilty for my lack of feeling.

"The others?" I said.

"Gabriel, Mick, and Jack will be fine. Smoke inhalation, a few cuts and abrasions, and I think Gabe's leg was broken. Although it might have already been broken."

"I'm so sorry."

I didn't know what to say. Some time passed. Couldn't say how long.

"And you know about Claude?" Greg said.

"I heard."

"Do you know how I found out?" Greg said. "Finn sent me a text. *A text.* I don't recognize this world anymore."

GEMMA RUSSO

I know we started the fire, but no one had to die.

When the boys realized that the door wasn't going to budge, Jack used a chair to smash the only window that wasn't blocked by flames. Gabe hurled himself outside, landing on his already broken leg. Mick and Jack crawled out after him. They told the police that they thought Adam had already escaped—that they couldn't see anything through all of the smoke. I don't know if Mick or Jack contributed to Adam's death or just didn't save him. Either way, the cops bought their story.

Jonah didn't know there was a fire until it was already raging. When the alarm sounded, and Jonah realized that the editors were locked inside the burning lounge, he couldn't find Carl or the key to his bike lock. Jonah tried to pick the lock but didn't know what he was doing. Then he went at it with a baseball bat. Eventually he got hold of the fire safety ax and attacked the door itself, throwing his whole body into the job. But those axes aren't like ours. The hallway was hot. Jonah's hands got sweaty. He said the ax slipped and sliced deep into his shin, hitting the bone. The paramedics found him as they were doing a sweep of the floor. That's when they broke the lock and found Adam.

Jack, Mick, Gabriel, and Jonah were taken to the hospital. Mick and Jack were released the next day. Gabriel was kept another twenty-four hours for observation. Jonah had lost five pints of blood and had nerve damage to his leg. Everyone kept talking about how he was going to make a full recovery. They meant that he'd be able to walk without a cane after six months and maybe jog again in a year. The soccer scholarship that had once been a sure thing wasn't even a longshot.

All of this I learned later.

We were at the Lowland precinct after the fire. They had us handcuffed to one another, sitting on a bench in a hallway. The one holding cell was taken up by a drunk.

Later, there was an investigation. We didn't talk. We weren't going to destroy our futures because of one mistake, and we'd learned long ago to keep our mouths shut. Chalk it up to inept police work, or the horde of lawyers retained by Stonebridge parents, or the prevailing code of silence, but no one was ever charged with attempted murder or arson or manslaughter.

But somebody had to take the fall, and it was easiest to fault the dead.

I don't know how the investigators reverse-engineered the evidence to reach this conclusion, but Adam was blamed for just about everything that happened that night. His unhinged mental state was ascribed to his relationship with Ms. Shepherd. Even the fire was somehow pinned on him.

Greg resigned, because there had to be an administrative

casualty for the sake of "optics." I know I ruined his career. I hope I didn't ruin his life.

Greg feels guilty about Adam's death. I know that because he's asked me more than once if I do. Usually I ignore his question or change the subject. When I think about Adam, I think about the kind of man he would have become.

Greg is still trying to figure out how it all went wrong and what he missed. Sometimes he'll remember a detail from the past year and realize he'd misread the situation at the time. Then he'll ask me about it.

"Your hair. It wasn't lice, was it?" he said just the other day.

I tried to explain it to him. I'm not sure whether he understood, but he really does try.

We moved off campus into some rich person's vacation home. Once I decide on a college, we'll move again. I'm being homeschooled for the rest of the term, which is interesting.

Greg's plan is for us to live together my freshman year. I'm not sure if the purpose of that is to save money or to keep an eye on me.

It won't be the college life I was imagining for myself, but it's better than jail. And it's better than the life I once thought was inevitable.

Time and space have separated me from my former allies. For some of us, the distance feels permanent. Emelia refuses to talk about the past, and without that, we have nothing in common. It took all of five minutes on the phone to figure that out. Tegan and I didn't even bother with the phone call. She also wants to forget. And I don't want to stand between anyone and their amnesia.

As for Jonah, the problem is that he can't forget. Every step he takes, every jab of pain, reminds him of that night. He knows I'm not a murderer. But I am, technically, an arsonist. Well, I was one once. I won't let that define me. Jonah wants to be with the kind of girl who was never an arsonist. I respect that. Really, I do.

With Mel and Kate, it's different. We're bound by spit, blood, and now ink. Mel and I copied Kate's tattoo of our preferred weapon. It was a gesture of solidarity at a time when we feared our bond would be broken. Mel and Kate wear their ink proudly. So far, I've kept mine hidden from Greg. He worries enough as it is. He even worries about the stupid red sweatband I wear around my wrist to cover it up.

It's important that people understand that we have a conscience. We know what we did. We won't forget that someone died as a result of our actions. Mel keeps trying to replay events, restructure the various points in our trajectory to find a way to destroy the status quo without taking a life. Kate, on the other hand, is confident that each variable was a necessary element in the equation that led to the final outcome.

"I've done the math," Kate likes to say. "It was the only way."

I'm not so sure about Kate's math, but I can live with what we did. It had to be done.

If I have one regret, it's for Linny. I should have let her fight by my side. Then she would have gotten it out of her system. I don't know that it will ever be over for Linny.

She never did get those pictures back.

MS. WITT

It's been a year since I left Lowland. The memories haven't faded as much as I'd like, and my life isn't as different, but I'm okay. I am still inside the machinery of my parents' universe. I'm not just a cog, in fact, but a wheel. Dad can't keep up with the book-a-year pace, so I'm pinch-hitting. As a ghostwriter, I don't feel quite like the god of the page, but I am perhaps a benevolent dictator. After everything that happened at Stonebridge, it's deeply satisfying to have one thing I can control.

When I drove out of Lowland, I thought I might never see Keith again. I would never go back there and I assumed he'd never leave. The first day he returned to campus after the fire, he decided he didn't belong there anymore. He sent his résumé to every prep school within twenty miles of Boston. He got a job coaching soccer and basketball at an all-boys boarding school with a competitive intramural program. The school has only half the acreage of Stonebridge, he reminds me often. I think he's happy. I think I'm happy.

Not a day goes by that I don't think about Stonebridge and whether I might have done something else, something that could have prevented the tragedy. I've never come up with a good answer. What I do know is that without the fire, Stonebridge would still be standing and so would the rot at its core, contaminating every student who entered those halls.

The headmaster at Keith's school offered me a part-time job as a fencing instructor. I declined. A few days later, I found myself in the offices of the sister school just a mile away, offering the same services for free.

Sometimes when I watch my students practicing their parries and ripostes, I see them hesitate. They're afraid of receiving pain, of course, but even more afraid of administering it. Above all, they're afraid of themselves—of the primal, euphoric thing that surfaces when they fight. They've been tamping it down so long that it's become alien, unrecognizable. I've come to see my job as reacquainting them with it. Sometimes it only takes one win to remind them how good it feels, how right. Once that happens, I know they'll be okay.

In a perfect world, they wouldn't need to fight. That's not the world I live in.

You can keep telling girls to be polite, to keep a level head and it'll all work out in the end. But don't be surprised when they figure out that you've been feeding them lies. Don't be alarmed when they grow tired of using their voices and playing by your rules. And don't be shocked when they decide that if they can't win a fair fight, they'll just have to fight dirty.

ACKNOWLEDGEMENTS

The Swallows is my tenth novel and it's safe to say it's the one that might have induced the most insanity. I am truly grateful to everyone mentioned below, and others, for somehow playing a part in getting it to this point. Many of these thank-yous should be accompanied by at least a small apology.

I'll begin with my agent, Stephanie Kip Rostan. Thank you for having faith in this book from the first draft to the last and all the versions in between. I hope I never put you through that again. And thank you to everyone else who makes Levine Greenberg Rostan so awesome, especially Sarah Bedingfield, who went way above and beyond, Melissa Rowland, Elizabeth Fisher, Miek (no, I did not misspell that) Coccia, Tim Wojcik, Matthew Huff, and the rest of the team that always finds time to eat cake with me.

Thank you to my editor, Kara Cesare, for all of your hard work, sage advice, and patience. Also at BBD: Kara Welsh, Jennifer Hershey, and Kim Hovey, I'm in your debt. Jesse Shuman, Loren Noveck, Karen Fink, Debbie Aroff, Colleen Nuccio, Kathy Lord, and Diane Hobbing, you are all awesome. Emily Osbourne, that bird is better than I could have ever imagined.

Jaime Temairik, thanks for the map and blowchart and the stuff we left out. Thanks, Kate Golden, for the tree illustration and the proto-blowchart.

Ellen Clair Lamb and David Hayward had to read an obscene number of drafts—consider this both a thank-you and an apology. I still owe many drinks (now it's in writing) to Katrina Holm for her notes on a very early draft. And thanks, Julie Shiroishi, for your excellent edits during one of those revisions. It's all a blur now. Sarah Weinman, thanks for all kinds of things. I'm glad you'll have the opportunity to read this book in its finished form.

Thank you, Morgan Dox for, yet again, reading a very early draft. And Steve Kim and Rae, Julie Ulmer, and Peter and Carol, just because . . .

Thanks to my cousin Jay (Fienberg) for all the hacker/technical help and for being really cool. And thanks to the rest of my family: Bev and Mark Fienberg, Jeff and Eve Golden, Dan and Lori Fienberg.

Last but not least: a huge thanks to my friend and comrade Megan Abbott.

ABOUT THE AUTHOR

Lisa Lutz is the author of the bestselling series, *The Spellman Files*, Her most recent novel, *The Passenger*, was described as "spellbinding" by the *Daily Mail*. She has received numerous accolades for her work, including an Alex Award, and nominations for the Edgar, Barry, Anthony Awards, among many others.

lisalutz.com
Facebook.com/lisalutz.author
Twitter: @lisalutz

ALSO AVAILABLE FROM TITAN BOOKS

THE BLACKBIRD SEASON

KATE MORETTI

In a quiet town, a thousand dead starlings fall onto a school playing field. As journalists flock to the scene, one of them catches a teacher, Nate Winters, embracing a female student. The student claims that she and Nate are having an affair, sending shockwaves through the close-knit community. Then the student disappears, and the police have only one suspect: Nate.

Nate's wife, Alecia, is left wondering if she ever really knew her seemingly loving husband. Nate's co-worker, Bridget, is determined to prove his innocence and find the missing student. But both women will have to ask themselves—do they really know what Nate is capable of?

"This cautionary tale keeps the reader guessing to the end"
PUBLISHERS WEEKLY

"The tale's suspenseful core should catch and hold most readers, especially Gone Girl *fans"*
BOOKLIST

"Exceptional" KIRKUS

ALSO AVAILABLE FROM TITAN BOOKS

RIVER ROAD

CAROL GOODMAN

Driving home in a snowstorm, Nan Lewis hits something with her car. She's sure it's a deer. What else could it be? Then one of her students is found dead, the victim of a hit and run. And there is blood on Nan's tyres. As friends and neighbours turn on her, and she starts finding disturbing tokens that recall the killing of her own daughter, Nan begins to suspect that the two deaths are connected…

"Emotion-charged twists and turns that you won't see coming"
TESS GERRITSEN

"An intense psychological thriller"
PUBLISHERS WEEKLY

TITANBOOKS.COM

ALSO AVAILABLE FROM TITAN BOOKS

THE DEVIL YOU KNOW

ELISABETH DE MARIAFFI

Rookie crime beat reporter Evie Jones is haunted by the unsolved murder of her best friend Lianne. Now twenty-two, Evie is obsessively driven to find the killer. She leans on childhood friend David Patton for help, but every trail seems to lead back to David's father. As she gets closer to the truth, Evie becomes convinced that the killer is still at large – and that he's coming back for her.

"[An] artful first novel"
PUBLISHERS WEEKLY

"Evie is a tough, wisecracking narrator worthy of the greatest private-eye pulp novels"
BOOKLIST (STARRED REVIEW)

ALSO AVAILABLE FROM TITAN BOOKS

IN HER BONES

KATE MORETTI

Fifteen years ago, Lilith Wade was arrested for the brutal murder of six women. After a death row conviction and media frenzy, her thirty-year-old daughter Edie is a recovering alcoholic with a deadend city job, just trying to survive out of the spotlight. Edie also has a disturbing secret: a growing obsession with the families of Lilith's victims. She's been careful to keep her distance, until the day one of them is found murdered and she quickly becomes the prime suspect. Edie remembers nothing of the night of the death, and must get to the truth before the police—or the real killer—find her.

"Captivating"
PUBLISHERS WEEKLY

"A slow burning and suspenseful psychological mystery"
CULTURE FLY